THE STORM PRINCESS
AND THE RAVEN KING

BY
JEFFE KENNEDY

A Broken Heart

Princess Salena Nakoa KauPo thought she was over her broken heart. She'd put her first love and childhood sweetheart, Rhyian, firmly in the past where he belonged. His bitter betrayal of her was locked away deep inside, along with her foolishly innocent hopes and dreams. Now Lena has been thrust together with him, the prince of shadows, the one man she could never resist, on a mission to save the world from a terrible cataclysm. Worse, Rhyian refuses to believe her when she says there's no hope for them.

An Irresistible Longing

Rhyian is rather accustomed to being a failure. Goddesses know, he's not magical enough for his sorcerous mother and not alpha enough for his father, the King of Annfwn. It hasn't helped that he's spent the last seven years trying to drown his sorrows—and to forget the one woman he ever loved, whose heart he carelessly shattered in a moment of weakness. Rhy knows he has to change to win back Lena's trust, but how?

A Love That Can't Die

As Lena and Rhy struggle to overcome the wounds of the past, they and their friends approach the final confrontation with the strange intelligence intent on rending apart the very fabric of their world. And it looks like it will come down to the pair of them to strike the final blow.

But only if they can build a new trust on the bitter past.

DEDICATION

To Kev

Everything I know about youthful first love, I learned from you.

ACKNOWLEDGMENTS

Thank you, first and foremost, to all the readers who love this series and gave me the perfect balance of cheering for this final book to come out without making me feel pressured. I'm sorry it took so long! You all are the best.

As always, gratitude to Carien Ubink for all the assisting and for beta reading.

Thanks to Darynda Jones and Kelly Robson for daily check-ins and having faith in me.

Love to Grace Draven in the hopes your crap year will turnaround.

Undying love to David, who is there for me every day and has been for over thirty years. Always and ever, my dear.

Finally, thanks and love to Megan Mulry and Charlie Whittock, for all the drinks, meals, and excellent conversation. I finished writing this book on the morning of your wedding and there's something magical about that. Frosé forever!

THE STORM PRINCESS AND THE RAVEN KING

BY
JEFFE KENNEDY

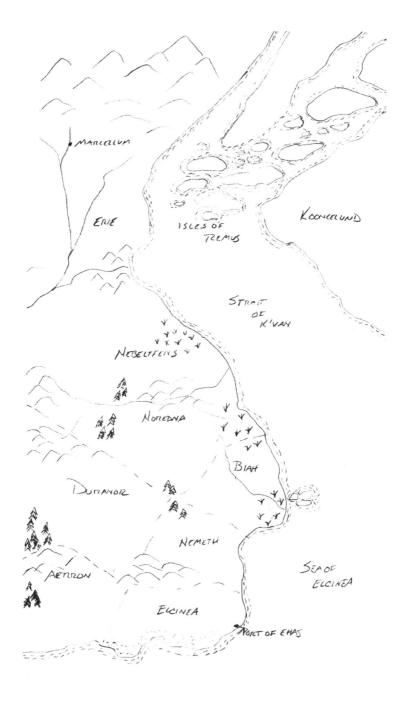

~ PROLOGUE ~

SALENA SHIVERED IN the sweet aftermath of passion, snuggling closer to Rhyian's skin. He smelled as beautiful as he looked, like sunshine on black feathers, his skin soft as the finest sueded silks from the high court at Castle Ordnung. Still joined to him in the most intimate way possible, she embraced him, inside and out. Never had she felt so complete, so thoroughly and ravishingly loved.

Everything was perfect.

Rhyian cuddled her closer, his long legs entwined with hers, his heart hammering under her cheek. He'd always been a sweetly attentive lover, showing her a side of himself he hid away from everyone else. With her he could be vulnerable, laughing at silly jokes and taking delight in simple pleasures. Away from the intrigues of his royal parents and the dominance games of the Tala, he dropped the coldly brooding façade he usually wore. That was a demonstration of trust that went beyond any declaration he might make in words.

She loved him and she knew he loved her, even if he'd never said so. Lena didn't need that from Rhyian—he wasn't the sort to talk about his feelings about anything at all, which she understood—because he showed her in countless tiny ways. Even now, the way his fingers trailed down her back, caressing her skin, spoke of how he cherished her. It was enough.

She tipped her head back, mostly to indulge herself in gazing on his beautiful face, gilded by candlelight, the shadows clinging lovingly to his angled jaw and high cheekbones. Her Prince of Shadows. He watching her, too, with heavy-lidded eyes, the deep blue sleepily sated behind thick black lashes. He lifted a hand, threading his long fingers into her hair and combing it back from her face, pressing his lips between her brows in a soft, lingering kiss. "Any regrets, love?" he murmured. There was that, too. He never said he loved her, but he always called her 'love.'

"Not a one," she answered, meaning it. "This is perfect. Exactly how I imagined it to be."

"You certainly planned it well enough," he replied with a purr of laughter, and she curled into the sound and the sweet intimacy of the moment.

Rhyian, along with their friends, liked to tease her about her inclination to plan everything. She couldn't help it if she had an orderly mind—besides, why shouldn't she plan losing her virginity as carefully as she'd approach every other life event? This had been a major life moment, even if she and Rhyian had been doing everything but actual intercourse for months now. She'd wanted it to be him and he, another of his wonderful qualities, had indulged her without protest, setting up everything exactly as she'd asked for.

They had this romantic nook in a private part of the cliff city at Annfwn—Rhyian being the son of King Rayfe and Queen Andromeda allowed him to commandeer the unoccupied space—near the top, where leaves rustled from the tree limbs that reached through the open windows. Flowers bloomed sweet on the soft night air, and an owl hooted quietly. Rhyian had scattered petals from tropical blossoms on the sheets, and candles flickered with warm light, gleaming over her lover's long, elegant body. Her friend, Stella, had warned her that planning everything wouldn't necessarily make it perfect, but her friend had been wrong. So much for Stella's sorcerous foresight.

"This is perfect," Salena repeated, pressing a kiss to the hollow of Rhyian's throat, tasting the salt of his skin twined with tropical flowers. "You're perfect."

He purred out a laugh, sliding his hand to cup her chin and raise her face so he could kiss her. Though they'd only just finished making love, his cock hardened inside her still-throbbing body, the heat rising between them. "You're the only one who thinks so, beautiful Salena," he whispered against her lips, and her heart ached for him.

"That's not true," she replied, winding her hand into his glossy black curls, which tumbled wild around his shoulders. "You're too hard on yourself."

Salena knew that, also, and understood how Rhyian struggled so against the many forces pulling him in different directions, never serious enough for his ambitious father, not magically talented enough for his powerful sorceress mother, not royal enough for the company he kept. The other folk of the Thirteen Kingdoms called him prince, because in their realms the acknowledged son of the king and queen would be exactly that. The Tala, however, conducted the business of determining succession differently, and most considered Rhyian too feckless, not alpha enough, to be king. His raven First Form didn't help matters, as no one considered a raven ideal for leading a wild and untamed people into battle.

Never mind that war hadn't touched Annfwn or the Thirteen in all their young lives, nor that Rhyian was only a teenager—the same as she was, though she was a few weeks older—still a young man finding his way. Old traditions and biases died hard. People whispered that Rhyian didn't live up to his father's ruthlessness in command or his mother's legendary heroism. Rhyian heard what they said, though he stoically ignored the comments in public. Only to Salena did he ever reveal his doubts.

"You'll be sore, love," he said with regret, stroking her cheek and withdrawing from her body, smiling when she mewled in protest. "I don't want to hurt you."

"I'm fine," she insisted. Certainly their many pleasurable interludes had stretched her passage, and she was athletic besides, having grown up surfing the waves of Nahanau. Rhyian had discovered how to slide a finger inside her, to stroke the exact spot that drove her wild. He was, however, definitely blessed in length and girth, stretching her tissues far more than the most vigorous use of fingers, and now the twinges made themselves known as the afterglow faded.

Still she didn't want this to end.

"There's blood," Rhyian told her, stroking her thighs clean with the warmed cloths she'd prepared. He glanced up at her, heat and love his eyes. "Which means you tore some. Besides, we have all the time in the world to be together this way."

Her heart thrummed, overfull, at his caring words, at the way he looked at her. Rhyian was all she'd ever wanted, and now he *was* hers. She didn't care if he became King of Annfwn or not. She was the eldest daughter of the King and Queen of Nahanau, after all, and she ruling there had never appealed to her either. She and Rhyian had their whole lives ahead of them and all that mattered was that they spend those lives together. *All the time in the world.* That he said so only proved that he loved her as deeply as she loved him. They were perfect together. Meant to be.

Rhyian placed a soft kiss on her belly, tongue flicking out to taste her exactly the same way she loved to taste him. Someday, she'd be carrying their child—not now, as they were too young yet, so she'd used an enchantment to prevent pregnancy—but someday, when they were older and ready, and he would kiss her belly just like that, with reverence and joy.

She reached down and ruffled his dark curls, blue-black in the true fashion of the purest Tala blood. He glanced up at her, beautiful lips curving in a sensual smile, feathering his fingers over her hip. "You are all golden in this light," he murmured. "My brown-skinned island girl. So breathtakingly beautiful, and all mine." The possessiveness in his face and voice moved her deeply, that wildness in him always near the surface. She understood that about him, too, and that his claiming her as his meant more than any declaration of love.

But she wanted him to know she felt the same. She was no shapeshifter, but Rhyian belonged to her on a profound level. This was the time to tell him, in this humming perfection, the time to speak the words she'd withheld for no good reason except for a last bit of shyness. That seemed so silly now, lying with him between her thighs, both of them naked, revealed to each other in the most vulnerable of ways.

"I love you, Rhyian," she told him, her voice coming out throatily. "You are my first and only love, and I'll love you for the rest of my life."

His smile stayed in place, his fingers stilling, and he stared at her, those cobalt-blue eyes intense and vivid. A shudder ran through him. Even knowing him so well, she couldn't quite interpret his response. Then he slid those clever fingers down to spread her wider, his mouth curling wickedly. "Too much talking," he purred, "when you could be begging."

Dropping his lips to her sensitized sex, he set to tormenting her. Indeed, all that escaped her were wordless pleas and the incoherent exchange of gasps and cries that formed the language of lovers everywhere.

A LONG TIME later, she awoke alone, dreamily replete, her entire body aching and zinging with Rhyian's passionate lovemaking. She'd lost track of her orgasms, finally passing out from the final one, and gauzily recalled him promising her breakfast. The sky outside the stone arches of the windows shone blue and clear, the leaves rustling green and gold in the morning light, while birds sang in a rising chorus, celebrating another day in the paradise of Annfwn.

Definitely time for breakfast, she decided, wriggling happily. On those nights she and Rhyian had managed to sneak away, when they'd greeted the dawn together, he'd always gone to find a vendor from the market, flying there in raven form and walking back to bring her Nahanaun coffee, just like from home, and her favorite cinnamon pastries. Another of their little traditions she loved.

On this special morning, of course, Rhyian had gone to get their breakfast so they could share it in bed together. One of the many small, thoughtful, and countless ways he demonstrated his love. Humming to herself, she rolled over, lazily contemplating that she should do something with her waist-length, incredibly tangled hair. She wanted to look pretty for him when he returned.

As she reached across the bed to grab the bag she'd brought with a few toiletries, anticipating this very thing, she found the sheets cool on his side. Odd. Surely he hadn't been gone that long? If it were anyone else she'd think he'd decided to let her sleep in, but Rhyian always said they could sleep when they were dead, loving to pounce on her like a cat pinning its prey, kissing and teasing her awake to play with him.

The thought making her smile, she climbed out of the low bed, stretching in luxurious satisfaction, before setting to the task of brushing out her hair. When the tangled length was at last glossy and flowing free, she sponge-bathed herself, then smoothed on the scented oil Rhyian had told her he loved to smell and taste on her. Though she'd lingered over her ablutions, he still hadn't returned with their breakfast by the time she was done, and her stomach rumbled.

After a long and largely sleepless night—not that she regretted a moment of the lost sleep!—she longed for the kick of that coffee. Perhaps Rhyian gotten caught up in conversation with someone. Or, the thought struck her with a pang of worry, hopefully nothing had happened to him. There hadn't been war in their lifetimes, but they still had enemies.

Pulling on the smoky blue silk dress she'd worn for their romantic evening, the one Rhyian said made her eyes look the exact shade of the sky where it met the calm waters of the sea before the last light fades from the sky, she went out through the front room. Like most of the living quarters in Annfwn, these rooms looked out on the main trail that wound and snaked up the side of the cliff face. Beyond, the calm seas of Annfwn gleamed turquoise in the midday sun, so much more gentle than the rambunctious surf of the beaches of her home.

Not many people traveled this secluded loop of trail, which was partly why these apartments stood empty, being a bit far from the center of social activity for the gregarious types and yet too much in the city for the solitary ones. Salena wandered out to the low wall, shading her eyes and looking for signs of trouble. Everything appeared to be normal, people carrying on the business and play of daily life in Annfwn. Then, on the next curve of the path down, she spotted Rhyian's tall, long-limbed figure, a giddy wash of pleasure rushing through her as it did every time she saw him.

He had his back to her, the sun kissing his tumbling curls to bring out the glints of blue in the black, and a tray sat on the balustrade beside him, coffee and pastries arrayed on it. He was bent over oddly, and it took a moment for her brain—which she'd always thought so very sharp and clever—to catch up with what her eyes reported.

Rhyian was bent over a woman, a Tala woman, by the flow of her wild, black hair. The pose was an awkward, strange one, and Lena couldn't seem to make sense of it. Until she realized...

It was a kiss.

Rhyian was *kissing* this other woman, passionately. Her long, Tala-slender legs were wrapped around his lean waist, one hand cupping his excellent ass and squeezing as if checking for ripeness. As Lena watched in stunned incomprehension, a second woman eased out from in front of Rhyian, looking sated and smug, kissing along his neck and tugging his shirt off his shoulder, following with her tongue.

Lena must have made a sound, because Rhyian froze, then looked over his shoulder at her. The woman he'd been kissing giggled, tossing back her hair, giving Lena an impudent grin, while the other continued in her absorbed devouring of Rhyian's now bare chest.

As for Rhyian, he met Lena's gaze unflinchingly, expression impassive, no attempt to extricate himself from either woman, or to protest the innocence he clearly lacked. Standing there on her short legs, her not-tall, too-curvy body still singing Rhyian's praises, Lena struggled to make sense of it all.

But she was no fool, no matter how foolishly she'd behaved. She should've known better than to give her heart to the Prince of Shadows. The blindfold of first love had fallen

9

from her eyes and she saw clearly now. Firmly, her brain stepped in, closed her heart behind a door where its desolate sobbing was silenced, and locked it with a key no one would ever lay hands on again.

Something crossed Rhyian's face, but she turned away, going back inside to efficiently pack her things. He never came in, which told her the last of what she needed to know to forget him and go on with her life. When she stepped out to the road again, he and his new lovers were gone, the tray of coffee and pastries cooling and abandoned on the rock wall. There was no one and nothing to stop her as she left Annfwnn forever, never to return.

~ 1 ~

Seven Years Later

"LENA, WHAT AM I going to *do* with you?" Zeph demanded, pushing a flute of sparkling wine at Lena where she lurked near one of the ballroom pillars. "You could skip puzzling over it and leave me alone?" Lena queried blandly, but she sipped the wine anyway.

"You should be dancing and having fun," Zeph said, plowing ahead blissfully, sipping her own wine and looking impossibly glamorous. With her mother's pale skin and her father's midnight black hair, and that long, slender Tala figure, Zeph was strikingly beautiful. As a talented shapeshifter, Zeph wore one of the gorgeous ballgowns she'd saved in a metaphysical cache until she needed it. Getting ready for the ball for her meant shifting to human form with hair done and wearing the dress she'd chosen.

Meanwhile, as a non-shapeshifter who'd lost everything but what she'd been wearing when they abandoned ship— literally—and dove into the sea on a rescue mission, Lena was relegated to wearing a borrowed gown. It was pretty enough, but was too long for her height and uncomfortably tight across her too-generous bosom. Feeling dowdy didn't help her mood at all.

"Remember the ball at Castle Ordnung on the night of the crystalline moon?" Zeph asked.

"As it was only a few months ago and my memory is excellent, yes, I do." In fact, Lena wished she *didn't* remember everything about that night with distressing clarity. Her memories were as crystalline as the moon had shone once she used her storm magic to clear the clouds away. For the first time in the seven years since that horrible morning after she lost her virginity—and witnessed his betrayal—she and Rhyian had actually talked.

And that had led them straight where she'd always fallen too readily: fainting with dreamy desire in his arms. She'd let the romance of the night sweep her up, the sensual allure of Rhyian to cloud her senses, and she'd kissed him up on that high tower with moonlight shivering silver around them. Making her a fool for the second time.

A mistake, to be sure, but one that might have had less impact if she'd left again in the morning as planned. Then she would've been spared enduring this endless battle with herself and him, made worse daily with them thrust together in such close circumstances. Fighting Rhyian's determined pursuit was enough of a challenge—she'd never been good at denying him anything—but resisting her own longing for what had been, and what could never be again, was gradually eroding her will. Even reminding herself of the pain and that nothing had changed, least of all Rhyian, wasn't working anymore. Seeing him every day, in all his brooding and sensual beauty, made her want to forget.

Against her will and better judgment, her gaze sought him out. Right there, on the other side of the ballroom, her Prince of Shadows lounged indolently against a pillar. Dressed all in black, his curling dark hair falling in glossy waves that blended seamlessly with his flowing coat, he looked like he wore a cloak of night. As always the goddess Moranu set her hand lovingly on her chosen son, his refined features glowing like the moon herself, his deep blue eyes fixed on Lena, returning her seeking gaze with banked fire. She wrenched her eyes away, heart pounding as she struggled to keep a bored, even disdainful expression on her face.

Rhyian could never know how deeply he still affected her. Yes, he wanted her in his bed again. He'd made that abundantly clear. And Lena knew that it was mostly pride and hubris driving him. Maybe desire, too, but he didn't love her the way she needed him to, the way she'd so naively believed he did all those years ago. Probably he was incapable of it, which she'd always understood about him, which made her foolishness all that much more embarrassing. Most humiliating of all, despite her keenly honed intelligence, the rational decision-making she'd developed as a scientist of storm magic, she had to acknowledge in the depths of her shattered heart that she loved him still. If Rhyian ever realized *that*, he could wrap her around his long and clever fingers—and wring her dry again.

"That was such a wonderful night," Zeph was saying dreamily, eyes lingering on the tall and handsome Astar. The blond heir to the high throne of the Thirteen Kingdoms was deep in conversation with a group of nobles representing the various islands that made up the Isles of Remus. Zeph transferred her sharp sapphire gaze to Lena. "You used to love dancing."

"I *used* to love doing my research in the Aerron Desert," Lena replied wryly. "This is work for me, just of a different kind. I'm here, aren't I? Her Majesty never said I had to have fun when she commanded me to go on this quest."

Zeph rolled her gorgeous eyes. "You and Rhy, both sulking when you could be having fun." Her glittering gaze went to Rhy, still leaning against that pillar, hands thrust in his pockets, and Lena couldn't help looking, too. Again.

Though he slouched broodingly, Rhyian still managed to look both elegant and like walking sex. Lena thrust that thought aside, yanking her gaze away before he noticed she'd looked in his direction, yet again. "Stop looking over there," Lena hissed at her friend. "You'll attract his attention."

"Like I have to," Zeph inserted drily. "He watches you all the time anyway, looking like a starving wolf."

Despite herself—and all her resolve never to feel anything ever again for the duplicitous Rhyian—sympathy and worry sabotaged her best intentions. She inadvertently glanced his way yet again, finding him indeed devouring her with that very hungry gaze, just as Zeph described. Then he looked away, giving some pretty girl a flirtatious smile as she cozied up to him. Typical.

"He was stuck in wolf form too long," she told Zeph, willing herself not to care about the guy who'd shattered her heart so carelessly. "In that alter-realm without food and water. That's why the gloomy, starving look."

"Oh, I'm sure that's all it is," Zeph replied with dripping

sarcasm. "Except that he's been soulfully gazing after you like a kicked puppy this entire trip, well before his adventures in the flat-grid alter-realm."

"*I* am the kicked puppy in this scenario." Lena tossed back the rest of the wine, tempted to smash the fragile flute to the cold marble floor. She was not one to throw temper tantrums, however. She was supposed to be the rational, level-headed one. "Just because *you* are blissfully in love... That you *all* are now," she amended as Gen danced by with the ivory-haired mage-king of the Isles of Remus, ecstatic in her joy. Lena begrudged Gen nothing, for if anyone deserved true love, it was Gen, who'd sought it with such a lonely and determined heart. "That doesn't mean that everyone is going to find a happy ever after," she belatedly finished.

"I think we find what we seek," Zeph said, eyes glinting thoughtfully as they rested on Lena.

"Easy for you to say when you've already landed your heart's desire," Lena shot back. She didn't begrudge Zeph, either. With her gríobhth First Form—what the mossbacks called a gryphon—Zeph had hunted down Astar with the skill of a true predator.

Zeph softened, glowing with love, as she sought out and met Astar's gaze. He immediately smiled back at Zeph, more than happy to have been her prey. "It's true," Zeph allowed. "You'll see. When you have your true love, then—"

"I had a shot at mine," Lena interrupted tersely, beyond done with this conversation. "Rhyian destroyed any hope of that. Deliberately."

"Will you forever be seeking revenge for Rhy's youthful

mistakes?" Zeph asked with quiet intensity.

Lena was taken aback. First of all, the flirtatious, mischievous Zeph wasn't the one to think about anyone else. Though, to be fair, Zeph had always had keen insight into the minds and motivations of others. Since settling into the intense love affair with Astar—including becoming engaged to him and accepting the responsibility of being the future high queen—Zeph had been more focused, determined to be, well, more responsible. Second, however, Lena had never expected Zeph to champion Rhyian.

"What's it to you?" Lena answered, well aware of how bitter and resentful she sounded.

Zeph shrugged in the elaborate Tala fashion, gracefully managing not to spill a single drop of her wine, though her flute remained quite full. Lena should not have drained hers so fast. Zeph sipped her wine thoughtfully. "I see a lot of myself in Rhy."

"You've certainly both had a similar number of lovers," Lena muttered ungraciously.

Zeph rounded on her, ebony brows arched, sapphire eyes sparking with anger. "Are you shaming me for enjoying sex? Because that's not like you, Lena."

"No," Lena answered, flushing with shame of her own. "I didn't mean it like that. It's just that what Rhyian did—"

"I know what Rhy did to you," Zeph interrupted hotly. "We *all* know, because it's been thrust in our faces daily on this quest. Rhy acted badly then, and arguably has behaved badly since, but you've hardly been a ray of sunshine."

Lena stiffened in outrage. "You can't blame me for that. I

do not want to be here."

"Yes, and you've made that painfully clear, haven't you?" Zeph snapped back. Lena could almost see her lethally curved gríobhth beak slicing through the short distance between them. "None of us asked for this quest, and it's taken a toll on everyone, including Rhy. You don't have to make it more difficult."

"I wasn't aware I was," Lena replied stiffly, mortified by the creeping realization that her internal pain had leaked out despite her attempts at rigid control.

Zeph snorted. "And everyone accuses *me* of being self-involved." She sipped her wine broodily, looking very much like Rhy in that moment: impossibly beautiful, full of raging passions, and completely herself. Zeph had the great gift of knowing, unapologetically, exactly who she was. Lena had thought she'd known who she was when she'd been buried in her work in the Aerron Desert. Once she'd been yanked away from that, it had become increasingly clear that her work had been a distraction. She was rootless and without any sense of who she was supposed to be.

And ever since her own terrifying experience in the forest alter-realm, she'd doubted on a heart-deep level that she was anyone at all. She'd let herself fall from Zeph's back, choosing to die rather than endure another moment. Stripped of her work and most of her magic, just another young woman in a brutally alien land, Princess Salena Nakoa KauPo had turned out to be a coward. The others of their group were all heroes. Even Rhyian had displayed new fortitude. Not Lena. She'd been tested and she'd crumpled. Her shattered heart had left her hollow and empty inside, nothing but a shell of a person.

"As for Rhy's supposedly bountiful array of lovers, I'd rethink your assumptions about what exactly he's been doing for the last seven years," Zeph finally said. "You never came back to Annfwn, so you don't know as much as you think you do."

"Are you trying to tell me he's been celibate?" Lena asked drily as she valiantly tried to recover her composure. "Monkishly reflecting on the error of his ways and forsaking all others?"

"Have you?" Zeph shot back.

"No," Lena answered in grim satisfaction. "As you well know." In fact, she'd taken a number of lovers, both for one night and a couple for as long as half a year. Lena had nothing on Zeph, but she'd made a determined effort of sleeping around, certain that she could erase the imprint of Rhyian's body from hers, eventually vanquish the memory of his ardent lovemaking. Unfortunately, there was no one like Rhyian.

She shook her head sharply to dispel the weakening emotions those thoughts evoked, succeeding in not looking in his direction this time. "Are *you* shaming *me* now?" she asked as lightly as she could. "Because I owe no one any kind of fidelity. I'm a grown woman who can do as she likes."

"Of course you are. The only shame is that you're cutting off your own tail because it got stepped on once," Zeph snapped, her own invisible gríobhth tail lashing in the air. "I feel I should remind you that, when you believed you were going to die, he was the first person you thought of and wanted me to give a message to. You wanted me to tell him you never stopped loving him."

"Shh!" Lena hissed through her teeth. Shapeshifter ears were acute and she did not want Rhyian overhearing that tidbit.

"He isn't paying attention." Zeph waved that off with raised brows at Rhyian, who was now surrounded by several flirting young women. The only surprise there was that it had taken so long. As Lena watched, Rhyian kissed the hand of a gorgeous redhead, and Lena gritted her teeth against the surge of jealousy, reminding herself that she didn't want him and he could put his lips on whoever he wanted to—and likely had. "Look at you," Zeph said more gently. "You still love him. You still want him. I know love isn't always easy, but maybe it's worth risking the pain?"

"You don't *know*," she bit out, so not in the mood to be chastised, especially by Zeph, of all people. "You've never had your heart broken. Leave the empathy to Stella," she advised. "It's not your forte."

Zeph arched her brows coolly. "It's true, I'm no empath. But at least I'm no coward, giving up before I know whether the battle is won or lost."

The words so precisely echoed Lena's own unhappy thoughts about herself that they took her breath away. She gaped at Zeph, torn between utter fury and complete devastation that Zeph—who'd always been a loyal friend—thought so little of her.

Zeph's glittering gaze softened with remorse. "Lena, I didn't—"

"Looks like you need rescuing, Salena," Rhyian drawled, his voice a sensual purr that scraped over Lena's skin like an intimate caress. "Care for a dance?"

~ 2 ~

SALENA'S SCENT FLUSHED toward fury, which was better than the desolation Rhy had detected as he surreptitiously observed the argument. The exchange had been growing increasingly emotional for some time, and he'd kept an eye on it at first because he was always watching Salena—couldn't stop himself—and then out of concern for her. Zeph was well-intentioned, most of the time, but her words could be as sharp as her predator's beak.

"A dance," he repeated helpfully, allowing a small smile in the face of Salena's ire. "It's when people cling to one another and move more or less rhythmically to music. A strange mossback custom, I'll admit, but it is customary when attempting to blend with the natives." He included Zeph in the smile, tilting his head meaningfully. "It *is* what we're supposed to be doing here. Frivolous young nobles out for a sightseeing tour, drinking, dancing, not spies for the high throne at all."

"Since when are *you* the champion of adherence to our mission requirements?" Salena demanded, apparently happy to turn her anger on him. But then, she always was, every slicing remark from her full lips a repetition of her undying grievance against him. No matter what words she used, everything she said to him contained the same meaning.

"I'm trying to do better," he told her with firm intent, willing her to understand that he meant in all ways. Two could play the subtext game. He held out a hand, daring her to refuse as she clearly wanted to. "Think of all the people watching us," he warned when it seemed like she might spit in his face.

For they were under scrutiny, that much was clear. The people of the Isles of Remus might be overjoyed to have their king restored, and willing—even if they were a bit less joyful about it—to accept his choice of bride in Gen. Isyn's subjects were polite to the rest of the group, grateful to their king's rescuers, affording them every comfort, but these were a people as unaccustomed to strangers in their midst as his own people. The Tala had grown more relaxed about allowing mossbacks into Annfwn, but nobody really loved it. Rhy recognized the the scent of suspicion, the subconscious bracing for possible attack a familiar tension in the air.

"Fine," Salena bit out. "One dance." Not taking his hand, she charged past him onto the dance floor, looking nothing like a frivolous young noble, but something more like a rampaging warrior storming the field of battle. She was a lot like her father that way. Salena might have her mother's petite and curving frame, but she had inherited King Nakoa KauPo's stormy disposition, fully the dragon king's daughter.

Zeph sipped her sparkling wine, eyes full of mischief equally as effervescent, all hint of argument vanished. "Have fun, you two," she cooed.

"Stop tormenting Salena," he told her, pointing a warning finger at her.

"She's standing out on the dance floor alone," Zeph replied, fluttering her lashes. "Humiliating her won't win you any points."

Biting out a curse, because she was obviously correct, Rhy spun on his heel and strode toward the fuming Salena. Pulling on a smooth, unruffled demeanor was much like shapeshifting—in fact, he was far better at it than actual shapeshifting—and Rhy gave Salena his most charming and seductive smile, not that it had ever fooled her, as he slid an arm around her narrow waist and lifted her delicate fingers in his. He whirled them into the swirl of music, noting how she stared firmly at his shoulder, refusing to meet his eyes, her posture far more rigid than even the formal mossback dance required. Her scent, however, held a hint of desire for him still, one that waxed and waned with her mood, but still lingered. She wasn't impervious to him, and that was all that kept his hope alive.

That and the conversation he'd overheard between Zeph and Salena back at Lake Sullivan. They'd thought him asleep, but he'd heard that Salena's wishes on facing death—something that grated in his heart like broken glass—were to tell Rhy that she still loved him. He'd had to lie there, pretending to no reaction, as Salena begged Zeph not to reveal that. She didn't want him to know how she felt because she couldn't trust him.

Now that he did know, it gave him hope. Conversely, knowing that Salena was certain she could never trust him again made him despair. He lived suspended between those two poles, rent every moment by that pain, uncertain how to escape them.

Especially when Salena's favored method of dealing with him was to pretend he didn't exist, even when she was in his arms.

"Remember the bonfire dances in Annfwn?" he asked. "Now *those* were fun." Salena was breathtakingly beautiful, looking exceptionally lovely in her deep red ballgown, her hair like sunlit caramel piled elegantly on her head. Still, he'd loved how she'd been back in Annfwn in those carefree days, her hair loose, her lushly curved body barely veiled by a translucent silk shift as she danced with wild abandon around the big bonfires, as unselfconscious as any of the Tala, laughing with easy joy.

"I don't want to talk about the past, Rhyian," she gritted through clenched teeth.

"What would you like to talk about?"

"Nothing." Her gaze, smoky blue as mountain valleys at sunset, flashed up to his and away.

"Everyone says I need to listen to you," he said after a moment. He was trying here. "You said that, too. But I don't see how I can do that if you won't talk to me."

"That's not my problem. I agreed to a dance, not a conversation."

"So we're to dance in silence?" he tried for a teasing tone. "Like a miserably married mossback couple with nothing to say to each other anymore." He dipped his chin toward an older couple dancing nearby. Their noses lifted, expressions impassive, they gazed steadfastly past each other, barely tolerating the contact. "I say they are the product of an arranged marriage. He was much older, though misery has aged her, and she was forced to abandon her illicit love—the family gardener—to marry and seal some sort of alliance so the mossbacks could acquire many *things*."

Salena didn't respond. Once they'd played that game with glee, speculating about the secret lives of the people around them. He supposed it was too much to hope she might unbend that much. "Not all marriages are miserable, Rhyian," she said finally. Not engaging in the game, but at least answering him, if with more slicing subtext.

"Just most of them," he observed cynically.

The air around them stirred with her storm magic, an uneasy turbulence shifting the previous steady state, a whiff of ozone in her scent. She met his gaze stonily. "My parents have a happy marriage, as do yours."

"Magically induced pairings don't count," he retorted, irritated that she'd bring up his parents at all. The nobly heroic Rayfe and Andromeda, brought together by the meddling of the goddess Moranu, and practically divine in their own right according to the majority of the Tala, were notable exceptions to everything. His mother, the powerful sorceress who saved them all in the Deyrr War? Some hero she was. No one talked about *how* she accomplished that. Nobody ever mentioned how she traded her unborn child—*him*—to the goddess Moranu for Her help. The great Andromeda reaped the rewards while he lived his life as not only a disappointment to everyone, but waiting for Moranu to take him up by the scruff of the neck and use him for whatever whimsy struck Her.

Oh, his mother *said* she was sorry, and his father routinely berated him for making her feel guilty, which was hardly Rhy's fault, but he was heartily sick of people holding up his parents as an example of anything. They'd sacrificed their only child to a goddess and waltzed happily through life. The gall. "Nobody in their right mind believes that *love* has anything to do with monogamy and fidelity," he added. "Those rules are either socially enforced or the product of an enchantment. Anyone who believes otherwise is a fool."

"I believe otherwise," Salena said quietly.

He snorted at that. "You'll eventually grow out of it. You're too smart to buy into that drivel."

The look she gave him then was so wounded that it finally penetrated the stale rage that overcame him at any reference to his wonderfully-in-love parents. He immediately and profoundly regretted introducing the topic at all. He'd need all his charm to move the conversation back to safer ground, to convince Salena that they *could* be together again, if she'd just open up her mind and let go of the past.

"You just never change, do you, Rhyian." Not a question, she pronounced the sentence like the doom it was.

"You can't know if I've changed if you won't talk to me, Salena," he replied with quiet logic. That was the best path: appeal to her rational mind. "Please, can't we talk this out?"

"We *did* talk," she said in that low, grinding voice. It meant she was barely clinging to control. Everyone thought Salena was so rational-minded, so logical and scientific—which she was—but she was also the princess of storms, building pressure just beyond the horizon until she unleashed her passion in all its stirring glory. "*Remember?*" she demanded, staring up at him now, her tone mocking his earlier remark. "On the night of the crystalline moon, you asked me to hear you out and I did."

Yes, she had. And he'd thought he'd gotten through to her, that he'd explained why he'd been so foolish. He didn't expect forgiveness for what he'd done. Moranu knew, he didn't forgive himself. But if she could just see her way to letting him start over again…

"We can't just pretend the past never happened, Rhyian." Her voice had lost the grating quality, but now throbbed with a different, darker feeling, and she stared up at him with grief-haunted eyes. Had he wanted her to meet his gaze? Now he felt pinned by the implicit accusation in them. She knew him better than anyone, better than his friends, his cousins, or his parents. She saw every flaw in him, which was saying something as there were a considerable number of those, and she'd always been able to forgive him. "I heard you out. I listened to your explanation as you asked of me, which I think was generous given… everything." Though she said the word slowly, her voice wobbled on it.

Rhy found himself holding her tighter, as if she might slip away if he didn't. "I apologized," he pointed out, feeling it should count for more than it had. Everyone always made such a big deal about apologizing, but what had it gotten him? Nothing. Less than nothing, because Salena only seemed to hold his explanation against him more.

"I know." She dropped her eyes, staring somewhere below his chin, the dusky blue luminous with what he was afraid were unshed tears. "And it's not that I don't appreciate and accept the apology."

That gave him heart. Maybe the stupid impulse had been worthwhile after all. "That night, you agreed to setting the past aside, so we could try to recover some of that joy together we once had." They'd kissed, and she had been like lightning and thunder in his arms, silky roiling surf and night-dark passion. Everything they'd been to each other before had clicked effortlessly back into place. The rightness of it still echoed through him. More, he knew she'd felt it, too, and he couldn't understand why she continued to deny her desire for him. Her love for him that she tried to recant. "It was good between us, Salena."

"I know," she said again, her voice small.

"Why can't we give this a second chance?" He was pleading, but such was the extremity her obstinacy had pushed him to. Nothing else he'd tried to win her back had worked so far. "Just try. One night. Then a night and a day. Small steps. See how it goes."

She chewed her lip, a tremble running through her that made him want to pull her closer. He'd tempted her to try. If he played this just right, she'd agree. Once she let him seduce her again, she wouldn't want to leave. She'd eventually admit to her enduring feelings. They simply couldn't be apart any longer. She had to know that, too. She *did* know that, because her thoughts had been of him when she faced death. She loved him still—he just had to get her to accept it.

"Please, love," he coaxed, sliding in just enough to brush his lips against her temple, breathing in her scent, the delicious desire tempting him to taste her skin.

"Don't call me that," she said, sounding ragged. "You lost the right to call me that."

Frustration ground at him. Not using the word didn't

change how he felt. "Fine, I won't. But I'm asking you to give me another chance. Give *us* another chance."

"I can't," she breathed, though she didn't pull away. "I'm not strong enough."

"You *are* strong," he insisted, lowering his voice, bending to whisper the words against her ear, kissing the sweet curve in the one spot that always drove her wild. "You're the strongest person I know."

She shook her head, pulling back, looking up at him. Tears were tracking over her cheeks. "I'm asking you to understand this, Rhyian," she said, her tone flat and uncompromising. "I know it's in the past for you, but what you did... you very nearly broke me. I just... I can't let you hurt me again. You have that power, whether either of us likes it. You are far too good at knowing exactly where I'm most vulnerable. If it happened again, I know I wouldn't recover."

"But I *wouldn't* hurt you again," he protested. "I'll make any promise you like," he added, a bit wildly, as he'd never been all that good at remembering things like promises and duties, all mossback inventions.

She was shaking her head, slow and steady, regaining her resolve. "I can't let you close enough to risk you hurting me again, because if you did—intentionally or not—it might kill me. My heart is fragile now in a way it wasn't before. And that's your fault, Rhyian."

Anger fired through him, exacerbated by the guilt, knowing it was true. "We could start over, if only you'd unbend," he insisted.

"Unbend?" She sounded dangerous again, that taste of

ozone in the air, lightning about to strike raising his hair in alarm.

"Yes! *Unbend.*" He gripped her harder. "Let go of your rigid mossback rules and your past hurts. I made *one* mistake. Am I to be punished for it forever?"

Their dancing had slowed as they argued and she came to a halt, now, as rigid physically as he'd accused her of being mentally. The dancers swirled around them, a rush of color and sound circling the fixed point of the pair of them. Her eyes blazed in a suddenly pale face. With a curl of dread, Rhy realized his fatal misstep. He'd lost his temper and his patience, something she could always make him do.

"No, Rhyian," she said with lethal quiet. "You do not have to be *punished forever.* Instead of suffering unspeakably as you are, you can do *exactly* what I've asked you to do over and over and over again!" Her voice had risen to a near shout, people glancing over with curiosity and concern as she wrenched out of his desperate grip. "*Leave me alone!*" she screeched, hands clenched into fists at her sides.

Outside, lightning cracked, thunder following in an immediate *boom!* The music came to a ragged halt as people gasped, some squelching startled screams, followed by nervous laughter fluttering through the sudden silence. A steady roar followed, rain pouring onto the high roof above, furiously battering as Salena's eyes glowed with matching rage.

"All right, now," Gen said, appearing immediately at Salena's side, wrapping an arm around her as Gen glared daggers at Rhy. Behind her, Isyn surveyed the scene with calm interest. "Let's get you out of here, honey," Gen murmured.

A lithe, dark-haired form wove through the crowd, Stella swiftly coming to Salena's other side. She'd retired for the night, exhausted from healing, her empath's senses not up to tolerating crowds even under the best of circumstances. Wrapping a hand around Salena's bare arm—working her calming magic through touch—she surveyed Rhy with wide gray eyes. "Time to step away, Rhy," she said, her firm tone making it clear she meant for more than just the moment.

The moment that had slipped through his fingers. The harder he tried with Salena, the worse he failed. Jak, disheveled from bed, had followed Stella and now clapped Rhy on the shoulder. "Let's go have a drink."

Rhy shook him off, viciously angry. He'd been so close to succeeding with Salena, and their interference helped nothing and no one. All he needed was for Astar and Zeph to step in and complete the forces arrayed against him. And—sure enough—there they were, the perfect couple already trying to rule him and all the world, standing on the dais on the far side of the room, watching with keen attention, whispering to each other, and looking disappointed.

"Let go of the storm," Stella was coaching Salena in a low voice. "You're safe. No one will hurt you here."

"I wasn't hurting her," Rhy grated out. All he'd done was ask her to *talk* to him.

Jak caught his arm, grip tighter. "Walk away, man. Now," he advised in a cheerful tone. "Don't be more of an idiot than you already are."

Rhy nearly snarled at him, ready to fight. His shapeshifter strength could easily best Jak's, no matter how clever the mossback was with his daggers. But Salena picked that moment to leave, sagging a little as their friends supported her. She stopped and looked back at him, silently asking the women flanking her to wait. "Rhyian?" she said, as if she didn't have his full attention already. As if she didn't always have it. "You claim you want to listen to what I'm saying, so listen to this."

"All right." He swallowed, nodded. He wouldn't like this, but he'd pledged to listen, so he would.

"You didn't make only one mistake," she said softly, a world of hurt in her eyes. "But tonight's is the last one I'll tolerate. Approach me again at your peril."

Thunder boomed to punctuate her words and Jak hissed an unnecessary warning in Rhy's ear. With a last baleful glare, Salena straightened her spine and strode out of the ballroom, Stella and Gen hastening to follow in her wake. Zeph cut across the dance floor like a dark arrow, casting Rhy a look of mixed rue and accusation as she went to join the women in their solidarity. Astar stepped off the dais, too, his tall figure still visible as he came straight toward Jak and Rhy.

Jak whistled, low and long. "Make that a number of drinks, eh?"

Rhy had no intention of sitting still for the lecture to come. Heedless of the injunction to avoid frightening the ignorant mossbacks with scary shapeshifting—as if anyone believed their ridiculous cover story, especially after they'd rescued Isyn—Rhy ditched Jak's insistent grip with the simple expedient of shifting into his First Form. As always, the raven form felt both natural and disappointingly lacking in power. If only his First Form had been something more impressive, his life would be different. People would respect him. He might have a chance at being King of Annfwn, rather than the not-really-a-prince.

But raven form was his, and no one could gainsay the will of Moranu. Such was his cursed existence.

Dodging Jak's attempt to waylay him, Rhy circled up to the ceiling, found a window open to the world, and flew out into Salena's emotional storm. Maybe he wouldn't bother to return.

~ 3 ~

"**I**'M *FINE*," LENA told the other women, for about the hundredth time that morning. Stella, Gen, and Zeph had all convened in her room, ostensibly to dress for the day, clearly to have another round of badgering Lena about her feelings. She could've told them all to stay in bed with their lovers. Time much better spent. "Of course I can attend a strategy meeting. That's why we're here, isn't it? To defeat the intelligence and save the realm for Her Majesty so we can all get on with our lives. I, for one, can't wait to get this finished so I can just go home."

"Home?" Stella asked gently. "Or back to Aerron?"

"Home is where the work is," Lena replied crisply. No, she had little desire to return to Nahanau either. She lacked the patience for court politics and her mother's well-meant, but searching questions. Also, the place was nearly as haunted with memories of Rhyian as Annfwn was. They'd spent so much time exploring the island together, when she'd shared her favorite hidden beaches with him. Where they'd first kissed and she'd realized with dizzying delight that the wildly gorgeous and enigmatic Prince of Shadows wanted *her*.

What a fool she'd been.

"Lena," Stella said in her patient voice, sitting with her hands folded serenely in her lap. "You haven't talked at all about what happened last night."

"What is there to talk about, Nilly?" Lena returned wearily, then held up a hand when Gen opened her mouth. "Let me stop you all there. I don't *want* to talk about it. I'm exhausted of thinking, feeling, and dealing with Rhyian. Please spare me having to put even a moment's more attention on him than I have to."

"But—" Gen began. Zeph, of all people, cut her off.

"Lena is a big girl," Zeph declared. "And this is between her and Rhy. If she doesn't want to spend more energy on the idiot, then we should respect that. Also, we'll be late for the meeting, so we should go."

"Weren't you the one chiding me about giving the relationship another chance?" Lena demanded.

"You *were*?" Gen asked with a level of astonishment Lena found most gratifying.

Zeph grimaced. "I was wrong, all right? Astar and I discussed last night and I can see that I should've stayed out of it."

"So much responsible growth," Lena observed. "Minding your own business and wanting to be on time for meetings."

"Miracles do happen," Zeph tossed back flippantly, though there was a grain of remorse in it.

"I really thought Rhy was maturing," Stella mused unhappily. "He gave me such good advice about learning from his cautionary tale, to work out my issues with Jak instead of giving into fear by taking the easy route and running away."

"I thought he was, too." Gen cast Lena a cautious look.

"He told me to stop seeking perfection and look for what would make me happy in the moment, since the moment is all we have."

"*I* told you that, too," Zeph put in with a hint of outrage.

"Yes, but I don't listen to *you*," Gen shot back with a cheeky hair toss. Truly, though they were first cousins, the pair of them fought like sisters.

"We're supposed to be focused on Lena, ladies," Stella reminded them mildly.

"No, we're not," Lena said with haste. "I know you all care about me and you mean well and I appreciate it, but the single relevant truth here is that it doesn't matter what Rhyian says. He's good at saying what anyone wants to hear; he may even believe it. But he's not going to change. Even last night he implied that I'm the problem for ever expecting him to be monogamous with me."

"Wait a moment," Gen burst out. "Setting up expectations with you is one thing. Going straight from your bed to someone else's on the morning you gave up your virginity is another matter entirely."

"To two someone elses," Lena correctly darkly.

"It's true, though, that the Tala are rarely monogamous," Zeph said.

"Does Astar know you feel that way?" Gen shot back.

"He knows that I've promised to be faithful to him," she replied calmly. "But I arguably have played the field to the extent that I've worked it out of my system. How about you, cousin? You've barely been with more than one man. When you marry Isyn, will you someday regret that he's practically the only lover you tasted?"

"Some of us don't have to taste a thousand flavors before we find the right one," Gen answered with cool confidence. "Isyn and I have been searching for each other, in countless ways, for years."

"You and Isyn are getting married?" Lena asked, hearing the astonishment in her own voice. "When did this happen?"

All three looked at her with various degrees of chagrin and sympathy. "Last night," Gen admitted. "He asked, anyway, though I haven't given a definitive answer."

"You haven't?" Zeph raised her brows. "I thought that was all you wanted."

Gen actually squirmed uncomfortably, glancing at Lena and away again. "It is. But the timing isn't right. We have the mission, and I just didn't want to throw it in Lena's face after..."

That did it. "All right," Lena declared, attempting to be as coolly rational. "No more dancing around my feelings. No more inviting me to talk about Rhyian and what happened between us a lifetime ago. Thank you, Nilly, for caring—I do appreciate it. Congratulations, Gen, on your engagement, because you are going to seize your chance for happiness and tell Isyn 'yes' like you want to. I'm truly happy for you. Zeph, you're absolutely correct that Rhyian is Tala to the bone and that means I never should have imagined he'd be what I was looking for. I am trying to be adult about this. And I admit that I've been letting the heartbreak of my younger self get in the way. But if Zeph can be responsible, so can I. Rhyian will never change and the fault is mine for ever expecting he'd be anything but who he is. We have a mission to accomplish. We've finally made it to the Isles of Remus. Let's do what we came here for. I can work with Rhyian as an old friend and current member of our team. That should be enough for everyone. Yes?"

She looked around at their encouraging expressions, easily reading the doubt in them. Well, she would show them different. She could do this: wall Rhyian out, treat him as no different than Astar or Jak, or even Isyn, who she'd barely met. Lock away her heart where it wouldn't influence her words or actions. She certainly was practiced at it. When none of her friends seemed to have anything to say to her little speech, Lena nodded crisply. "Let's get to this meeting on time."

THE COUNCIL CHAMBERS at Isyn's newly acquired palace were as lovely and spacious as the rest of the rambling structure. Not fortified like the citadels of the original twelve kingdoms, the palace of the rulers of the Isles of Remus boasted enormous windows that looked out onto the verdant surrounding rainforest. Fitted with real glass kept sparkling clear, the windows gave onto a breathtaking vista of the lush canopy that rolled toward the distant sea, all swathed in streams of mist and gentle rain.

The edifice was also clearly a place built by and for a people who were not shapeshifters. While paradisical Annfwn was undeniably beautiful, it was a place of the Tala, wild in their ways, most of them strongly driven by their animal natures, so the comforts of the human body weren't always taken into account. They disdained the written word and "things" in general. Lena had always felt a bit out of place in Annfwn, even at the best of times, longing for the library at home in Nahanau, and the creature comforts there.

In fact, the Isles of Remus reminded her of home with an aching nostalgia. Though considerably cooler than her tropical island home, the mild climate came as an intense relief from the bitter winter they'd been traveling through. Lena felt like her bones were finally thawing. These isles were also a chain of islands like the Nahanaun archipelago, and the lush foliage— though of a different variety—was very like the landscape of home. She'd never been homesick all those years working in Aerron, but now it hit her hard. Part of the emotional fallout of the scene with Rhyian the night before, no doubt. Nevertheless, for the first time she found herself contemplating going home to Nahanau when this was done. To lick her wounds, figure out who she was without the Prince of Shadows and their torturous past haunting her. To begin again.

So, she found herself staring out the generous windows more often than not during the meeting, listening to the conversation with only half an ear. A whole lot of the discussion involved bringing Isyn up to speed on what had happened to them thus far. The other five of their crew recounted their adventures with enthusiasm and she was happy enough to leave that to them.

Rhyian, naturally, hadn't bothered to show up for the

meeting. He hadn't been seen since he shapeshifted into raven form—in the middle of Isyn's ballroom, no less—and flew off into the storm Lena had accidentally brewed up. She doubted he'd gone far, not out of any sense of responsibility, but because the isles were magically removed from the rest of the world. Unless Rhyian found some store of hitherto hidden sorcery in himself, he was around somewhere.

No doubt sulking.

Which was his own cursed fault and she refused to feel bad about it.

"That must have been terrifying, Princess Salena Nakoa KauPo," Isyn was saying, the sound of her name, in all its grand formality, snagging her attention. When she glanced at him, a bit startled to be called out, he inclined his head gravely, bright green eyes somber. "When I first fell through into the Winter Isles alter-realm, I was so disoriented by the transition, so completely confused, that I immediately fell to my attackers. I'm impressed that you had the wit to find high ground and defend yourself from the tentacle monsters with only a dagger."

Normally Lena had no problem with being the center of attention, but at this moment—with everyone looking at her with warm, encouraging smiles—she felt very much on the spot. They didn't need to be worrying about her. Much as she appreciated her friends' concern, her personal troubles and stupid love life did not merit this kind of attention.

"Call me Lena, please, King Isyn," she replied. "And everyone else at this table has suffered far worse since." It was true, because after her one harrowing experience, Lena hadn't returned to any alter-realm, not until they'd all gone to the Winter Isles to rescue Isyn. Even then she'd had light duty, especially as a non-shapeshifter, mainly assisting Stella in healing Isyn and then hiding while everyone else handled things. And yet, she'd still been filled with icy terror the whole time. Completely irrational, as she'd been in the least amount of danger of any of them. She'd barely been able contain her internal panic.

Stella, with her empathy, had known and even now watched her with wide gray eyes that saw far too much. Irrationally, Lena hated the grave sympathy she saw there.

Isyn was nodding thoughtfully, considering her words. "Then you must call me Isyn. As to your point," he continued in a musing tone, "it seems to me that just because others have worse troubles, that doesn't diminish our own struggles. Our problems are our problems and don't decrease in scale in relevance to what someone else endures."

Gen, clearly completely dazzled by her ivory-haired lover, took Isyn's hand and squeezed it. "You're so wise, Isyn."

"It's a fair point," Stella acknowledged, exchanging a speaking glance with Astar. The twins sometimes spoke subvocally, their version of a private language, so they were no doubt conferring. "We've all been tested by our adventures, and we each have coped with those intense pressures in our own way. It's important to remember not to judge one-another for how we've handled the trials we've endured."

Lena didn't have an empathic or telepathic bone in her body, but she knew with uncomfortable clarity that Stella was speaking of Rhyian. "At any rate," she said, hoping to divert the discussion from uncomfortable emotional morasses, "all credit to Jak for teaching me how to use a blade and making sure I was wearing a pair of daggers. That saved my life."

Jak grinned easily, flipping a small silver blade between nimble fingers. "You're a quick study and you practice diligently." He slid his dark gaze to Stella beside him. "Unlike *other* people we could mention."

"Don't start," Stella replied equably. "I'm still mad at you about the boat."

"I kept us alive," Jak argued, eyeing her warily.

"Which is the only reason I'm still allowing you in my bed."

"I don't recall making it to the bed last night," he purred meaningfully.

Stella blushed, still managing to slide him a stern look. "It's a metaphor, but you can find yourself literally out on your adorable ass if you want to continue poking at me."

Jak opened his mouth to retort, then looked past Lena and raised his brows. "Well, look what the raven dragged in."

~ 4 ~

R HY SURVEYED THE gathering, trying to quell his irritation over the obvious fact that the others evidently had been meeting for some time. Salena had her back to the door, her hair upswept so it was all coiled on her head to reveal the enticingly vulnerable hollows of her swanlike neck, deep golden skin tempting his lips. The immediate tense rise of her lovely shoulders at his entrance quelled any pleasure at the sight, however.

As did the near-universal scowls from his so-called friends.

"I see you didn't wait for me," he noted, keeping himself to a lazy stroll as he took the remaining empty chair at the table. The one farthest from Salena, he noted, as if he couldn't be trusted not to leap on her like a mad dog. He had himself tightly leashed. Flying and running himself to exhaustion had guaranteed that much.

"Should we have waited?" Astar asked blandly.

"Or informed me there *was* a meeting," he answered in the same oh-so-neutral tone. "Unless you intended to exclude me."

Zeph rolled her eyes. "Don't be a gruntling. It's difficult to send a message when no one knows where you've gone."

Rhy snorted, deliberately sprawling so the golden prince

42

and his prospective princess bride would know their censure bothered Rhy not in the least. He'd been scolded all his life by the mighty Rayfe, King of the Tala, and young Willy had a long ways to go before he had even a quarter of the impact. "As if I could go anywhere." He leveled a look on Isyn, seated at the head of the table. "These isles of yours are as impossible to exit as Annfwn once was to enter."

Isyn sat back, expression guarded. "I'm as new to these isles as you are, Prince Rhyian. Though being king here has long been my destiny, I've only just arrived, and have had little time to learn much about my new realm. Still, it seems to me that your kingdom of Annfwn benefitted greatly from its enchanted insularity. The protections here, however they work, also serve to keep anyone from coming in."

"Not really a prince," Rhy pointed to himself with a thin smile. Mossbacks with their thick skulls and obstinate assumptions. He decided against mentioning that Annfwn's barrier had always allowed animals to pass—or shapeshifters in animal form—whereas the intangible force that separated the Isles of Remus from the rest of the world didn't. Not that he'd truly been trying to leave. It was just that something in him rankled at not being able to.

"It brings up an interesting point, though," Astar said to Isyn. "Are the Isles of Remus in truth functioning as an alter-realm?"

"They're different," Zeph added, "in that the Isles are at times connected to the overall reality of the rest of our world whereas the alter-realms seem to be entirely cut off."

"And the isles aren't warped landscapes like the alter-realms," Salena said. "We've been here only a short time, but from what I've observed, these isles are a fully functioning ecosystem. As opposed to the alter-realms, which are all skewed in some way and unable to sustain life without magic."

"And we can shapeshift here," Gen added, "unlike in the alter-realms."

Rhy suppressed a shudder. The alter-realm he'd been stuck in as a wolf had been a huge, flat grid of polished black stone with bottomless defiles that sliced through it at intervals. No food, no water, no life at all. And time passed oddly there, feeling like days. Until Zeph had appeared in gríobhth form, he'd been growing despondent at the prospect of dying as a wolf, and seriously considering hurling himself into the abyss instead of slowly withering from thirst.

And from never seeing Salena again.

Zeph was frowning at Salena, thinking. "Are they all warped landscapes though? The forest alter-realm seemed pretty complete."

Salena shook her head, warming to her topic, eyes lighting. She was always happiest talking about ecosystems, something he didn't understand, but nevertheless had always liked about her.

"Ah, but it *wasn't*," she said. "It may have seemed that way on the surface, but we observed only a few varieties of macrofauna and they were of wildly different species. Most important, there were no insects." She looked around at their bewildered faces—not incidentally skipping over Rhy—and smiled at their puzzled expressions. "You can't have a healthy ecosystem without insects or even smaller life forms. That's why the leaf detritus only accumulated without decomposing. The broken cycle of life is a key indicator that the alter-realms aren't self-sustaining."

"The Winter Isles were not self-sustaining," Isyn said, nodding to Salena. "Though that place seemed as if it was once connected to the rest of the world, it had at some point become cut off and encapsulated. From the tales the folk told, their land had once been a balanced and thriving landscape, which gradually changed and became a land of eternal winter."

Gen shuddered. "They basically lived on fish. No greens. It was awful."

"We had seaweed," Isyn reminded her with a wry smile.

"I know." The smile she returned blazed with far more happiness than any conversation about seaweed deserved. "And I shouldn't complain. I was only there for a few weeks; you endured it for nearly a lifetime."

"My life began when you arrived." Isyn lifted their joined hands and kissed the back of hers.

Rhy barely contained an eyeroll at the display and found Salena at last acknowledging his existence. She regarded him with steady appraisal, clearly noting his discomfort over the billing and cooing of the new lovebirds. He raised one brow, daring her to challenge him on it and she looked away, disengaging with such an utter lack of interest that it pierced him to the bone. He'd take fighting with Salena over her not caring at all.

"What's key here," Astar said, bringing them back on track, dutiful leader that he was, "is that the intelligence we've been sent to defeat has almost certainly created these alter-realms for some reason of its own."

"Created them or cut away pieces of other places and isolated them?" Salena asked. "The latter seems more likely."

"Does it matter?" Zeph asked with genuine curiosity.

"It might," Salena answered. "The more we understand about the intelligence's abilities and methods, the greater our chances of defeating it. We need to consider why it's doing what it's done so far—and what it will do that causes the catastrophic event Her Majesty sent us to prevent. We need to pool everything we've observed about the intelligence and the alter-realms."

"We know that we each have affinities for certain alter-realms above others," Stella volunteered. "Certain alter-realms will drag us to them when we enter portals if we don't direct them otherwise." Jak, watching her, ran a comforting hand down the long fall of her hair and she leaned into him. Her confrontation with the intelligence apparently obsessed with her, declaring itself in love, had been grueling. "I had visions all my life of being stuck in that tower in the alter-realm that was the field of lilies. Maybe that's why it felt so familiar when I landed there, but somehow I think there was something else that tied me to it."

"Lena went to the endless forest world," Zeph mused. Salena shuddered, probably imperceptible to anyone else's eye, but Rhy saw. And, unlike Jak, he was helpless to comfort his beloved. Just as he'd been helpless to do anything when he felt her suddenly disappear from the world, the most harrowing experience of his life.

"You went to the forest realm also," Astar said, touching

Zeph's arm gently.

"I went because I was going after Lena," Zeph pointed out. "So I followed her path. We have to consider only those realms we ended up in by happenstance." She narrowed her eyes at Rhy. "Rhy went to the flat-grid alter-realm."

And what did that say about him? Stella got lilies, Salena a forest, Isyn and Gen went to an entire, if small world with an intelligent race living in it, and his fate drew him to a lifeless landscape of precipitous death. Bleak and mercilessly sharp-edged as his soul. Not a cheerful thought to contemplate.

Perhaps Salena was thinking the same thing, because she winced a little. "But Rhyian was only following the people from the inn," she argued. "Maybe that portal was keyed to one of them."

Ever the soft heart, she had. "I wasn't following them, Salena," he said, since at least in this it was important to be honest. "I fell through the portal by accident. One moment I was chasing the tentacle monster and the next I was falling." He stretched to ease the agitation the memory evoked, hoping to look nonchalant. Salena glanced at him and away, and he wondered if he was as transparent to her as she was to him. Probably. Except that she was determined not to care about him. And he had only himself to blame for that.

"So, the only ones of us who haven't gone to an alter-realm on their own, rather than chasing someone else," Stella mused, "are Jak, Zeph, and Willy."

"Are you suggesting we each go to see where we end up?" Astar asked dubiously.

Zeph shuddered. "Please no," she declared.

"Could be interesting," Jak suggested, spinning his blade thoughtfully. "I wonder if mine would be endless ocean."

"Allow me to make it clear that I am *not* suggesting this course of action," Stella said repressively.

"We can draw tentative conclusions based on the information we have," Salena agreed, "without risking lives to gather more."

"Isyn and I have been discussing this," Gen said into the thoughtful silence that ensued. "First, we feel strongly that we cannot leave the folk to their fate in the Winter Isles alter-realm. They'll die out before long. We have to go back there. If there's not a way to save their dying world, then we need to bring them here."

"And second, I owe it to Falada to find her," Isyn said. "She set sail with you all to help rescue me and was lost along the way. If your theory is correct, it's likely she was pulled into some alter-realm that matched her in some way when you all entered the portal to the Winter Isles."

Privately, Rhy didn't know how one would go about locating an incorporeal faery horse that only a few people seemed to be able to see, but he kept that opinion to himself. Still, from the way no one offered a response, it seemed everyone was thinking that.

"Meanwhile," Astar said finally, "we need to discover why this was our destination. Queen Andromeda saw in visions that the cataclysm would occur in the Isles of Remus. That's our priority: to stop it. Have you glimpsed anything more, Nilly?"

Stella shook her head, looking tired. "What with the sailing expedition and rescuing Gen and Isyn, I haven't had it in me to explore the possible futures. It's something that requires quiet, solitude, and long periods of concentration. Now that we're here, I can do that."

"It's also something that requires you to be fully rested," Jak said firmly, looking to Astar for support. "Which Stella is not yet. She needs to take a couple of days to rest and recover."

Astar nodded. "We all need to recover our strength. It seems that we have an opportunity to breathe and collect ourselves. We'll need to be in top condition for this final battle—whatever form it takes. So consider yourselves ordered to do exactly that."

Rhy wondered how much any of them could truly rest when they all were on edge, anticipating another attack by the intelligence, but again he said nothing. Witness his restraint.

"In the meanwhile," Isyn said, lifting his and Gen's joined hands, "I suggest we add a bit of celebration to our schedule. How about that wedding?" he asked her.

Gen stilled, eyes going wide. "Wedding?"

"When I said last night that I wanted to marry you and make you my queen, those weren't idle promises. I mean to marry you, Gendra. The sooner, the better. If you'll have me?" added, acting sweetly humble.

Rhy nearly rolled his eyes, but Lena glanced sharply at him just then. He raised his brows at her in all innocence and she scowled mightily, seeming convinced that he'd do something to ruin the moment for the lovebirds. *Fine, then.* Rhy wouldn't be the one to point out that Gen and Isyn had barely known each other for a month, even given the accelerated time in the Winter Isles alter-realm.

Besides, Gen was looking all dewy-eyed and overcome. "Of course I'll have you," she whispered. "But it can wait until—"

"No," Isyn interrupted, kissing her lips to stop the words, then caressing her cheek. "I've spent a lifetime waiting and I'm not taking any chances. We're facing uncertainty in the near future, but we have a few days of reprieve. I want to spend them marrying you and being married to you."

"Isyn," she breathed, clearly in raptures, "yes, I'll marry you, but I want to be married to you for a whole, long life."

"I want that, too." He threaded his fingers into her hair, oblivious to the rest of them, apparently. "I've been given a second chance and I intend to demonstrate to your goddess that I'm going to use that time making her favored daughter as happy as possible."

"What's that about her goddess?" Rhy asked, enduring the near-universal scowls from his friends for interrupting the moment.

Gen, however, didn't frown. Instead she looked vaguely embarrassed, disentangling herself from Isyn's embrace, but staying close. "I still have dragon form," she told them all. When there was a murmur of confusion—as they'd all seen her take dragon form in the Winter Isles—she shook her head. "I'm telling this badly. I thought I gave it up, to fit through the portal to come here. I thought I'd only borrowed dragon form to save Isyn, like Astar did with Zeph."

Astar took Zeph's hand and they exchanged a long look. That was another relationship Rhy didn't understand. Zeph had been one to play the field in true Tala fashion. Of course he understood her single-minded pursuit of Astar, but not that she'd agreed to marry him and live in his mossback castle all her days. It made no sense. There was practically a plague of monogamy going around, like a mossback pestilence infecting everyone.

"When the intelligence had Isyn underwater, I prayed to Moranu." Gen looked to Rhy, defiance and sympathy in her gaze. Another child of war heroes, Gen had grown up on the same tales Rhy had. She understood, perhaps better than Salena did, how much the dread onus of belonging to Moranu weighed on Rhy. "Just as Mother called on Moranu back in the day. I needed Her help, so I offered to trade my life for Isyn's."

"You *what*?!" Isyn exploded, dangerous magic shimmering around him. Rhy regarded the ivory-haired mage-king with renewed interest. He'd thought the man entirely mild-mannered, but apparently there was more to him than met the eye. "You had no business, Briar Rose—"

"Hush!" She snapped at him, full of fire herself. "There's nothing I wouldn't do for you. *Nothing.*"

He subsided, but only simmered down his anger. "Finish the story. But we're going to talk, Gendra."

She turned back to the rest of the group. "I'm only telling this in case it's important. I offered my life for Isyn's and She refused. She told me that one doesn't pay for favors, that they must be freely given, that there is nothing more precious than the gift given freely."

Rhy snorted at that. Or the gift given freely of someone *else's* life.

Gen narrowed her eyes at him, but continued. "I told Her that I had nothing to give. She said that wasn't true. I didn't know what She meant, and there wasn't any time to think, so I offered Isyn, and She said, 'done.'"

"What do you mean, you gave him up?" Rhy demanded. These women, so eager to hand Moranu their lovers and sons.

Gen was weeping, focused on Isyn now. "I gave up having you love me. That's why I thought you wouldn't—didn't— anymore."

"Oh, Briar Rose," Isyn whispered, drawing her close again. "No power in this world or any other could change my love for you."

She nodded against him, catching her breath. "I know that now," she replied, her voice too soft for any but shapeshifter hearing to catch. Dashing away her tears, she faced the rest of them again. "So, I thought I must have misunderstood Moranu, and that I'd given up dragon form instead, but I still have it. And then Moranu restored Isyn's youth."

"Then what bargain did you make?" Rhy asked, a deadly fear settling over him.

"That's just it, Rhy," Gen answered, "I don't know. I feel sure there's a price to be paid."

"A favor, freely given," Salena murmured.

"But we can't know what it is until the time comes," Astar declared with such certainty that it was clear he intended to end the discussion. "Such are the ways of the divine. It's good to know we have the aid of Moranu in this venture and that Her help will be worth it to stop the cataclysm."

With sick dread, Rhy felt certain he knew exactly who would be paying that price. The shadows seemed to gather, the brush of black wings in them, and he suppressed a shudder. *Mine,* a dark voice whispered.

~ 5 ~

A S ABSURD AS it seemed to be to plan a wedding in the midst of a quest to save the world from a rapacious, alien intelligence intent on consuming it for its own whimsy, Lena found herself enjoying the simple fun of it. She and Zeph had volunteered to do most of the work, as Stella was under strict orders to do nothing for a couple of days, an undertaking Jak had embraced with whole-hearted enthusiasm. He'd snapped up Isyn's offer of a remote cottage on an isolated cove, and had whisked Stella off immediately, declaring that he'd make love to her until she slept, waking her only to feed her and lull her into sleeping again.

Astar had looked pained, but managed to say nothing more than to wish them well and give strict instructions for them to remain vigilant for danger. So far the inherent magic of the Isles of Remus seemed to be holding the intelligence away from the charmed place. There'd been no incursions of strange beasts here.

Although, as they all knew far too well, their presence could change that. If it was still searching for Stella in particular, the intelligence might be able to hone in on her location. But Jak would be on the alert and they all understood that for

Stella's sensitive mind to fully recover, she needed to be away from people, their noisy thoughts, and invasive emotions. Stella was just hugely blessed that Jak could touch her and be with her without impinging on her internal peace. Physical affection was something Lena knew that Stella had been resigned to never having, and it was nothing short of miraculous that Jak could give it to her.

So, Zeph and Lena spent the next couple of days working with the palace staff on gathering flowers and creating the perfect space for the ceremony. As a child of Annfwn, Gen would want to be married outdoors, they'd decided, an oddity for the locals, who were so accustomed to the presence of rain in the misty isles that they'd never plan an outdoor event. Good weather, however, was something Lena could guarantee, and the lush foliage offered plenty of material for recreating the feel of Annfwn's blooming landscape.

Zeph had declared herself to be in charge of Gen's wedding gown, which Gen agreed to with relief. In fact, both Gen and Isyn had been happy to turn over planning, both of them busy with sorting out the long-ignored problems of their new realm, so long without a ruler on the throne. Astar spent the majority of his time with them, lending advice and insight. He'd been trained by Her Majesty High Queen Ursula in everything he'd need to know to succeed her on the high throne, so he was an ideal consultant.

Astar also, Zeph confided, was looking ahead to the future when he hoped to make the Isles of Remus an ally of the Thirteen Kingdoms. There had been rumors, long before the intelligence had thrust itself into the center of attention, that the kingdom of Kooncelund, across the water from the Isles of Remus, was looking toward the Thirteen Kingdoms with acquisitive interest. If trouble came, as Ursula's spies suggested it might, the Isles of Remus would be in the best position to hinder—or assist—any advancing navy.

Lena listened to Zeph's chatter about politics as they wove flower garlands to decorate their impromptu outdoor ceremony, bemused by her flighty friend's newfound interest in the weighty affairs of mossbacks. But then, unlike some of the others, Lena had always thought Zeph had it in her to be Astar's queen. Zeph possessed a wily intelligence and her First Form lent her a predator's keen insight into the strengths and weaknesses of others. She'd just never had cause to use it in service of anything beyond hunting down a desired lover before.

Everyone was busy but Rhyian, who'd disappeared after the council meeting and hadn't been glimpsed since. Probably off somewhere sulking. Again.

"I'm sorry about Rhy," Zeph said abruptly, startling Lena with the change of subject. "Sorry that I pressed you about him."

Lena took a breath. Much as she'd prefer to ignore Rhy's existence in the world, much less talk about him, that wasn't to be. "It's all right, Zeph," she said. "I'm sorry, too, that the bad blood between Rhyian and me keeps affecting all of you. I'm terribly embarrassed that we had that fight in the middle of Isyn's ballroom. Just when I think we can be grownups, we go right back to being unhinged adolescents again." Like the hot pots of northern Aerron, where a thin crust of apparently solid ground disguised the molten death below. She and Rhyian seemed to traverse that same territory over and over, she thinking that they'd found their footing at last, only to be scalded when the slightest misstep had them plunging through again.

"It wasn't your fault," Zeph said, shaking her head, glorious ebony curls snaking over her shoulders. "Astar lectured me for hours on being insensitive and pushing you into an uncomfortable position."

"I could have said no to the dance." And why hadn't she? Because some stupidly idealistic part of her always hoped that this time would be different, that Rhyian would be... what? Someone other than who he was.

"I thought Rhy would behave, finally," Zeph said with a bite, "but apparently he never learns."

"You know," Lena said slowly, "I think the problem is that we expect him to be learning something, to become this person that we think he should be. Maybe what Rhyian needs is for us all to just accept him for who he is."

Zeph pinned Lena with her sharp sapphire gaze. "Can you do that—accept him as he is?"

"Yes," Lena answered with perfect honesty, "if we're only friends."

"But can you do *that*?"

"I have to. I can't let him into my heart again, but I can let him go be who he is."

"That's awfully generous."

"Well, it occurs to me that all his life, everyone has been expecting Rhyian to become someone in particular. You know how Rayfe and Andi are—it's not easy to live up to the expectations of parents who've gone through what they did."

"I don't know, you and I, our parents are heroes of the Deyrr War, too," Zeph pointed out, but Lena shook her head.

"Not in the same way. Your parents were ordinary people who got caught up in events. Karyn was just a refugee from Dasnaria and Moranu knows Zyr was the last person anyone expected to be selflessly heroic."

Zeph smiled with affection. "Dad manages to surprise people that way. He seems all flirty and superficial, but he comes through when it counts."

Much like Zeph herself, Lena thought, returning the smile. Zeph also had plenty of her mother's spine. The blonde Dasnarian beauty was deceptively sweet looking, with her mild and sometimes apologetic manners, but she possessed a fiery spirit. "And my mother was a *librarian*," Lena continued, "a quiet spinster, dedicated to books."

"Your father was a warrior king who could make storms, though," Zeph replied wryly.

"Yes, but she married him by accident. Caught up in events, see? Whereas Rayfe and Andi, they were both destined for greatness from the beginning, marked by the goddesses for extraordinary deeds. When the histories tell the tales, they start with Rayfe and Andromeda."

"Many of them start with Queen Amelia marrying Hugh of Avonlidgh," Zeph mused, then glanced up, bright eyes wide. "Why so surprised? I listen to the stories."

Lena nodded, amused. Yes, Zeph was very like her father, easily underestimated. "Granted, but again—that marriage resulted in Astar and Stella's birth, and they are both arguably living up to great expectations."

"Those expectations have certainly shaped Astar," Zeph agreed somberly, holding out her hand, examining the ring Astar had given her to seal their engagement, the cabochon ruby a luminous bloodred.

Yes, Astar had dutifully followed every expectation, until he relinquished adherence to the rules and fell in love with Zeph, the first time Astar had stepped out of the rigid path set for him. When they returned to Castle Ordnung—if they all survived to return—Astar would have to give Her Majesty the news that, instead of delivering a planned marriage of state with one of the approved brides on the list the high queen had given him, he'd given the ring to Zeph instead. The ring had belonged to Astar's grandmother—and Rhyian's grandmother—the first Salena, and Lena's namesake. Perhaps it was more correct to say that the long history began with her, with Salena, sorceress queen of the Tala, who left Annfwn and sacrificed her health and sanity to save her beloved people.

Lena shook off the skin-crawling sense of prescience. Foresight was Stella's talent, not Lena's. Her magic only affected weather and even then wasn't all that extraordinary. Queen Andromeda had tried to include Lena in scrying for more visions of the future that loomed over them with catastrophic intensity, but Lena hadn't been able to contribute much. Andromeda and Stella were so much alike, with their intense presence, wild and rippling rusty black hair, and storm gray eyes that looked right *through* you. Lena supposed that she was her mother's daughter, the librarian in this scenario, destined to become a spinster in truth, married to her work. Better that by far than a life of heartbreak and misery, being buffeted by Rhyian's pathological inconstancy.

"Anyway," she said, determined to shake the gloomy thoughts, "Rayfe and Andromeda are so extraordinary, they loom so large in the histories, that everyone expected the same of Rhyian. But he's not a sorcerer like his mother, being the son of the king and queen of Annfwn doesn't mean he'll be king, and he doesn't have the ruthless drive that made Rayfe overcome all odds to win the throne and then wage an impossible war to bring Andromeda back to Annfwn to save them all. Rhyian isn't a bad person he's just not…" She trailed off, realizing what she'd been about to say.

"He's not the kind of person they tell stories about?" Zeph finished for her, brows raised.

"It sounds bad, put that way."

Zeph shrugged. "Not everyone has to live a huge life. You've made a really good point. I never wanted to be high queen—I just wanted into Astar's tight velvet pants." She threw back her head in a hearty laugh, her joyousness so infectious that Lena laughed, too. "Like you say, sometimes events grab us up and make us do difficult tasks that later become the stuff of stories, but in the moment, we're just doing the best we can to save our friends. They may put this quest of ours in the histories. Rhy is part of that. He may not seem like the noble heroic type, but he's been here with us, part of the team. That counts for something."

Chastened, Lena focused on weaving her garland. "I didn't mean it to sound like I thought otherwise."

"You didn't." Zeph sounded uncharacteristically gentle. "We all know this has been hard on you and that Rhy hasn't had the wit to make it easier. If Rhy has a magical ability, it lies in creating turmoil, unfortunately."

"I sometimes think he has so much turmoil inside that it just... leaks out."

"Spattering everyone with gore," Zeph agreed. "It's a decent metaphor."

"At any rate," Lena said, letting out a cleansing breath, "I'm done expecting Rhyian to be anyone but who he is. I think that was my mistake all along, thinking that he'd turn into this ideal version of himself, like a kind of shapeshifting miracle."

Though Lena smiled at her attempt at humor, Zeph didn't return it. Instead she looked sad. "I don't think there's anything wrong with seeing the best in the people we care about. When you and Rhy fell in love, all those years ago, you were the perfect couple. We all thought so. My mother once said you'd be the making of Rhy."

Lena paused, taken aback. "What does that mean?"

Zeph bent over a tricky bit of weaving. "I don't know exactly. Maybe she thought like you did, that Rhy was floundering and that being with you would somehow bring him through his own muck to being a better person."

Something stabbed at Lena's finger and she cried out, popping her bleeding finger into her mouth. Zeph looked up with sudden concern. "I didn't mean to upset you."

"I pricked my finger is all," Lena said, holding up the offending digit to show the blood welling bright red. The light flashed off of Zeph's cabochon ruby and Lena wondered if she was supposed to be interpreting these signs as some sort of omen.

"We all know Rhy fucked it up with you," Zeph said, very seriously. "It was never your job to make him into a better person."

"Then why were you bugging me about forgiving him and having fun dancing?" Lena had to ask, the bitter salt taste of blood and greenery in her mouth.

"For *your* sake, Lena," Zeph replied, a half-smile twisting her lovely mouth. "All you ever wanted was Rhy. We all knew it. You were so happy when you were together. Maybe it was foolish of me—all right, it *was* foolish of me, as Astar explained over and over—but I wish that you could enjoy what Rhy is capable of offering, in the moment. As I tried to explain to Gen, it doesn't have to be true love. There's so much to be had from simply bedding someone who makes your body sing."

"Clearly the lecture didn't take with Gen," Lena replied wryly.

"Clearly," Zeph agreed with a heavy sigh. "Can you be-lieve she's *marrying* Isyn, already?"

"I can understand it, yes." Wary of the lurking thorn, Lena resumed weaving her garland. "Remember that for us it's been less than a week, but for them it's been much longer."

"I know, I know," Zeph grumbled.

"And that's not taking into account how extreme circum-stances make everything more intense," Lena added. "In normal life, things *can* move slowly. Not so when every moment feels like it could be your last. All of us have come so close to dying—or worse—that it feels like we can't afford to waste a moment of happiness." When she raised her head, Zeph was giving her a significant look. "I know what you're thinking," Lena said with an exasperated huff, "and no, that doesn't apply to me and Rhyian, because he makes me as miserable as he makes me happy and the up and down isn't worth it."

"Even if one or both of you doesn't survive this?" Zeph asked softly.

"Even so," Lena replied firmly. "Rhy may not be capable of changing, but I am. I'm going to break this vicious cycle we've embroiled ourselves in, if it's the last thing I do."

A fraught silence settled and Lena realized what she'd said. "I don't mean literally."

Zeph snorted. "Tell Moranu that. If Gen is right, She is still waiting to claim her price."

"The gift freely given," Lena corrected.

"Right," Zeph agreed, but she didn't sound like she meant it.

~ 6 ~

R HY SPENT A lot of time in raven form, exploring the isles and testing the odd boundaries that protected them. It wasn't that he wanted to leave—far from it—but his inherent Tala nature rebelled against the confinement, however large and verdant the cage.

He also needed the time to think. Or, rather, to *not* think, as raven form didn't lend itself to brooding. The raven brain was a canny and inventive one, but the large birds didn't worry much about whether they were assholes, if their friends hated them, and if they could ever persuade the one woman they'd ever cared about that he was truly sorry, that he *did* want to listen, and that he would never hurt her again, if only she would give him one more chance.

Oh, wait—that was him, not the raven.

There were other ravens on the island, ones with a vibrant community. They let him join in their activities cautiously, as they weren't quite sure what to make of him. In Annfwn, the natural animals had grown accustomed to the shapeshifter varieties, accepting them as friends and sometime visitors. These ravens knew he was wrong in some way, but hadn't decided exactly how. The story of his life, right there. If he, or anyone, could figure out what was wrong with him, what drove him to always say and do the wrong thing, then maybe he could fix it. Maybe he could win Salena back.

I find it interesting that you used the word 'win.' Is that what this is about—you simply can't resist the challenge? Astar had asked him back in Gieneke at the start of all this and Rhy had been deeply offended. It wasn't his fault the mossback Common Tongue conflated seducing your heart's desire with triumphing in a conflict. All he wanted was to be with Salena. That was all he'd ever wanted—the one sure thing in his confused and miserable life. The seven years they'd spent apart were a blur. He could see that now. He'd been lost without her, aimless, shapeless.

Once Salena had entered his life again on the night of the crystalline moon, standing on that balcony in Castle Ordnung in shimmering white, blazing like a star, he'd known with absolute certainty that he needed her.

For a while, he'd convinced her of it, too. She'd forgiven him that night, he knew it. If their lives had proceeded normally, he could have wooed her. He'd have visited her at her worksite in Aerron, spent time talking with her, the way they had back when they'd been only friends, before sex had muddied the waters. Eventually they'd have regained what he'd carelessly destroyed.

Then the stupid quest had disrupted his plans, thrusting them together and scaring her off. Salena didn't like being trapped any more than he did. They were alike that way, even if she wasn't Tala. Still, there had to be a way to get through to her. Perseverance wasn't his forte, but he did have obstinacy.

In this, if only in this one part of his feckless, wastrel life, he refused to give up. If he wanted to be a better person, like everyone was forever exhorting him to be, then he needed Salena.

He returned to the palace for the wedding. Gen would be hurt if he didn't—and Salena would chalk up his absence to his dislike of the mossback institution, which would be fair. He did think it was a bunch of foolishness. Saying some words amid flowers didn't seal your love for another person. He and Salena had never made any vows and he loved her with an unrelenting intensity that hadn't faded one whit over the years apart.

From what she'd confided to Zeph, it hadn't faded for Salena either.

So, he winged in and found the room that had been assigned to him, returning to human form in the basic black pants and loose shirt that was all his skill allowed for. He'd drilled for ages, it seemed, to be able to do that much. They'd lost all their bags when they'd abandoned the sailboat to dive into the portal to the Winter Isles to rescue Isyn. Not that he, true child of Annfwn that he was, cared much for *things*, but it got old borrowing fine clothes from other people in order to play frivolous noble for the locals. Zeph, Gen, and Stella could store all kinds of outfits when they shapeshifted, so they had it easy, but the rest of them had to make do.

He'd planned to wear the suit of black clothes he'd been given for the welcome ball that first night, but instead found a different outfit laid out on the unused bed. Raising a brow, he used two fingers to pick up the fussy jacket the color of blueberries, examining the black embroidery of raven's feathers. At least it wasn't entirely wrong for him. Still... *blueberry?*

"The entire wedding party is wearing shades of blue," Zeph said from behind him. "An army of people have been working tirelessly to create these wedding clothes for us, so stop holding the jacket like it's a venomous worm. It won't bite."

"Are you sure of that?" he asked sardonically.

"Yes, but these folks might—and not in a sexy way—so behave." Zeph waved forward a quartet of determined-looking people armed with various sewing implements. "You haven't been here, so you're getting fitted on the fly."

Figuring himself outnumbered, Rhy relinquished the jacket to one fellow and allowed a young woman to begin undressing him. "Why are you here, suddenly in charge of what I wear?" he demanded of Zeph.

She rolled her eyes and leaned against the bed post, arms folded. "I'm here to ensure your compliance, since I'm charge of dressing the wedding party," she retorted. She was resplendent in a low-cut gown in a paler shade of blue than his clothes, also decorated with embroidery, hers in gold thread of tiny gryphons. They weren't much like her actual gríobhth First Form, so she clearly hadn't shapeshifted to demonstrate the reality to the army of mossback embroiderers.

He eyed her askance. "That isn't the best color for you," he said, not above sniping at her. "With your pale skin, your face looks blue also."

She snorted, not bothering to look away as the efficient team shucked off his pants. The Tala weren't much for modesty. "Look who's the king of fashion now," she replied. "And I'm not supposed to look my best. This is Gen's day to shine and I'm being considerate by taking a step back. So are Nilly and Lena."

As if Salena could ever be anything less than the most beautiful woman in the room, no matter what they dressed her in. But he kept the thought to himself, wincing as the team wrestled him into the very tight velvet pants.

"And you're in the wedding party because we all are," she continued. "Gen can't have her parents here or any of her mossback family from her father's side, but she *can* have us. You, Jak, and Astar are standing up with Isyn, while Lena, Nilly, and I are standing with Gen. It's balanced."

He said nothing as they dressed him in a finely made shirt. Tucking the shirt inside the pants, two of the dressers fastened the pants and began sewing him into them, while another put a vest on over the shirt and bent to the task of doing a row of tiny buckles to close it.

"I don't see why I need so many layers," he muttered ungraciously, giving the vest—more shining black feathers than fabric—a dark look. He missed raven form already.

"You need them because I say so. We're representing Annfwn and doing something special for Gen." She paused. "You *will* behave, won't you, Rhy?"

"I'm wearing the stuff, aren't I?" The team of dressers was fitting him into the jacket, adjusting seams and doing buckles, while others were messing with getting the pants tucked just so inside a pair of high boots. At least they were black, not blueberry.

"I mean in all ways." Zeph gave him a meaningful look. With her glossy black hair pulled away from her face and piled into a tumble of curls that fell down her back, she looked different. More grown up maybe. More like the high queen she was going to be and less like his younger quasi-cousin who'd followed him around, pestering him to play with her.

"Remember playing I Eat You?" he asked suddenly.

Zeph wrinkled her nose. "I remember beating you every time."

Yes, because he had only a few forms. "And Gen could beat both of us." Gen also possessed a kind of genius for shapeshifting, always seeming to be able to pull out the exact form that could defeat them. And Salena would always cheer for him, no matter what. "Those were good times."

The quartet finished and stood back, looking to Zeph for approval. "Well done," she told them, dismissing them, then regarding him somberly. "Turn around and I'll fix your hair."

"My hair is fine." He wore it loose, in Tala fashion, and it didn't need fixing.

Zeph held up a comb, sapphire gaze gríobhth sharp. "Behave."

Giving up, he turned, wincing as she tugged at the thick curls. He at least could shift back to human form clean, but— as with his lack of skill at saving anything other than his basic clothes—his hair tended to be in disarray. After his mother berated him for it one too many times, he'd stopped trying, taking that small satisfaction in thwarting her.

Zeph worked quickly, pulling the stuff back into a tail that she tied off with a bit of black ribbon. "There. You look very handsome. You're welcome. The wedding is in one of the back courtyards. I suggest you get down there sooner rather than later."

"That's it?" He asked, surprised. He'd figured Zeph's appearance to see him suitably dressed had been a cover for a deeper agenda, one in which she lectured him about Salena and his many faults and lapses.

Zeph turned back. "What else is there?"

"I thought you'd have something to say, about Salena," he supplied, feeling awkward, as if he'd given up ground having to broach the subject first. He'd been prepared to counter her arguments and now his aggression had nowhere to go.

Zeph gave him a long look, resignation in it. "What can anyone say that you haven't already heard, Rhy? You know full well where the problem lies: in you. The solution also sits with you. None of us can fix this for you."

"Usually you like telling me what to do," he offered with an attempt at a cheeky grin.

She didn't return the smile. "Everyone is sick of trying to talk to you. You just don't listen."

"This again," he growled. Always with the *listen listen listen*. "I listen!"

"Today is not about you, Rhy," Zeph said with pointed gentleness. "I was only here to make sure you look nice for Gen. Now I have other people to help get ready."

Oh. "Is there anything I can do to help?"

"Of course." She flashed a brilliant smile and immediately dropped it. "Be pleasant. Be on time. For one day, try to keep a low profile. Don't stir up any trouble."

"We used to enjoy stirring up trouble, back when we were kids, remember?"

"Yes. Then we grew up." She strode for the door, blue skirts swishing, invisible gríobhth tail lashing. Glancing over her shoulder, she paused at the door. "At least, *some* of us did."

Ouch. Tempted though he was to show Zeph she wasn't the boss of him, Rhy nevertheless decided he'd better go find this back courtyard. Maybe Jak would've brought a flask to share.

It did take a while to find the right spot in the sprawling palace that had so many gardens and courtyards that it seemed foolish to expect anyone to find a particular one. He finally had to ask the way, of several different servants. When he made it to the right one, he paused a moment to take it in. A pang of harsh homesickness hit him at the sight of the flower garlands, so like the blooming tropical vines of home. The sun had emerged, for the first time since they'd arrived, the skies a clear aching blue that beckoned him to fly up and up and up. It was warm, the sunshine a tawny liquid heat that went to his bones. After all the winter they'd traveled through, being warm again felt miraculous.

Astar met Rhy and handed him a little silk pouch. "Flower petals," he explained to Rhy's confused frown. "We're to toss them—gently Zephyr says, or there will be a price to pay—at the end of the ceremony."

"Why does anyone want to be pelted with floral detritus?" Rhy wondered, but he pocketed the little bag.

"I do as I'm told," Astar answered with an amiable grin. He wore light blue that matched his summer-sky eyes. Rhy had expected bears in the embroidery, as that was Astar's First Form and that seemed to be the theme, but instead Astar bore Ursula's crest of a stooping hawk. Apparently being heir to the high throne took precedence over Astar's Tala nature, and didn't that just figure? Zeph had tied Astar's hair back, too, in a tail like Rhy's, with a light blue ribbon.

"Lena came through, huh?" Jak said with a grin, offering the hoped-for flask. Zeph had dressed him in a very dark blue that was almost black, with silver embroidery of small daggers tumbling over it. His hair was too short for the ribbon treatment.

"Salena?" Rhy echoed, drinking gratefully, the whiskey's bite welcome. "Where is she?"

"The girls are all with Gen," Astar said, taking the flask and a judicious sip. "They'll come down together. Thank you for being here, Rhy. Gen will be happy."

"I wouldn't have missed it," Rhy protested, snatching the flask back and taking a healthy swallow.

Jak nimbly slipped it out of his grasp. "Hey, that's good stuff. Treat it with respect. And I meant that Lena came through with the weather magic." He toasted the sunny skies.

Ah, of course Salena was responsible for the weather. The buttery sunshine felt almost like Annfwnn's tropical warmth. "She's really gotten good."

"Lena said it's easier to clear away rain than make it, which I don't understand, but…"

"But we don't need to understand to enjoy," Jak declared. "I feel warm for the first time in months."

"As do I," Isyn said in fervent tones, joining their small

group, and holding out a hand for the flask. "Only make that decades. May I?"

"It's your party," Jak said with a wide grin, extracting a second flask from his vest pocket and handing it over, "which means you get your own." He swept a bow. "A wedding gift, from Stella and me."

Isyn studied the silver flask with a pleased expression, then sipped, raising his brows in pleased surprise. "Branlian whiskey?"

"Only the best," Jak agreed.

"How did you get that?" Rhy demanded. "I know you came here with only the clothes on your back like the rest of us."

Jak winked. "I'm resourceful. Necessary for us lowly moss-backs who can't shapeshift our troubles away."

Rhy snorted. If only he could. He turned to Isyn, surveying the man. The groom was dressed in ivory that matched his flowing hair, which he'd been allowed to leave loose. Isyn returned Rhy's cool stare, eyes a grass green like the embroidery of leaves on his pristine wedding suit, with ghostlike horses in white on white glimpsed between. Leaves for the verdant Isles of Remus, Rhy supposed, along with the ghost horse, Falada. "Nerves?" Rhy asked, dipping his chin at the flask as Isyn sipped again.

Isyn smiled thinly. "Only that something will interfere. I've been waiting for this moment for a lifetime."

"I'm surprised there's no audience." Rhy made a show of looking around the smallish, otherwise empty space. "Shouldn't this be a big court event?"

Isyn canted his head. "You forget, perhaps, that I've lived alone as the only human in an isolated realm for decades, and have only recently arrived in this court. I'm no more at home here than Gen is. There will be the wedding ball and reception after this, but for the ceremony we both preferred something small and intimate with her friends." His mouth twisted ruefully. "As I have none."

"*We* are your friends now," Jak said.

Isyn narrowed his gaze at Jak. "With the suffering you've been putting me through in the name of regaining the strength and agility in my bad leg, I sometimes wonder."

Jak grinned easily. "You're welcome."

Astar clapped Isyn on the shoulder. "As Gen has always been like a sister to me, you will now be my brother."

Jak and Astar both looked expectantly at Rhy, so he held out a hand to shake Isyn's. "We're a strange and twisted little family," he said with a smile. "but don't worry—Jak tortures all of us. That just makes you one of us now."

Isyn laughed. "Thank you, I think."

"To Gen and Isyn," Jak said, lifting his flask and clinking it to Isyn's. Astar and Rhy echoed the toast, Rhy feeling oddly moved. He didn't know what was going on with him, reminding Zeph of their childhood games, being nostalgic for Annfwn when he'd always felt throttled there, beset with this restless need for Salena, unable to bear her determined refusals a moment longer.

"Ah," Jak breathed, his face lighting with wonder. "There she is. A beauty to light the darkest night."

Rhy turned, expecting to see Salena, but realized Jak meant

Stella. His cousin did look pretty, but she was also just Nilly, who'd always lorded her being a few years older with irritating authority. Stella led the way, walking slowly and carrying a bouquet of lush, tropical-looking blossoms Rhy was surprised they'd managed to find in the isles.

Then Salena appeared and Rhy lost his breath for a moment. If Zeph thought she'd dressed Salena so as to not outshine Gen, then she'd failed utterly. Yes, the gown Salena wore was of a muted hue, but the dusty gray violet was exactly the shade of Salena's eyes when she was happy—or in the languid aftermath of passion. And her eyes shone with happiness now, misty with emotion. Salena had always been a soft touch for romance, a sentimentality he'd enjoyed indulging when they'd been young. The simplest romantic gestures had moved her and he'd loved seeing how she melted for him.

Using his shapeshifter vision, he focused in on the embroidery of her gown, wondering what she'd chosen. Smiling to himself, he noted how the violet-gray velvet had been coaxed into patterns like storm clouds, with forks of silver lightning glittering here and there. A perfect representation of her.

He took a step toward her, unthinking, just wanting to be near her. Maybe to tell her how beautiful she looked, but Astar snagged his arm. "This way," Astar said, jerking his head at the flower-bedecked arch. "Remember what we're here to do."

Yes, Rhy thought as he obediently followed Astar. He was here to make Salena admit to his fact that she still loved him, to persuade her it was worth it to give him another chance. Whatever it took.

~ 7 ~

L ENA MADE HER usual determined effort to ignore Rhyian.
Despite all the practice, she still wasn't any good at it,
however. It was even more difficult to pretend he didn't exist
when he watched her with that avid look, deep blue eyes
intent in his gorgeous face. He no doubt hated the mossback
outfit, but the tailored fit clung to his lean, elegant body with
loving attention. Someone—probably Zeph—had tamed his
wild hair into a sleek queue that set off his carved cheekbones
and sensual mouth. The black feathers scattered over the
velvet the exact shade of his eyes emphasized his darkly
brooding good looks and gave a sense that he might take flight
at any moment.

Perfect for him.

Chiding herself for looking, Lena wrenched her gaze from
Rhyian's sexually potent one, wishing for the nth time that she
didn't have such a weakness for him. Instead she focused on
Isyn, his eyes all for Gen, approaching on Zeph's arm. In lieu of
Gen having her parents here, and the rest of her Tala and
mossback extended families, Zeph was her closest relative, and
so won the honor of escorting Gen. They'd all gotten misty
more than once helping Gen get ready, until Zeph threatened

to cut off the hair of the next person to smudge her makeup.

It was worth the effort of the last few days to see this small courtyard now so reminiscent of Annfwn, everyone wearing symbols inherent to their identities. Gen's white gown had been lavishly embroidered with dragon scales of the same shade, making her seem to glimmer all over, small green hummingbirds glimpsed here and there. Her final form and her First Form, so appropriate for this celebration. Lena was viscerally happy that Gen and Isyn had decided to keep this to the eight of them. It felt like a celebration of their quest, of their survival thus far, for them all to be together. Even Rhyian, who'd at least made the effort to be present. A low bar, perhaps, but she was working on expecting less of him, after all.

As Gen and Isyn spoke their vows to each other—as king of this realm, Isyn was the highest authority, and neither of them had cared to invoke any meddlesome goddesses—Lena's gaze strayed past Astar standing solemnly beside Isyn, inevitably landing on Rhyian. Blue eyes blazing, Rhyian made no pretense of paying attention to the ceremony. One thing you could rely on about Rhyian was that he'd never pretend to anything, just to satisfy propriety or please other people. He smiled, very slightly at her, a hint of sadness in it. For what she wasn't sure. It wasn't any sentiment from him about marriage or weddings, that was certain.

Then Isyn and Gen were embracing, indulging in a long kiss as the rest of them cheered and tossed flower petals to shower the deliriously happy couple. The entranced pair finally broke apart to accept hugs and congratulations from the rest of the group, and discreet servants wheeled out a cart with iced sparkling wine. Isyn poured and they all toasted, the moment intimate and convivial, poignant in a way Lena knew she'd remember for the rest of her life.

She even clinked glasses with Rhyian, feeling as if she acknowledged all they'd gone through to come to this point—and sent up a fervent wish for all they'd yet to endure. Lena had never had much connection to Moranu, or any of the goddesses of the Thirteen Kingdoms, in truth. Her mother's daughter, Lena had always placed knowledge at the top of her belief system. But she also couldn't deny that Moranu's shadowy hand lay heavy on Rhyian, and she offered a prayer to Moranu that, however She decided to make use of Her tribute, that She'd set him free of all that haunted him.

Rhyian, perhaps sensing something of Lena's thoughts, gave her a curious look, but it was easy to avoid any direct conversation with him amidst the convivial giddiness of the gathering. They were taking turns making toasts, each more absurd than the last in the good fortune they imagined for the newly wedded couple, laughing to the point of tears, all of it a welcome release from all they'd endured thus far and worried they may yet still face.

Then it was time to make their procession to the ballroom for the formal reception and dancing. Isyn and Gen led the way, naturally, as their small group processed through the graceful halls, servants and others not grand enough to be invited to the party lining the way and sending up cheers and congratulations, throwing the flower petals Zeph and Lena had distributed. Unfortunately, for all their careful planning, Lena had not predicted how this set-up would fall out. For Astar naturally offered Zeph his arm, following behind Isyn and Gen, and of course Jak and Stella did the same.

That left Rhyian and her to bring up the rear. He offered his arm with a sardonically crooked twist of his lips, challenging her to make a scene of refusing. But it would look odd if the final couple in their little parade were walking side by side with hands swinging free, so she locked down her trepidation and slipped her hand through the crook of his elbow, doing her best to ignore the feel of his lean muscles and the wild, enticing scent of him. Sunshine on black feathers, warm skin, hot sex.

"The sunshine for the ceremony was the best part," Rhyian murmured to her.

She cast him a sharp, sideways glance, suspecting him of mocking her, but he met her gaze with apparent sincerity. "I thought it would be nice for everyone to enjoy a bit of summer warmth, if only for a short time," she replied defensively. "It might seem like a frivolous use of weather magic, but it was good practice for me, so it wasn't wasted."

Rhyian arched a raven-winged brow. "I'm the last person to criticize *anyone* for frivolity. Frivolous is practically my middle name—if Tala had more than one name, like the mossbacks seem to."

"I don't have a middle name."

"No, but you have a lot of them, Princess Salena Nakoa KauPo."

She grimaced. She'd never loved her very long surname—which Rhyian knew full well—but it was also her family. "Be nice or I'll call you Prince Rhyian," she retorted, fixing a smile on her face and waving to the people.

"What *is* with mossbacks and their insistence on calling me that?" Rhyian growled under his breath.

"They're trying to accord you the proper respect, you idiot," she growled back. "Stop expecting complete strangers to understand your arcane personal pain. Not one person understands why hearing yourself addressed as 'prince' is like a dagger to your heart."

"You do," he countered immediately and unexpectedly, giving her a warm, even intimate smile.

"Yes, well, I'm different."

"Unique, I'd say," he purred. "My point is that saying 'not one person' is flat wrong."

"*My* point," she retorted, annoyed with herself for responding to that sensual purr with a flush of pleasure, "is that your friends here understand how you feel about it, but you're so busy having temper tantrums over minor shit that you don't notice."

He was quiet a moment. "You think so little of me anymore. I'm sure I deserve it, but it's still painful. I wish I knew what to do to earn your respect again."

Gah. Her heart twisted with sympathy at his words, exactly as she'd promised herself she wouldn't allow. She couldn't soften toward Rhyian, or her heart would be more than twisted. "You're going about it backward," she said through smiling teeth, "just as you always do."

Cocking his head, he regarded her seriously. That was surprising in itself, as she'd expected a sarcastic or annoyed reply. "I seem to be unable to dig myself out of that particular burrow," he replied, sounding almost... introspective? Surely not. "Can you explain what I should be doing?" He flashed a grin. "Pretend like I'm five years old and use small words."

Goddesses help her, she very nearly laughed. "I don't have to pretend. It's not a stretch."

Again, instead of a slicing retort, he nodded. "I'm trying, Salena. I really am."

"All right." She took a breath. One last try and then she was done. "Stop trying to earn my respect. Stop getting upset when people call you on your shit. Instead, put your attention on what we're supposed to be *doing* here. None of this is about you, or even about me. All of that is incidental. We're trying to stop a cataclysm, and any time you put attention on anything but working toward that goal, you're going to piss everybody off."

She braced for the rebuke, the mockery, the sarcastic defensiveness, but Rhyian said nothing. In fact, he was silent so long that they reached the ballroom and associated fanfare without another word from him. Risking a glance at Rhyian's face, she expected to see his expression taut with anger. Instead he looked... thoughtful. Catching her glance, he tipped his head. "Thank you for explaining, Salena."

Because they were halted, he disengaged her hand from his arm. She was ready for him to drop it and stalk away, but he lifted her hand kissed it. Not lingeringly, but a polite brush of lips—which still sent her senses flying because they were Rhyian's lips. The music struck up the notes of the first dance, Isyn leading a radiant Gen into the center of the cleared dance floor. Rhyian watched also, expression politely attentive.

When Astar led Zeph out, and Jak and Stella followed, Rhyian raised a brow at her. "Sincere question: am I to dance with you now or would you prefer to be exempted from this particular ritual?"

A rush of relief filled her at the question, along with astonishment that he'd asked, and... a hint of disappointment? Surely not. "I believe we can be excused," she answered unsteadily.

He nodded, showing no hint of his feelings in either direction. "Then I shall mingle and do what I can toward our purpose here. Anything specific you suggest?"

"I, ah, no." She wasn't at all certain what to make of his reserved, almost humble demeanor. It felt like a trick, but maybe that was unfair. "You could ask Gen to dance. That would be a nice gesture."

"All right. That's what I'll do." He brushed a wave of black hair from his forehead, his soft smile almost wistful, reminding her piercingly of how sweet he'd been back then, during their youthful love affair. "I won't pester you, Salena, but if you'd like to dance, I should be easy to find. And I'm always willing." His eyes glinted meaningfully, making it clear he meant more than the dance. "Just say the word."

He prowled off, sleek and graceful, leaving her thoughts scrambled, and her pulse pounding with heat—her body taut with sudden longing for what she didn't dare take.

"Is something wrong?" Stella asked, appearing at Lena's side and studying her with wide gray eyes, looking *through* her. "You feel... rattled."

"A good assessment," Lena replied with a smile. Black

jaguars leapt around the neckline of Stella's gray-blue gown, an intertwined chain that matched her upswept dark hair. Zeph had declared that only Gen would wear her hair loose, so she'd stand out. Stella so rarely fussed with her hair that she looked very different with it styled. Older, somehow, and wiser. The widow's peak she'd once hated until Jak loved it showed clearly, giving her a more witchy look than usual.

"But I'm fine," Lena continued. "Rhyian," she added by way of explanation, and rolled her eyes, then changed the subject. "Are you withdrawing now?"

"No, I can hold out a while longer," Stella answered, "especially for Gen and her special day. Astar is dancing with Gen now, so Jak stepped up to distract Zeph by dancing with her. The last thing we need is a jealous gríobhth threatening to eviscerate the bride." Her eyes sparkled silver with merriment. "So I begged off to take a break. It's not as if I'm going to dance with anyone but Jak, and the more I'm out of the crush, the longer I'll last at the party."

Lena nodded in sympathy. "How were the few days away? You seem restored."

"Wonderful." Stella positively glowed. "I *am* restored. It's truly miraculous, being with Jak. He somehow fills and soothes the raw and empty places in me. As you know, I never expected to have that with anyone. I was resigned to living my life alone and I wasn't bothered by it. I was happy on my own. But now that I know what I would have missed, I can't imagine life without Jak loving me, without loving him. It's transformative and—" Stella caught herself, stricken. "And I'm a blithering, insensitive idiot, going on this way." She laid a hand on Lena's bare arm, a rare physical gesture of affection, a waft of calming green energy suffusing into Lena. "I apologize, Lena, sincerely."

Lena had been struggling to keep her expression—and, more important, her unruly emotions—in check as Stella gushed, and now she felt terribly guilty on top of the rest of it. Stella was so rarely self-absorbed, almost never spoke of her own feelings, always so sensitive to caring for everyone else. And now Lena had failed to be a good friend and simply enjoy Stella's happiness along with her. "No apology needed, Nilly," she told her friend, as honestly as she knew how, knowing Stella would read the sincere emotion behind the words. "It's truly wonderful to see you so happy and to hear that your love affair with Jak is such a healing part of your life. No one deserves it more than you."

"Everyone is deserving of love," Stella corrected with a gentle smile, a hint of sorrow in it now that was entirely Lena's fault. "Is it so wrong to want that for you, too?"

"Not at all!" Lena answered, a bit too emphatically, and Stella sobered further, no doubt feeling Lena's despair. There was no hiding emotional truth from an empath. "I want that for myself, too," Lena explained more steadily. "It just can't be with Rhyian and I'm having to take the time to come to terms with that. I thought seven years was enough for me to heal and it…" She let out a long breath. "It clearly wasn't. Everything is still as raw as it was back then. How long will it take before I'm over him?"

"Seven years of avoiding dealing with the hurt isn't the same as seven years of recovering as you move on with a healed wound," Stella observed, in all her gently brutal wisdom.

"Then how do I heal this wound?" Lena demanded. "Tell me what to do and, believe me, I'll do it." And didn't she sound exactly like Rhyian just then? *Pretend like I'm five years old and use small words.*

Stella was considering the question seriously, however, answering before Lena could retract her words. "Emotional wounds aren't the same as physical ones. There's no step-by-step procedure for 'fixing' what's broken, no stitching or bandaging to be done. But there are metaphorical parallels. Remember how we had to break Isyn's thigh bone again to heal it properly?"

Lena nodded, wincing. Helping Stella heal that leg had been harrowing. Jak had used his precisely aimed strength to snap the badly healed bone and they'd had to pull the fractured ends apart and align them properly before Stella could work her healing magic. Isyn had bruised Lena's hand, gripping it so hard as he endured the agony. Even metaphorically speaking, the prospect of trying to do the same emotionally was daunting. "So," she said slowly and carefully, "are you suggesting I let Rhyian break my heart again so I can somehow realign the edges correctly this time?"

Stella looked startled, and even huffed out a laugh. "Moranu, no! What an image."

Beyond relieved, Lena let out an echoing laugh. "Good, because I don't think I could survive that." She thought of what she'd told Rhyian. *It might kill me. My heart is fragile now in a way it wasn't before.*

Though Lena hadn't said it aloud, Stella followed anyway. "A heart, the metaphorical variety anyway, cannot be truly broken. It is not a bone. It's a part of who we are and how we operate in the world. Our hearts are what allow us to love, to trust, to hope, to be intimate with each other. Your heart cannot heal if it's locked away from what it's meant to do. Like a flower deprived of sun and rain, a closed heart will wither and die."

Lena caught her breath, her heart—metaphorical or otherwise—clutching hard at Stella's words. She remembered that day, seven years ago and as vivid as a moment ago, when she'd locked her heart away. "I was only trying to protect it," she murmured.

Stella smiled in infinite compassion. "Of course you were. That's what we do, in the moment of pain, when the agony is too much to bear. But it's time, past time, to unlock that vault you've sealed your heart in."

"And do what then?" Lena asked, her voice sounding young to her own ears.

"Give it what it needs," Stella answered simply. "The equivalent of rain for a parched desert. You know how to do that."

She did know how to bring rain to the desert—and she was scientist enough to know healing a broken heart wasn't the same thing at all. Stella smiled at Lena's consternation, not bothered by her doubt in the least. "Sit with the metaphor for a while," she suggested. "What serves as rain for a parched heart?"

"My star," Jak said, stepping up behind Stella, wrapping his arms around her waist, and drawing her back against him so he could kiss her temple. "Another dance? If the lovely Lena will excuse you from whatever intense conversation you two were having. Willy asks me to remind you that you're meant to be full of gaiety."

Lena grimaced and replaced it with a sunny smile. "Sorry. And, of course, go dance. I shall go do the same and offer the groom my best wishes." After all, wedding or no, she was still here to do a job, not maunder on about disastrous past love affairs. Ironic that she'd only just chastised Rhyian for that very thing.

"We can talk more tomorrow," Stella promised her. "We have the strategy council in the morning anyway to talk next steps, given what I've seen."

"Not too early," Jak cautioned, giving them both a cheeky grin as he took Stella's hand and pulled her toward the dance floor. "Tonight is for celebration, which means we're sleeping in tomorrow. Anyone who isn't hungover will answer to me, personally."

Lena laughed and waved them on. Gluing her happy smile in place, she resolved to do her best, parched and shattered heart notwithstanding.

~ 8 ~

RHY WASN'T THE last one to arrive at the strategy council this time. In fact, he was the first, besides their host. Isyn turned from the windows, giving Rhy a welcoming smile and nodding at the sideboard. "There's a variety of breakfast food and beverages there, if you're interested. I'm told there's also any number of remedies appropriate for hangovers."

"A benefit of being a shapeshifter," Rhy replied, "is we don't get hungover. Metabolism is different or some such." He surveyed the offerings, beyond surprised to see hot coffee among them. He poured a cup, sipped, and closed his eyes in utter bliss. "Is this real Nahanaun coffee or have I been so long away from home that I can't tell anymore?"

"I understand it's the real thing," Isyn answered, coming up beside him. "I thought it would be pleasing to all of you traveling such a long time, when I heard they had a store of it. Enviable, on the no-hangover perk."

Rhy topped off the coffee and filled a plate with pastries and fruit, setting aside the poignant memory of bringing Salena breakfasts very like this. If he made her a plate and a cup of coffee the way she liked it, would she be pleased or annoyed? It didn't matter, he reminded himself, as he'd promised not to approach her. Not for a dance, not for a pleased smile. He'd wait for her to come to him.

What if she never comes to you? A snide voice whispered in the back of his mind. *Will you just give up then?*

Yes, he replied firmly and yanked himself out of his own head. "I'm surprised no one else is here yet."

Isyn looked faintly guilty. "Ah, about that. Gendra told you half an hour earlier than everyone else, saying that would ensure you'd be on time."

"Is that so." Rhy said, not really a question. He'd be irritated if Gen hadn't pegged him so accurately. "Did she do the same to you?"

Isyn gestured for Rhy to sit, taking a cup of coffee to his place at the head of the table. "No, I volunteered to keep you company, as she was still getting dressed. And I didn't trust myself to resist the temptation to drag her back to bed." He offered a conspiratorial smile that Rhy couldn't quite share in.

Gen was a beautiful and talented woman, but she was also like a sister to Rhy. He found himself surprisingly uncomfortable imagining her engaged in sexual games with Isyn. For the first time, he was happy about the wedding thing, because at least he could soothe his surge of protectiveness with the knowledge that Isyn would take care of Gen forever. Gen deserved that. "So, how's married life so far?" he asked, not above poking at Isyn a bit, expecting the man to protest it hadn't been even a night and a day and that it didn't make any difference anyway.

Instead, Isyn looked thoughtful. "It's different. I wasn't sure it would be, but it is. Gendra is my wife now, and my queen. I find that changes things, makes them... shinier somehow." He offered a sheepish smile. "Knowing we'll be together for the rest of our lives means something, deep down."

"However long that might be." Rhy was far too cynical to keep himself from adding that.

Undaunted by that caution, Isyn nodded. "I've already *had* a long life," he mused. "Over those fifty years that passed in the Winter Isles, as my body aged and my hopes dimmed, then faded out entirely, I had plenty of time to reflect on what I wished had filled those years instead of loneliness and despair." His uncanny green eyes met Rhy's. "When I was a young man still, my thoughts were preoccupied with all the things I didn't do, the dreams unrealized, the accomplishments I'd never attain. But after a few years, those things paled compared to a much deeper regret: that I'd never share my life with a woman. That this idea I'd had of a someone who'd share those dreams and celebrate those accomplishments with me would never come to be. That realization devastated me as nothing else had."

They were quiet a moment, Rhy for once entirely without a clever response.

"You must understand something of what I mean," Isyn continued. "You were trapped in that alter-realm, having to face that your life might be only that until you died."

"Except without food and water, I figured my life wouldn't last all that long," Rhy returned, regaining some of his sardonic insouciance. "And I was in wolf form and wolves aren't given to contemplating philosophy."

"What *does* a wolf think about?" Isyn asked curiously. "Or a raven, for that matter? When Gendra was stuck in whale form for so long, when she returned to her human mind she says she thought obsessively about fish. Which was fortunate for me, as fish was about all I could offer her." He grinned, affectionate nostalgia in it.

Rhy found himself relaxing and returning the good humor. "Food tends to be a preoccupation regardless of the animal form," he answered. Normally he didn't like answering mossback questions about shapeshifting, but Isyn had a guilelessness to his curiosity, a lack of judgment. Possibly from being such an old person inside his now-young body. And what Isyn had endured dwarfed what Rhy had suffered. It rather put Rhy to shame that he'd felt sorry for himself at all. "With practice and training, however, you learn to maintain some human priorities, regardless of the shape. It's just that over time, that human mind and resolve erodes as the inherent animal instincts grow stronger."

"That's very interesting," Isyn replied thoughtfully, clearly meaning it as opposed to simply offering a standard conversational gambit. "I understand it's rude to ask how many forms you can take or what they are, so I'm absolutely not asking that, but I'm ever so curious about what it's like to be different animals. How is being a wolf unlike being a raven?"

"How is a raven unlike a writing desk?" Rhy murmured, paraphrasing one of Lena's mother's favorite riddles, which was saying something as Dafne, the former librarian, was fond of all sorts of literary riddles like that.

Isyn pointed a finger. "I remember that one. From a book,

long ago."

To his bemusement, Rhy was actually enjoying the conversation. And Isyn's interest was so genuine, without subtext, that Rhy didn't mind answering his questions. More, he began to understand why Gen liked the guy so much. "I don't have many forms," he said, answering the question Isyn had been too polite to ask. "I'm not nearly as talented as Gen and Zeph, or even Stella. I have more forms than Astar, who only has his First Form, but he and I are otherwise pretty much on the same level." Except that Rhy could heal while shapeshifting back to human, but he didn't think he should mention that.

"And that's what it comes down to, inherited talent?"

"Some." Since Rhy was working on being honest, he admitted, "It's also a function of practice. I've never been much for diligent study, to the great chagrin of my parents and teachers." He toasted their absence with his coffee.

Isyn considered that. "When I was a young man—which I know sounds odd, given that we're probably of equivalent physical age now—I hated doing anything my parents demanded I do. Looking back, I can see my feelings weren't reasonable. I loved them both, and they're not awful people, but I felt like... Like they wanted to shape me into smaller versions of themselves."

"I met them, you know," Rhy replied, "when we stayed in Erie. They seemed pleasant enough, but people think that about my parents, too."

"I have not met King Rayfe and Queen Andromeda, but I've naturally heard the stories. I imagine you grew up on them. My own folks would tell their own story countless times of how they were nearly tricked out of marrying one another. Marjie, Wim, and I had a whole secret game where we gained points according to which details they included, deleted, or embellished with each retelling."

Rhy grinned back at him. "An innovative way to relieve the tedium." It would've been nice to have siblings to share that with. Interesting, in truth, to talk to another son of a king and queen, and ones with a legendary origin, too. Astar was the only other guy he'd known who'd grown up in that same scenario, but Astar was hopelessly noble, utterly determined to live up to all expectations, no matter how unreasonable or warped. Getting engaged to Zeph was the first time the golden prince had in any way shrugged off the chains of duty they'd put him in. It would be most interesting to see how Her Majestyness reacted to the news. Rhy very much hoped to be there for that entertaining event—and not only because it would mean they'd lived through this grueling quest.

"We'll no doubt do the same to our children," Isyn reflected ruefully. "But that's part of the job of being a parent, to torture our children. Otherwise they'd live happy, but uninteresting lives."

"I'll leave that to you, as I won't be a father." And repeat the sins of his parents? No. Moranu would no doubt want to sink her shifty claws into any child of his, too. "It's gotten better," he added, "but the Tala tend not to be terribly fertile. Gen may not conceive."

"She warned me," Isyn replied easily. "If it happens, wonderful. If not, all good. I understand from Gendra that the Tala are freer with lovers than mossbacks, in general." He offered a wry smile for the insulting nickname. "The lack of fertility explains why you don't already have children?"

"Not that I know of, anyway."

Isyn chuckled. "Have you been with so many women then?"

"Relatively speaking, though only one that ever mattered," he confided before he thought about it. This honesty thing got to be a habit. "Please keep that to yourself."

"Of course," Isyn replied immediately, and Rhy knew he could trust Isyn to do just that. "Though I'm naturally curious about the story there."

Rhy contemplated his empty mug, oddly tempted to tell Isyn the tale of Salena and him, though he strongly suspected Gen would have already, and Isyn was only offering the courtesy of apparent ignorance. Then his sharp shapeshifter hearing picked up the voices of their group coming down the hall. "Here comes everyone else," he advised Isyn.

They arrived *en masse*, Gen looking so pleased at Rhy sitting beside Isyn that he immediately suspected her of wanting to foster the conversation as much engineering a timely start. Salena, naturally, didn't look at him at all, though everyone else offered greetings before they gathered around the breakfast buffet. As they settled in their chairs with laden plates, Gen sat beside Isyn, exchanging a lingering kiss first, and Salena picked the chair as far from Rhy as she could get, everyone else conspiring to aid her effort. Rhy set his teeth and instructed himself not to be annoyed, though his good humor from the amiable conversation with Isyn dissolved.

"All right, Nilly," Astar said, taking charge of the meeting.

"We might as well get straight to it. What did your foresight reveal?"

Stella sighed a little, looking around the table. "I don't suppose I have to preface this with the warning that what we have yet to face will not be easy." Was it Rhy's imagination, or did Stella's stormy gray eyes linger on him? It would just figure. "Also, what I've seen is not clear. I have only fragments to go on, and best guesses about which scenarios will most likely bring about the desired outcome."

"Which is why everyone hates prophecies," Jak noted with uncharacteristic grimness as he flipped a dagger in the air, catching it neatly again. Probably Stella had already discussed what she'd seen with him.

Stella paid Jak no attention. "There are, of course, many branching pathways and possible futures dependent upon which choices we make, sometimes within a narrow margin of time. I can caution every person at this table that you will be tested in the days ahead, and our success—indeed our survival—will depend upon keeping our mission goals firmly in mind."

"Nothing like knowing a split-second decision under pressure could mean the end of the world," Rhy commented drily, restless with the doomsaying. Jak threw him an appreciative glance, but no one else was amused. Typical.

"I don't offer this warning lightly, Rhy," Stella said, her sorceress's gaze so like his mother's with its ability to see to the flawed heart of him. "Nor to increase the pressure on you. I'm walking a narrow line here between giving you all enough information to work with and giving you so much that it paralyzes you with indecision. It's not easy for me."

"I know that, Nilly," he replied softly. "I apologize."

Everyone looked at him with varying expressions of astonishment. "What?" he demanded. "I've apologized for stuff before." He very carefully did not look at Salena. She'd been the first person he'd apologized to, after years of resolutely refusing to apologize for himself to anyone.

"Well," said Jak. "At least we have solid confirmation that we're facing the end days if Rhy apologizes for being irreverent."

They all laughed, even Rhy joining in sheepishly. It was a valid point. Stella sobered first, her gaze lingering on him. "Rhy has always been the unpredictable one among us," Stella said, a resonance to her voice that Rhy recognized. Andromeda sounded exactly like that when the magic—or Moranu—spoke through her.

"Unreliable, you mean," Rhy retorted, misliking the direction of this.

Stella tilted her head, an inhuman silver glow to her eyes. "At times, yes," she agreed, "it has been seen that way. Where Astar is the fixed point, Rhy is the element of chaos."

"The trickster has a long history in mythology," Salena spoke up unexpectedly. She was even looking at him. "While some are bothered by the disorder the trickster brings, that dislodging of what is entrenched is also part of nature."

"Balance," Stella agreed. "We've known from the beginning of this quest that our primary goal is to restore the balance disrupted by what we now know is the intelligence. We will have to come at that problem from a number of directions, which will require something from each of us, but Rhy most of all."

He forced himself to relax, deliberately kicking back in his chair and grinning at the irony. "Then surely we're all doomed," he drawled, "if the solution depends on me. If we'd known that in the beginning, we could've given up then and saved a lot of trouble."

Astar fixed him with a stern glare. "You're too hard on yourself. You always have been."

"Funny," Rhy retorted, "I've always been told the opposite, even by you at times, Willy. I'm the feckless wastrel who never tries hard enough. Believe me, I've heard it enough times to have the variations memorized."

"Yes," Zeph snapped in exasperation, "and you've been at pains to reinforce that reputation. But we are your friends and we know better."

Oddly warmed by that, he smiled at her. "Love you, too, gruntling."

"Is there anything specific you *can* tell us, Nilly?" Astar asked, redirecting them to the task at hand, as usual. The fixed point, indeed. "Do we stay here and wait for the cataclysm to begin or...?" He trailed off, leaving the question open for infinite possibilities.

Jak huffed out a humorless laugh. "Just wait for it. You're going to love this. And by that, I mean, no one is going to love this."

Stella, more herself and less vessel for the goddess, flicked her lover an irritated glance. "Don't make me regret confiding in you."

He grinned at her, unperturbed. "I made it worth your while."

Unaccountably she blushed, and Gen cleared her throat. "The suspense is killing me. Can we just get to whatever we have to do out there? Then at least we can be efficient and worry about the specifics rather than a host of possibilities."

"Very practical," Isyn murmured to her.

"From all I've seen," Stella said, "there is a course of action that is the most likely to guarantee success. In fact, if we don't do this, I see only disaster."

"That makes the decision a simple one," Astar said. "I agree with Gen. Just tell us."

"Jak is right. None of you will like it," Stella replied glumly.

"You're only the messenger, Nilly," her twin said with gentle compassion.

"I know. But I'm also the one sifting through the choices and I'm aware that by telling you this I'll influence your decisions." She held up a hand to stop further interruption. "If we wait for the intelligence to strike, we fail in every scenario I've seen. Also, just as we've only temporarily defeated it in the past, we cannot hope to win decisively in our own world. Therefore, I believe we need to travel *to* the intelligence, to find its home realm, in order to destroy it."

~ 9 ~

A FRAUGHT SILENCE settled over the table, Lena doing her best to calm her immediately panicked reaction at the prospect of traveling to more alter-realms. Even Rhy had no pithy remark for that one.

"Which alter-realm is its home one?" Gen asked with remarkable calm.

"I don't know," Stella admitted. Her eyes strayed toward Lena before she shook her head at herself. "I've seen it, but I don't recognize it as one any of us has yet visited." Lena immediately caught the subtle prevarication in Stella's words. It wasn't an alter-realm they'd encountered so far, but Stella did recognize something about it—and that something had to do with Lena. The question was, had Stella meant for Lena to draw that conclusion or had it been a slip on the narrow line the sorceress walked? "I do see us traveling through a number of different alter-realms," Stella added, "as part of the process of discovering where the intelligence's home realm is."

"Is the Winter Isles alter-realm one of the ones we travel to?" Isyn asked.

"Yes." Stella smiled at him. "I see us going there and working to fracture the enchantment that walls it off from the living world. In fact, I'm guessing that's what we do in triangulating on the intelligence: travel from one alter-realm to the next, fracturing the enchantment that holds each, causing the intelligence to flee each in turn."

"Hounding it into a corner," Zeph murmured, a predatory light in her eye. "It's a good plan. I should have thought of that."

"In a way, you did," Stella said to her with a smile. "I simply created a short-cut in that process by telling you now."

"Thank you, future-me," Zeph said, bemused.

Stella's smile went uncertain, lines of white tension bracketing her mouth. "I really hope I'm doing the right thing by telling all of you this. You can see how it's a risk—creating informational loops."

"You must have a reason to think it's a good idea," Astar replied gravely.

"She does." Jak flipped the dagger, a set expression on his usually mobile face.

Everyone waited, but they said nothing more. Lena held up her hand, stuck on a major point. "Let's move on then. I need to know what you mean by 'fracturing the enchantments.' Do we even know how to do that?"

"We'll work on figuring that out," Stella answered. "You, me, and Isyn, with the assistance of the Star of Annfwn."

Isyn's face lit with anticipation. "I'm excited to see that magical jewel. I glimpsed it during the rescue, but didn't get to see it up close. This is like getting to use something mythological. I'd always heard the tales about the Star, of course, and its role in winning the Deyrr war, never imagining I'd get to use it."

Rhyian made a sound of disgust, sprawling languidly in his chair, studying the ceiling. The Star was a sore point for him, as Andromeda had given the jewel to Stella. Never mind that Rhyian had never displayed any sorcerous talent—that his mother had given the Star to her niece instead of her son was yet another way that Rhyian felt disinherited by his parents, another dagger to his heart that he enjoyed twisting to torture himself.

Stella shifted, becoming a small cat and returning immediately to human form holding the Star in her open palm. She extended the perfectly round and smooth topaz to Isyn. "Go ahead and take it. It focuses and amplifies magic, very powerful. Queen Andromeda loaned it to me for this quest."

"It's all right to say she gave it to you," Rhyian inserted, no longer pretending to be nonchalant. His deep blue eyes gleamed with some emotion Lena couldn't name, but he was holding himself together. "You are Mother's protégé and rightfully so, Nilly. You don't have to step delicately around my tail."

Stella gave him a look that clearly transmitted she knew better—you can't fool an empath about your emotions, after all—but that she'd pretend for his sake. "It *is* a loan," she said to all of them. "The Star belongs to no one and everyone. I'm simply the current bearer of the jewel."

"It's remarkable," Isyn said and handed it back to Stella. "I didn't expect it to be hot."

"It responds to your magic," Stella explained.

"I feel I should point out," Lena said, feeling a bit like Astar in wanting to steer them back to a focused discussion of practical considerations, "that going to an alter-realm and planning to just 'figure out' how to break an enchantment beyond anything anyone understands, then flinging ourselves on a hunt through other alter-realms with monsters inclined to kill us is not exactly a sound strategy."

Nobody had a reply to that. Jak met Lena's gaze ruefully, nodding in agreement, but saying nothing.

"I don't know what to tell you, Lena," Stella finally said. "You are, of course, absolutely correct. And yet I don't see another path for us that has a chance of succeeding."

"But you *do* see us succeeding this way," Gen put in hopefully.

"Yes." Stella seemed to be about to add something, but closed her lips on the words. "I really shouldn't say more. You all already know more than is ideal for you making decisions in the moment."

"Then we all go," Astar said. He glanced at Isyn. "To the Winter Isles first?"

"That would be my preference," Isyn answered, "in lieu of other directives."

Stella indicated nothing by word or gesture, her expression carefully neutral.

"At least we're all familiar with the Winter Isles," Gen said, "and the folk will provide us with food and shelter. It's a good place to start."

"The alter-realms will no doubt get progressively more lethal as the intelligence tries to shake our pursuit," Zeph noted, sapphire eyes glittering with gleeful anticipation at odds with her dire prediction. "We should take weapons."

"*Lots* of weapons," Jak emphasized. "Everyone should be armed. No exceptions." That last was directed at the shapeshifters. "Remember that you will likely be stuck in human form in the alter-realms. You won't have claws to rely on."

"I can assist with providing additional weapons," Isyn said.

Jak nodded his thanks. "It wouldn't hurt to do some practice, too. When do we leave?"

He'd asked the last of Astar, who glanced at Stella. When she gave no clue, Astar made the decision. "No reason to delay any longer. Let's begin as we mean to go on. We leave in the morning. Everyone report to Jak this afternoon to be armed and checked out on technique. Train as you like. Otherwise, rest yourselves. This might be our last reprieve for some time. Make good use of it."

"Are you going to impose a no-sex moratorium on this excursion?" Zeph wanted to know.

"A no-sex moratorium?" Isyn echoed, his startled gaze going to Gen with obvious dismay.

"Astar has occasionally seen fit to set that rule on this trip," Zeph explained sweetly, then glared at Astar. "If you're going to command that, I want to know now, because you are going to be *very* busy for the rest of the day, *and* all night, and it won't be playing with blades."

"Hey," Astar protested, "the sailboat no-sex rule was Jak's idea, not mine."

"For good reason," Jak agreed amiably, "but as we are no longer on a boat, this one isn't up to me."

"I have to say, I'm not favor of such a moratorium," Isyn said, exchanging a torrid look with Gen. "I have a lot of catching up to do and I'm not inclined to delay those efforts."

Astar threw up his hands. "Fine. Everyone can have as much sex as they can fit in between fighting for our lives and saving the world."

Well, not everyone, Lena thought to herself as the others cheered, pushing back from the table and gathering their empty plates and cups. She braced for Rhyian to say something. He didn't, however, and she risked a glance at him. He was watching her steadily, no hint of salaciousness or irreverence in his manner. She didn't know what to make of it. Probably that was his intent and this was simply another trick of his.

To Lena's surprise, Rhyian actually showed up for weapons practice that afternoon. He was late, naturally, arriving after Lena had already been working out for more than an hour, and after most of the others had been and gone, leaving only Jak, Stella, and her. Still, Rhyian had showed up. Taking in her expression, he cocked a questioning brow. "Willy did say everyone should report to Jak for this."

"Since when do you obey all commands?" she asked. "That doesn't sound like you. Are you certain you feel well?"

Rhyian gave her a long look, one with enough pain in it

that she immediately regretted needling him. She was supposed to be treating him like a friend, but sometimes the words seemed to just leap out of her., "I'm trying to do better, Salena," Rhyian answered quietly. She pressed her lips together, having to look away. "Where is everyone else, anyway?" Rhyian asked more loudly.

"Been and gone," Jak replied with some disgust. "Got their weapons and took off again. Probably planning to have lots of sex before that rest Willy also ordered."

"Which is what *I* would be doing," Stella put in archly, "if my lover wasn't a tyrant and a taskmaster."

"You like my tyrannical ways in the bedroom," Jak pointed out. "Like when I hold you down and—"

"Jak!" she cut him off, blushing vividly.

Jak grinned at her, unperturbed. "Remember our deal, my star. We agreed that if you put in the time on this to my satisfaction, and I will put in my time seeing to *your* satisfaction."

Stella clapped her hands to her flushed cheeks and gave Lena and Rhyian an apologetic glance. "Please forgive his poor manners. It's especially inconsiderate to behave this way around you two," she added, glaring at Jak reprovingly.

Ouch. Lena knew Stella hadn't meant to call attention to her strained relationship with Rhyian. Stella only ever meant well, wanting to spare others the emotional pain she sensed in them, but the words still made Lena wince. Rhyian met her gaze ruefully, the pair of them in temporary solidarity in their discomfort.

Fortunately, both Jak and Stella seemed to realize their

gaffe and ceased their byplay. "What can I do for you, bro?" Jak asked.

Rhyian held up his hands, waving his elegantly long fingers. "No claws and no talons in the alter-realms, yes? I'm here for some mossback weapons, lest I be the first one eaten."

"We can only hope," Lena muttered, the bitter words bursting out of her more from habit than any real ire. Rhyian studied her, exasperation replacing the hurt in his gorgeous face.

"It's something I can do," he pointed out, seemingly without sarcasm for once. "Sacrifice my worthless self for the cause. You won't have to outrun the tentacle monsters; you'll just have to outrun me, and I promise to go slowly."

"I didn't ask for that, Rhyian," she said on a long sigh, annoyed with herself for continuing to be so petty. "I don't want you dead." Even articulating the possibility struck her with fear.

"Comforting," he replied with dry sarcasm, before turning to Jak. "So, I'm thinking a really big sword like Willy's. Something to strike fear into the hearts of giants before I slay them."

Jak snorted. "With your long, lanky build? No, you get something much slimmer and lighter. Easy to swing."

"You forget I have shapeshifter strength," Rhyian shot back. "I'm as strong as Astar. Stronger, maybe."

"It's not a contest," Jak returned mildly. "It's a question of matching the weapon to the fighter." He selected a sword from the supply Isyn had provided and swung it experimentally. Satisfied, he tossed it to Rhyian hilt-first, nodding his respect when Rhyian caught it despite the lack of warning. "Besides, you're faster than our Willy and that's an advantage for our team we don't want to lose. Try that."

Lena backed up a safe distance as Rhyian snapped the sword through the air, then broadened his strokes. His body moving with liquid ease, he danced through more intricate steps, spinning, lunging, blue-black hair flying as he increased speed. Lena was entranced, unable to tear her gaze away. Rhyian had always been so alluring to her with his sultry elegance and indolent grace. Seeing him in this new light only intensified her reluctant attraction. He'd matured over the years, sharpening himself like the blade he held, and he seemed even more her Prince of Shadows now, Moranu's hand so clearly in the lines of his body and elastic swiftness as he accelerated, moving like black and liquid lightning. Watching him now, she couldn't help remembering how it felt to have him naked against her, all that contained passion and intensity focused on and within her.

"He's been learning sword work," Stella murmured in her ear, bringing Lena abruptly back to the present moment.

"Really?" Lena couldn't quite imagine how that had happened. Rhyian had always been so disdainful of mossback tools and approaches. "When did that happen?"

"It *has* been seven years," Stella answered. Was that a hint of mild reproof in her voice? "And Rayfe is a demanding father. Rhy has made some concessions here and there."

Yes, Lena had known that. She loved Rayfe and Andi like an aunt and uncle—and had even dreamed one day of having them as her heart-parents, back when she'd been young and stupid enough to fantasize about marrying Rhyian someday. Rayfe had often been frustrated with his son's lack of direction, seeming to think that if he pushed Rhyian hard enough, eventually Rhyian would... well, become more like Rayfe.

But Rhyian was equally his mother's son, fey and slippery, not easily browbeaten into anything at all. Andi had famously defied her own tyrannical father, as few people had ever had the guts to do. Neither Andi nor her trickster son should be underestimated.

Jak had taken up a sword of his own and was trying out a few attacks and counterattacks with Rhyian. Though Jak lacked shapeshifter speed, he'd trained all his life in Danu's martial arts, honing his lithe body and gymnastic agility into a keen edge. The two men were surprisingly well matched, at one moment going at each other with lethal intensity, blades flashing, the next moment laughing with the ease of their long friendship. Stella didn't suggest moving away, equally fascinated by the display, until Jak looked over at a pause in the action, frowning at them. "This isn't a show, ladies."

"On the contrary, it's an excellent show," Stella purred with rare carnality, an answering spark lighting Jak's keen, dark eyes. Lena mentally patted herself on the back for her role in making sure Jak and Stella had been alone in that carriage back at Lake Sullivan, giving him the opportunity to give his salacious demonstration of what he had to offer. She wished she'd had a man willing to put on a show like that for her.

Rhyian met Lena's gaze before she caught herself, a slow, curious smile curving his sensual lips. To her horror, she found herself blushing. "Jak is right. I should be practicing."

"Or not," Jak suggested. "Willy told us to rest as well. You've been at it a while. Let's call it good."

Oh. Lena really didn't want to spend the rest of the afternoon and evening doing nothing, alone but for her regrets and disappointed hopes. "I thought maybe you could correct my technique with the paired daggers."

"Lovely Lena," Jak said wearily, though not unkindly, "you're not going to learn anything you don't already know in the next hour. You've got this. Now you just need to trust yourself." He considered Rhyian, looking thoughtful. "You acquitted yourself well with that sword. Try this one." Jak took up the Silversteel sword, flipped it, and handed it hilt-first to Rhyian. No irreverent tossing this time, he presented the shining weapon with a hint of ceremony.

Taken aback, Rhyian set aside the sword he'd been practicing with and clasped the hilt of the Silversteel sword. "This is yours," he said, sounding tentative, though his eyes shone with acquisitive interest.

"Technically it belongs to Willy," Jak replied, lifting one shoulder and letting it fall, his sharp eyes on Rhyian's face. "Isyn used it in the Winter Isles. Seems like you should have a go at it. I like my daggers best anyway." He clapped a hand on Rhyian's shoulder. "Don't get eaten by a tentacle monster, my friend. You'd be sorely missed, no matter what you think."

"Thank you," Rhyian replied, clasping Jak's shoulder in return, so clearly moved that Lena felt guiltier than ever. She hadn't *meant* she wanted Rhyian to get eaten.

Jak stepped back, saluted Rhyian, then swaggered up to Stella. Taking her hand, he bowed over it gallantly. From where Lena stood, she could see him press a lingering kiss to her palm. He looked up, dark gaze full of promise. "I believe it's time to uphold my end of the bargain?"

"Indeed it is," Stella replied in a seductive murmur, threading the fingers of her free hand through Jak's short, dark hair.

Lena had to look away, tamping down the stab of envy—and the shiver of desire incited by the charged atmosphere around the pair. For once Rhyian wasn't watching her, his own gaze on Jak and Stella also, his expression a blend of that same desire and envy Lena felt. As if sensing her gaze, he flicked a glance at her, shrugging ruefully.

"I'll work with you, if you like, Salena," Rhyian offered with only a hint of hesitation as Jak and Stella departed.

Oh, *that* was all she needed. Already feeling the prick of sexual frustration, on top of unreasoning loneliness, if she worked physically with Rhyian, she might forget herself and succumb to—She shook that image away. "No, thank you," she said, attempting to be neutrally polite but her tone coming out terse and prim. She hated the way she sounded, so she tried smiling at Rhyian. Friends. She should be able to treat him like any other friend. "Your sword work is excellent, though."

"Thank you," he replied, a note of surprise in his voice.

"I didn't know you'd learned that," she said, then was immediately sorry when his face hardened.

"I'm not a complete wastrel, and you don't know everything about me anymore, Salena."

"I'm aware of that," she replied stiffly. "We've spent more years apart than we were together. In truth we hardly know each other at all now." *Which was how it should be,* although she didn't say so aloud.

He closed his eyes, pressing his lips together as if restraining words that way, simmering with frustration. When his eyes snapped open, ablaze like molten cobalt, Lena braced herself for a slicing retort. Rhyian had always had a knack for the cruel remark that breathed fire, turning his unwitting victim to ash. Instead, he blew out a breath, visibly releasing his anger. Sheathing his sword, he stood there a moment, watching her and flexing his fingers, as if trying to decide what to do with his hands. "Why do we always end up fighting with each other?" he finally asked, seeming to be genuinely seeking an answer.

Lena sighed, finding it helped her, too, to release that tight breath. "Too much old hurt and anger, I suppose."

"We're not really arguing about whether you should know I learned sword work," he mused. "Instead we're having the same fight over and over again." He laughed without humor, tilting his head to study her in that quintessentially raven way of his. "Will we ever stop?"

"I don't know," she answered honestly. "It doesn't look that way. Seven years apart didn't do it. Talking it out didn't do it."

"But *have* we talked it out?" he persisted. "You still seem to be telling me that I haven't listened to you."

"Maybe that's unfair of me because I really don't know what I want you to hear," she said helplessly. "I don't have any idea what would fix *this.*" She thumped her closed fist over her heart, impacting harder than she'd intended, the wound there aching as if freshly dealt. "If anything even can. Maybe it's all my problem and not anything you can do."

He glided toward her, footsteps soundless on the wet grass, mist beading on the blue-black hair curling wildly to his shoulders. Though she knew in her mind that she shouldn't let him get close, she stayed riveted to the spot. Tentatively, with infinite gentleness, he slipped soft fingers over her clenched fist, easing it away from her breast and cupping her hand in both of his.

Inclining his head over the tightly knotted fingers, he examined her fist, coaxing her tense fingers to unfold, smoothing open her hand. There was nothing overtly sexual in it, and yet the moment, every caress, simmered with tension as sexual as anything that had ever passed between them. Lena's mouth went dry, parched for the taste of him, and her body swayed with longing beyond her control.

When he slowly lifted his gaze to hers, his face echoed everything she felt. "I want to, Salena," he whispered. "Whatever it takes, as long as it takes, as difficult as it might be, I want to find a way to begin to repair what I carelessly broke."

~ 10 ~

SOMEONE WHIMPERED, AND Lena realized it was her. She simmered with need, unable to step away as she knew she must. Still moving slowly, Rhyian laid her now-opened palm over his own heart, his lean body tight with tension that mirrored her own, his heart pounding in time with hers. They used to do that, lie with their hands on each other's hearts, feeling them synchronize as they gazed into each other's eyes. In all the innocent foolishness of youth, they'd believed that it meant something other than a trick of physiology.

"Maybe our mistake has been counting on words," he suggested. "We never needed to discuss everything back then. We just understood each other. We could find that again," he murmured, voice full of dark promise. "You and I, we've always had this." Still holding her palm flat against his thrumming chest, he set his other hand lightly on her breast, sealing his palm to her heart, a chaste touch, though his eyes burned with the memory of more. "Remember how we used to do this?"

"Yes," she managed to say, knowing that he'd feel her trembling need, that he'd get the wrong impression—and still not quite able to tear herself away.

His fingers curled ever so slightly against the curve of her breast tightly constrained by the fighting leathers. Her nipples went taut as if they remembered how he'd tease them with such skill, begging for a return of that meticulous attention. Yes, all of her remembered, all too well, how it had been between them, and how she'd never found anything that came close with anyone else. She craved Rhyian with a deep and grinding thirst, as if she'd spent the last seven years in the desert, parched and drawn thin to snapping, and now she'd found the oasis, and she need only drink the sweet water.

Even knowing that water would poison her, she still wanted it.

Rhyian's eyes, his face, his entire being, physical and magical, radiated the same need, the same long mourning and a mirroring, desperate desire. "Salena," he whispered, narrowing the space between them, his blazing gaze going to her lips, dark head tipping to that perfect angle perfected over so many kisses. They'd spent hours only kissing, long, languorous sessions she missed with all the longing for lost youth. So help her, she couldn't move, breathless with the driving need to feel his mouth against hers, already drunk on his breath, that wild scent of him that always made her think of sunshine on black feathers, though that shouldn't smell like anything in particular.

Unable to resist a moment longer—reckless and fatalistic, like flinging herself off a cliff—she moved into him.

His lips touched hers, and she sighed in every pore, shuddering with the delicious feel of him. She moaned with her entire body, going lax and boneless as he gathered her to him, wrapping her up in those strong arms, mouths feasting on each other, so familiar and simultaneously freshly new. She pressed herself to him, feverish in her need, threading her fingers through his silky locks that seemed to curl lovingly around her hands.

His hands roved over her in a frenzy of desire, seeming to touch her everywhere at once, and she wanted it. Oh, how badly she wanted this.

And she could have him, the knowledge a burning brand in her mind. She could take him to bed and instead of a lonely afternoon and evening kicking her heels and stewing with dread, she could spend it entwined with Rhyian's glorious body, giving herself over to his dazzlingly skilled lovemaking, sating this overwhelming need that had built up over the years, layers of sand driven by harsh winds to pile into dunes that smothered her soul. She arched into Rhyian's caresses, welcoming them like the dark opiate they were, dulling the pain in her heart and mind, salving the aching, empty, lonely places.

Rhyian broke the kiss to trail his lips over her jaw and down her throat, murmuring words in the liquid Tala language, describing her beauty, his need and desire. His teeth, ever so slightly sharper than usual—a hint of the wolf's fang in them—nipped at that exact spot on her neck that drove her wild. She cried out, the orgasm shivering close from only this much. With his uncanny expertise and the intimate knowledge of long familiarity, Rhyian touched her in other places. Even over her fighting leathers, his clever hands erotically stoked those fires he'd been the first to ignite in her and that it seemed only he knew how to fan.

"Yes," he murmured. "This is right. Your body knows me. We belong together. Trust in that, if nothing else."

Those words—or perhaps that one potent word, *trust*—penetrated her desire-fogged brain. With a cry of something close to despair, she wrenched herself away from him, putting several steps of cooling distance between them. "We can't do this," she gritted out, holding up a hand when he moved toward her.

"We *can*," he insisted, but halted where he was. "There is nothing stopping us."

"*I'm* stopping us," she replied firmly. "I don't want this with you."

"Liar," he snarled, teeth still sharply snapping like the wolf. "I know full well that you want me as badly as I want you."

"No, I won't lie." If he had his wolf senses sharpened, he'd scent her desire anyway. She firmed her chin and her resolve, holding his gaze. "And you're right—we have always had this." She waved her hand back and forth between them, acknowledging the simmering passion and deep connection that persisted, apparently whether she wanted it to or not. "It *is* good and yes, I still feel the same desire for you," she added, helpless to deny the urgent onslaught of that desire.

"Stay back," she said, sharpening her voice when he swayed toward her. "Physical desire isn't enough. I am more than my body. You, of all people, should know that I value my mind. I will not succumb to sexual needs when I know that being with you will only damage me."

"So very controlled, aren't you?" he bit out.

She tried not to let him see how much that stung. "Don't you see, Rhyian?" she tried, pleading with him. "We had this then, too, and it didn't *work*. If I allow it, I'll be right back where I was all those years ago."

"You don't know that," he replied with quiet intensity. "Maybe this time we *can* make it work. We can't know unless we try. That's all I'm asking, Salena—that you give me a second chance, and a last one."

Tempting. Oh, so very tempting with her Prince of Shadows simmering with such seductive power, there for the taking. But she shook her head. "I can't risk it. I'm sorry. Maybe I'm a coward, but I just... I know myself and it won't be only sex. I can't be vulnerable to you that way."

He nodded, his anger and determination bleeding away as he lifted his hands and looked at them. "I wish I knew how to earn your trust back. Astar says to be trustworthy, and I'm trying to be that, but..." He lifted his gaze to hers, the blue muddled with pain and need. "I seem to be as inadequate at figuring out how to do that as I am at meeting every other challenge in my life," he finished bitterly.

"Oh, Rhyian." Her heart ached for him, for the troubled boy he'd been and the tormented man he'd grown into. She'd always felt like the only person who forgave him everything—until he did the one thing she couldn't forgive. She'd also been the one person who never thought Rhyian was anything less than exceptional. They'd had so many conversations about that, where she'd expressed her belief in him, her certainty that he simply had to find his own way. She wanted to be able to tell him he'd figure it out, but she didn't believe it. She couldn't be that person for him anymore. "I don't know what to tell you," she finally said, knowing it for a weak reply as she said it.

He knew it, too, sliding his hands into his pockets and focusing all that brooding intensity on her. "Why should you be any different?" he asked philosophically.

The hopeless resignation in his tone stung, and guilt stabbed her, as if she'd broken some promise she'd given him long ago. "I'm sorry," she added quietly. It was ever so much easier when she was seethingly angry with him. "For the record, I still think you're an exceptional person, Rhyian."

He slanted her a reproving look. "Just not exceptional enough for you."

"No," she corrected steadily, meeting his gaze and willing him to understand. "That has nothing to do with anything. Maybe we need to look at it like this: you and I simply have a fundamental incompatibility. It's a dealbreaker. It's not your fault. It's not my fault. It just *is*."

He was quiet so long, studying her, saying nothing, that she'd begun to search for something more to add, something final enough to put an end to this excruciating conversation. She couldn't help feeling she was breaking the heart of the one person who'd ever meant anything to her, even as the rational part of her argued that this *had* to happen.

"I'm practicing this listening thing," Rhyian said, just as she was opening her mouth, his tone wryly self-deprecating. "So please tell me if I've got this wrong. I think what you're telling me is that you believe we're incompatible because you want the mossback life of monogamy—marriage, children, living by rules—and that I don't."

"You don't have to make my idea of a good life sound so contemptible," she replied. "Those aren't the only things I want."

"But that's where we don't match up," he persisted, serious and intent. "Correct?"

"It's not that simple, Rhyian. There are a lot of ways that we are very different people."

"Zeph and Astar are very different people," Rhyian pointed out. "So are Jak and Stella. Gen and Isyn…" He paused, then huffed out a laugh. "Well, I didn't think Gen could find someone so very much *exactly like* her, but she did, so that's a bad example."

Lena couldn't help smiling. It was true about Gen and Isyn. Still, she couldn't let Rhyian pursue that argument to its logical conclusion. "It's not the same thing," she told him gently and firmly.

"Because I screwed it up," he said. "Tell me this, Salena, if you would indulge me a moment longer: if I hadn't done what I did—and I'm not excusing it—but if I hadn't done that, would we have been compatible, like you're talking about? Would we have lasted?"

"How should I know that?" she demanded, suddenly feeling like she had to fight back tears. This came far too close to those girlish fantasies, how she'd once believed they were perfect for each other. "I was so young then. We both were. We were kids, no matter what adult games we got up to."

His sensual lips twitched, ever so slightly, his heated gaze making it clear he remembered those games as well as she did. Then he sobered. "We were friends first. You were my best friend, always. Doesn't that count for something?"

"Friends don't treat each other the way you treated me, Rhyian," she bit out, abruptly furious again. She put her fingers to her temple, overcome, her head throbbing with stifled emotion. "I apologize. That wasn't fair."

He smiled ruefully. "It's what you need to say to me, which means I need to listen. And you're absolutely right." He sighed heavily, canting his head back to look up at the mistily raining sky, his profile heartbreakingly gorgeous. "Everyone, including you, keeps telling me I need to let you go and I... I *can't*." His voice broke a little and he lowered his gaze to hers. "I can't, Salena. You're the only one for me. Without you, I'm nothing."

She managed not to say that she'd been far from the only one for him. "You lived without me just fine for seven years, Rhyian. You're just overcome by proximity, and an extended lack of other lovers."

"Is that that what you think?" he asked tersely. "That I'm only looking for sexual release and you're the nearest warm body?"

She reined in her temper. "All the shapeshifters are struggling with their animal natures, probably because of the intelligence exerting influence on you. Go find someone else to give you the release you need. Moranu knows there were plenty of willing females giving you longing looks at the wedding ball."

His lips quirked as his annoyance faded, a glint of pleasure in his eyes, his gaze intent. "You paid attention."

Oh, she always paid attention to him and the hordes of

women who wanted him. And she battled jealousy every time he bestowed those toe-curling smiles on someone else. "Find someone else, Rhyian," she repeated, leaving that alone. "That's the path forward for us. Then, perhaps, one day we can be truly friends again, without this—" *will-sapping, overwhelming, undying passion* "—between us."

"Is that what you've done?" he asked silkily. "Because I pay attention, too, and I've noticed you haven't taken any lovers all this time."

"I've been busy," she snapped. And she'd certainly considered taking several different someones to bed, if only to stop herself from fantasizing about Rhyian. She'd discarded the notion almost immediately in every instance, despite several offers that should've been more interesting than they were. And she really hated having to admit it was because Rhyian's presence in her life again made it impossible to think about anyone else that way. He was like a dark star of sexuality, drawing all her thoughts to him.

"I haven't been with anyone else either, Salena," he confided somberly, telling her what she'd suspected and didn't want to know. Yes, she'd paid attention, and she'd never once seen him taking anyone up on their flirtation. It made her irrationally angry because of course he showed that restraint *now*, when she couldn't let it matter. "Not since I saw you again on the night of the crystalline moon," he continued, apparently oblivious to her consternation. "You are the only one I want."

The words were what she'd always wanted from him, needed him to give her, had assumed he'd given her until he made it blatantly clear she was a fool. And now it was too late.

What he meant now, he wouldn't mean later. She'd learned at least that lesson, to her lasting sorrow. "You should find someone else to want, Rhyian," she finally said. "I need to do that, too. We both need to move on. If we keep doing this, we'll only tear each other apart."

"I'm already torn apart, Salena," he confided, dark blue eyes somber. "What if the answer to healing is for us to come together? If that's the path forward and we turn away, we might never get over this."

A daunting thought. A tempting offer. The risk was too great. "I'm going inside to rest," she told him, instead of the hundred other things she might have said, and then wished unsaid.

"Alone?" he asked, lifting a brow. "An empty room and a cold bed don't sound all that enticing. I speak for myself also."

She nearly laughed. "Alone," she confirmed, turning to go.

"Salena," he called after her, waiting for her to look back. "How about a game of *kiauo* then?"

"What?" she asked, too taken aback to dissemble.

"*Kiauo*," he repeated. "There's a set in the little library over by that one courtyard. I can find it again. We could order a late lunch or early supper, have some wine, play a few games. Restful, and not alone."

She was absurdly tempted by the offer. The Nahanaun strategy game always felt like home and comfort to her. Focusing on the complicated game in a cozy parlor with wine and snacks sounded exponentially better than trying to make herself nap in her cold bed in her lonely room. Rhyian knew her far to well and had offered something she didn't want to refuse. "You hate playing *kiauo*," she said, not at all sure how to handle this invitation, or what this new approach from Rhyian heralded.

"No," he said carefully. "I hated that I wasn't good enough to beat you. It occurs to me that I won't get better unless I practice. And I'd like to spend the time with you, being friends." He grinned briefly. "Another kind of practice."

It would be surly of her to refuse, besides that she really wanted to do this. "All right," she agreed. "I'll change out of my leathers and meet you there."

He nodded, expression calm, and she recognized that he was trying not to scare her off. His eyes sparkled with happiness, however, and perhaps a bit of triumph. Ah well. He wouldn't be Rhyian without that. "I'll make arrangements," he said. "See you there."

IN THE MORNING, they all convened, along with their supplies. Isyn had also provided for those of the group who'd left everything behind on the sailboat, giving them clothing, including gear for the bitter weather of the Winter Isles. Lena wore her own fighting leathers, as she'd worn them to the Winter Isles and out again, but the cloak and gloves were new—and greatly appreciated even in the minor chill of the misty morning. She wasn't relishing revisiting winter.

They were leaving early, before the palace denizens would

be up and about to be dismayed at the sight of their newly recovered king departing again. Rhyian had sardonically noted that they'd be sure to notice Isyn's absence eventually, but Isyn had only shrugged with good-natured resignation, commenting that he didn't have to throw it in their faces.

They walked a short distance into the surrounding forest, where they'd be screened from any chance onlookers, and Lena stepped up to use her magic to hold one side of the portal that Stella would open. Isyn moved up next to her, ready to learn by doing. Technically, Stella could open a portal by herself, but having help impacted her magic reserves less. Also, in the eventuality that Stella couldn't open a portal at some point, Astar wanted Lena and Isyn to be the backup team. Astar was careful to specify that this eventuality would likely be because Stella was in animal form and thus unable to work magic, but a muscle ticked in Jak's jaw as he stared stonily into the distance. All of them were keenly aware that it was more likely that Stella would be incapacitated in some other way. Any of them could disappear or be killed. Still, Lena wondered if Jak knew something that the rest of them did not.

Lena was on edge and trying to disguise the low-level, grinding terror. When they'd abandoned the sailboat to travel to the Winter Isles to rescue Isyn, that had been a fast decision, and a necessary one. Also, Lena had been preoccupied with having to jump in the icy water to travel through the portal and hopefully not drown on either the way in or the way out, along with working her weather magic to warm the water somewhat. The logistics of the rescue had consumed most of her attention then, leaving little time or energy for her to worry about what might happen to her there.

The evening before, she'd played a number of games of kiauo with Rhyian, winning all of them handily, though he'd improved markedly for the last few, showing more interest than he ever had back in the day. It had been far more fun and relaxing than she could have guessed. Rhyian had a gift for being charming when he wasn't brooding, and he'd clearly come to some decision because he'd been a delightful companion. Though she'd been braced for it, he hadn't said or done anything sexual, behaving like one of the other guys. Less so than Jak, even, who was a pathological flirt.

Rhyian had taken her mind off her worries, but that had ended when they knocked off early with the intention of getting a decent night's sleep. He'd walked her to her room, bidding her good night without touching her or seeming to have any other thought in his mind. She'd been almost disappointed, to her great chagrin, as if by not having to fend off Rhyian's advances had her dwelling more on what she was missing than she might have otherwise.

Her past fears and unresolved sexual tension had combined to make her restless and wakeful, Rhyian's words about a cold bed returning to mock her. Unable to get comfortable, she'd laid awake contemplating just how horribly all of this could go wrong. She'd known Stella all her life and she could tell when Stella was withholding something terrible. It seemed very likely at least one of them wouldn't live through this final confrontation. Stella had promised taking this path gave them the greatest chance of success in their mission, but that wasn't a guarantee they'd succeed, nor was it the same thing as everyone making it home safely.

Lena had never been superstitious—her academic training didn't allow for that—but she couldn't rid herself of the foreboding that she would be the one to die. When she'd let herself fall from Zeph's back in that first alter-realm, she'd been half dead already and hadn't expected to live. Maybe she was supposed to have died then and that death had been chasing her ever since and had nearly caught up. She shook her head to dispel the morose thoughts and caught Rhyian watching her with a moodily dark gaze. He didn't look like he'd slept either, and she wondered—almost in a panic—if she'd been wrong to refuse him. What if one or the other of them died and the night before had been their last chance to be together?

What if the answer to healing is for us to come together? If that's the path forward and we turn away, we might never get over this. Rhyian's words haunted her, and held her gaze as if he'd spoken them again.

~ II ~

"EVERYTHING ALL RIGHT?" Isyn asked, startling Lena and making her self-consciously aware she'd been staring at Rhyian with nothing short of abject longing.

"Yes," she assured him, offering a smile she hoped didn't look as fake as it felt. She turned to face Stella across the short distance they'd established. Everyone was going through in human form, so this portal didn't need to be big, which also helped conserve their magic. "Set one hand on my shoulder," she suggested to Isyn. Focusing on practical actions would distract her from useless worrying. And imprudent desires. "I don't know how your magic feels to you, but see if you can shadow what I'm doing."

"I've stabilized existing rifts before, but creating one is new to me," he replied, putting a careful hand on her shoulder, his sword in the other.

"Remember that Stella is doing most of the work. We're just assistants."

Stella, nodding her readiness, tucked the Star into the neckline of her shirt under the fighting leathers, then drew her daggers, one in each hand. Lena drew her blades also. Creatures from the other side of the portal had a tendency to hurtle through any gateways they opened. While it was unlikely anything from the Winter Isles would come through to attack, there was always the possibility that the portal would open to a different alter-realm, or that the intelligence would interfere in some way. Jak insisted they all treat each portal opening as a potential attack, which meant weapons at the ready.

Stella drew on the focusing power of the Star, her magic reaching to Lena like a golden hand. When Lena and Stella had done this together before, they'd stabilized an existing rift, just as Isyn had learned to do on his own. Since then, Stella had developed the skill of opening an entirely new portal, one to the destination she chose. Much like the intelligence could do, Lena realized, and stored that thought away to contemplate later.

Lena focused on weaving her magic into Stella's, whose magical grip felt solid and assured. Stella's silvery gaze met Lena's, her long, dark hair stirring in a breeze that hadn't existed a moment before, the magical currents disrupting the atmosphere. Sometimes Lena wondered if the weather magic she'd inherited from her father's people wasn't simply a sorcery particularly disruptive to the environment. All magic disturbed the area where it was invoked to some degree, and weather patterns were especially sensitive. Attuning that disruption specifically to making rain was just a subset of that.

Lena's scalp prickled as her own hair lifted, the small hairs on her arms and at the back of her neck rising as the current between Stella and her began to grow in intensity, becoming greater than either of them separately. With their magic interweaving, Stella guided their mental hands, Isyn following along. His magery had a different flavor, somehow fresh like pristine snowfall. Lena observed with careful attention as Stella opened the portal, braiding in the instructions for the destination. Lena doubted she could replicate the process—Stella was magnitudes more powerful than a simple maker of rain—but Lena could perhaps assist Isyn, if necessary. Or maybe the pair of them could combine to attempt to replicate Stella's ability, but...

She just really, really hoped they wouldn't have to.

A sharp winter wind blew through the verdant rainforest. Since Lena stood to the side of the portal, she couldn't see into it, but Astar nodded crisply. "Gateway to the Winter Isles confirmed," he declared, broadsword at the ready in his big hands. "Isyn, if you'll do the honors, please?"

Isyn patted Lena's shoulder. "Well done," he murmured. "That was fascinating to witness." He stepped away and offered an arm to Gen. "My queen?"

Gen blushed faintly, which was lovely to see, still so new to being loved. "I sure hope the folk aren't angry about you absconding on them," she fretted as she looped her hand through the crook of his elbow.

"I'll explain to them—and when they understand that we've shattered the walls of enchantment that isolated their world, making them dependent on my magery, then all will be well."

If they could figure out how to accomplish this feat they had no clue how to approach. Across from Lena, Stella met her gaze and smiled encouragingly, clearly aware of the cynical direction of

Lena's thoughts.

Isyn and Gen stepped through the portal and vanished. Astar and Zeph followed, both ready to fan out and defend in case of trouble. Rhyian swept Stella and Lena a bow, brandished the Silversteel sword with a theatrical gesture and leapt into the portal.

"Go ahead, Lena," Jak directed. He'd wait to accompany Stella through, as she had to go last, holding the portal to the end.

Extricating herself from the anchoring position on the portal felt much like disentangling from a sticky spider's web. Stella handled the transition easily, however, taking all the work onto herself without even a tremor of disturbance. Lena pulled up the fur-lined hood around her face, already cold just from that wind, and—determinedly ignoring the curl of dread in her gut—made herself step through the portal.

The final phase of their quest had begun. For better or worse, it would all be over soon.

RHY PULLED HIS new fur-lined, black-leather cloak—a gift from the generous Isyn—as tight around himself as he could and still keep his sword-arm free, the bitter air bruising his lungs. Why their quest couldn't involve *warm* places, he didn't understand. He eyed the empty air, the aching sense of Salena's absence clawing at his guts as he waited for her to step through the portal.

Though the sensation of the connection joining them being abruptly severed by being in separate alter-realms was no longer so disconcerting—it helped to know what was going on—it still drove his animal selves wild. Besides which, though they'd become almost accustomed to this bizarre mode of travel, it was hardly safe or secure. Anything could happen, including some of them going to another alter-realm entirely.

And, of all of them, Salena was arguably the most vulnerable. She was a scholar and a scientist, with magic to make the rain fall or the sun shine. Her intellect might have claws sharp enough to shred, but otherwise she was no warrior. He'd feel better when she—

The connection snapped back into place as Salena appeared, stepping onto the frozen sea, a green tinge to her dusky golden complexion. The heel of her boot skidded a little on the slick surface and without thinking, Rhy grasped her elbow to steady her. Her smoky blue eyes flashed to his in startlement, and he muttered an apology. He was *trying* to stay away from her—hadn't he been on best behavior the evening before, despite the desperate longing to touch her?—but sometimes instinct took over. Everyone might agree that Rhy was a feckless asshole who'd failed to live up to expectations of any kind, but he couldn't stand by and see Salena hurt in even the smallest way.

Ravens might not be a fierce creature like the First Forms of the others—well, except for Gen with her little hummingbird, though she could also be the white saber cat and a dragon—but his own First Form was intelligent and communal. Also, he'd been the wolf for so long in the alter-realm that its hot-bloodedness lingered in him. *All the shapeshifters are struggling with their animal natures, probably because of the intelligence exerting influence on you,* Salena had said. *Go find someone else to give you the release you need ... find someone else to want.*

For the smartest person he knew, Salena just didn't seem to get this. He burned with consuming desire, yes, but unfortunately only one woman could slake it. The verdict was in and it was indisputable. All those years apart from her, he'd *tried* to find that same thing with any number of someone elses. And his life had become an empty shell, something he couldn't go back to.

So, when—after kissing him with molten passion, her desire heady to his senses—and she'd *still* turned him down, he'd done his level best to be Salena's friend. At least that way he got to be in her company, and it had salved some vicious need in him to spend those hours playing *kiauo* with her, to see her lose that guarded mien she had around him all the time, to hear her laugh with genuine pleasure. It had strained his self-control to bid her goodnight and walk away, but he'd done it. The surprise in her face had been almost worth the resulting night of miserable restlessness.

Now, he'd lost the ground he'd gained, thoughtlessly taking her arm lest she fall.

To Rhy's surprise, however, Salena didn't immediately jerk her arm away. Their gazes met for a long humming moment, the bronze fur lining her hood the same color as the richly streaming hair surrounding her face, both a few shades lighter than her skin. Those eyes, a blue that neither of her parents possessed, were a throwback to the Tala ancestry buried in her family tree on both sides. Rhy marveled, not for the first time, at her astonishing loveliness. She'd been beautiful in their youth, freshly blossoming and artlessly enthusiastic about trying everything, and time had only honed and polished that beauty. Her intelligence and experience made her both more alluring and more intimidating. With a stab of stark realization, Rhy suddenly understood that he wasn't good enough for Salena anymore. That very likely he never had been.

"Thank you," Salena murmured, and he quickly released her arm, looking and moving away from the temptation she represented. He might know he wasn't good enough for her, but that didn't stop the eternal craving for her. A bitterly ironic fate, that he could have any woman except the one he truly wanted.

Jak and Stella stepped onto the ice just then, the portal closing behind them with a snap. Jak spun in a circle, confirming the safety of the group, and relaxed marginally. He squinted at the settlement of the folk on the distant shore, then cast a frown at Stella. "Did you have to land us half-an-hour's walk away?"

She wrinkled her nose at him, unperturbed. "I thought that was better than landing us in the middle of a group of startled and angry folk, Captain Safety First. This is not an exact science and I'm still learning."

"We might as well commence that walk," Astar said in a mild tone, pointing for them to get going. "It poses an interesting question, however, in that the intelligence *is* so precise at opening those portals. Remember when it opened one directly in front of our carriages on that narrow road around Lake Sullivan?"

"Strategically placed, indeed," Jak agreed sourly. He'd been the one to control the terrified horses as they were bombarded with frenzied monkey-lizards pouring through the portal—and had nearly gone over the cliff. "But do we really care how the intelligence does it?"

"It's a relevant question," Salena spoke up. "I was thinking about this earlier, that Nilly is learning to do what the intelligence has been doing. Does that mean the intelligence is some sort of sorcerer too? Where did it learn? How did it practice?"

"Why did it suddenly start opening portals into our world now?" Gen asked over her shoulder, expression grave.

"Yes, and what is its purpose?" Rhy asked, scowling when several of them threw him surprised glances. "I've been paying attention, too," he said, making sure he didn't sound surly. He might not love sitting around with his parents talking strategy, but he'd absorbed plenty of it. "You all have been talking about it like the intelligence is capricious and childlike. But what if it only seems that way to us? Maybe there is a method."

"Experimentation," Salena put in, nodding at him, for once not sounding like she hated him.

"Exactly," Rhy replied, warmed that Salena thought he'd said something worthwhile. "But to what end—what does it want?"

"We know what the intelligence wants: Stella," Jak answered crisply, an edge of violence in his voice. "That's inescapable. It's also not going to have her."

"I'm fine, Jak," Stella said soothingly, taking his hand.

"But it didn't want her from the beginning," Rhy argued, returning the glare Jak threw at him, sharp as one of his blades. "Yes, once Nilly drew its attention, it became interested in her. But back when Isyn was drawn into the Winter Isles, when the giant attacked at Gieneke, when the blood eclipse happened during the crystalline moon—all of those occurrences were the intelligence starting whatever its doing before it ever met Stella."

"Rhy is right," Zeph commented. "I know we thought the giant was trying things out at Gieneke, tearing people and animals apart and putting them back together all wrong, but just because it didn't work, does that mean whatever it was doing had no purpose?"

"Or that it's only our perception that the results weren't something that 'worked,'" Gen mused.

"I know from listening to Salena talk about science and research that a negative result is useful information," Rhy said.

"Hypothesis testing," Salena said, eyes going wide, her canny brain working away.

"So we need to figure out what its been testing and to what point," Astar suggested.

"Yes," Rhy replied. "My father always says understanding what the enemy wants is more than half the battle."

Astar tossed him a grin. "Our Auntie Essla says it, too."

"Further debate on the topic will have to wait," Isyn cautioned them. "A troop of folk, heavily armed, are heading in our direction."

"Here's hoping this ends with food and shelter and not bloody warfare," Gen said.

FORTUNATELY, FOOD AND shelter it was—*such as it was*, Lena added with a wry and silent observation. The main hall where Isyn had resided during his long tenure in the Winter Isles had been built primarily to accommodate the waist-high, furry folk. Thus, the only human-sized bedchamber was the one Isyn had used. Gen and Isyn could share that—as they had during Gen's time there—but the rest of the group would be uncomfortable at best, miserable at worst. Lena was accustomed to rough conditions from field work in the Aerron Desert, but at least there she didn't have to worry about freezing. The thickly-furred folk didn't have much accommodation for their thin-skinned visitors.

Also, with the folk already strained for food supplies, it would be especially inconsiderate of their well-fed, and well-supplied group to impinge on their hosts' hospitality until they knew they could break the enchantment isolating the Winter Isles. Thus, everyone was motivated to get immediately to work on figuring that out.

Lena still didn't see how they could pull this off. She wished for the confidence of Stella's foresight as the two of them, plus Isyn, gathered in the main hall. The last time any of them had been there, they'd been fighting a pitched battle against two enemies: the folk wanting to retain Isyn, their life-giving mage, and the monsters being hurled at them by the intelligence via portal. That is, the others had been fighting a pitched battle while Lena cowered in Isyn's bedroom. Rhyian had fetched her out when it was all over, but she still hadn't shaken the sight of the blood and gore-covered hall, filled with still-twitching creatures. They seemed to haunt the inhospitable space, and she shivered from more than the biting cold.

Not exactly prime conditions for her to concentrate and attempt a magic she had no idea how to accomplish.

Though there'd been no sign of the intelligence being aware of their activities, the other five of their group not involved in the sorcerous effort arrayed themselves in a loose circle around their triad of magic workers, brandishing weapons of choice and ready to defend against sudden attack. Gen muttered darkly about preferring her claws, but took up a place at Isyn's back, holding her dagger in one hand and a shield in the other. Jak, naturally elected to guard Stella's back. Lena more than half expected Rhyian to insist on taking up a position at her back, and she couldn't decide if she was relieved or disappointed when he elected to be a roving guard along with Zeph, while Astar took the place behind Lena, giving her a sweet and encouraging smile as he did.

Isyn, who spoke the folk's strange language fluently, had explained to them what they were attempting, so most of the small, permanent population of the Winter Isles had gathered in the hall. They ringed the room, their bright eyes glittering with hope, their chatter excited until Isyn asked them to be silent. Lena seriously doubted there would be anything to see, especially as it was unlikely they'd get it right the first time. It might take them days or weeks to discover the trick to undoing what the intelligence had so expertly accomplished.

Setting aside those concerns, Lena conscientiously instructed herself to ignore Rhyian as he prowled with distractingly sinuous vigilance in her peripheral vision, making herself focus only on Stella—and on Stella's certainty. Magic was funny that way: it tended to follow what you believed. If Lena allowed doubt to creep in, she would be the weak point of their triangle, and her crumbling would drag them all down into defeat. For a moment, she felt as if she was falling again, tumbling through the air in utter despair, wanting only to die, failure an inevitability.

Stella gave her a penetrating look. "Are you all right, Lena?"

"I'm fine," she answered firmly.

Though Stella clearly knew better, she accepted Lena's assurance at face value. She withdrew the Star from the secure pocket inside her fighting leathers, holding it on her open palm. The round jewel shone like a small, golden sun, radiating more than light and heat. A susurrus of wonder ran through the watching folk, subsiding as Isyn shook his head in reproval.

"Both of you cup your hands over the Star, also," Stella directed quietly. "As best we can, I'd like us to find a position that will allow the three of us to touch it an equal amount." She stretched her fingers back so the Star was more exposed, perched with just enough contact to keep it from rolling off.

"If Isyn and I each put a fingertip on the Star," Lena said, "that will be close to the same amount of contact." She demonstrated, the surface of the Star molten against her skin, just shy of being too hot to bear. Isyn followed her lead, doing the same.

"That works," Stella acknowledged, her eyes going silvery as she summoned her sorcery, hair stirring in the nonexistent wind of magical disturbance. "I take it back. We need more contact than that, and with each other, too. I'm going to cup my palm more. As I do, both of you curl your fingers around the Star, gradually increasing your skin contact with it."

It was a delicate balancing act, an awkward bit of metatarsal acrobatics that took several tries to accomplish, as Stella called a halt and had them start over. Eventually they found a point of equilibrium, the three of them clustered close together, hands equally holding the Star, heads bent close. The pose put Lena in mind of old stories and the archetypal three witches gathered around a cauldron. With Stella's dark hair, Isyn's ivory, and her own gold-streaked bronze, they likely made a striking image, too. Had Andi seen this in her visions? Some deep intuition made Lena think that was so.

"Sink into the aura of the Star," Stella murmured, a hint of singsong in her voice, alluring and hypnotic. Lena did her best to let go of doubts, fears, and any lingering reservations. Trusting in Stella—for they'd done this sort of thing before—she gave herself over to her friend's lead.

It took a bit longer for Isyn to mesh with them. His masculine energy, his different flavor of magery, and the bare truth that he hadn't been their friend all their lives, made dissolving the instinctive barriers their conscious minds wanted to throw up more difficult. But his long years of isolation hadn't been wasted. Isyn had a meticulous control of his magery and his conscious mind that Lena could envy, were she willing the pay the monumental price that he had. In the end, it was Isyn who found his way into being part of the connection between Stella and Lena, not their skill that admitted him. His wintergreen magic wound through Stella's silver and Lena's darker storm-sense, the final click of harmonious convergence sending a shiver of completion through Lena.

"Expanding outward," Stella murmured, her voice echoing in their minds as much as in their ears. "Let's find the boundaries of this world."

Their sphere of awareness moved, slowly at first, then gaining momentum, escalating equally and evenly in all directions at once, moving through floor, walls, and ceiling. The hall dwindled as their shared bubble moved out farther, through soil, sea, and sky, reaching and stretching ever more...

Until they hit a wall.

~ 12 ~

THE SENSATION WAS almost bruising, a shock to the senses in the barrier's wrongness and impenetrability. In the ecstasy of shared purpose, the sheer delight of magical harmony inebriating, Lena had nearly forgotten their objective. Now that she recalled what they sought, she had no doubt they'd found it.

"Stay with me," Stella urged softly, speaking entirely on a shared mental plane now. *"Settle, calm. We expected this. Now to assess."*

Explore and assess, yes. Gather data. Lena centered herself in that familiar expertise. She knew how to go about this. She touched, tasted, and tested the encircling barrier. The unnaturalness of it was repellent, but she pushed past her intuitive desire to pull back. Even had they not been certain the intelligence was responsible for sequestering the alter-realms, she'd have known it now. The familiar and decidedly distasteful feel of its magic permeated the barrier. She had a vivid sense of the enchantment it had imposed, like a sphere of glass that had encircled this section of living world and excised it, leaving it to stand alone in space and time.

And to wither and die.

Now that she had a better feel for the barrier, too, she sensed what lay beyond it. More bubbles like this one suspended like an array of glittering micro-worlds. Like a collection of prizes, perhaps. Somewhere out there among them had to be the forest alter-realm she'd first stumbled into. Much as she loathed the place and had zero desire to ever revisit it, she felt a pang of sympathy for it. And she wondered—if these places had been cut out of living worlds, had they left a hole behind? Had that been what caused the strange phenomenon the night of the crystalline moon? Something big had passed across the face of the full moon, temporarily occluding it. A chunk of another realm could do that. Could it have been from theirs? But no, surely they'd have heard about it. Lena's mother's spies had reported in from all parts of the known world.

In the midst of her musing, the barrier around the Winter Isles shivered like a bell struck with a precisely tuned hammer. Intuitively, Lena knew that meant the intelligence had sensed their intrusion. Worse, it sensed Stella's presence and reacted with a flare of avid hunger that terrified Lena, even though she wasn't the object of it.

Connected as she was to Stella, Lena experienced with her friend the debilitating terror as Stella flinched in alarm, their unified sphere of magic wobbling dangerously. There was no prevaricating when sharing thoughts, and Stella's fear of the intelligence rippled like dirty ice in Lena's mind. The sense of Jak as safe harbor also shone clearly, the essential trust in him, that he'd care for and protect her if she could only reach him. Lena accepted the stab of envy for what it was. She wanted that for herself, but in rejecting Rhyian and the danger he posed to her heart, she'd given up any hope of having it. Instead she was on her own, maybe forever. In that case, she'd have to learn to be good at self-sufficiency. Starting now.

"Contract," Lena suggested, trying to project calm. So far as they knew, the intelligence couldn't attack them magically on this plane. All of its aggression had occurred via the portals and creating creatures to animate. *"We withdraw, slow and smooth,"*

Stella agreed with fervency, a vibrating undercurrent of alarm in her mental voice. *"I'm informing Jak, just in case."*

Dimly Lena heard shouted orders to be ready, a scramble of reaction from the folk. She screened it out. Her job was to maintain control, so she concentrated on that. Their combined globe of power must remain unbroken and even, not lopsided or weakened in any one place. She would not be the weak link who made them fail.

RHY PACED RESTLESSLY as the sorcerous trio stood still as stone in the center of the rustic hall. The back of his neck prickled with awareness of the watching folk. In his human mind, he understood that Isyn had spoken with the folk and that they wouldn't attack, but his animal side remembered all too well how those same creatures had done exactly that.

People who stuck you with spears and knives didn't just become friends with a few words. All of his animal selves understood that—and understood also that this was simply a temporary truce. Everything could go sideways in a moment. With pretty much everyone he cared anything about all in this room—including the one person who meant everything—that put him on edge.

"Brace for incoming!" Jak shouted, sending Rhy's nerves into even higher alert. He'd much rather be in wolf form for this. Or any animal form, really. His human self always seemed to be lacking when it came to a fight. The Silversteel sword hummed light in his hand, however, ready to serve where claws and fangs were lacking.

"Incoming from where?" Astar demanded tersely, scanning the area. "Zephyr, do you sense anything?"

Zeph's gríobhth senses made her sensitive to the formation of rifts, but she answered in the negative, prowling in her black fighting leathers, hair bound back, eyes glittering with predatory light. She'd no doubt prefer to have claws and talons, too.

"Stella says only that the intelligence is aware of their actions," Jak answered.

"Are they close to breaking the barrier isolating this realm?" Astar asked.

Rhy thought he could answer that one by the expression on Salena's face as the sorcerers emerged from their trancelike state. She looked disappointed and annoyed with herself as she did when she failed to master some task she'd set herself, and something else, too. She looked sad and resigned, beyond whatever unhappy mood had been clouding her earlier.

"I called a retreat when I sensed the intelligence was aware of us," Stella answered. "We were close, though, to figuring out how to break the enchantment. When the intelligence arrived... I'm sorry to admit I panicked. I wasn't sure what it would do."

"You did the right thing," Jak told her reassuringly.

Nobody else said anything, though Rhy felt sure he wasn't the only one to wonder about the truth of that. A disappointed mutter ran through the assembled folk when Isyn told them what hadn't happened. Rhy's instincts prickled. The folk were small, but they were vicious fighters, had the advantage of home territory, and outnumbered their visitors by probably ten to one. It wouldn't be difficult for a mob of the wily folk to overwhelm the eight of them. No evidence of a rift forming or any attack by the intelligence, either. Rhy snuck a glance at Salena, to gauge her reaction, and found her looking right at him. Something in her gaze made him think she wasn't sure retreating had been the right decision.

They waited a while longer, tense minutes dragging out while nothing at all occurred.

"What is it doing, can you tell?" Astar asked the trio.

Everyone looked at Stella. "I can't," she confessed. "I simply felt its awareness of our presence and... well, as I said before, I panicked."

"You were calm and controlled," Salena corrected with an encouraging smile.

"I was afraid," Stella said quietly, pressing her lips together. Jak was beside her immediately, putting his arms around her.

"Of course you were," he said, glaring over her head at Astar. "It's understandable, given what you went through with that... thing. No one expects you to face that again."

Astar looked as wretched as Rhy felt. Stella was the best of them, always kind, always ready to be there for any of them, for healing or for a kind word. When the intelligence had held her captive in the tower of her lifelong nightmares, Stella had rallied and triumphed, but no one could walk away from an experience like that unaffected. Certainly not someone with Stella's sensitivity.

"You have to try again, Nilly," Astar said, clearly trying to be firm, but sounding more like he was pleading. "Not right now, or even today, but you, yourself, said this was the way. The only way."

Stella, face buried against Jak's shoulder, didn't reply. Then she pulled back, visibly steeling herself, and faced the rest of them. "I don't think I can be the guiding hands. I'm so sorry, but—" She bit off the next words, her usually serene face crumpling as tears spilled down.

Jak soothed her and Astar—noble Astar, so determined to do a good job, so torn between duty and love for his twin— actually looked to Rhy. As did everyone else. Maybe it was because Jak and Astar were so caught up in their shared need to protect Stella, but Rhy also remembered something Stella had said to him on that night of the crystalline moon. *This group has always followed your lead...* He'd immediately countered that their group had always followed Astar's lead. Stella had only given him a pitying look and called him thick-skulled as only Stella could do and still sound sweetly compassionate.

Rhy had dismissed Stella's words at the time as a ploy of hers to get him to play nice with Salena, but now he wondered. "If Stella can't be the guiding hands, then Salena needs to do it," he declared, meeting Salena's somber gaze and nodding his confidence to her, as if she'd asked a question. "Isyn is too new to this kind of working." The ivory-haired mage nodded his agreement, unbothered. "Besides," Rhy continued, "Salena is a trained observer and has a logical mind."

"Stella has all the power," Salena countered, though she didn't argue the rest. Instead she seemed to be considering an approach, thinking already to next steps.

"Then use her power," Rhy said, "and you supply the control." When she looked doubtful, he gave her a deliberately cocky grin. "Remember how you told me that clearing an opening in the storm for everyone to view the moon on the longest night was child's play? You have a great deal of magic and the control to wield it deftly."

Salena had an odd expression on her face as she listened. For the first time in ages she looked... almost like he'd gotten through to her, past the hurt and anger. Her eyes had a softness to them, a feel to her that he remembered from so long ago, when they'd understood everything about each other without the need for words. "But it's only weather magic," she said, doubt in her voice.

"No 'only' about it," he told her softly, willing her to believe. "My mother said she had a vision of you wrangling powerful magic. This is now."

"I don't know how to break the enchantment, though."

"*Nobody* does yet," he pointed out. "Not even Stella. But you *do* know how to alter entrenched patterns, like the weather that makes a desert over the course of years and decades. You said it required so much more finesse, that it needed meticulous work over time to account for all the ripple effects, and that you'd gotten really good at it."

Zeph chose that moment to break in, snickering. "And here I thought Rhy had only paid attention to your prodigiously displayed bosom that night, Lena."

Salena flicked Zeph a look full of all the irritation Rhy also felt. Yes, he'd been entranced by Salena's beauty that night, and he'd never forget how she looked in that white gown that so brilliantly displayed all her lush, brown-skinned curves. But that wasn't what this was about. Salena needed to believe in herself. "You can do this," he insisted softly, speaking only to Salena. "And you won't be alone. Isyn and Nilly will be with you magically, and the rest of us will be here to guard your backs."

Salena glanced toward Astar who stood squarely behind Stella now, flanking her with Jak, and Rhy moved behind Salena, nodding to Astar for confirmation. "I'll be right here. You concentrate on your job," he told Salena.

With a long and canny look, Zeph took up pacing the perimeter for both of them. Gen, at Isyn's back, gave Rhy a thoughtful smile. Stella, steadier, squared. "You hold the Star this time," she told Salena, "and I'll follow your lead. You know what to do."

LENA DIDN'T KNOW what to make of Rhyian's sudden step into a leadership role, nor of his surprising declaration of faith in her. Or perhaps that wasn't fair. Rhyian had always believed in her, had been warmly admiring of her innate magic, and even back in the day had been interested in her plans to help alleviate the drought that created the Aerron Desert and caused it to expand. That had never been the problem between them.

And this wasn't the time to think about the problem that had destroyed it all.

Holding the Star in her palm, Lena stretched back her fingers, waiting as Isyn and Stella curled their fingers around it, then softened to cup it more. They found the sweet spot faster this time, the three of them falling into a rapt communion facilitated by the jewel. Stella was there in all her vast power, a sense of resolve over the tremulousness of her recent scare. Of course Stella was afraid of what the intelligence might do. Jak had been beyond lucky to be able to save her once. If the intelligence managed to capture her again, finding her might not be so easy. Lena quickly banished that thought, lest Stella read it in her mind.

It helped to give Lena perspective, however. What she'd experienced in the forest alter-realm wasn't anything compared to what the others had suffered. They were all wounded in their invisible ways and it was time for Lena to step up and be a useful member of the team.

Without Stella as the interface, Isyn's magic harmonized even better with Lena's, both of them inclined toward the natural magic of the world. Stella's magic derived from living things also, but in a markedly Tala way. Isyn's magery had been born of non-Tala lineage just as Lena's was, and their like magic formed a firm handshake.

Stella was still with them, but more as the power behind the effort, as she'd promised. Perhaps that would also help shield her from the intelligence's notice. Hopefully it had only briefly looked their way and then moved on.

Still, Lena proceeded cautiously as she led them to form the globe that she then expanded to encompass all the realm. Rhyian was right to some extent that this did feel to her like moving the core of a weather pattern. Those weren't spherical, but working with storms did require finding the whole of them, the origin and the manifestation, and holding it all in her mental hands. With weather, however, there was an infinite connectedness, a chain of incidents that led back from one condition to the previous.

She wouldn't have thought to do it that way, but Rhyian had triggered an idea. Holding their sphere just inside the boundary of the alter-realm bubble that was the Winter Isles— which would hopefully keep them just beyond the notice of the intelligence—Lena observed what she could. While she'd been thinking of the alter-realms as excised from normal reality, unconnected, was that accurate? Nothing was truly disconnected.

So she explored, observing from enough distance so as not

to cause an effect from her study. She knew how to do that, too.

And then she found it.

Yes, the Winter Isles had been cut away, but the alter-realm also had a tether. It was connected to and sustained by something else. Something massively powerful that could be working to feed magic to keep the Winter Isles alter-realm as it was. It reminded Lena of the connection she and Stella had found to the stone giant in Gieneke, that Lena had severed to collapse the rampaging creature while Stella flung all the grief and horror she'd absorbed from the terrorized townsfolk back at the force animating it.

Just as they were working on the assumption that the intelligence was behind the rift and the existence of the alter-realms, it stood to reason that this connection was also powered by the intelligence itself, wherever it was.

She might be able to sever that connection. She had experience with something similar—though it still surprised her that Rhyian had recognized that fact—as breaking up the chain of conditions that created drought was much the same. But then what would happen to the Winter Isles? It would do no good to sever the Winter Isles from the source that sustained it if the alter-realm would then die. She needed to reconnect it with its home realm, wherever that might be.

And that wasn't even considering that the intelligence would absolutely notice, react, and probably retaliate violently. Though... if she severed the connection, would the intelligence be able to open a portal into the world again? Would *they* be able to open a portal out? She wished there were a way to test it.

"*We could test it on an unpopulated alter-realm,*" Stella suggested mentally. Lena startled, having forgotten that Stella, and probably Isyn also, could follow Lena's thoughts in this meshing of magic. "*The flat-grid world would work.*"

"*Another thought: can we follow those connections back to the intelligence?*" Isyn asked. "*It would be a way of finding where and what that intelligence is.*"

"*If we trace the connection from another alter-realm—with Lena in the lead—the intelligence might not be on alert as it surely is now,*" Stella agreed, sounding remarkably steadier.

"*Let's contract and discuss with the others,*" Lena decided, already delicately withdrawing, guiding them backward. It was both easier and harder this time. She was more practiced at the method, but she also noticed an energy drain. When she disengaged from Stella's seemingly endless and effervescent supply of magic, Lena swayed dizzily, temporarily woozy from the immediate deficiency.

A strong hand caught and steadied her, a welcome sense of comfort in the touch. She opened her eyes to find Rhyian right there, wickedly gorgeous face full of concern, wild blue eyes intent on her. "You should sit," he said.

Reflexively, she opened her mouth to argue, but realized that would be foolish. She nodded, and Rhyian guided her a few steps to a nearby bench, then let go of her and withdrew to a polite and measured distance. Friends only. Missing his touch immediately, Lena dropped her head in her hands, ready to blame the magic drain, whereas she mostly needed a moment to reflect bitterly on the irony of getting exactly what she'd asked for and being disappointed in the result. That had always been the problem, though: she craved Rhyian even knowing he wasn't good for her.

"Salena?" Rhyian asked tentatively, going down on one knee to peer at her. Alarm tightened his expression and he cursed. "You need healing."

"I don't," she protested, though weakly.

"You forget I've seen you knocked unconscious for hours from magic use," he countered bleakly. "Nilly, over here!"

"No, no." Lena made herself lift her head—*ouch*, a dull headache was forming at the base of her skull—and pasted on a smile. "I'm fine. I just needed a moment."

Rhyian snorted. "You forget I know all of your smiles, and that it your pretending-to-be-fine-when-you-feel-lousy smile."

She had to laugh, he'd nailed it so perfectly. Then Stella was at her side, slipping a cool hand under Lena's hair to the heated back of her neck, the incipient headache immediately dissipating with the flow of green healing magic. Lena sighed her relief even as she looked up at Stella. "You have to be drained, too."

In truth, Stella looked better than she ought to. Steadier and no longer so fearful. "You and Isyn were much harder hit," she explained with a rueful smile. "If we're going to the grid world, we'll do it tomorrow, however, after we all have rested."

Rhyian tensed palpably, his apprehension zinging straight to Lena's nerves, despite the physical and emotional distance between them. "The grid world?" he repeated in a dangerous tone.

"*You* don't have to go," Lena reassured him, easily seeing the shadows that haunted him still from his sojourn in that sterile world.

"Neither do you," he snarled.

Astar came up and set a hand on Rhyian's shoulder, reassuring or restraining, or both. "It sounds like they might have to. But we also need to discuss. *After* everyone rests."

~ 13 ~

R HY DIDN'T LIKE it. Obviously, he didn't like any of this, but he *really* didn't like how his friends seemed to have lost their collective minds. His only solace lay in the questionable comfort that Jak was also completely against this plan.

"You all have lost your minds!" Jak declared, sweeping a dagger point at everyone but Rhy. For his part, Rhy tossed him an irony-filled salute of solidarity.

"It's a good plan, Jak," Stella insisted with her gentle gravity. "Lena's theory is a sound one. We went into this knowing we'd have to discover how to break the enchantment severing the alter-realms from their more complete realities. Lena's identification of the cord connecting the Winter Isles to a magical source that logic tells us must be the intelligence is the only answer we have so far. This is the best solution we have."

"A logical solution isn't necessarily a sane one," Rhy noted sardonically, kicking back against the wall and forcing his body to relax. Not easy as he truly wanted to rend and tear to release this savage worry. Jak, once again spinning his dagger instead of pointing it, threw him an appreciative look. Salena gave him an exasperated one. At least she looked better for a night's sleep and a couple of good meals. She hadn't fooled him with her fake smiles. That magic working had drained her far too much. Now she wanted to extend herself even more. Insanity. "Why go to the grid world, of all places?" Rhy added, the wolf inside feeling particularly growly about that.

"We've been over this," Astar said patiently, though he was clearly no happier about this plan. "If Lena is able to sever the connection but it destabilizes or destroys the alter-realm, it could kill everyone in it."

"We can't test it here," Isyn inserted with quiet determination. "I can't risk the folk that way. I owe them that much."

"The grid world is the only alter-realm we can be sure has no life in it," Stella said.

"There was that snake," Jak pointed out.

"Which you killed," Stella replied evenly, "and which was arguably ported there by the intelligence to attack you. This won't take long. I can port Lena, Isyn, and myself to the grid world. Lena can determine if the same connection is there and see if she can trace it to the intelligence's location. Logically, those connections will be rooted in whatever realm is the intelligence's home. Once she's identified that home realm, she can sever the connection and liberate the grid world."

"This is the part I don't like," Gen put in.

"There's only *one* part?" Rhy demanded.

She ignored him. "What if the grid world does collapse or implode or whatever?" she asked. "Then we lose all three of our magic-workers."

"Not to mention people we love," Rhy pointed out silkily.

Now she flashed him an annoyed glance. "I'm trying to keep to *rational* arguments here."

"Why should you when they're not?" he retorted.

"If only one or two of us go," Stella inserted calmly, "then we might not have the same power and stability the complete triad has."

"Nilly has to go," Salena said, "as only she can portal us back out again."

"*If* she can even open a portal with the connection severed," Zeph said. "If the severing disrupts that magic, too, then you're stuck there. You need me with you."

"The whole point of only us three going is to save at least some of us if things go wrong," Salena argued.

"I'd rather die with you than live without you," Jak told Stella with quiet ferocity. "I'm going. You need me to protect you."

Privately, Rhy thought the same about Salena, though he'd at least gotten smart enough not to say so out loud.

Astar held up a hand, silencing everyone. "We're going in circles. Every argument being aired has already been discussed. There is no perfect solution that I can see here, no option that is risk-free except going home and we already know that failing to act only seals our doom at a later date." He sighed heavily, shaking his head, his grizzly bear First Form clearly as restless as the rest of them facing being left behind to stew and wonder. "Nilly, can you do this with just you and Lena?"

"No," Rhy bit out. "Salena was exhausted by—"

"Is your name Nilly?" Astar growled. "No. Be silent."

Rhy subsided unhappily. Salena and Stella were considering. "I think so," Stella offered. "At least for the test attempt. If we can't do it, we can always add Isyn."

"Then the two of you go," Astar decided. "If everything goes wrong, we'll still have Isyn. Besides, we need him here so the folk don't murder us in our sleep," he added with a grim attempt at humor.

"The girls need a guard," Jak argued and Rhy—muted by royal command—pointed at Jak in agreement. "You've seen them, Willy," Jak wheedled. "When they're in that trance state, they're oblivious to everything around them. The intelligence could port a snake on top of them and they wouldn't notice."

"I'm pretty sure I'd notice being eaten by a giant snake," Salena said drily. The sarcasm was a cover, Rhy saw through that much. Salena was afraid, which was a good sign, because at least then she'd be smart. He raised his hand, but Astar shook his head.

"I don't need to hear it to know what you're going to say, Rhy," Astar said. "You're not going and neither is Jak. Zephyr is right. She should go." He frowned ruefully at Zeph's excited straightening. "If any of us have a chance of finding a rift if Nilly can't create a portal home, it's Zephyr in gríobhth form."

"Dragon form might be able to," Gen said quietly.

"Maybe," Astar allowed, "but that's untested. If you like, you can spend the waiting time practicing, but my decision is final: Zephyr, Nilly, and Lena are going. Isyn can use his magery to shift Zephyr to gríobhth form, and back again when you all return. Find out what you can, try severing the connection if you think it's safe. No heroics. Under no circumstances are any of you to take on the intelligence on your own. Lena, I'm primarily talking to you here. Find that home realm if you can, then withdraw. All of you get back here as fast as you can. Keep in mind that time is going faster for us here, so the wait will be torture." His gaze lingered on Zeph, his expression speaking loudly of his own fears.

At least Astar would be risking his own beloved, too. It was uncharitable of him, Rhy knew, but he also took a certain comfort in it. Reluctantly, he also allowed that Astar displayed a courage in leadership Rhy himself certainly lacked. He doubted he could make the decision that was best for the mission and potentially sacrifice the one woman he'd ever loved. He already knew how it would feel when Salena stepped out of their shared reality and into an alter-realm without him. Contemplating what it would be like if she never returned... well, it *didn't* bear contemplating.

Salena stood, breaking the fraught silence that had settled over the small group. "No reason to delay, is there? Let's do it and get it over with."

While the others prepared—Isyn readying himself to trigger Zeph's shapeshifting, Jak checking Stella's and Salena's store of blades—Rhy stood back, reminding himself to give Salena the distance she'd asked for, even as the wolf in him frothed to act. Gen sidled up to him, her own worry clear in her sober expression. "Is it wrong to be relieved Isyn doesn't have to go?" she whispered.

Rhy shrugged, not in elaborate Tala-fashion, but subtly, then produced a careless smile for her. "Enjoy the reprieve, I say," he told her. "You'll get your turn to be eviscerated worrying about him taking ridiculous risks at some point, no doubt."

Across the way, Salena nodded at something Jak said, looking very serious as he adjusted her grip on her dagger. That was all well and good, but Rhy didn't see how she'd be in any state to use it if she was locked in a magical trance.

"You really do still love her," Gen said, giving him a searching look when he jerked his gaze back to her in annoyance.

"You say that as if it's not common knowledge. Of course I still love her. I never stopped."

"What I mean is," she continued unperturbed, "this is the real thing. Not a youthful infatuation. Not simple lust. Not a stubborn determination to win. It's love as true as it gets."

He supposed he'd been accused of all the alternatives Gen mentioned, so that was fair. "I tried to stop loving her," he said quietly enough that even the other keen-eared shapeshifters in the room wouldn't be able to hear. "I can't seem to get it to take."

"That doesn't surprise me," she replied just as quietly, giving him a sympathetic smile.

"Doesn't it? Everyone else seems to think I should be able to."

She snorted softly. "Well, I *am* the one who believes in true love—and I don't believe it simply vanishes just because you wish it so."

His voice came out unexpectedly hoarse. "What I wish doesn't matter," he finally said, feeling rather pitiful. "Salena has made it abundantly clear she wants to be only friends, if that. What do you do when you can't stop loving someone who doesn't want you?"

Gen considered that question thoughtfully. "You make

giving them what they want part of loving them. You can't stop loving her, but you can give her the gift of letting her go her own way. Sometimes loving someone means sacrificing your own happiness for theirs."

Her quiet words reverberated between them like a chime rung once, its notes humming on with soft significance. How had he not understood this before?

"Everyone is ready," Astar declared, waving them over and breaking the spell.

Astar caressed the curve of Zeph's neck. She was glittering golden in gríobhth form. Jak embraced Stella, giving her a long, lingering kiss, then tipping his forehead against hers and murmuring something too quiet for Rhy to hear, even if he had been inclined to eavesdrop on the private moment. Salena stood back slightly, looking a little afraid and lonely.

Rhy wasn't sure if he should say something to her or not. At that moment, Salena—as if sensing his torn feelings—looked his way and met his gaze, offering a tremulous smile. To his utter shock, she came to him, Gen discreetly drifting away.

"Don't worry so much," Salena said, trying to make her smile wry instead of wobbly. "We'll be back before you know it."

Rhy attempted to match her chosen attitude, quirking a brow at her. "You forget that time passes faster here. I'll know every long moment of your absence." All right, that was a failure in nonchalance. He sounded far too intense, too wrecked. "Just make sure to come back," he added.

I'll be waiting for you, he didn't say.

Stay safe, if only for me, he also didn't say.

His deepest fear stemmed from the way Salena had given up and let herself fall from Zeph's back, that Salena had so easily sacrificed herself in part because of the pain he'd dealt her. *My heart is fragile now in a way it wasn't before. And that's your fault, Rhyian.* He needed her to have a reason to want to live. He needed words to convince her, other than that he loved her, since that wasn't anything she wanted to hear—Gen was right about that. But he had no idea what he should say or do, since he always seemed to be saying and doing the wrong thing, even as others castigated him for not doing enough.

Salena hadn't moved away yet, gazing up at him, her eyes that shadowed blue that hinted of purple tropical evenings. "Rhyian," she said softly. "If I don't come back..."

He bit down on the urge to interrupt, to assert that she *would* come back, that she must. But he was trying to do better, to listen, and that meant not interrupting, even if she trailed off temptingly like that, practically inviting him to fill in that potentially devastating hole. Was she going to repeat the message she gave to Zeph, that she loved him? He held his breath, forcing himself to be still, to wait, despite the lethal anticipation.

"Never mind," she said on a sigh, starting to turn away. "It's not important."

Cursing himself mentally—as apparently, she *had* expected him to step into that inviting pause—he caught her hand. "Please finish, Salena. I'm listening. I want to hear what you have to say."

She very nearly smiled in truth, brows rising in feigned

shock. "No wonder I didn't recognize the behavior."

"Yes, well, you've always been a keen observer." She hadn't pulled her hand away, so he savored the feel of her slender fingers, her skin silky against his. Even so chaste a touch fired the grinding desire in him unbearably, but he'd rather touch her than not. The sweetest torment.

She looked down at their loosely tangled fingers. Cleared her throat. "I want you to know that I... appreciate how you supported me, suggesting that I take the lead magically."

He nodded, containing his disappointment. It wasn't the declaration he'd hoped to hear, but he made himself listen to what she *was* saying, rather than what he wanted her to say. Her thick fringe of lashes fluttered against her high cheekbones, a hint of gold in them shades lighter than her skin, before she raised her gaze to his. "It meant—means—a lot to me that you believe in what I can do."

He waited a beat, in case she wasn't done. "I've always believed in you, Salena."

Her full lips curved. "Yes, you have. That was always one thing..." She didn't finish, shaking her head and pulling her hand away. "I'd better go."

"Salena," he said, low and urgently, casting caution to the winds, just in case this was the last time he'd ever see her. "I know you don't want to hear this from me, but I can't leave it unsaid."

"I'm listening," she replied with a hint of amusement when he didn't continue. "You did me the courtesy of listening, so I can do the same for you."

Now he wondered if this would be a massive mistake. One

to add to his top ten lists of disastrous mistakes, with the number one position belonging to that day when he ran from Salena's sincerely and sweetly offered love, sure that he'd destroy it eventually and—unable to stand the suspense— ensured that it happened immediately.

"Say it, Rhyian," she said softly.

He took a breath, mustering his courage. He'd rather face the grid alter-realm than this all of a sudden. "Remember Astar's command," he said, instead of what he'd wanted to say. "No risks. Don't try to take on the intelligence yourself."

She cocked her head, not acknowledging that reminder, which worried him. "That's what you *couldn't* leave unsaid?" she asked doubtfully, raising her brows.

"No." He took a breath. *Coward.* "I want you to know that I love you, Salena." She flinched, unhappiness clouding her face, but he plowed on. "I'm not asking anything in return, except that you know and remember that. If you ever… have cause to doubt if it matters if you live or die, I want you to know that it *matters.*" He cleared his throat. "It matters to me, more than anything in the world, even my own life."

She pressed her lips together, nodding somberly. "I'll re-member," she said, so softly that even he almost couldn't hear it. "After all," she said more loudly, a bit of cheekiness to her smile, "no one wants to be a dead hero."

He laughed at her throwing his words back at him, though it was mostly to cover the way it struck his heart that she'd paid enough attention to have heard his griping from the beginning of the trip and remembered it all this time. "Go get 'em, Princess."

He looked up to find their friends studiously not watching them and he was immensely grateful for the courtesy, that no one had tried to hurry them along. Salena strode over to Stella, the pair of them efficiently creating a portal big enough for Zeph's bulk. The familiar non-scent of the sterile grid world cut through the pervasive atmosphere of snow and frozen sea that was the Winter Isles. The wolf in him remembered and quailed, but Rhy made sure not to show it. "Don't fall off a cliff," he called out helpfully, and the three women—even Zeph—rolled their eyes at him.

They stepped through the portal and vanished, the sight and scent of the alter-realm disappearing with them. He nearly staggered at the rending absence of her, his personal moon excised from the sky.

He settled in to wait for her to return and restore light to his eternal night.

~ 14 ~

LENA HAD NEVER been to the grid world before, but the others had described it accurately. A flat expanse of polished, gleaming stone black as obsidian stretched apparently unbroken to the horizon in all directions, featureless, lifeless. It wasn't unbroken in fact, however, as the others had discovered. Instead, bottomless defiles cut through at regular intervals—forming the grid—so seamless that the careless didn't notice them until they'd nearly fallen to their deaths.

It was uncanny in a horrible, heartlessly menacing way. Almost as if the place had been meticulously designed to incite despair in living beings. Lena began to worry they'd made a dreadful mistake in their reasoning. This alter-realm surely had been deliberately manufactured and not cut out of some other world.

Too late to change their plan, however.

She and Stella lost no time meshing magics while Zeph stood guard. It put Lena in mind of the true start of their adventures, when they'd battled the giant at Gieneke and she and Stella stood on that pier while Zeph stood between them and the giant. They'd used a chant, a children's rhyme from Nahanau, at Stella's suggestion, to help Lena relax into bending her storm magic into such a strange conformation. Now she needed no such rituals, far more practiced at using her magic this way. Which was fortunate, as that first time with Stella had knocked her unconscious for hours, as Rhyian had recalled, to her embarrassment.

It was both easier and more difficult to use the Star without Isyn. Stella could simply cup her palm over Lena's, no need for adjustments to make their contact equivalent, but Lena missed Isyn's firm handshake of magic so like her own.

She also missed Rhyian being at her back, which made no sense because she'd been so certain he only caused her pain. Those things he'd said... It defied logic that this most recent declaration of love somehow felt different. Maybe because he only offered it and asked nothing in return.

She couldn't allow that to distract her. Taking only the warmth that she'd felt at his words—*If you ever have cause to doubt that it matters if you live or die, I want you to know that it matters*—and setting the rest aside, she shaped the sphere of magic.

Only it didn't work. The sphere felt all wrong, not expanding above and below as it had in the Winter Isles.

Then an insight occurred to her: this was a world of lines and squares. Rethinking, she reframed the shape of their shared magic, then expanded. It worked. The cube felt clumsier, but also sharper—and definitely congruent with this alter-realm. She slowed them as they neared the outer boundary, this experience very much the same as in the Winter Isles. With part of her attention and from a dispassionate distance, she noted the shape of the grid world. It was a cube, with apparently identically grid-marked sides all around. Did that mean if someone fell into one of the defiles, they'd land at a center point?

"Or perhaps fall all the way through," Stella noted, following the thought with a shiver of apprehension.

A place designed to induce despair indeed. Not unlike the forest realm had been, just in a different way. And the alter-realm of lilies, and the Winter Isles, too. *Hmm.* Something else to think about later. Focusing on her tasks of here and now, Lena extended her attention carefully beyond the square barrier encapsulating the grid world, while Stella hung way back, present only via the Star, her magic almost completely disguised behind Lena's. There was that same constellation of alter-realms, floating in nothingness. In one part of her mind, she contemplated whether there would be a way for them to bridge that nothingness, to leap from world to world in this space, rather than retreat from each alter-realm and portal to the next.

Then it occurred to Lena that perhaps that was how the portals and rifts worked—they felt like a fold in reality, an overlap of two places with a slice of nothing between. She set that question aside, too, putting it with the others in her back brain for her subconscious mind to chew over. Looking for a connector, she found it snaking away from the cube, vanishing into the nothingness abruptly—as if threading into a rift. She traced its path all the way to the edge of the rift, pausing just outside its border.

What would happen if she followed the cord into the rift? Would it portal her consciousness away from her physical body? That could be very bad. Magic-users of all types were cautioned on out-of-body exercises, as it was all too easy to be cut off from the physical body and be unable to return. Still, they needed to know where this connector went. If it led to the intelligence's physical location, the information would be worth the risk.

"Not if you can't get the information back to us," Stella said from a distance.

Better some chance than no chance at all, though. Andi had said she'd had a vision of Lena being critical to this mission—what if this was it and she ruined everything by being a coward? After all, what was Lena's life, compared to the importance of the others?

If you ever… have cause to doubt that it matters if you live or die, I want you to know that it matters. It matters to me, more than anything in the world, even my own life. Rhyian's haunted gaze, intensely blue in his gorgeous face, floated in her mind. The Prince of Shadows was like an entire alter-realm of his own. No wonder she felt pulled into his reality, separate from all others and all-consuming.

If she and Stella tried breaking the enchantment holding this alter-realm without following this connector, they could die in the process without finding out more about the intelligence and its home base. But if her gambit worked, Lena could pinpoint the location of the intelligence, Stella could break the enchantment, and they'd return a success. It was worth it. In the far distance, Stella called a warning, but Lena was determined to ignore that. She was tired of being afraid.

Aware that this felt like another version of letting herself fall from Zeph's back, Lena plunged mentally into the rift.

HOURS PASSED WITH excruciating slowness for Rhy, far more slowly than they had while he endured boring lessons on mossback history or yet another parental lecture on applying himself. The gnawing sensation of Salena being *not in the world* was driving him insane on an instinctive level. Whatever atavistic, possessive, protective sense he derived from his animal forms—or perhaps his own admittedly lonely and decidedly unhealthy psyche—the wildness in him absolutely *loathed* doing nothing to recover Salena from the nothingness she'd vanished into.

When it happened the first time, when Salena fell through the rift to the forest alter-realm, he'd been off flying in the remote wilds of northern Annfwn, trying to reconcile his driving need to win Salena back with Astar's explicit orders to leave her alone. The foundation of his world had suddenly dropped out, sending him into a near panic. Knowing the reason for it didn't seem to help calm the frantic need to *do* something. Everything in him cried out for action and there was no action to be taken.

Normally he'd scrub off this restless energy by embracing the wildness within and letting it run its course—by shapeshifting, then flying or running until his human brain had stopped the endless circling over the exact same territory. That wasn't an option in the Winter Isles alter-realm, obviously, unless he asked Isyn to trigger a shift, which would be a waste of magery they might need later. Besides Rhy wanted to be right here, in human form, when Salena returned.

If she returns, the panic in him whispered.

He swiveled at the scrape of a blade, bringing the Silversteel sword to bear. Jak stood there, grinning tightly, Astar behind him, shirtless and swinging his huge broadsword in a limbering arc. "We're going to spar," Jak informed him.

"When Moranu grows pink roses," Rhy retorted, not at all in the mood for Jak's games.

"All three of us are going out of our minds with waiting," Astar said, his normally sunny smile strained. "We've got nothing to fight."

"So we'll fight each other?" Rhy drawled.

"Why break with long-standing tradition now?" Jak retorted cheerfully. "If you're going to be a moody bastard, you might as well put that crankiness to good use and get some practice with your new weapon."

Rhy idly spun the Silversteel sword, sizing up the pair of them—Jak, shorter, no shapeshifter strength, but graced with a gymnast's agility and an almost uncanny gift for aiming his blades; and Astar, taller, broader, stronger, well-muscled and trained in wielding that big sword.

This could be fun.

"What are the rules?" he inquired, already plotting how to best them.

Jak's eyes widened in disbelief. "You never pay attention to the rules!"

"Yes, I'm not giving you rules just so you can break them," Astar replied, more than a little bear in his voice as he advanced on Rhy.

Rhy danced back, not allowing Astar to force him into a retreat so soon, aware of Jak gliding in at an oblique angle. Flanking him? *Oh, I don't think so.* "Two against one hardly seems fair."

"Afraid?" Jak taunted. "Poor little baby shapeshifter can't resort to claws in order to cheat."

Rhy narrowed his eyes at Jak—keeping well back from Astar's longer reach. Let them think he was retreating. Picking your perfect moment to ambush someone could look that way. "You've been waiting for the opportunity to fight me when I couldn't shapeshift."

Jak's dark eyes sparkled with genial menace. "It *is* a once in a lifetime opportunity."

"I'm still faster and stronger."

"I'm still better." Jak leapt into the air, turning it into a tumble, a throwing knife whistling past Rhy's shoulder as he nimbly dodged. It *thunked* into a wooden pillar behind him and Rhy breathed a laugh.

"Throwing your weapon away? You're always scolding us not to do that."

Jak sprang up and smiled thinly. "Yes, but I have more."

Rhy was wise to Jak's tricks. Ignoring the bladesman, Rhy gauged Astar's approach precisely, and ducked just as the flat of the broadsword whooshed over his head. The maneuver put him inside Astar's considerable reach, and he gave his royal cousin a sharp jab in the ribs with his elbow on his way up to lay the sword at the man's throat. "My kill, I believe," he informed the crown prince silkily.

The point of a blade jabbed his kidney. "Yes, but you turned your back on me and now I've killed you," Jak informed him with good cheer.

Rhy used shapeshifter speed—he always had that, whether he could actually shift or not—to flicker out from between the two, laughing as they belatedly lunged. "If I'd wanted to cut Willy's throat, it would've been done before you got that blade into me."

"Vengeance works for me," Jak declared, palming several small throwing blades and assessing his next move.

"Hey," Astar protested. "What good is your vengeance to me if I'm dead?"

"Sorry, Your Highness," Jak declared, not sounding sorry at all, dark eyes darting between Rhy and Astar. "I promise to pour whiskey on the feet of the statue they erect for you."

"Notice he didn't say Branlian whiskey, Cousin," Rhy said. "It would probably be the cheap stuff."

"Why waste the good stuff on stone?" Jak asked, dancing back as they advanced on him. "You two can team up, but you still can't take me." He flung a dagger, which grazed Astar's arm, drawing a bright line of blood.

Rhy exchanged glances with Astar. "Get the Dasnarian," Astar ordered on a roar.

Something of a melee followed after that. In the exhilaration of the mock-battle, Rhy forgot to worry about Salena and the other girls. It felt like being a kid again, fighting his cousin and friend, though they'd all grown considerably more skilled since the last time they'd brawled like this, ages ago. As always, they switched off partnerships, generally two going after whoever seemed to be gaining the upper hand. By the time Astar called a halt, they were all panting, sweating copiously, and bleeding from multiple shallow wounds—except for Jak who appeared to have only bruises and scrapes.

"I can't believe you three," Gen declared with asperity, plunking down a tray of cloths and scary-looking bottles. "You're not adolescents anymore, even if you behave like it. You first, *Your Highness*." She stressed Astar's title meaningfully.

Looking sheepish, Astar sat obediently, allowing Gen to wash his various cuts. "I thought you were closeted with Isyn," he replied. None of them had begrudged the newlyweds going off together. If Rhy had been on good terms with Salena and had access to the sole human-sized bedroom, he'd have wanted to do the same. No doubt Jak and Astar felt likewise.

"Was," Gen replied crisply, jerking her head at Isyn coming down the stairs to the main hall. "It's too nerve-wracking, though, waiting." She splashed some liquid from a bottle on Astar's worst cut and he hissed. "Serves you right, having to suffer through mossback healing."

Rhy grimaced in sympathy and rose to take Astar's broadsword, cleaning the weapon for his cousin now that the Silversteel one shone clean and dry again. Gen gave him a sharp look. "Don't go far, Rhy. You're next."

"What about Jak?" he complained.

"Jak is unwounded," Jak answered with a jaunty salute. "Which means you both owe me a forfeit."

"We never agreed to terms," Rhy muttered.

"It is our standard agreement, however," Astar said with good-natured resignation. "Liquor, coin, or future favor?" he asked Jak.

"Why not all three?" Jak countered, rubbing his hands together in piratical glee.

"Are they always like this?" Isyn asked, joining them and surveying the disarray of the hall with mild curiosity.

"Worse," Gen answered, tying off a bandage. "This is them being mature."

"Oh, that's unfair," Rhy protested. "You were—" He broke off at the stab of something, lunging to his feet. Jak and Astar did likewise, eyes on Rhy as Astar shook off Gen.

"What?" Astar demanded.

"I don't know," Rhy answered with grim honesty. "Salena already felt gone to me, but this is somehow worse." If possible, the tension in the room thickened. The inside of his skin prickled with the driving need to shapeshift, to fly, to run, to go to Salena...

Astar put a firm hand on Rhy's shoulder, steadying, holding his gaze. "Describe it to us. Take your time."

How Astar did that, Rhy would never know. Maybe it was his cousin being alpha in a way Rhy never could be, but Astar had a knack for bringing clear focus during a crisis. Rhy took a breath, willing himself to approach Astar's level of determined calm. "When Salena goes to an alter-realm, I feel her absence, here." He struck the meat of his fist against his solar plexus, the shock of the strike helping him to be more alert and less crazed. "Now, it's as if she's... especially absent."

"How does he know this?" Isyn murmured to Gen.

"He and Lena have always been like that," Gen replied quietly. "Connected on a level that defies comprehension."

The wolf in Rhy sent up a keen of mourning and the man struggled to contain it. "Is she... dead?" he choked out, asking it of Astar, as if he would somehow have an answer.

Astar squeezed his shoulder with bracing affection, his expression taut with worry that he tried to contain. "Don't give up hope before you know."

"After all, *I* was dead for a while and it didn't take," Jak offered, a weak attempt at humor, his expression grim. "I'm just lucky Stella woke up and healed me before all of you burned me on my funeral pyre."

"Not me," Rhy argued, for form's sake. "I was stuck in an alter-realm at the time. It was these other assholes who raced to light you up."

"Hey!" Gen interjected, indignant. "You were a frozen corpse. What were we supposed to do?"

"Maybe check for a pulse?" Jak shot back.

"Of course we checked," she retorted, stomping a foot. "What do you—"

"Portal," Isyn interrupted crisply, pointing to a section of the floor. They all drew or dove for weapons, racing to encircle the area, blades at the ready.

"I should be a saber cat for this," Gen whispered, sidling closer to Isyn. "Or a dragon."

"Dragon is too big for the hall," Isyn replied tersely.

"If Nilly is incapacitated, we might need your human hands," Astar added, staring fiercely at the wavering air that was the forming portal.

Rhy stared also, willing Salena to step through, perhaps make a cutting remark about why were they all standing around, doing nothing. The air shimmered, and Zeph stepped through, still in golden gríobhth form, Stella following after.

But Rhy only saw Salena's lifeless form draped over Zeph's back, facedown, hair trailing. And still entirely gone.

~ 15 ~

THOUGH THE WOLF in him howled in agony, and Rhy felt as numb as if he, too, had died, he still managed to propel his body forward. In a moment, he had Salena in his arms, carrying her to a table Isyn hastily uprighted and laying her bonelessly limp body on the hard surface. Unable to find a pulse, he laid his ear against her breast, ordering his instincts to be wrong that she was gone forever, willing her heart to be beating.

After a long moment of shattering silence... he heard it. Low, barely there and far too slow, a fading attempt of her heart to live. Stella rushed to Salena's other side, laying healing hands on her. Salena's heart beat faintly stronger. "My magic works better here," Stella said, "but not as well as the real world. I can keep her body alive for a time, but it still might not be enough."

"We need to take her back to the Isles of Remus then," Rhy said, preparing to lift Salena in his arms.

"That's a bad idea," Stella declared firmly. Rhy became aware the others were gathered round. "Every portal we take Lena through is a step farther from her spirit. It does no good to heal her body if she can't find it again."

"Then what can we do?" he asked, wrestling the profound sense of helplessness.

She pinned Rhy with a gaze bright and sharp as Silversteel. "Keep ahold of her, Rhy. Don't let her go."

Dazed and uncomprehending, Rhy nodded, taking Salena's hand in both of his and gripping it tightly, not quite sure if that was what Stella meant. Isyn must have shifted Zeph back to human because she was talking in the background. "She just collapsed. Nilly thinks Lena followed the connection from the grid world through a portal to find the intelligence on the other end and determine its location. Her body began dying immediately. Nilly kept her alive, but you know her magic isn't as strong in the alter-realms. So we got her back here as fast as we could."

The others replied, but Rhy let their voices fade into the background. Now he understood what Stella was asking. Salena, out there in the void, separated from her body. It wasn't her hand he needed to hold onto, but her spirit. *He and Lena have always been like that. Connected on a level that defies comprehension.*

He didn't need to comprehend the connection to believe in it, however, and he refused to let Salena go.

Except there was nothing to hold onto. Salena was as *gone* from the world as if her body wasn't there, as if her hand wasn't clasped in his. What he held was an empty shell and holding onto *that* wouldn't make any difference. Salena was going to die and he could do nothing to save her. Worthless, feckless wastrel that he was, he would fail—and at the single task he'd ever truly cared to succeed at.

"Rhyian," Stella said, a rare demanding edge to her voice. "You *must* do this. You're the only one who can reach her."

"I don't know how," he pleaded. "I would, if I only knew *how*."

"Stop whining. You're the only one with a chance of knowing," she replied with brutal intensity. "All this time, you've been saying that you want to prove yourself, that you love Lena, that you would do anything for her. Well, now's your chance, Rhy. Don't you give up on her. Because if you do, she's lost to all of us."

Rhy nodded mutely, massively not up to this task. Holding Salena's hand, he caressed her long brown fingers that had once touched him with such affection, such trust. She'd grown her nails longer and painted them red, something she'd never done when they were younger. He tried to feel for her familiar presence, her bright intelligence and fundamental radiance of spirit that had always made her shine so brightly for him. Though he trained his keen hearing on each labored beat of her heart, the sound brought him nowhere closer to her living essence. Salena's beautiful face looked waxy and sunken, none of her animating personality in it. *She's lost to all of us.*

A strange sound grated out of him and he became aware that tears were streaming over his cheeks and down the back of his throat. He blinked his eyes clear and focused on Stella. "I can't," he said. "There's nothing to hold onto. She's not there."

Stella held his gaze a moment longer, then nodded somberly, grief clouding her being like dirty fog. "Then we've lost her. Time to let her go." She took her hands away, brushing gentle fingers over Salena's forehead. "Goodbye, my lovely friend."

Now Stella was weeping freely.

The others had gathered round. Coming up beside Stella, Jak put an arm around her waist, his expression grave with none of his usual jaunty humor. Gen was sobbing against Isyn's chest, apparently unable to look. Zeph stood somewhat off to the side, staring at Salena with ferocious and wracking guilt that Rhy understood well. Zeph meet his gaze, shaking her head minutely, as if agreeing that they'd both failed to protect Salena.

Astar put a supportive hand on Rhy's shoulder. Rhy nearly shook him off—he didn't deserve comforting—but he couldn't quite make himself. "I couldn't reach her," Rhy said, speaking to them all, that pleading tone in his voice that he still didn't fully understand.

Astar squeezed his shoulder. "If you couldn't, no one could. We all know you'd do anything and everything in your power for Lena. It's not your fault."

But *had* he done everything? There was something he hadn't tried. Something he'd never done in his entire life, a thing he hadn't thought of because it was such anathema to him, to the point that he'd sworn he'd never do it. Out of pride, out of resentment, out of sheer terror of what might become of him. Now all those things seemed frivolous and without meaning compared to Salena's life. "Keep her body alive," he instructed Stella savagely.

Her eyes wide with hope, she laid her hands on Salena's still form, the current of magic stimulating the slowing and weakening heartbeat. Salena's body warmed with the increased current of blood, her breast rising and falling as her lungs drew air, but that was all Stella's magic. Salena was still gone, utterly separated from her body, beyond the reach of any mortal mind, no matter how invested or powerful, let alone a good-for-nothing fraud like himself.

Fortunately, he had a direct line to someone who did have the power.

Moranu, he called silently, closing his eyes to shut out everything else. *Goddess of the Tala, of shapeshifters and shadows, She of the many faces. I ask you a favor.*

There was a long pause where nothing happened and no one answered. Rhy cursed himself viciously for his self-absorption and self-pity. If he'd simply accepted his fate as belonging to Moranu long ago, he wouldn't be in this fix now. The goddess had to be aware of his bitter resentment, how little he loved Her. Why should She answer him now? He certainly wouldn't, if their positions were reversed. If some little shit had spent his entire life taking every opportunity to blacken Rhy's name and then suddenly showed up one day begging for favors, Rhy wouldn't be inclined to help. No, he'd likely take the opportunity to kick that little shit in the teeth and tell him he'd gotten what he deserved. He wouldn't blame Moranu at all for doing the divine version of a good teeth-kicking.

Thing was, Rhy would accept whatever punishment Moranu wished to deal him, if She'd only help Salena. *It's not for me, Moranu,* he added, in case She didn't know every thought in his head. *I'm asking for a friend. She needs help. I'll pay any price.*

With bitter chagrin, he realized he trod in his mother's

footsteps in this. Had his mother, the mighty, all-powerful Andromeda felt this level of desperation? For the first time in his benighted life, he understood the impulse that had led her to offer up her unborn child to Moranu's service. He'd likely do the same in this moment, if it meant saving Salena in the here and now.

To save Salena's life, he'd even offer up all of their theoretical children. Of course, that was an easy offer to contemplate, as Salena would never accept him into her bed again, let alone her life. Nor would Moranu answer his call, because he'd fucked that up, too. He could've had everything and had let his fear consign him to a life of nothing. Too little. Too late. Never had anyone been so deserving of such a pitiable and pitiful epitaph.

So, what are you going to do about it? The darkly amused voice was resonant of night and deepest shadows, filled with the birdsong, growls, purrs and howls of a million animal voices. Rhy didn't have to ask if it was the goddess. He'd heard that voice all his life, in the back of his mind, speaking through his mother, and in the countless myriad sounds of the world around him.

Anything, he answered. *I'll do anything You ask of me.*

A bit late for that, isn't it? She replied, no longer so amused. *You, yourself, realize you've done nothing to predispose Me to grant you favors. I'm rather amazed at your temerity Prince Rhyian of the Tala.*

He bit back the mental correction that he wasn't really a prince. One didn't correct a goddess, even a little shit of a mortal shapeshifter like him knew that. *I know I deserve nothing from You, beyond any disdain or misfortune You care to deal me, but Salena is Your daughter, too, and she's done nothing wrong. In truth, she sacrificed herself to try to save all of us. All I'm asking is that You help her now. And I'll pay the price.*

You are already *a price paid, Prince Rhyian,* the goddess replied, *and a poor bargain I made there, too. Your mother and her mother before her—your Salena's namesake—served Me and My purposes far better than you ever have. And now you offer Me your service, which you already owe Me? Twice nothing is still nothing, My wayward son.*

Nothing and twice nothing—it described him all too well. *I am aware of my worthlessness and yet I have nothing else to offer.*

Salena would make a fine servant, the goddess mused. *Will you offer that in exchange for her life?*

No. His answer was immediate and certain.

No? But you offered Me anything I wanted. Do you renege already?

Begging Your pardon, Moranu, but Salena's life and service aren't mine to offer. I cannot betray her trust that way.

Hmm. The goddess didn't sound happy. More growls and hisses underscored Her mental voice. *How about your firstborn child? You and Salena would make a powerful child. I'll take them.*

Again, he refused. *I cannot promise that,* he said with increasing desperation. *I doubt we'll have a child, but even if by some miracle that occurred, I can't give You that person. I cannot put someone else through what has been a torment to me. I can only offer my own suffering, which You admittedly already own.*

The goddess was silent so long he feared She had turned her back, going off again to wherever it was that goddesses spent their time when they weren't meddling with mortal lives. He'd nearly resigned himself to facing their friends, to confessing to yet another failure, when Moranu spoke again.

Has it been such a torment then, belonging to Me? The goddess's voice gentled in the inquiry, sounding almost … hurt? She sounded much like his mother did when Rhy was deliberately cruel to her, railing at her for ruining his life, for giving him away so callously. With a stabbing catch of his breath, he viscerally regretted being so awful to his mother. Andromeda hadn't deserved such a shitty son. And Moranu hadn't deserved such a poor bargain for Her assistance, which had saved so many lives. Including Salena's and his own worthless one.

No, he admitted. *All the pain has been self-inflicted, all in my imagination, as You have never asked anything of me.*

There's a reason for that.

She didn't say more, instead leaving a hole for him to fill, a technique he recognized well from both his royal parents and Her Majestyness. They put statements out there and then waited, allowing the silence to draw out until whatever pitiful wretch they were interrogating spilled his guts, incriminating himself for their judgment. In the back of his mind, he wondered who'd learned the technique first and who'd emulated it. Maybe they were all born knowing how to deal with little shits like him. He certainly didn't feel like he'd been born knowing anything at all.

I'm more sorry than I can say, Mother Goddess, he confessed, hoping She would feel his very real contrition, *but I don't know the reason You haven't asked. I've always wondered. I suppose I thought You were waiting for the right task.*

Could a goddess sigh heavily? If so, Moranu did at that moment. *Sometimes I wonder what you, My children, think of Me. It seems you imagine Me with nothing better to do than concocting schemes to meddle with your lives.*

That was uncomfortably accurate. And startlingly snide, for a goddess.

You sound like me, he noted before he thought better of it.

If I do, that's because I'm a reflection of you, Prince Rhyian. I am nothing more than your higher self reflected back at you.

If that's true, he retorted, *You wouldn't call me "prince," as I don't think of myself that way.*

Part of you doesn't, but part of you knows the truth and does.

The riddles were giving him a headache. *I don't understand.*

No, that much is clear.

He viciously restrained the urge to snap that conducting circular mental conversations wasn't helping any of his parts. But that wouldn't fit well with the whole beseeching-a-goddess strategy. *How about I promise to think about it? Meanwhile, time is slipping by and Salena needs help.*

I've waited your entire lifetime for you to have a conversation with Me and you want to hurry it along?

The circumstances are somewhat dire, as I've explained, he gritted out mentally, close to losing patience entirely. Talking to Moranu was very much like trying to argue with his mother, and surely that was no coincidence.

No, Andromeda and I share certain...aspects. Also, this conversation is occurring outside the flow of time, so you need not be concerned.

Which time? he shot back. *There's been so many lately.*

Ah, at last you ask a relevant question. While it may seem, from your mortal perspective, that there have been times moving at different rates, those are all constructs.

Rhy waited, hoping She would say more, since he didn't at all understand, nor did Her insight seem relevant. She said nothing more, however, so he asked, tentatively, *So, will You bring Salena's spirit back to her body?*

No, Prince Rhyian, I will not.

She could have said so to begin with. All for nothing. Salena was dead, forever gone to him. He couldn't quite grasp the enormity of that. Surely there was something he could do. Stella believed he could and she was another like Moranu.

There was that sense of a sigh again, so like Andromeda's that Rhy felt an unexpected twinge of love and misery, the twin emotions that always seemed to twine simultaneously around his heart when anything had to do with his mother. With his father, the relationship was more straightforwardly strained, and usually ended up with them both shouting. With his mother... Rhy always came away from interactions with her feeling like a guilty failure and like he wanted to run back, climb into her lap, and beg her to love him again. Which was foolish, as he knew his mother loved him.

And this had nothing to do with anything. More of him thinking about his own problems instead of Salena, who needed him. Salena, who was dead.

She is not dead, the goddess said, almost gently.

He wrestled the wild surge of hope, knowing that it wasn't enough if Salena was only teetering on the edge of death, rather than fully dead. *And yet You won't help her.*

I cannot. There are reasons the divine "meddle" in mortal lives.
She stressed the word wryly. *We cannot act directly, only assist you in acting. I have been waiting for you to ask Me for assistance, because trusting in Me is you trusting in yourself.*

Can You please just spell it out? he snapped. Apparently he'd used up his meager supply of sounding humble. *Tell me what to do and I'll do it.*

You could begin by making decisions and sticking to them, She said, sounding more like his mother than ever.

He wanted to grind his teeth, but he made himself accept that advice without argument. He'd asked the goddess to tell him what to do and She had. *All right, I'll stick to my decision. What should it be?*

This time her sighing voice sounded amused. *The trick with decisions, My wayward son, is that you must be the one who decides. Having someone else decide for you cancels the point. It makes you the pawn you so fear to be.*

Valid point, but... *How do I know what the right decision is?*

That's part of what you have to learn, but I can tell you that making any decision is better than making no decision at all. There's power and magic in deciding on a course of action and sticking to it.

Thank You, he said, trying to sound sincere and humble. He was still confused about what to do, but he had more now than he'd had before. *Any other advice?*

Yes: follow your heart.

What? He forgot to be humble. *This isn't a fairytale!* he shouted, railing at the many-faced goddess, who only smiled.

Isn't it? What are fairytales but stories that contain truths so deep that they are told and retold? It's up to you to decide what sort of story you're in, Prince Rhyian.

And She was gone.

Rhy opened his eyes, finding everyone standing in the exact same pose as before, which at least saved him the humiliation of having them wait a long time while he ostentatiously accomplished exactly nothing.

"Whatever you have in mind," Astar said encouragingly, "go ahead. We'll have your back."

Coward that he was, Rhy nodded crisply, as if just now accepting the mission, and closed his eyes again. He'd observed enough sorcerous types at work to feign the correct attitude, even if he'd never experienced anything that felt like sorcery in himself. Moranu knew, his mother had delved the depths—or perhaps it would be more correct to say the shallows—of Rhy's soul, searching for any glimmer of magical ability, only to come up empty.

Any decision is better than making no decision at all. There's power and magic in deciding on a course of action.

All he had was this subconscious connection to Salena. Seven years they'd been apart and he'd buried the deep mourning for her in every way he could find or invent. Nothing had erased the imprint of her silken, perfect body from his skin, from his heart, from his mind. And apparently from his spirit. He'd thought about her every day—or, rather, had ruthlessly banished the regular appearance of her in his thoughts—but he'd never been aware of that connection between them.

Until that moment he'd seen her again at Castle Ordnung on the Feast of Moranu, when the sight of her had hit him with all the magical force of that enormous crystalline moon. When the mossbacks had written down their regrets to be burnt and their promises to be shared or kept secret, he'd written down the Tala rune for the moon. Salena, his personal moon. Not the sun of his universe, but the ever waxing and waning moon, like the many-faced goddess Herself, now shiningly present, now hidden in shadows.

Always, always there. *Follow your heart.*

Rhy wasn't all that fond of his heart. It had tumbled him into hopeless love with Salena, making him vulnerable to her in terrifying ways. His heart had been the fickle organ that sent him running that morning, when he'd lain there, wide awake with Salena curled trustingly against him. She'd offered him everything, especially that f ull and utter trust, and he'd known with sickening terror that he'd fail her. Sooner or later, he'd disappoint her, break that trust, and he couldn't bear the suspense. Something in him—his heart?—had driven him to make it happen then and there. Forcing her to do what she must inevitably do: set herself free of him.

Over and done with.

Only it hadn't been.

Because he hadn't been able to let go, even after she begged him to, even after it made no sense to keep trying. And now she was out there, crying to him for help via whatever tether still connected them, despite her avowed desire to lose that connection. Salena deserved far better than the likes of him, but if they couldn't sever this bond, then all he could do was try to be what she needed.

You make giving them what they want part of loving them. You can't stop loving her, but you can give her the gift of letting her go her own way. Sometimes loving someone means sacrificing your own happiness for theirs.

He would sacrifice more than his happiness for hers. Which made the answer seem so glaringly simple, he marveled that he hadn't seen it before.

All he had to do was allow that love for her, the love he'd never stopped feeling, draw him to her. Thinking back to those times before he wounded her so terribly, recalling how close they'd been and how it had felt to be bathed in her unstinting affection, and also of that scintillating, magical night when they kissed again at long last under Moranu's moon, he mentally tore out his heart and offered it to the one person who'd always been the keeper of it.

He didn't need his heart, because it had always been Salena's, and always would be. Giving up all concern for his own welfare, he hurtled the rest of himself after it, following the trail of blood and love.

~ 16 ~

LENA WAS NO longer in the grid alter-realm. The realization provided the only evidence that recklessly flinging herself into the void had worked.

Astonishingly enough, the landscape seemed incredibly familiar. Lush green foliage spilled over itself until it reached the pale golden sand of a beach that sloped toward a tumbling surf as in tropical Nahanau. It could be the favorite beach of her childhood, with the very waves she spent so many joyous hours body surfing, the fine-grained sand where she and Rhyian had explored each other's bodies with such innocent pleasure. To all appearances, she could be home.

Except for the growing sense of wrongness.

Turning in a slow circle, she took in the landscape—the vivid turquoise sea, the idly smoking volcanic peak rising against a lovely, soft blue sky. The trees bore sweet blossoms and heavy fruit. The waxing and waning of the waves made a soothing rhythm. Otherwise, however, it was silent. That was the wrongness. There were none of the constant bird calls of her island home. None of the cheerful chirping of the tiny, jewellike tree frogs.

Pinpointing another wrongness, she noticed there was no

scent. Nahanau was redolent of so many things—blooming flowers, ripening fruit, the pervasive brine of the sea, and even the darker notes of fecund vegetation rotting back into the soil. This place was as sterile in its way as the grid alter-realm. It wasn't the rich ecosystem that was the Nahanaun archipelago, but another lopsided slice of one.

Also, she realized as she thought past the initial delight of seeing such a dear and familiar place again, the weather was wrong. The skies around Nahanau were almost never cloudless. Especially around the volcanic peak, wisps of clouds always formed and caught, clinging with tattered affection to the high prominence. Reaching with her magic, she tried creating a small cloud, something she'd been able to do since she was a child, wiling away sunny afternoons by brewing up clouds in whimsical shapes and dispersing them again.

Nothing.

With a shiver of terror, she realized she must be in an alter-realm, one tailored specifically for her. And she was utterly alone. She knew that with bone-deep certainty. There were no other people here. Worse, she'd brought herself to this landscape that would no doubt embody her personal nightmare. There would be no lingering rift to lead the others to rescue her. Stella wouldn't even know where she'd gone, as she'd hung back so carefully. Lena was on her own.

"At least there aren't tentacle monsters lurking under leaf litter," she observed aloud, her voice sounding odd in the pervasive silence of living things. Belatedly realizing that there could be other creatures silently poised to attack—and that Jak would have her head for being so off guard—she went to draw her blades.

And her hands passed right through where they should be.

Vertigo overwhelmed her, like a rogue wave swamping her and dragging her under, and Lena fought the panic that threatened to send her screaming. *You came here on purpose,* she firmly instructed herself. She didn't speak aloud, since that had felt so oppressive. *You are the hunter this time. You followed that connection to the alter-realm where the intelligence was hiding and this is where you ended up. That's why you're incorporeal. You left your body safely behind with Zeph and Nilly to accomplish this important task. So get busy.*

At least, she hoped her body was safe—and alive—and that taking her spirit so far from the flesh that had borne it hadn't killed her. Maybe this was what death was like. She'd never really believed, as others did, in the bower of Glorianna's arms that was some sort of ideal afterlife. It actually made more rational sense that, if there was a persistence of consciousness after death, which she'd also always doubted, it would be more like a recapitulation of the person's life. Maybe she'd died and become a ghost haunting her home island, unable to detect the presence of living beings of any kind, just as the living were unaware of the presence of their ancestors lingering only in spirit.

A truly depressing thought.

With effort, she made herself focus. At least she didn't have to worry about physically defending herself, that was a positive. And she needed to work on the assumption that she *wasn't* dead, that she'd succeeded in chasing the intelligence to where it lived—lurked?—and that this was it messing with her head. Quite effectively, too.

"Show yourself!" she shouted, deciding to continue the offensive she'd begun, and not to be intimidated by the repressive way the atmosphere tried to drown her voice. She would not be silenced. "I know you're there."

Nothing happened. Lena fervently wished she had some of Stella's abilities. There must be a way to sense the presence of the intelligence. Hopefully it was here and hadn't fled upon her arrival. But she hadn't thought so before. This place had felt like its anchor and was only dressed up to mimic her homeland to distract her. Which had been working so far, but no longer.

Concentrating, she closed out what her senses reported, and felt for that connector she'd followed in the first place. It had led her here, and she'd never consciously released her mental grip on it, so it must be within her grasp still.

And there it was.

With a surge of triumph, she fastened onto that connector with all her will, and followed it. Never mind that it felt like walking—whatever metaphor worked for movement—she pursued her target with determination. She refused to be afraid of what the intelligence might do to her. She'd come on a mission because she was the only one who could do this.

A blast of fiery breath incinerated her, everything going up in flames, her nerves shrieking with the agony of it. *Dragon fire.* The dragon filled her vision and the strip of beach, immense, glittering bronze. Kiraka? Her mother's dragon friend readied herself to blast Lena again, which made no sense. Kiraka had been the kindly godmother of Lena's youth, always mitigating her curmudgeonly nature for Lena and her sister, Bethany, allowing them to scale her like a personal plaything. Kiraka would never hurt her.

Also, that first blast of dragon fire should have killed her. It *would* have killed her, if she still had a body. Small mercies.

Taking a stand, she focused on the imposter. Unlike its previous incarnations, the intelligence had manifested this time in exquisite detail. The dragon was incredibly lifelike, and imitated Kiraka perfectly, except in behavior. Curious if the realistic rendering of the dragon, no doubt plucked from her own mind, represented a leveling up by the intelligence—as its last form had been more detailed, but nothing at this level—or an image as immaterial as herself, Lena walked up to it.

The false-Kiraka opened her huge mouth, caged with terrifyingly sharp teeth, and roared, flame shooting out to engulf Salena. She cringed, as she didn't have that much self-control as to convince her atavistic self that the fire meant nothing. Besides, she still felt the searing pain of it. Then she straightened and walked on.

"You can't hurt me," she told it. Which was only partly a lie, depending on how you defined "hurt," but it sounded better than "you can't permanently damage me." Especially in case it didn't realize it could inflict the illusion of pain on her. People could go mad from pain, even if their bodies weren't harmed. "What are you, really, that you must borrow the forms of others?"

The dragon swiped at her, phantom talons passing right through her. Painful, but with no other result. Clumsy, too. If she hadn't been already confident that the real Kiraka wouldn't harm her, this jerky motion would've convinced her. The intelligence had been like that all along—puppeting its creations as if unfamiliar with how those bodies worked. Perhaps it was.

The dragon that wasn't Kiraka stilled, cocking its head to examine her, curious and stymied both, she guessed. "Yooo dohn blonng heer," it said, its voice distorted by the dragon's mouth. Still, it spoke better than it had in the beginning.

"You don't belong in our realms," she replied evenly. "What is your intention in coming to our reality, in taking pieces of it for yourself?"

"Mine," it growled.

"But it isn't," Lena pointed out, lightheaded at the surrealism of the situation, and taking refuge in cold logic. "You can't exist in our realm without co-opting local materials to form a very crude, often ineffective physical form. You corrupt the pieces of the realms you cut away, destroying what makes them part of a living world and dooming them to slow but certain annihilation. The rifts you create between realities only cause more damage and destruction. None of this is yours. Everything you touch begins to die. You are wrong to attempt it. You must stop."

"I dohn wantoo." If anything, the dragon seemed to pout.

"If you refuse to halt your destructive behavior, I will stop you," she insisted, hoping she seemed more confident than she felt. Somehow these edicts always sounded better coming from her father. Probably being a huge warrior-king helped with that.

The dragon cocked its head. "How?"

An excellent question. One she had no answer to. Andi had

said that it would be up to Lena to close the cataclysmic rift, but could she do it from this side? And would she have the courage to do it if that meant trapping herself forever in this dissonant reality? Maybe, if that meant trapping the intelligence here with her. "I have power you cannot imagine," she answered steadily. "Give up now and I'll allow you to live." There: that sounded nicely warriorlike and threatening.

The dragon laughed. Lena had thought she couldn't be disconcerted further, but the very human-sounding laugh emerging from the false-Kiraka's toothy maw created a dissonance that unsettled her profoundly. "You're a child," it said, quite clearly and distinctly. "Your piddling abilities are nothing to mine. I could swat you from existence at any moment."

Lena struggled with the disorienting sense of having dreadfully underestimated their opponent. Gone were the childish mannerisms and distorted speech. In its place was a true intelligence, sharp of wit and clever enough to have dissembled all this time. "Why haven't you then?" she inquired with what she hoped was academic-sounding interest. "Clearly you have no regard for our lives. If you want to destroy us and easily can do so, why all these games?"

False-Kiraka lowered her head, resting her chin on the sand so her great, glittering eyes were on a level with Lena's. Lena refused to give ground, though she was shaking with nerves. *It's remembered physiological response,* she reminded herself. *An artifact of the body you no longer have but your mind thinks is still there.*

"I'll let you in on a little secret, ghost girl," the intelligence said. "I haven't ended your pitiful existences because I find you interesting. These games, as you call them, are entirely for my own entertainment and elucidation. You're something of a scientist, aren't you, Salena?"

It knew her name. Worse, it knew *about* her. It had paused, expecting an answer, so she nodded. "Something of one."

The dragon winked. "More than that. I've been watching you for some time, how you tinker with weather patterns."

That gave her a chill, the dread condensing in her heart. "Have you now."

It chortled. "I have. Your efforts are rudimentary, of course. And it should be noted that your clearing of the sky so your silly friends could moon gaze was an absolutely frivolous use of power."

So, it had come around to that. She and Andi had wondered if the admittedly frivolous use of weather magic the night of the crystalline moon had somehow set these events into motion. That seemed to be the case, although the intelligence indicated it had already been watching her work in the Aerron Desert. "So your intent is to punish us for that?"

"Punish?" If Kiraka's form had eyebrows, the intelligence would have arched them in surprise. As it was, it counterfeited the expression surprisingly well. "Not at all. I enjoy the frivolous use of power, as I would think an observer as clever as you purport to be would've figured out by now."

Yes, she had, and she also contained the satisfaction at having gotten the intelligence to confirm as much. "You mentioned science earlier, however, which is arguably the opposite of frivolous application."

"Ah, yes. You, I feel certain, understand the core concepts of experimentation."

"Experimentation implies intelligent design," she countered. "A question posited and an answer sought. Your methods have evinced no such design, no hint of purpose."

A smile stretched the false-dragon's mouth, truly an uncanny sight. And a revealing one, because it seemed that the intelligence was finally showing its true self—and that smile was a sign of emotion. "Perhaps the design is simply too advanced for your limited mind to comprehend."

"Or there isn't one," she retorted, "and you want me to believe there is."

"It's true that the value of intellectual stimulation cannot be overestimated, especially for someone such as I. My purposes are varied and arcane."

"Who and what are you then?" she inquired, as it didn't seem to want to be forthcoming about its rationale—if it even had one—but might give her a clue as to how to defeat it.

It tsked at her, chuckling. "I wouldn't worry your tiny brain about such details. That information is inconsequential."

"What information *is* consequential?"

The grin spread wider, full of teeth and imagined heat. "That would be telling."

"Am I to solve your riddles then?"

"I suppose you could try, though I doubt you'd succeed. Whether you do or not is immaterial to my purposes, though I do find the scrabbling efforts of you and your little cadre of would-be heroes rather stimulating, regardless."

Lena set aside the bristling irritation at its condescension.

Her friends had faced life-threatening injuries, sanity-disturbing horrors, and even death, and this supercilious creature smirked at them. Making a show of idle curiosity, she looked around. "So, is this where you're from?"

"This is where *you* are from," it answered, just an edge of doubt in its assertion. Very interesting. "Don't you recognize it?" It sounded almost disappointed, like someone who thought they'd offered the perfect gift only to realize it was entirely the wrong thing.

She frowned, taking in the smoking volcano and cloudless sky. "This is not where I'm from at all." She could say that with perfect confidence. This was not Nahanau, regardless of the surface resemblance. Cocking her head, she tried to appear apologetic. "Oh, did you try to make it look like that for me? Sorry to sound ungrateful. You can put your home realm back to its usual configuration now."

"You will *not* see my home as it is!" the false dragon snapped, smoke billowing from her nostrils.

Ha, Lena thought to herself in satisfaction. *Gotcha.* "It's awful, isn't it?" she asked, oozing sympathy. "That's why you steal pieces of other realms and create poor illusions to disguise yours."

"Poor illusion?" it demanded, so affronted it lashed its tail. "You can't accomplish anything close to this, little weather witch."

Another supposition confirmed. "No," she agreed sorrowfully. "I wish I had even a portion of your magic and skills. How have you become so strong?"

The dragon considered, then curled up a talon, beckoning

her closer. "I'll whisper it in your ear.

The thing couldn't hurt her, not physically, and yet she hesitated. "I can hear you fine from here, even at a whisper."

"Indulge me."

Lena weighed the cost and benefit ratio. It couldn't kill her, but it also loved to play games. She doubted it planned to give her any useful information, not deliberately, but she'd already gleaned more about it than she'd known before. What it cagily refused to tell her could be as illuminating as the tidbits of information it dropped. She was her mother's daughter, by blood and by training, and she couldn't resist attempting to solve the puzzle. Taking a step forward, she mentally braced for whatever trick it had planned.

"Salena!" Rhyian's shout penetrated her non-existent being.

~ 17 ~

Astonished, Lena jerked around to see Rhyian racing toward her down the beach. He was in human form, but moved also with the liquid grace of a loping wolf and seeming to fly like the raven, black hair streaming, cloak billowing behind him like great wings, eyes a blazing cobalt visible at a distance. He focused that predatory gaze on the false-dragon and howled a challenge. "I'll kill you!"

Cold terror that she hadn't felt for herself flooded her. She couldn't be killed—unless her body had already died, but that was beside the point—but Rhyian could be. "Rhyian, no!" she screamed.

Undaunted he catapulted toward them, full of vengeful fury. "Don't you touch her!"

"And the hero arrives to rescue the lovelorn maiden," the intelligence said on a chuckle. "This will be ever so interesting." With a breath of air, the false-Kiraka vanished, the assembly of scales forming her image hovering in the air a moment before shivering to the sand in a glittering heap.

Rhyian flung himself past her, carried by his momentum and kicking futilely at the discarded scales, which seemed to be disintegrating back into sand. Fingers curled into claws, he threw back his head and bayed at the empty sky, anguish and fury in it, before he rounded on her, eyes wild. He seemed momentarily confused, staring at her.

"Salena. You're alive." A bit of sanity returned to his gaze as he ran to embrace her—and passed right through her.

Astonished, he wheeled around again. "Are you...?"

"A ghost?" She managed a calming smile. However Rhyian had managed to find her, he'd contorted more than his skin to do it. He was more than a little wolf at the moment. "A disembodied sprit, perhaps," she suggested, then sobered. There were only a few reasons Rhyian could have known to chase after her. "Unless my body is dead?"

His face collapsed into such a rictus of grief that she knew she'd hit the truth squarely. She *was* dead.

"No," Rhyian said firmly, in that tone she knew well, him at the fullest of denial. "Nilly is keeping your body alive until I can bring you back."

She took a moment to assimilate that. Not that Stella would use her magic to keep Lena's body alive, but that Rhyian had somehow successfully followed her. "How are you even here?" she asked, uncertain how she felt about it.

His beautifully carved lips quirked in a rueful smile. "I failed to come after you once before. I couldn't make that mistake again, not when it mattered most."

Her battered heart cramped with emotion. She'd never really acknowledged to herself how much it had tormented her—salt grinding in the fresh wound—that Rhyian had never made the effort to follow her to Aerron. He'd let her go with apparent ease, not even caring enough to try to explain or argue with her or make the tiniest attempt to get her back. She'd told herself she didn't *want* him to come after her, that she'd throw him out on his ear if he did, but when he never arrived... Well, if possible, that had hurt most of all. "Oh, Rhyian..." she said, feeling the tears she couldn't shed.

He came closer to her, reaching out a tentative hand, touching where her arm would be, his fingers passing through her. "You really are just your spirit here."

"How did you find me?" she asked, her throat tight.

"I followed our connection," he said, as if it were the obvious answer. "Stella said I was the only one who could."

"Just like that?"

His gaze darkened, muddled with shadows. "Yes."

"Don't lie to me, Rhyian. What did you do?"

"I asked a favor, all right?" he bit out. "It was mine to ask."

"A favor?" she repeated, shocked and growing worried. "Of Moranu?" she squeaked.

Rhyian shrugged, elaborately and ruefully. "Your body will die without you in it. Who better to apply to in order to meddle with mortal lives than the goddess of shadows? Besides, I figured She'd be the most likely to answer me."

Utterly stunned, Lena grappled with the implications. "But you... You've worked so hard, all your life, to escape Moranu's notice."

"Yes, something She just *had* to mention right off." Rhyian grimaced, then tilted his head, gazing at her. "She wasn't particularly helpful, but she did give me the information that got me here. So." He shrugged with liquid grace, giving her a cocky smile that didn't disguise his deep unease. Whatever had transpired between Rhyian and the Goddess who held claim to him, it had cost him.

"At what price?" Lena demanded tightly.

"Salena," Rhyian said softly, smile dimming and voice suffused with emotion, "there is no price I wouldn't pay for you. I know I've been shit at showing you that—and don't think for a moment that I expect anything of you in return—but I had a chance, the one chance, of finding you and bringing you back. I took it."

Lena nodded, overcome, wishing she could throw herself into his arms. If he tried to seduce her at that moment, she'd likely yield entirely. "Did you come through a portal?" she asked, making herself focus on the practical. Could her spirit return through a portal—after all, that's how she'd gotten here—and then somehow merge again with her body? And a further consideration, *should* she go? She hadn't yet discovered all she could about the intelligence. She'd made it this far, had determined this was its home realm, and should be close to being able to destroy it. She didn't know exactly how yet, but she had a feeling—that familiar sense of a problem nearly solved. An epiphany hovered at the edge of her mind, she just knew it. To abandon her purpose at this stage would be the height of cowardice.

Rhyian's brows had lowered and he frowned at her, perhaps divining some of her thinking. "Not a portal," he said. "I... followed our connection. I don't really know how."

A creeping suspicion took hold of her. "Try picking up some sand."

He glanced at the sand and back at her. "You want a handful of sand?"

"Indulge me." Belatedly, she realized she sounded like the intelligence.

"I suppose it's the least of tasks I'd undertake for you," he mused, crouching to dig his fingers into the pale gold sand.

They passed right through it. As she'd feared.

Rhyian jumped back, alarmed and bristling with suspicion. "What is this?" he demanded.

"It's all right," she soothed, speaking to the animal in him, though she very much doubted anything would be all right for either of them. "You're simply here as a spirit, too."

IT TOOK HIM far longer to process what Salena said than it should have. Once his—now immaterial—brain caught up, Rhy realized that *of course* he was present only in spirit. He'd followed that non-physical connection between Salena and him and he hadn't done that with his body. That realization led inevitably to worrying about what must be happening with their empty bodies back in the Winter Isles. "I hope that, if Nilly can only keep one body alive, she chooses yours."

Salena glared at him. It was amazing how exactly herself she seemed. Until he'd tried to touch, she'd looked perfectly solid to him. Now, however, as his panic at seeing her facing down a dragon receded, he noticed what his shapeshifter senses didn't detect: she had no scent at all. It struck him as profoundly wrong. So much about Salena was her physical presence, her scent of sun-warmed skin that reminded him always of those first early pleasures of the flesh, simple joys he'd never been able to replicate or recover. Worst of all, he could no longer reassure himself with the scent of her desire for him. Now there was nothing but her coldness, hurt, and anger. He was adrift with nothing to go on to read her, but what she wanted him to see.

That and her words.

"I hope she's able to keep *both* of our bodies alive," Salena snapped.

A grin at her feistiness cracked through his worries. A Salena who could snipe at him was a Salena unbroken by what had happened to her. All he needed was for her to survive this intact. "The question is," he said, "how do we go back?"

Salena shook her head slowly and thoughtfully. "No, the real question is, should I even try?"

His heart went cold. Salena had tried to give her life to save Zeph, yes, but that had been the impulse of the moment, born of exhaustion, blood loss, and despair. Surely she couldn't be determined to get killed in some heroic effort to martyr herself. "I thought you weren't interested in being a dead hero."

She gazed back at him evenly. "That was you."

She'd agreed with him, though, he remembered that clearly. "You are coming with me," he snarled. "I came to you—mortgaged my soul to Moranu—to get you back."

"I *never* asked you to do either of those things." She'd clenched her fists by her sides, clearly distressed, perhaps...

guilty?

He reined back his desperate fear for her and tried to think this through before speaking, something that he'd never been any good at, as he was so frequently reminded. "Do we only do things for the people we love because they ask us?" he said, testing out the words as he said them. "It seems to me that if we only do what they articulate, then it's too late. We forced them to say what they needed when we should've known already, if we'd been paying attention."

She softened, perhaps mostly in bemusement, but no longer so upset. "That sounds oddly mature for you."

"I told you, I'm trying to do better." He made himself sound even-tempered and not annoyed at her thinking any hint of maturity in him was odd. "And, as I say that, I realize that I'm supposed to listen to you. So, tell me, why do you question whether you should try to go back?" After all, he only had her words now, so he'd concentrate on those.

She opened her mouth, a quick retort on her lips, then closed them over the words. Cocking her head, she seemed to be considering him. Her lovely, intelligent gaze roved over his face, assessing and analyzing, giving no hint of her conclusions about him. She looked... resigned, even sad. Turning, she gazed over the uncannily still landscape. He observed it with her, making himself be silent and wait for her answer. It looked like Nahanau, without any human or animal life in it, and that dragon had looked exactly like Kiraka. Rhy recalled Salena's musings on whether the various alter-realms had been tailored to torment each of them in particular ways. Had this place been shaped specifically to cause her pain?

"That dragon was the intelligence," she said, still gazing out to sea.

No surprise there. "It took Kiraka's form then."

Salena glanced at him, her thoughts opaque. "I'm surprised you recognized her. You only met her a few times and it was a long time ago for you."

"Meeting a cantankerous dragon who hates you and can incinerate you with a sneeze is a memorable experience," he observed wryly.

"Kiraka never hated you," Salena replied, brows knitting. "I don't know why you always say that."

"Because Kiraka hates everyone but you, your mother, and your sister," he replied, smiling a little at the memory. "She barely tolerates your father."

Salena shook her head at something, looking amused and nostalgic. "You're wrong, Rhyian, but it hardly matters now. But yes, the intelligence took Kiraka's form, precisely detailed, as you observed, and we... had a conversation. I learned things."

His interest sharpened, even as the feeling of dread deepened. "A conversation with Lord Wuv Wittoo doesn't sound all that enlightening."

She didn't laugh as he'd hoped. "It's gotten far more articulate since then. Even in the Winter Isles, it was far more coherent. In fact, talking with it now, I'm of two minds on the subject: either it's always been able to speak as well or better than any of us and it was dissembling for some reason previously, or the forms it took—or puppeted—in those alterrealms limited how it spoke and thought. Anyway, that's not relevant."

"It's so interesting though."

"Don't be patronizing, Rhyian."

"I'm not," he replied, making an effort not to retort in kind. "Don't pick a fight with me over something I said or did or sounded like before *this* conversation."

Summer-storm magic gathered around her, her eyes flashing like lightning striking a restless blue ocean. Then, as fast as it had gathered, the sense of storm vanished again, and she ran a hand through her hair. "I apologize," she said grimly. "You're absolutely right that I keep doing this and can't seem to break out of the pattern."

"At least you're trying."

She narrowed her eyes. "Is that sarcasm?"

"Why would you think so?"

"I don't know..." She frowned at him. "In the absence of other cues I find I'm having a difficult time sorting it out. Something about our communication has changed."

He believed it. "I wasn't being sarcastic," he answered in perfect honesty. "Though I understand why you'd think so. I've discovered one of the greatest drawbacks of living the life of a feckless wastrel given to sarcasm is that everyone seems to suspect me of being sarcastic even when I'm sincere."

"See, even that sounds sarcastic," she noted.

He shrugged, elaborately, in the tradition of his people. "I'm doomed, clearly."

A trace of a smile tugged at her full lips. "Perhaps you're not capable of true sincerity."

"I wouldn't be surprised. Moranu isn't the goddess of clear

lines and bright justice, now is She? No, Mother just had to hand me over to the trickster goddess and then she's surprised by how I turned out."

"That is a valid point," Salena acknowledged.

It is? Would wonders never cease.

She sighed, gazing at him wistfully. "You know, I never minded that about you, Rhyian."

"The sarcasm?"

"That, too. Or any of it—the tricks and jokes, how you never take anything seriously. I always kind of loved that about you, that you were the agent of chaos in our group. Chaos is a critical element in weather patterns, you know."

She was looking at him like she loved him still, even though she'd used the past tense. If he could have, he'd have touched her then—caressed her cheek, or a lock of her hair. He'd have sidled close enough to scent her desire and delighted in stoking it, even if she refused to admit her longing for him that mirrored his for her.

Yes, she said in his memory, *I still feel the same desire for you. But physical desire isn't enough. I am more than my body. You, of all people, should know that I value my mind. I will not succumb to sexual needs when I know that being with you will only damage me.*

He'd answered in the wrong way then. Maybe it was just as well that he couldn't smell or touch her. The last thing he wanted was to damage her trust and her loving nature more than he already had. "Thank you," he said gravely, acknowledging the compliment and not pressing her further. "You were telling me about your conversation with the intelligence," he prompted, "and why you feel it's important to stay here instead of trying to get back to our bodies."

"I think I'm close," she confided. "And I went to all this trouble—risked my life already, and now yours—to follow it to this place. If I leave now, I might waste what could be our only opportunity to destroy the thing."

"Or, at least," he qualified, "discover the information we need in order to destroy it." He nodded. "All right, what's the next step then?"

She blinked, focusing her penetrating gaze on him. "Just like that?"

He shrugged, not so elaborately, trying to look as sincere as he felt—however *that* looked. "I chased you here to help you. This is what you want to do. I'm at your service, Salena."

Studying him, she softened, though he wasn't sure what he'd said that got through to her. "You know, when you call me 'Salena,' it still sounds like you're saying 'love.'"

"I'm sorry. I know you asked me not to call you that anymore, but I can only govern what I say to you, not what I think," he replied seriously. "I can't change how I feel about you, even if I wanted to. And I did want to, for a very long time. I tried to forget you, to stop loving you." His voice caught, surprising him with the anguish, remembered and immediate. "I really tried, but…" He couldn't seem to finish.

"It didn't work for me either," she said in a small voice, her eyes full of turbulent emotion that made them look depthless and deep blue.

He curled his fingers in helpless need, imagining plunging his hands into her hair, holding her like a cup he could drink from endlessly as he savored those gorgeous lips. "Salena, I'm truly sorry for what I did."

"I know you are. You said so already."

"No, I mean, I know I apologized, but I'm not sure I've told you how deeply I regret what I did. If I could go back in time and change my actions that morning... Well, I'd say I'd give anything to do it, but I already promised that to Moranu."

"I wouldn't change it," she said slowly, with firm conviction, surprising him no end.

"You wouldn't?" he echoed, faintly enough that the waves crashed through his words.

She heard him, however, shaking her head furiously. "No, because that morning brought us here."

The incredulous, tremulous hope was almost too much to bear. He made a show of looking around, knowing he was deflecting, but needing to stave off the intensity of his emotions. "Here—to a fake-Nahanau alter-realm where we can't even touch other and where we might be trapped for eternity because our bodies are dead?"

She laughed, merriment in it, a hint of the sweet music she'd had in her youth. Radiant, she smiled at him. "Exactly."

~ 18 ~

LENA FOUND HERSELF off balance in the best of ways. Something had changed between Rhyian and her, something profound and yet unquantifiable. As if she'd suddenly found something she hadn't realized was lost, recalling its preciousness at the same moment she remembered its existence. She still hadn't quite grappled with the shocking reality that Rhyian, so wary of drawing Moranu's attention, had asked for a favor from the goddess of night, in order to save Lena. She was also viscerally, dangerously happy—giddy, even—that he'd come after her.

If it were a tale of romance and epic deeds, this alone would have proved his true love and enduring faithfulness. But this wasn't a ballad, romantic or tragic, and if Lena had learned anything, it was that true love wasn't enough on its own and faithfulness endured only until it was broken. The rational part of her knew that.

The irrational part wanted to believe. It warmed those cold and bleeding places in her that Rhyian was here, of his own free will in her personal nightmare, pledging to help her any way she wanted. And making jokes about it.

"I don't know what's next," she said, answering his ques-

214

tion from before she got distracted, making herself concentrate on the mission and not on Rhyian's heartbreakingly beautiful face. It helped, however, more than she'd imagined, that she could relax the leash on herself. She *couldn't* throw herself into his arms and succumb to his drugging kisses, yielding him everything, utterly. It was oddly restful. She wasn't able to give in to desire and betray herself, even if she lost all control.

"You said you found out things about the intelligence," he prompted. "Things that were helpful."

"Yes." She focused on that and not on Rhyian. "It was expansive, even chatty, though it seemed to be trying to be cagey. It thought it was giving me riddles, confusing me, but one thing it revealed that I suspect is important is that it had noticed me messing with the weather in Aerron. It had studied me."

She saw the flash of protective ire in Rhyian's face—and how he contained it. *Huh.* Guess he really *was* trying. "You and Mother thought, back in the beginning of this at Ordnung, that perhaps your magic had factored into the sudden change that set all of this in motion."

"Yes." Though Andi and Ursula both had attempted to take responsibility for it themselves. Lena had always felt the prick of guilt for it, feeling in her bones that she'd somehow caused that initial rift that resulted in an apparent unpredicted eclipse of the moon and the resultant violent foresight that gripped their sorceresses. "The intelligence hinted that it does have a purpose, and said outright that it's aware of our efforts to stop it and finds them both pitiful and entertaining. It also slipped and revealed that this is its home realm, but disguised because it doesn't want me to see how that place truly is. I was trying to get more information about its nature when you arrived."

Rhyian looked stricken. "I interrupted. You'd have gotten more vital clues if I hadn't misinterpreted what I saw. There I was, thinking I was charging to your rescue, and instead I fucked that up, too."

Oh, how she loved him. It never failed to warm her heart that Rhyian was so ready to protect her. That had never been the problem. "You did come to my rescue," she pointed out, giving him a smile she hoped wouldn't be misleading. "And— to answer your prior question—no, I don't want to die here, so I fully expect you to effect that rescue. Finally, I doubt you disrupted any truth-telling. It was playing games with me and I went along, in order to prolong the conversation, garner more clues. I don't believe it had any intention of fully confessing much more."

Rhyian nodded, considering. "I hope you're not just saying that to make me feel better."

She raised one brow. "Would I do that?"

He smiled ruefully. "Not anymore. Once you would have, though," he added, almost wistfully. "You were always good to me. I can see that now, that I didn't value what I had, in you and everything else. I regret a great deal."

"Well, stop," she told him with a bit of impatience that clearly surprised him. "Regrets are a waste of time and emotional energy. You can't change the past and the future hasn't occurred. All you can change is now, so do it."

His rueful smile went crooked. "As my lady commands."

"Good." She felt oddly exposed, as if she'd changed something between them with this conversation, though she couldn't say what. "Anyway, you asked what I'm thinking we should do next."

"We?" He seemed surprised by that, too.

"We," she answered firmly. "You're here, aren't you? I think the mission is the same: find where the intelligence is holed up—it originated in this alter-realm, I'm sure of it—and determine its nature."

"Have you thought, though..." Rhyian frowned, concerned. "Why did it make its home alter-realm look like Nahanau?"

"I have thought, and I'm not sure." This was good, talking out the problem with Rhyian. They'd always understood each other—in their youthful love affair, they'd even believed they sensed each other's thoughts and emotions, but that had been a fancy of youth and first love—and Rhyian was very clever when he applied his intelligence. Talking with him had always helped her sort out her thoughts. "I have a few theories."

He grinned with genuine warmth. "You wouldn't be you if you didn't."

"Ha! True." She ticked off the points on her fingers. "First, it could be that the intelligence morphed this place specifically for me upon my entry. I think that's the most likely, as it seems to enjoy tormenting us with specifically designed landscapes."

"I thought the forest realm was the one designed to be your personal nightmare," he replied tightly.

"What if it isn't predicated on who enters it first? Maybe the forest alter-realm was for Zeph—a world in which she couldn't shapeshift and that made flight in her gríobhth form nearly impossible."

"That would assume the intelligence knew Zeph would come after you."

"It would be arrogant of us to imagine we are the only ones with the ability to glimpse the future."

"That's unsettling to contemplate."

"And yet critical to remember. I think we've been making a grave mistake in underestimating this intelligence. From the beginning we called it childlike and took its distorted speech and apparent emotional tantrums to mean it wasn't doing everything in a precisely calculated way."

"Unsettling," he repeated. "If your theory is correct, that it made this alter-realm look like Nahanau for you, what about that is so torturous?"

"It's home, but not," she said in a bleak tone. "It lacks the life that made home special to me. And, I feel compelled to point out, if the intelligence is using foresight to predict our actions, then it knew you would be here, too. This landscape might not be for me, but for *us*. It almost said as much, that it would be entertained watching us."

He took a moment, visibly grappling with that. Then he looked around. "But why here? If we're to suffer from being forced together, and if this intelligence knows so much about us, then why not put us back in Annfwn where I committed the crime against you and broke both our hearts forever? That would be the keenest torment." He spoke lightly, but Lena knew he felt the pain of his words as acutely as she did.

"This is where it started, isn't it?" she asked softly. "That first kiss. When you kissed me on my favorite beach and I knew you liked me as more than a friend."

His lips quirked in a quizzical smile. "Surely you knew before that."

She shook her head, remembering those heady days when Rhyian seemed to be paying special attention to her. Everyone had wanted him and he'd been surrounded by fawning admirers everywhere he went. She'd been dashed from the heights of ecstasy, certain of his interest in her, to the nadir of insecurity and despair when he turned his intense focus onto someone else.

But that day he'd asked her to teach him to body surf in human form, while their friends were off doing other things, and it had been a rare and special occasion, for it to be only the two of them. They'd had so much fun, too, and Rhyian had been shirtless, wearing only small swimming trunks—and those only as a concession to her father who wasn't so lax as the Tala on matters of undress—and she'd been mesmerized by his bare chest, the way the water beaded on his golden skin, his lean muscles defined and tempting her to touch, to taste, to have. "I hoped," she said, trying to put those feelings firmly in the past where they belonged, "but I could never be sure with you."

"I could never tell with you either," he replied. "I couldn't think about anything but you and meanwhile you always seemed so above it all, off in your thoughts, dreaming away, or nose in a book. All you did was read." He shook his head in mock sorrow. "I used to wonder if you'd notice me more if I were a book."

"I did more than read," she defended herself indignantly.

And, oh, how many times had she been pretending to read while she surreptitiously admired Rhyian? He'd always taken up all the light in the room. No one could fail to notice the Prince of Shadows.

"You did *one* thing besides read." He held up a single finger, blue eyes sparkling with amusement, looking so much like the boy he'd been that her heart skipped a beat. "Body surfing. I schemed for weeks to get you alone that day," he confided. "Our friends were always hanging about and I could never seem to find a moment alone with you. And I *knew* if I let drop any clue that I was trying to get rid of them, they'd be contrary and make it even more difficult."

It was true. Their little group had always been loving and loyal—and terribly interested in any hint of flirtation. They'd have pounced on the opportunity to tease Rhyian about his interest in Lena. Indeed, later, when Lena and Rhyian had utterly failed to keep their nascent love affair secret, they'd pounced with glee.

"So I came up with that excuse, wanting you to teach me to body surf," Rhyian remembered, "and then I had to suffer through that entire afternoon of lessons before I could find the right opportunity to kiss you."

"*Suffer!*" she exclaimed, but she was laughing. "You claimed you were having fun."

"I did have fun, but all I could think about was making my move, how to approach you, what would happen if you refused me." He grimaced for his younger self, raking a hand through his dark curls. "I was terrified you'd be shocked and upset and say you only wanted to be friends. I didn't think I could bear it if that happened, if I lost my chance with you forever and…" He trailed off, their gazes connecting and holding, fraught with all that had happened since that sweetly innocent day, the awareness that his fears had been realized later, and in a way neither of them could have predicted then.

"Why did you do it, Rhyian?" she asked quietly, both of them knowing she wasn't referring to that first kiss. "I know you regret it, and maybe that should be enough for me, but it isn't. I need to know the why of it. You told me before that you were scared that I said I loved you, but surely you knew that already. It couldn't have been a surprise at that point, how I felt about you."

He winced and scrubbed his hands over his face. "No, I knew it. And I've told you I felt the same." Pausing, he stared intently at her. "Do you know—I very nearly said it back. The words were right there on my tongue. I wanted to tell you. But it was so… intimate, being with you that way. I didn't think it would be any different than everything else we'd done, but it *was*, you know?"

Her mouth dry, she nodded. She did know. It had been transcendent, making love with him, and she'd never before or since felt so connected to another person. Not even in sexual intercourse with her other lovers since, which should have felt exactly the same—it was the identical physical act, after all—and yet never did.

"Maybe 'afraid' is the wrong word," Rhyian continued, eyes fastened on her, beseeching. "I felt … vulnerable. Exposed. All my life, till then, I'd worried about what Moranu would do to me, and in that bed with you, inside you, I suddenly realized that *you* held that ultimate power over me. That you could destroy me without even trying. That some day you'd figure out I was a fraud and not good enough for you and you'd kick me out of your life. Or, worse, that you'd simply forget about me and go off thinking about more important things."

"Rhyian..." Her chest was tight, her heart strangled. "I could never have forgotten about you."

"But you did, didn't you?" he returned swiftly, accusation in every line of him. "You went off to Aerron and thought only of work, took other lovers, and never looked back at what we had. You never gave me another thought."

"Because I had to!" she shouted, the tears flowing from nowhere. How could she weep without a body? It didn't matter, because the tears were as real and not real as the rest of her. "You are so wrong saying I never gave you another thought! I thought about you every day, no matter *how* I tried to forget you. You did that, Rhyian! You forced me into a life without you and it was awful! I never felt again what I felt with you. It was as if you'd ripped away all the color and scent and music from the world and I lived like a woman already dead. *You* never tried to contact me either. Of course I tried to move on. What else was I supposed to do?" A sob wrenched out of her, painful as the dragon fire that burned even though she had no flesh to feel it. "I don't know what you expected of me."

He gazed at her for a long, torturous moment. "I don't know either. Maybe... maybe part of me thought you loved me so well that you'd truly forgive me anything. In my idiocy, I might have been testing that."

"The irony there is, I probably *would* have forgiven you," she replied, feeling bitter and weary. "If you'd only asked."

"I did ask. I'm asking now."

"It's too late."

"Is it? If you could have forgiven me then, when even I didn't understand myself, why not now that I do understand why I did such a terrible thing, when I can promise I'd never betray you like that again?"

He sounded so earnest, appeared completely sincere, and yet... "But *can* you promise that?"

"I *do* promise it," he answered instantly, as if he'd just been waiting for her to ask the question. "I vow to be faithful to you, Salena, if you'll have me back. I'll be monogamous, if that's what you need."

She felt like she was losing her mind. Perhaps this was all a dream, born of desperate hope and dissolving connection to her corporeal form. "That's not what you said to me only days ago. You mocked monogamy as a stupid mossback tradition."

"It *is* a stupid mossback rule," he shot back, definitely sounding like himself. "But I'm willing to abide by it because *you* mean more to me. You mean more to me than anything in the world. I'll sacrifice anything to have you back."

Gazing at him, unbearably torn, she turned over the decision like some foreign object she'd discovered washed up on the shore, trying to determine what it might be or do. Hope— and debilitating desire for the sole object of her love and passion—surged in her, demanding a yes. But the risk... No, the risk was too great. "No, Rhyian," she said softly. "That won't work. My decision remains the same."

"Why won't it work?" he demanded, eyes wild, hair rippling like the blackest storm-tossed ocean. "This is what you require from me and I'm offering it to you."

"Our relationship isn't a contractual exchange of goods, Rhyian!" she fired back.

"Isn't it? That's what mossback monogamy is, a contract. I listened to the wedding vows Gen and Isyn exchanged. I was paying attention, as you asked me to. They promised to love each other and to be faithful. I'm offering to exchange those same vows with you."

She nearly choked on her shock. "You're *not* offering to marry me."

"That's exactly what I'm offering."

"Well, I will *never* marry you," she spat, unreasonably enraged. Of course he asked her to marry him now, after all this time, when she was probably already dead, after she'd lost the last of her romantic illusions. In truth, he hadn't proposed at all. She'd imagined this moment so many times, with various romantic trappings, and *none* of those fantasies had included an incorporeal argument about contractual obligations.

"Why not, Salena?" Rhyian pleaded. "You said you never found with anyone else what we had. I haven't either. You and I are connected, bound together by something we maybe don't understand, but that's so real I used it to follow you past death. Marry me and make that real, too. Be with me forever."

That was closer to the fantasy proposal. And tempting, oh so tempting, but... "I don't want marrying me, being faithful to me to be a painful sacrifice for you!"

He clenched his jaw. "I didn't mean it to sound like that. Mossback rules don't always make sense to me, but I've learned to abide by many of them. I'm willing to accept this one in order to make you happy. I don't want to be with anyone but you—I've demonstrated that to myself these last seven years—so I'll observe any rule at all out of love for you."

Rhyian meant it. Lena could see that. But they were also in an extreme circumstance. And she was too afraid of what would happen if he broke his word to her. "I can't," she said, her voice breaking. "I just don't trust you to keep your word."

He was silent a long time. "It seems like your unwillingness to try is your problem, not something I can change."

She acknowledged that. "I accept that. I told you I was broken."

"You're not broken, Salena," he returned evenly. "You're simply afraid to be vulnerable. I recognize that, because that's how I was. We've traded places is all."

All. But he was right, angry as the accusation made her. "The difference is, I never deliberately inflicted pain on you," she replied defensively.

"Haven't you?" he asked, not belligerent, but softly, sadly. "I think you've been deliberately inflicting pain on me at every moment. Even now, I think you're refusing in part because you won't let go of wanting me to suffer for what I did."

In that moment, she knew the truth of it. If she couldn't let go of this anger, this bitterness at his betrayal, if she couldn't find it in herself to honestly forgive him, then they truly could never be together. "I'd only make us both miserable. You're better off away from me."

"Better off." He laughed without humor. "It hardly matters as I'm miserable either way." He fastened his gleaming, intent blue gaze on her. "I elect to suffer *with* you."

"Rhyian..." She actually stomped her foot from frustration. "How can I convince you?"

"You can't. I gave up on us twice before—once back then, when you ran to Aerron, then again at Gieneke when I very nearly took you at your word and didn't return." He shook his head slowly, watching her with full attention. "I won't give up a third time. You don't want my vow, but you have it anyway. I will never take another lover but you."

"And if I won't have you?" she asked on an astonished gasp. Surely he couldn't mean it.

He shrugged, elaborately, fully trickster Tala in his languid, mischievous grin. "Then I'll be celibate all my life."

She barked out a laugh. "I'll believe *that* when I see it."

Going perfectly still, deadly serious, he pinned her with that wily raven's gaze. "My plan, exactly."

~ 19 ~

R HY FELT SURPRISINGLY energized by the emotional exchange with Salena. For once he had her off-balance— and he was finally on solid ground, knowing exactly what he needed to do and secure in his decision, while she was the one scrambling for how to react. He was oddly happy. Oh, *she* wasn't happy with him, palpably fuming as they walked down the beach, throwing him occasional speaking glances that ranged from frustrated to confused to angry to... something else. He was getting better at interpreting those expressive eyes, discerning her thoughts without her scent to give her away.

Even the prospect of a celibate future should she remain stubbornly entrenched in her refusal to ever again admit him to her bed and life didn't bother him as it once might have. After all, he'd had plenty of lovers in the past seven years and, no matter how enchanting to begin with, they'd all left him disappointed in the end. Because none of them was Salena.

If he couldn't have Salena, then he'd have no one.

He had no idea what she'd ultimately decide, but it felt good to have chosen his stance. At least he was no longer groping in the dark, trying to figure out how to listen, how to change, how to be better. This was what she'd asked of him and what he could give her. Whether she accepted or rejected the gift was as immaterial as their bodies. The essential truth was the gift given. The freedom of the firm decision made him almost giddy. It almost didn't matter what happened after this. Rhy finally knew exactly what he wanted and what to do about it.

Funny to recall that younger self from their first kiss, how nervous he'd been, so wary of her aloof and sensual beauty, her absolute power to crush him with her disinterest—or possibly, her revulsion. She'd been so incredibly lovely that day, her gorgeous violet-blue eyes alight with sparkling joy, her lush body shining brown with sun and seawater, her bathing garments soaked and clinging to her curves. When he'd finally worked up the nerve to close the distance between them, brushing a wet strand of dark-caramel hair from her cheek and following the movement to caress the back of her neck, those eyes had filled with surprise and that something more. And that kiss, the way she'd yielded, responded, and met his inquiring lips with reciprocal fire... It had been the answer to everything.

Through all those delicious, intimate months they'd been together, he'd never really lost that anxiety, he realized now. He'd been always on edge, waiting for her to come to her senses, to take it all back, to withdraw the generously offered love he was certain deep down he didn't deserve. Ever since then had been an anguish of continued uncertainty, as he'd never been able to reconcile himself to the outcome of his actions.

Now he was committed, hers to cherish or discard, but the decision was made. It was restful.

"It's not like the *Elskathorrl*, you know," Salena said abruptly, staring determinedly down the beach. Neither of them knew their destination, naturally, but swimming out to sea seemed fruitless and they'd quickly discovered the bordering foliage was impenetrable. There were only two directions to go to try to determine more about this place, so down the beach they went.

"The *Elskathorrl*?" he echoed, vaguely aware that he'd heard the term before, but not quite sure where. It sounded Dasnarian.

"You know," she answered impatiently. "Don't feign ignorance."

"I don't have to feign ignorance," he replied laconically, "it comes naturally to me."

She huffed out an annoyed breath, but he saw her suppress the smile of amusement. "The vow Harlan made Ursula, that comes from the *Skablykrr* discipline he studied after his sister disappeared. I know you know what I'm talking about. This promise of yours is *not* like the *Elskathorrl*, if that's what you're thinking."

It hadn't been at all what he was thinking, as he hadn't really remembered that bit of history. Who paid attention to the love affairs of their older relatives? Now that Salena brought it up, however, half-heard bits and pieces assembled in his head. His Uncle Harlan, at that time a hired mercenary in her father's court, had made this vow to Auntie Essla without telling her. It *was* very similar to Rhyian's promise—lowering to admit that perhaps he hadn't been so original in thinking it up—in that the promiser of the *Elskathorrl* gave up all others from that point forward, loyal only and completely to the object of their devoted affection.

"Why can't it be like that?" he wondered aloud. If they ever got back to Ordnung, he'd have to ask Uncle Harlan about the particulars. Harlan would be happy to explain, Rhy felt sure. Of all his immediate and extended family, Harlan had been singular in never scolding Rhy for not amounting to more. "It seems like the exact same thing to me."

"Oh, *now* he remembers." Salena threw up her hands, looking to the sky for sympathy. As usual, the sky didn't care.

"You prompted my memory. Once I thought about it, I recalled hearing various stories."

"You always were good at that," she said grudgingly, sounding irritated by it. "Everyone always thinks you're not paying attention, but you absorb everything, pulling it out for use when you decide you actually care."

"Thank you." The compliment warmed him.

"It wasn't meant as praise. It's only further to my point that you *were* thinking about the *Elskathorrl*, despite your disclaimer otherwise."

He wasn't bothered. Salena was simply off-balance, irritated as she always was when not in control of a situation. "Uncle Harlan makes that special gesture at Auntie Essla," he mused. "It's kind of a salute, really. That's the *Elskathorrl*, isn't it?" He paused in his walking, turning the backs of his first two fingers to his forehead, thinking of his promise and looking to Salena as he did. It felt good and right.

"Don't *do* that," Salena hissed, looking around as if someone might witness it.

Rhy grinned, not above being pleased with having discomfited her. "I wonder if Ursula was as annoyed by that as you are, back before she accepted him."

"No doubt," Salena ground out, marching on. He caught up easily, matching his longer stride to hers. "And it can't be like that," she continued in a more scholarly tone, the one she used when she was trying to be logical and not emotional, "because you're not a graduate of the *Skablykrr*. Harlan has been very clear that, in order to pledge the *Elskathorrl*, a student of the training has to have demonstrated they have the strength of character, judgment, and perseverance to make such a vow."

Even better. Moranu had said that he needed to improve his character by making decisions and sticking to them. Without realizing it, Rhy had stumbled upon a discipline that would help him do exactly that. It was even a family legacy, of a sort, that Dasnarian decisiveness to counterbalance his inherent Tala mutability that sometimes led to fickle behavior.

"Then that's what I'll do," he told Salena, saying it out loud for himself, too, to confirm the decision, putting it out there with resolve to the witness who mattered most to him. "Once our mission is done, I'll ask Uncle Harlan to sponsor me in this training. If he can't teach me, I'll travel to Dasnaria to undergo whatever is required."

Salena slid him a look of patent incredulity. No fine interpretation or observation needed there. "Don't be absurd."

"I'm not." Her doubt stung a bit, but he could hardly

blame her. It wasn't as if he had a reputation for doing hard and difficult work. "I'm going to do it. If I live through this," he amended.

"It could take years," Salena pointed out relentlessly. "I don't know how long Harlan spent there, but it was after he helped Ivariel escape her horrible marriage. He did it out of desperation, so his family couldn't make him tell where she'd gone, not even by torturing him or his other sisters. That's the strength of the *Skablykrr* training, that even those monsters recognized they couldn't break him after that and gave up."

"Sounds like a useful skill to have." He hoped he'd be up to it, but this idea also sounded good and right, like the answer to all his questions. Maybe this training would finally make him into a better person, one with character, discipline, and the ability to apply himself as everyone wished he would.

"You're not thinking this through, Rhyian." Salena stopped and faced him, punching fists to her generous hips. "You and I are over. In the past. Don't get some idea that I'll be waiting around for you if you go off to Dasnaria."

"I wasn't thinking that," he replied with some surprise.

She threw up her hands. "Then why do it? I don't understand."

"You are not the sole reason for all of my decisions, Salena," he answered. "Yes, proving myself to you, wanting to be someone you can trust not to betray you again is the spark that lit this fire, but it's a light that's helping me to see clearly. Your contempt and disdain has been the impetus for me wanting to do better, to become a better person, but I can see now that I need to do that for myself, too. And perhaps for Annfwn, my parents, my people. I may not be a real prince, but I do come from a royal family. I've always tried to duck those obligations. I've even tried to escape a vow my mother made to Moranu, and I'm not proud of that. Even if I can never be with you again, perhaps the *Skablykrr* training will at least help me to become someone I, and maybe others, can be proud of."

She pursed her lips, then blew out a breath, chewing on her lower lip as she studied him with an oddly plaintive expression. "Do you swear you're not doing any of this just to get between my legs?"

He nearly laughed and settled for a smile. Maybe she was right that it was good they couldn't touch, because the thought of doing exactly that, of bearing her naked to the sand and being enfolded against her voluptuous body again beckoned with a sweet agony greater than the thought of going home. Salena was his home, and always had been, he realized, even more than Annfwn. It was a day for realizations, apparently.

"Salena, my love," he said gently, fervently. "There is nothing I wouldn't do to be with you again that way, it's true, but all of this has finally opened my eyes. You, my cousins, our friends, my family, have all been trying to tell me for a long time that I need to do something about myself. I'm finally listening."

She rolled her eyes, shaking her head, pretending to be done with him, but he'd caught the glimmer of respect in her eyes and took heart. He'd been looking for that light from her for a long time and the sight of it filled him with ebullient joy. This was the right thing to be doing. It seemed that Moranu, a dark and shifting presence in the back of his mind, laughed mistily in agreement. *Finally.*

"Well, I won't stop you," Salena said. "Nobody ever could stop you from doing anything, once you set your mind to it. Andi used to remark that we were fortunate you set your mind to very few things." She caught herself, pausing awkwardly. "I didn't mean that badly, the way it sounded."

"It's a fair point," he observed, bemused that he'd had no idea his mother had said such a thing.

"But I'm warning you, here and now, Rhyian," Salena continued. "Save your *Elskathorrl* vow for someone else. Go and do the *Skablykrr*, if you must, though I hope Harlan can teach you and you don't have to go to Dasnaria because you'll hate it there. But retract this promise you made me."

"I can't." He shrugged in the face of her disbelieving, irate glare. "It's already made. If I retract or break that promise, then I've failed before I've even begun." *There's power and magic in deciding on a course of action and sticking to it.*

She stomped her foot. "I'm the only one who knows!"

"You are the most important person who knows," he corrected, "and I'm the other person who knows. I can't break faith with either of us. Not again, not anymore."

"I don't even know who you are anymore," she marveled.

"Yes, you do," he replied, very seriously. "You've always known me better than anyone. Even if you'll never have me again—and I do understand if you won't—then I'll always be glad that it was you who was the making of me. *If*," he added with a self-deprecating grin, "I actually manage to make anything of myself."

"I think maybe you already have," she whispered, eyes full

of emotion. Her body yearned toward him, ripe and lovely, inviting him to touch and take, so familiar from back then. He'd longed for this moment, yearned in return to take her up on the offer.

And he was beyond grateful he couldn't. Not until she truly believed in his promise. "We should keep moving," he suggested softly, "continue the search for the intelligence."

"Right," she replied in the same tone, but sounding unconvinced.

"Have the star-crossed lovers reunited at last?" a sardonic voice asked. "Or is this another temporary reconciliation, as when they kissed on the night of the crystalline moon?"

Rhy flicked his gaze at the woman standing on the sand. She wasn't anyone he'd ever met, but he recognized her immediately. With her flowing dark hair, black waves gleaming with deep crimson highlights like banked coals, and storm-gray eyes like his mother's, like Stella's, the image could be of only one sorceress: the long-dead former High Queen Salena, his Salena's namesake and his and Stella's grandmother. He set his teeth at the sacrilege, figuring the intelligence had chosen this form to goad him.

"Were you there that night?" he inquired silkily. Salena had said that the intelligence had been watching her, observing them, but no sense giving that away when asking questions might yield more information.

"Here. There. I am everywhere and nowhere," the intelligence answered carelessly. "Truly, Rhyian, for one of the Tala you are certainly mossback in your thinking, clinging to such limited concepts of place and time."

"And which are you, Grandmother-in-appearance?" he shot back. "Tala? Mossback? Sorcerer?"

"All and none," she replied with a thin smile. "I don't know why you're all so obsessed with discovering my exact nature."

"All the better to destroy you," Salena observed with cheerful and lethal intent, aligning herself beside him to confront the uncanny creature. "For example, why employ such cheap, sideshow magician's tricks by taking forms beloved to us? It's a strange choice."

The false Salena's eyes flashed with silver, convincingly very like his mother's or Stella's when their magic rose. Rhy observed carefully, seeing through the illusion easily. He knew the feel of both his mother's magic and his cousin's. Their ancestress should feel like them and didn't.

"I'm answering the question you've asked so persistently," the intelligence said, sweeping a hand at itself. "I *am* Salena, your progenitor and powerful sorceress. I've been observing you both, my grandson and my namesake, and I'm displeased with how you've conducted yourselves. Thus I've returned to correct your ways."

Though he probably should've cozened the thing along by pretending to believe, Rhy couldn't help himself and barked out a laugh. "Do tell," he sneered. "How are we meant to correct our ways?"

The false-Salena drew herself up imperiously. "You must strive to discover that for yourselves!" she declared.

"By experimenting?" his Salena asked cannily. "I wonder if, were we to waste our time pretending to chase this ridiculously transparent challenge, would what we eventually discovered be the very thing you're seeking?"

The intelligence hissed, the image of his grandmother contorting and blurring as it lost its grip in fury.

"Now!" his Salena shouted. Rhy had only an instant to wonder what action she was signaling to him when she leapt at the shivering image of the intelligence. Without hesitation, he flung himself after her, experiencing an alarming dislocation of reality as his noncorporeal self collided with and merged into that of the intelligence and Salena.

And erupted in a storm of violent magic.

~ 20 ~

I T HAD BEEN pure, possibly insane impulse that prompted Lena to throw herself into the maelstrom of magical energy that was the intelligence's manifestation. Worse, she'd called for Rhyian to follow, which he'd done, of course. Foolish, devoted man.

She didn't have the least idea of what she hoped they'd accomplish, either, except that—for a fraction of a moment— she'd detected a shift in the intelligence's presence. It was like the line of demarcation between air masses, where a cold front abutted a warm one, the border between them tangible without being solid. It didn't mean anything, necessarily, but it was a fault line in the intelligence's otherwise seamless projection of itself. A rift, as it were, very much like those folds where one reality overlapped another, creating that pocket that became the portals between worlds.

The intelligence emitted a shriek that had no sound but boiled with emotive energy. At Gieneke, Stella had banished the intelligence by taking the its emotions and hurling them back at it. Lena was no empath, and not a fraction of the sorceress Stella was, but considering what she sensed of the intelligence in terms of weather—especially storms—her next steps made intuitive sense to her. Digging her mental claws into that fissure, she held on as the intelligence hurtled itself away. And Rhyian was with her, his raven's talons gripping and tearing into the fault lines, too.

They tumbled through non-space, a dimension where surely no beings like herself or Rhyian belonged. If she thought about it too hard, or tried to make sense of the experience, she thought it would indeed drive her mad. Minds such as theirs weren't equipped to comprehend this sort of thing. She managed by concentrating on the entity in her grasp, digging in and holding on, and she could only hope that Rhyian would do the same, that she hadn't doomed him to a life as a raving lunatic or—worse?—a somnolent vegetable by dragging him along with her.

But they were in it now, no going back, so she focused on those aspects of the intelligence that reminded her of weather patterns, bringing her magic and her scientific understanding to bear on the problem. *You know how to do this part.* If nothing else, spending the past seven years relentlessly focused on her work, trying not to think about Rhyian, had taught her to compartmentalize her attention. She'd spent more time with her head literally in the clouds, gently tweaking the weather patterns to bring rain back to the desert, than she had on anything else.

Changing the weather was as much breaking up established patterns as creating new ones. Lack of rain wasn't solely the absence of precipitation-producing clouds, though that was naturally a factor. Pressure systems that prevented the formation of clouds became entrenched, sometimes far away from the affected landscape. Other factors affected whether rain would fall, such as the temperature of the air, the dryness of the sand and soil, baked by season after season of aridity, so that if rain did fall, it evaporated before ever reaching the ground.

This process was as delicately complex as that, built of layers, requiring time and attention they didn't have. Already her sense of self was shredding, losing cohesiveness, as if the non-wind of their headlong plunge through this fold of nothingness was tearing at the integrity of her spirit. When Zeph had fallen through the too-narrow portal from the forest alter-realm back to their reality, it had stripped her gríobhth form away, leaving her falling through the sky in naked human form. This was like that, in a way—only Lena had no other form to lose.

Beside her still, Rhyian seemed to be shredding also, losing feathers and substance. With every moment that passed, she was killing them both. Letting go, however, would strand them in this non-place and be even more disastrous.

So she kept drilling with her magic, finding the layers of the intelligence, its many aspects and levels, the high and low pressure assembly of it. Much as she'd destabilize an entrenched pattern over the Aerron Desert, she plucked apart the core of the intelligence, starting a cascade that gradually accelerated as it howled its agony and fury. The concatenation of collapse grew, and the thing desperately tried to shake them off, even as it began to lose its own integrity.

She and Rhyian might be destroyed with it, but at least they'd succeed in taking down the thing determined to shatter their world. Rhyian's like sense of triumph echoed through their connection in grim solidarity. Without him there, she couldn't have held on and worked her magic at the same time. She'd never felt she had much of a predatory or killer instinct, so she borrowed Rhyian's to keep from flinching as the intelligence cried its death agonies, her magic relentlessly keeping it from recovering from the relentless cascade of dissolution.

It couldn't fight them off or flee, and they were winning. Her storm magic had been the deciding factor after all. Exultant and despairing, grimly thrilled at their victory and mourning that she and Rhyian would not survive this, she poured her magic into the expanding inferno of collapse that had been the intelligence.

Then, so suddenly she didn't immediately comprehend the change, she was flung off, hurtling through the non-space at impossible speed. Something flew toward her at equal velocity, on a collision course she couldn't alter. They seemed irrevocably drawn to each other and they crashed together, agonizing and melding.

Everything went black.

CONSCIOUSNESS RETURNED WITH excruciating immediacy, every pore of her body throbbing, her skin feeling as if it had been sanded away. Lena couldn't seem to catch her breath.

When she tried to breathe, it became alarmingly clear that her lungs weren't working. Was her heart even beating? No.

Did she *have* a body?

Something niggled in her memory about that, but she was too panicked about not being able to breathe to think, to remember anything.

Then firm lips closed over hers, forcing air into her mouth and down her throat, expanding her lungs, which creaked in furious protest. If she could feel those things, she must not be dead...

The mouth disappeared and strong hands pumped down over her heart, a ragged voice commanding her to breathe, to live.

She tried to obey—she really did because she had reasons to live, didn't she?—but she couldn't seem to connect to her body. It felt wrong and heavy. The mouth returned, a familiar flavor, a sweet bliss, but this wasn't a kiss. The air hurt going into her. *Everything* hurt and she wanted to back away from the pain, to flee this cage of flesh that gripped her with such agonizing force.

"Salena, curse you!" the voice shouted. "Don't you dare die on me now. Not after all of this!"

Rhyian. Yelling at her. Like *she* was doing this to spite *him*.

Indignant fury flooding her, she sucked in a breath to tell him exactly how infuriating he was—and choked on the agony of it. It was as if all the fiery, sun-heated, drought-stricken sand of the Aerron Desert poured down her throat and filled her lungs. The coughing wrenched her body and she flung herself onto her side, feeling as if she must be coughing up sea water—had she nearly drowned?—but nothing came out. Her heart kicked into a frantic beat, hammering against her ribs, and she still couldn't really breathe.

A warm body curled at her back, knees tucked up behind hers, arms wrapped gently, comfortingly around her, one hand on her belly, another bracing her forehead. "Just breathe," Rhyian murmured in her ear. "Slow and smooth. You're relearning your body is all. The instinct is there, let it take over. You don't need to think. Relax and let your body and mind realign. You're fine. You're healthy and uninjured, just relearning. Let it happen."

Oddly, since she still couldn't quite grasp what had happened and what Rhyian was talking about—relearning the what?—his litany soothed her. More important, it worked. As she let go of trying so hard to breathe, the intuition of her body took over, her heart slowing its panicked racing, her lungs relaxing into their familiar flexibility. They weren't full of sand after all, or of water, but sweet air that filtered into her bloodstream. With the return of oxygenation, her mind sharpened and she could actually think again.

Rhyian was holding her, his body pressed all along the back of hers, bracing her in that oddly comforting way, his lips in her hair as he murmured his lullaby of reassurance and instructions. She should push him away—why, she couldn't quite recall just yet, but she should—and yet she didn't want to. He filled the ragged, frantic places in her, calming what had nearly torn itself apart.

"Better now," he finally said, not a question, but on a relieved sigh.

"Yes," she managed to say, blinking her eyes open against hot sunshine. The beach at not-Nahanau still. Again? The same rolling surf and otherwise lack of sound and scent. Except she could smell Rhyian, warm sun on black feathers, skin and sex and love intertwined. She inhaled it, holding it soft and familiar inside, another healing balm. It felt so good to be with him, to be held by him again. And she remembered why she shouldn't let this happen.

Yet... she couldn't make herself push him away. "Rhyian," she breathed, a plea in it.

"I know," he said, equally hushed, sounding as ragged as she felt. "I know and I'll move, I promise. Just give me a moment more and I'll let you go. I just... I can't—" His voice caught and broke, tears in it.

She turned in his arms, not pulling away, but pressing herself closer to him, the sense of flesh, of having a body again, was immensely grounding. Rhyian was weeping, eyes closed so the tears emerged from the lavish dark fringe of his lashes, sand in his flowing black curls. She wiped the tears from his high, carved cheekbones, and his beautiful lips curved into a lopsided smile. He was almost too pretty, with his heart-shaped face and winged brows—until he opened his eyes, the intense blue sharp, blazing, burning away anything so soft as prettiness.

Her heart, so battered, so worn, and so recently resurrected, turned over with a thud. This, too, was instinct, the intuition that overrode all else. She belonged here, with Rhyian, regardless of all else. Unable to resist the temptation he presented—she never had been able to—she kissed the tears away, then pressed her lips to his, savoring the taste of salt and surprise before he returned the kiss with desperate vigor. It was sweet and passionate, lingering and loving, expressing all they were so terrible at putting into words.

Cherish.

Together.

Love.

Forever.

Belong.

Mine.

"I love you, Salena." Rhyian's words whispered against her lips, through her mind, and filtered through her being, suffusing her. Though she'd heard him say it before, the sentiment resonated thickly, infusing her bones and blood. She believed him. More, she trusted him, with her life, and with her heart.

"I know," she answered, brushing his lips with hers. "Just as I know I love you."

He caught and held his breath and her gaze, searching her eyes. "Are you sure? Even now, after everything?"

"I never stopped," she confessed. "No matter how much I wished I could."

Sorrow darkened the deep blue. "Do you wish it still?"

"No." It didn't even feel risky to admit it now. "I might as well wish the sun not to rise, the moon not to wax and wane. Loving you is part of who I am, for better or worse."

That crooked smile again. "I delivered worse already, so I promise to give you better from here on out."

"Be careful of those promises," she warned. "You're throwing a lot of them around."

"No," he correctly gently, brushing her lips with a kiss as sweet as Annfwn honey, "I'm holding onto these promises. No matter what we face, I promise to give you better, the best I have in me. That may not be much, but love—I mean, Salena, I—"

She laid a finger over his lips. "Your best is beyond what anyone could wish for. You've always had that in you. And you have official permission to call me 'love,' again. I missed it," she confessed.

He smiled fully then, kissing her fingertip, then drawing it into his mouth, sucking lightly and laving the sensitive pad with his tongue. The sensation flooded through her newly awakened body, her pores singing of desire rather than pain, and she moaned. He echoed the sound, low and incoherent, releasing her finger with a last nip of his teeth that had her shuddering, returning his mouth to hers, kissing her with relentless passion. He threaded his hands through her hair, holding her and kissing her as if he couldn't get enough. Her mind, heart, spirit, and body hummed with the joy of it, feeling as if she'd at last returned to the place where she felt whole.

She clung to him, aware of sand and surf and sun, wanting the moment to be endless.

Knowing that it couldn't be.

Rhyian either felt the change or thought the same thing at the same time. Withdrawing from the kiss with all the reluctance she felt, he took her hand, lacing her fingers with his, then eased them into a sitting position. "Much as I long to lie here and kiss you, love," he said, "you had a near miss there. And we could still be in danger."

"What happened?" she asked, memories coming back, but still making little sense.

"I thought you were dead," he told her somberly. "You weren't breathing. Your heart wasn't beating. Your body was cold as death. If I hadn't sensed you inside, I'd have despaired. As it was, it was closer than I can bear to contemplate."

"How did we end up in bodies again?" she asked, feeling somewhat more ready to face reality—whatever version of it they might be in. "I think we're back in the same alter-realm, but corporeal now."

"I think so, too. Somehow our bodies got sucked through a portal to meet our spirit-selves here."

"They could be new bodies," she mused, holding up a hand to study it, fanning her fingers. She recalled the sensation of collision, that feeling of racing toward something hurtling toward her at equal velocity.

"Same clothing though. And we have the weapons we were wearing." He tapped the Silversteel sword on his belt, unmistakable. "Also, you have that scar, here." With a quiet finger, he traced the faint, old scar on her left shoulder, white against the tan. "Where you cut yourself on that coral."

She smiled, feeling wobbly. Rhyian knew her as no one else did, and it was strange to be part of that again. She'd mostly forgotten about that scar, but of course he hadn't. "Why did you do so much better rejoining your body than I did?"

He grimaced slightly. "First of all, I'm only glad it worked that way, because I was able to perform those tricks of Uncle

Harlan's to get your body going again. I shudder to think what might've happened if I hadn't been here." He looked so bleak that Lena had to kiss him, and he leaned into the contact, feeding greedily upon her mouth, less in passion than seemingly in a need to feel her continued vitality. Finally he released her, leaning his forehead against hers, closing his eyes and letting out a rueful sigh. "Please endeavor to never do that to me again."

She nearly promised, glibly, then stopped herself on the realization that she might have to risk such a thing, if the intelligence had survived their attack. She wanted to think they'd destroyed it, but... "Do you think we defeated it?" she asked, hoping he'd have a more optimistic opinion than she did.

Rhyian considered, grimaced, and shook his head. "I think it's wounded, perhaps severely. You were tearing it apart, it was nearly done for, and then—I suspect it pulled our bodies here to drag our spirit selves away from its throat, so to speak. A desperation move. So I think it's alive still."

Curse it. "I agree, unfortunately."

He smiled, releasing her hand to comb his fingers through her hair, shaking out the sand that apparently adorned her as well. "As to why I recovered faster, your body was empty longer than mine. Also, I'm also more experienced at finding myself back in human form after a time away from it."

"Does shapeshifting feel like *that*?" she asked, aghast and gripping his wrists for reassurance—for herself or for him, she didn't know. Somehow they'd never talked about this. She supposed when she was younger she'd considered the topic of his shapeshifting off limits. The Tala didn't much like to discuss it, especially with non-Tala. One effect of their long-separation, the anger and arguing, was that in reconciliation no topic seemed too sensitive to broach. They'd already survived the worst they could do to each other. "I wonder how any of you brave shapeshifting at all, if it feels like *that*."

"It doesn't, exactly." He slipped his wrists from her grip and turned her hands over in his, kissing first one palm, then the other. "But it can feel foreign, like a bad fit, especially after a long time in a different shape. More than that, when you try a new form, it doesn't always work correctly at first. Like when you try to breathe as a fish when you have gills instead of lungs. Or learning to fly if you never have before. Animals grow to adulthood learning to use those bodies. When we become a new form, we have to consciously learn to work those bodies, while still allowing the intuitive aspect of that shape's brain fill in the details. It's difficult to explain."

She contemplated how that would feel. "I had no idea."

His lips twisted in a self-deprecating smile. "I never told you. You know how the Tala love their secrets."

She nodded slowly. "No wonder you don't enjoy acquiring new forms. I'm even more in awe of people like Zeph and Gen who have so many."

"Their confidence and competitive spirit compensates for the inherent terror," he commented drily. "Though I suspect those two are totally lacking in the insecurities that seem to plague me."

Lena nearly asked who this man was. Had hard-shelled, brooding Rhyian just admitted to being insecure, afraid even?

He must have observed the thought in her, because his sardonic smile faded and he folded her hands between his. "This is me being completely honest with you, love. I've realized there are ways I've been deceptive by pretending to be someone I'm not, by failing to disclose how I really feel. So, in the interests of keeping my promises to you and to myself, I'm telling you things I never would have before. But this is obviously new territory for me, so please tell me if I'm screwing this up."

"You're not screwing this up," she told him, her mouth dry. She was almost more afraid of this new Rhyian than of the cuttingly cruel one. This one could possess her heart even more entirely than ever.

"Then why are you afraid?" he asked softly, freeing one hand to tuck a strand of hair behind her ear, then caressing her cheek. "I thought this is what you wanted from me."

"It is." She leaned into the caress. "I had no idea how terrifying it can be to be offered what you want most in the world."

"Because having it means facing the possibility of losing it," he replied gravely. "I understand."

Yes, she supposed he did.

"I understand, too," he continued, "if you're unwilling to take that risk. You owe me nothing. I was wrong to pressure you, to pursue what I'd lost. I had my chance with you and I was too much of a coward to handle it. I would not blame you in the slightest if you decide to walk away."

"You're not a coward, Rhyian," she replied firmly. "Never that."

"I have behaved in cowardly ways," he said ruefully. "I

have to be honest with myself about that."

"You persisted despite your fears and insecurities. That's bravery."

"You always did see the best in me." He said it as if he doubted her judgment, though in affection.

"I know you better than anyone," she reminded him. "Just as you know me, even after all this time. The important things about each other. And I know you're no coward. Rhyian..." She gathered her own courage. "I don't want to walk away. I want to try again."

Still somber, he searched her face, the smile dawning on his lips like the sun rising, burning away the mist and gloom. "Are you sure?" he whispered.

Was she? Yes, she absolutely was. "Yes." Taking his face in her hands, she splayed her fingers over those sharp cheekbones, framing his staggering beauty. Kissing his tempting lips, she tasted him, inhaled his beloved scent and feel. "Yes," she breathed into his mouth. "And I want you, Rhyian. You can't take me to bed, but we have the solitude of this beach."

To her surprise, he hesitated. Oh, he kissed her back, passion and sweetness blended—but then he drew away and caressed her cheek. "I think we shouldn't," he said to her utter shock.

"You don't... want me?" she asked, struggling with the sting of his rejection.

A smile broke over his face, radiant with longing. "Oh, Salena—how could you think it? I want you with everything in me, always. I just wonder if we should wait until I complete the *Skablykrr* training. So you'll know you can trust me."

She nearly laughed. "I've already nearly killed myself with wanting you and not having. Either or both of us could die tomorrow. I am *not* waiting another moment."

"Here?" he asked softly, as if wary of breaking a spell. "Now?"

"Here," she answered. "Now."

~ 21 ~

R HY STRUGGLED TO grasp this change in his fortunes. His friends and family were right to criticize him for being brooding and gloomy. It seemed that had always been in him, those dark shadows that undermined his every effort. Except for the time with Salena, his storm princess who brought the fresh winds to dispel the dampness and pessimism that shrouded his soul.

Not to be overly dramatic about it, though that was his special gift, Salena *had* been the saving of him. Those long years without her had nearly destroyed him. Still... "It's not your job to save me," he told her, feeling that he should.

She smiled, radiantly lovely. "I'll consider it an avocation, then. I understand the pay is terrible anyway."

Unbearably moved, he threaded his fingers through the silk of her long hair, bronze and suns-hot gold from her time in the desert, though their winter travels had the recent growth at the roots a deeper caramel color. "It's something to consider," he warned her, knowing she wouldn't be taking this step lightly. Salena was a monogamous soul. If they did this, it would be forever. "You better than anyone know what it means that Mother gave Stella the Star of Annfwn, that I'm not really a prince at all. I have no idea what to do with my life."

She smiled, sensual and mischievous. "You can always do me."

He laughed, arousal quickening. Moranu, how he wanted this woman. The distinct possibility that he just might be able to have her had him hard and needy. "Wherever you go, I want to go with you."

"I never needed thrones," she said, more seriously. "All I ever wanted was my work and you."

It did his heart more good than he'd have guessed to hear those words from her. Deep down he'd wondered if she'd ever truly want him again—or even if she'd wanted *him* to begin with. "I'll spend my life making sure you have both," he promised her.

"I'll take that deal." She smiled, then laughed—breaking off with a gasp as he pulled her close, inhaling her laughter and her passion before sealing the promise with a kiss.

She melted under his touch, yielding sweetly, with the utter trust she'd given him once upon a time and that he'd hardly dared to hope she'd offer again. Drawing him down to the sand, she embraced him, lush and voluptuous, a feast for his senses. Salena. His only love.

Murmuring a protest when he drew back slightly, she subsided when he drew her to her feet. "I think we're wearing too many clothes that are difficult to get out of." Not like in their youth, romping on the shores of Nahanau and Annfwn, wearing very little in the tropical heat.

"I *am* hot in these fighting leathers," she observed wryly. "They're not exactly beach wear. But I can take them off. You have to be roasting in that fur-lined cloak."

He was—but other things were more important, so he stilled her hands as they went to the complicated fastenings. "I'd like to undress you." He posed it as a question, still tentative, part of him still shy of her changing her mind, rejecting him, though he refused to let that drive his behavior any longer. "Savor the moment like the gift it is."

She took a shuddering breath, eyes misty with emotion, surrendering the field. "I never could deny you anything."

"You did it well enough for seven years," he replied.

"I didn't." She shook her head, face and eyes full of sorrow. "I didn't do well at all."

"I'm so sorry." He needed more words to express to her the depths of his anguish and regret.

"It's in the past," she replied with her logical surety. "This is now."

Not delaying a moment longer, he swept off the cloak and laid it leather-side down to make a bed for them. The fur wasn't ideal in the heat—though the sun was sinking so the air was cooling—but Salena had always hated getting sand in her crevices, as she put it.

Returning to her, he examined the fastenings of her leathers, undoing the first and rewarding her with a kiss. To the best of his ability, he wanted this to be perfect for her—already a challenge in this alter-realm where their only choice of bed was this beach. He hesitated at the thought. "We don't have to do this here."

"I don't want to wait. What if…" she trailed off, not needing to finish.

What if this was their only chance? Death lurked so close. "We could be in danger."

"We've been in danger since we left Ordnung," she replied. "I'm tired of being afraid."

He pulled her close, kissing her deeply, drinking her in, the need riding him hard. All the more reason for this to be perfect and all the more difficult to accomplish.

"Rhyian," she said against his lips, her breathing ragged, her full breasts surging against him, "I respect your desire to savor this moment, but please hurry."

With a laugh, he obeyed—though he still kissed her after each unfastening, either her mouth or the skin he uncovered. She was paler under her clothes than she used to be, no longer a daughter of sun and surf, but still that golden brown, her skin flawlessly lovely. He freed her breasts, savoring her gasps as he kissed the generous globes, her nipples deeper brown, an erotic contrast to all the bronze and gold of her. Her narrow waist tapered, then flared into rounded hips. Stroking his hands over the seductive curve, he fell to his knees in the sand, pressing a kiss to her gorgeously soft lower belly, not quite able to finish stripping the leather pants down her thighs.

Salena combed her fingers through his hair, murmuring a soft question, and he looked up at her. Gloriously framed by the sun, her expression nearly sundered his heart with all the love and compassion she showed him. Again. At long last. "Are you all right?" she asked again.

"I'm overcome," he confessed. "I thought I remembered how beautiful you are, but seeing you, touching you..." He flicked out his tongue to taste her dimpled belly button, the sweet salt of her skin haunted by a trace of leather, her sex steaming with animal arousal and beckoning him to go lower, to feast on her. Now that he could scent her again, it drove him nearly wild with the need to bury himself inside her. "Tasting you," he groaned, tugging down her pants and revealing the vee of her mound, the curls a dark bronze. "I need to taste you, Salena."

She echoed his groan. "Then finish undressing me already."

But he couldn't wait for that. Cupping her delectable ass, holding her in place, he plunged his tongue into the sweet gap between her thighs, just enough room there to slide through her juices, parting her plump and swollen nether lips, her clit hard and welcoming. Salena threw her head back on a strangled scream of pleasure, small sparks like lightning scattering over his skin as she fisted her hands in his hair, pressing him to her. She didn't need that fierce grip to hold him in place, but he welcomed it, loved the demonstration of her answering desire.

It reassured him on a fundamental level that she hadn't changed, not in this way. He still knew her body and her rhythms, knew how to suck and lick at that demanding clit to keep her hovering on the edge, now pushing her, driving her wildly toward the peak, now backing off the intensity. At least he still knew how to do this for her, and focusing on her pleasure helped him leash the ravening wolf within that wanted to plunder, feed, and ravish.

This was for her. Always and ever for her.

LENA HAD FORGOTTEN, impossible as it seemed, how viciously expert Rhyian was at extracting the extremes of pleasure from her body. She'd enjoyed her other lovers—most of them, some had been better than others—the harmony and chemistry varying from one to the next. But none of them, no matter how willing to be patiently instructed in what she liked, had ever possessed Rhyian's wickedly intuitive knowledge of how to drive her wild.

And wild she was, thrashing in his unnaturally strong shapeshifter's grip, giving herself over to simply feeling and experiencing. She didn't have to tell him anything, didn't have to retain any control of the situation, because this was Rhyian, first love and first lover, who knew her in every way.

She was sobbing with need, crying his name, begging to be released—and yet he somehow kept her balanced on that excruciating edge. She'd have fallen long since, if not for him holding her, and she finally did collapse back onto his cloak, a controlled fall that he eased her into, at last and finally stripping off her boots and peeling off her leather pants, rendering her naked and vulnerable to his every kiss and caress.

He took full advantage of that vulnerability, too, rising over her, blue eyes nearly black with the ferocity of his passion, face taut, lips full and wet from her, golden grains of sand glittering in his dark curls like fairy dust. She could believe this was a dream, her Prince of Shadows, *hers*, again and at last.

His mouth fed on her taut nipples, traveled to her lips and down her throat, his wolf's teeth sinking into the join of her neck and shoulder, making her arch and scream and beg for more while he chuckled darkly and only teased her more. His long, clever fingers cupped her slippery sex, slipping inside and out again to torment the engorged tissues, never enough for her to come, just enough to send her mindless with need and longing.

And he was still fully dressed. When he traveled up her body again, pausing to linger over her breasts, his leather-clad knees wedged between her thighs to keep her splayed for his occasional feasting, preventing her from easing her own desperate need, she fisted her hands in the black curls framing his wickedly gorgeous face. "Rhyian, please. Enough teasing. I am begging you."

"I like hearing you beg me," he answered with a smolder-ing smile, giving her a lingering kiss, almost sweet, as if she weren't naked, sweat-sleeked, and panting beneath him. Holding her gaze, he lowered his body in a long undulation, animalistic and languid, his fighting leathers teasing her nakedness unbearably. "And it will never be enough, Salena," he added with devastating intent. "I could feast upon you for the rest of my days and nights and never have enough."

"Enough for now then." She wriggled trying to free herself, to no avail. Tsking, he edged his knees a bit more apart, spreading her wider. Easily extracting himself from her grip, he pinned her by the wrists over her head, holding her stretched with his long arms and superior, lanky strength. Almost casually, he trailed a hand down her body, smiling absently as she pressed into the caress. Dipping his head, he circled her sensitized, tormented nipple with his tongue. When she mewled a protest, he nipped her sharply, making her convulse. "Rhyian!" she screamed.

He kissed her, humming, his eyes all fierce wolf on the hunt.

"Inside me, now," she commanded, trying very hard to make it sound like an order and not a plea.

He pretended to consider, cocking his head raven-style now, toying with the nipple he'd been subjecting to his special brand of exquisite torture. "I have a conundrum, love," he confided, mischief glinting his eyes, though he kept his expression serious.

She groaned in frustration, bucking against his grip. She'd forgotten this playful side of him, the delight he'd always taken in driving her to a frenzy. Forever the trickster, Rhyian couldn't help toying with his prey once he had her helpless. "No more games. Please."

"I don't see how I can get undressed," he continued, not at all moved by her struggles, "and hold onto this wildly seductive creature I've captured at the same time."

"I'll be good," she promised recklessly.

He narrowed his eyes in suspicion. "Will you though?"

"Yes!"

"I think you'd say anything at this point to get what you need." His hand trailed down her body, tantalizing, fingers tangling in the soaked curls at her mound, then circling to caress the sensitive skin of her inner thigh. Nowhere near close enough to where she needed them.

Lena threw her head back, gritting her teeth against the grinding need for release. "I'll stay still," she ground out. "Just like this, so you can get undressed."

"That will take a great deal of self-control," he purred. "Are you sure you're up to the task?"

She glared at him. "I have excellent discipline and willpower."

"I know you do." He rubbed against her making her moan in desperation. "I also think you're sorely pressed. But I'm willing to make you a deal. You stay exactly like I've put you, without moving—no matter what—and I'll get naked and inside you."

She groaned her agreement. "Yes, yes. Do it now."

"But if you move, even a little, then I start all over again," he warned.

Closing her eyes in despair, she rocked her head in the sand. "I don't know *how* you're restraining yourself! It's been so long. There's time enough for these games later."

"I'm doing it because I love you, Salena," he replied with utter seriousness. "Because you love this."

She did love it. No one else could play her this way, had the strength of will to resist her, to push her past her limits. Only Rhyian. Always and ever him. Prince of Shadows and sweetest tormenter. "I can't believe anyone ever says you don't apply yourself."

A wicked smile broke over his taut expression. "I just have to be appropriately inspired, my love. Now, do we have a deal?"

"Yes," she agreed helplessly, not at all sure she was equal to this task but quite sure she wouldn't be able to dissuade him.

"Good, because I want to look at you." Gradually, as if expecting her to leap away, he released his hold on her, easing away slowly, ready to seize her again should she try to escape him. Concentrating, she closed her eyes, willing herself not to move no matter how exposed she felt. "Look at me, love," he urged in a rough voice. "I need you to see me, to see me looking at you."

Unable and unwilling to refuse his hoarse plea, she opened her eyes, seeing him standing over her silhouetted against the rose and gold sunset, a slim, lethal shadow, blue eyes blazing out of darkness. That molten cobalt gaze raked her and she shivered, watching him strip away his own black leathers, revealing his long, leanly muscled body. How she managed not to move, she didn't know, because she wanted more than anything to lick her way up his body, to take that perfect cock in her mouth and drive him as wild as he'd made her.

Next time, she promised herself, she'd turn the tables on him and he'd know what it was to be in a frenzy of need for her.

"I already know how it feels," Rhyian said, seeming to read her thoughts.

~ 22 ~

R HY RECOGNIZED THE frenzy of need in Salena's straining body, the way she devoured him with her gaze, and he only contained himself through sheer force of will, trembling inside with the roaring need to slake his desire—second only to the fierce determination to imprint himself on Salena's body, heart and spirit. She said she loved him, had never stopped, but before he could believe in that, he had to know he could give her the pleasure she'd always craved from him, whether she'd wanted to or not.

He was doing better, but he suspected he'd always have to fight that insecurity, that debilitating fear that she'd stop loving him, that she'd find him wanting. It helped, though, to stand fast in his love for her, his devotion to her, and his vow to cleave only to her. It also helped, he admitted in his restless, predatory heart to have her helpless under his caresses. Even now she strained to obey, holding still with her gorgeous thighs spread, her swollen sex ripe and vulnerable. With her gold-shot hair rippling over the lighter sand, framing her lush, brown curves, she was transportingly beautiful.

He could stand there and look at her for hours.

She read it in him. "Don't push me farther than I can take,

Rhyian, or I'm calling a stop to this game."

Charmed by her, tempted to test her resolve, he neverthe-less lowered himself to the soft fur of the cloak. Naked as she, he crawled over her, noting the way she trembled at his advance. "You wouldn't," he purred, deliberately adding a bit of threat to heighten the edge.

She still didn't move, still held his gaze, but her lips parted in anticipation. "Not when I'm so close to getting what I want—but don't you dare withhold a moment longer or I will take matters into my own hands."

"You wouldn't," he repeated, pausing to lick her taut and trembling calf, the golden brown skin sweet. She made an incoherent sound, still not moving. Almost disappointed, he continued licking his way up between her widely splayed thighs. "You wouldn't," he said a third time, "because you love this."

She moaned an acknowledgment as he seated the head of his cock at her entrance. It was a good thing she'd managed to keep her end of the deal, as he doubted he could wait any longer. Propping himself over her on straining arms, he drew in a long, shaky breath, willing himself to last. "Because you love me," he added, almost a question, and slid inside her. Her slick sheath welcomed and clasped him, taking his breath away again.

"Yes!" Salena cried, an affirmation of the joining and an-swering his question in one. Freed from constraint, she wrapped her arms and legs around him, an embrace he'd been living for these last seven years, and he nearly wept from sheer relief.

If not for the driving need, he might have, but already their bodies—always wedded, never part of the separation they'd created—eagerly moved together, fitting, finding, meeting and retreating. They moved together in a dance they'd memorized long ago, instantly finding that rhythm again, and he buried his face against her swanlike throat, inhaling her, nibbling at her skin, savoring her breathy moans.

He didn't last long, but fortunately neither did she, the first, fierce climax taking her and ripping him with her as her internal muscles gripped him. He emptied himself inside her, drinking her cries of completion from her lips, then—finding himself as relentlessly hard as ever—he continued thrusting. She met him, hips lifting and sinking, bearing him up and in, deeper and more intimate.

Nothing had changed between them and everything had. As twilight deepened her smoky blue eyes, he gazed into them, their bodies knowing one another and yet marking the journey they'd taken. Before there had been an innocence, a frank and artless joyousness in their lovemaking. Some of that lingered, but it had been marinated in pain and anger, burnished in the crucible of their harrowing adventures. He knew to savor and value this as he never had been able to before.

He regretted what he'd done, how he'd hurt her, and he wouldn't forget it. Still, this finding each other again with the sober understanding of how easily this precious thing between them could be shattered made him cherish her all the more. As she climbed the second peak, her movements and cries growing more urgent, he rode with her, stroking inside her to amplify and heighten the climb, watching her beautiful face.

Her eyes met his and she smiled, beatific, heavy-lidded. "I do love this, Rhyian, and you," she breathed. "I love you, forever and always."

Though she'd said the words before, something about this moment convinced the animal inside him. A knot loosened within, a tight band of dread giving way to sheer relief and release. As Salena threw back her head in a convulsion of utter pleasure, he threw himself after, trusting her to bring them safely back to the ground.

"I CAN'T BELIEVE I thought it was a good idea to do this on the beach," Salena complained. "Even with your cloak, I have sand everywhere." She stood over him, trying—futilely—to dust the sand from her skin. It made for a delightful show, what with the wiggling and supple bouncing, so Rhy continued to loll in his nest of furry, sandy cloak, watching avidly. Truth be told, he doubted he could move just then, he felt so languid and replete. Amazing that Salena possessed so much ready energy.

"It's not as if we had other options," he pointed out. "You were the one who just *had* to have me right away, no waiting for a sand-free bed."

She gave him a narrow look, eyes heating as her gaze raked his body. "I seem to recall you being eager to comply."

His co ck hardened, stretching readily as if obedient to her interest in it. "Anytime, anywhere, love," he agreed, gesturing to himself. "I lie here awaiting your least desire."

She sniffed, pretending to disinterest, though he could tell she was considering the offer. "I'm not interested in putting anything in my vagina, even your gorgeous cock, while I run the risk of having sand up in there, too."

"You could put my gorgeous cock in your lovely mouth," he invited, the member in question twitching of its own accord at the thought.

"I could," she mused, tapping her lip thoughtfully. "Or I could rinse off in the ocean." Sauntering away, her hips swaying seductively, she glanced over her shoulder. "The wise man would join me."

It turned out he *could* move, and quite quickly. Chasing after her, he swept her into his arms, a sensual bundle of sex-heated flesh. She shrieked, giggling, laughing as she protested and threatened him as he galloped into the surf, the water bracingly cool. Laughter erupted from him, also, freed from some deep, dark place where he'd stored it away. This part he'd forgotten, how time with her could be playful in a different way. How they'd romped like children, her commanding him to take different forms to please her. Now a horseback ride, then a dolphin so she could hold onto his fin and glide through the sea. He'd accommodated her least wish, shapeshifting with joyous ease, a sensation he'd forgotten until that moment.

Holding her still, he stopped in chest-deep water, the swells gentle. Salena relaxed in his arms, body lax, arms and legs floating like the seaweed mass of her hair, as she allowed him to swirl her through the buoyant saltwater. They'd done this, too, playing floating games, and her dreamy smile looked the same as it had then. His heart ached for all the time he'd wasted away from her.

Barely cracking her eyes open, she gazed at him. "Am I allowed to ask what you're thinking?"

He frowned, not liking her phrasing. "I don't allow or forbid you anything. Except during sex," he added quickly, giving her a grin. "Because you indulge me in that."

Her sensual smile deepened. "I think it's indulging myself, but so long as we agree on the result." She sobered. "I ask because you never used to like it if I asked what you were thinking about."

It was a fair point, to his chagrin. "I was always afraid you'd see through me," he told her softly. "I didn't want you to know what I was thinking because it was always about you and how desperately I loved you."

She lifted a hand from the water, crystal drops falling and catching the moonlight as she traced his cheekbone, then his lips. Unable to resist, he flicked out his tongue to taste the sea-salt and her, her nails sharp and skin soft. "And now?" she asked quietly.

"I was thinking how desperately I love you," he answered promptly, then nipped her fingertip. "And how easy things used to be between us, innocent, in a way. I sometimes feel like when I lost you, I lost my childhood." He winced at himself, bracing for her to remind him that it was his own cursed fault. "I don't mean to excuse—"

Salena pressed her finger back against his lips, tugging the lower one down to stop him as she regarded him gravely.

"Let's put it behind us," she suggested. "No more apologies. No relentless claiming of responsibility. I forgive you and part of that is forgetting for me."

"Not for me, love," he felt he had to say. "I must never forget."

"All right. I suppose I can understand that, but I don't need that from you, Rhyian."

"What *do* you need?" he asked softly, wondering if he was up to hearing the answer, what she'd require of him. Whatever it was, he'd have to find a way to give it to her.

"You," she answered simply, winding her arms around his neck, fingers combing through his wet curls, tugging his head down to receive her lavish kiss. "I want you, and this feeling. I know it can't always be like this moment, this perfect peace and harmony, but that's my ideal."

"Yes," he agreed, his being humming in understanding. This was perfection. "Then we should—"

Something strummed across his senses, sending him to high alert and Salena stiffened, tense in his arms. "A portal," she gasped.

He whirled, cursing himself for leaving his sword on the beach, for letting down his guard. This time with Salena had felt so dreamlike, a reprieve from the grueling mission and their long years of estrangement, that he'd nearly forgotten that it wasn't over. And now he'd failed to protect Salena. Reflexively, desperately, he reached for his shapeshifting ability, but the alter-realm rules held true and the sense of his other forms stayed just beyond his reach.

Then a shout and screech echoed over the water, human

and gríobhth combined. Enhancing his night vision, Rhy saw—with a mix of relief and exasperation—Jak leap from Zeph's back and spin in a circle, daggers glinting. He crouched over the pile of their clothes, then scanned the area. Zeph clacked her beak and pointed at the water. Jak strode to the verge of the waves, peering directly at them. "Hey, you crazy kids," he called, "fuck you for swimming and cavorting when we've been worried sick."

Zeph called an agreement, then turned and disappeared, stepping back through the portal. "Well," Rhy said to Salena, "this solves the problem of what to do next."

"At least in part," she agreed, giving him a kiss, "though being dressed would've been nice."

Resigned, Rhy carried Salena back toward shore, setting her down in water shallow enough for her to stand with her head above water and still be covered. "Turn around," he instructed Jak.

Jak's grin flashed white in the moonlight. "I dunno. This could be my big chance to see Lena naked. I couldn't—ow!"

Stella, having just stepped through the portal, smiled serenely as Jak flapped his hands, putting out the fireball she'd hurled at him. "Serves you right, you scoundrel."

"The scoundrel you love above all others," he corrected.

"Wait," Salena said, frowning at Stella. "Who's holding the portal open?"

"Isyn," Stella answered, surveying the area with raised brows. "All that faster passage of time in the Winter Isles, remember? We had plenty of opportunity to practice. Is this Nahanau?"

"What is the status?" Astar asked, having followed Stella through the portal, Zeph—back in human form—with him and both of them carrying packs in one hand and a blade in the other. "Zephyr gave the all-clear for us to come through, so we brought food and water, along with all our other supplies."

"We're fine," Rhy answered, realizing he was ragingly thirsty. They wouldn't have lasted long in this alter-realm now that they had bodies to care for again, another bit of reality crashing in. "We are naked, however—so everyone has to give us a moment to dress."

"Who's naked?" Gen asked. She and Isyn also carried blades and more packs. Her gaze lit on Rhy and Salena where they stood in the ocean, rather humiliatingly stranded by their so-called friends' inability to give them a morsel of privacy. "Oh, look," Gen cooed. "Here we thought we were mounting a rescue mission and these two have been frolicking."

"Given said frolicking," Zeph said coolly, folding her arms, "I assume it's safe here?"

"Not necessarily a good assumption," Astar answered in a low voice, nearly a growl, and glaring at Rhy. "What is this place?"

"This is the intelligence's home alter-realm," Salena answered. "Or, at least the one it's anchored to. It's a long story, but Rhyian and I injured the intelligence and we believe it's off licking its wounds. It should be safe for now."

"Not exactly a rousing endorsement," Jak pointed out, also leveling an accusing glare at Rhy—one that included a pointed glance at the weapons he and Salena had discarded along with their clothes.

"I was careless," Rhy acknowledged.

"*We* were," Salena corrected, taking his hand under the water. "But I did scan for a hint of the intelligence's presence— or any life at all, as you'll note there's nothing here but us— and there's been nothing until you all portaled in. Still, I'd love for Nilly and Isyn to confirm my findings."

"That sounded really good," Rhy whispered, bending to nuzzle her ear and whisper into it, while Stella and Isyn used the Star to extend their magical senses.

She sighed, a breath of pleasure and self-recrimination. "It's mostly true. I admit I got caught up in you."

"Same," he replied wryly. Being with Salena was as addictive and utterly distracting as ever, possibly even more so.

Isyn and Stella emerged from their brief trance. "Lena is right in this much," Stella announced, Isyn nodding in confirmation. "There is no sign of the intelligence anywhere near. We're as safe here as anywhere."

"Which isn't saying much," Jak pointed out, Astar grunting in agreement, but overall the group relaxed.

"It's enough for me," Zeph declared, shrugging out of her fur cloak. "I was bored to death in the Winter Isles, not to mention really tired of being cold, and now we finally get to be somewhere tropical. I want to hear the tale of how our star-crossed lovers have finally reconciled." She sniffed the air pointedly. "And by reconciled, I mean sex."

"Yesss," Gen agreed, drawing out the word in a pleased hiss. "I want to hear *every* detail."

"No," Salena said firmly. "Naked here."

"You made *me* tell *you* details," Stella pointed out. "With no mercy."

"This is very true." Gen nodded decisively. "Seems to me we have them by the tail. Should we hide their clothes?"

"That *is* the traditional move," Jak remarked, stroking his short beard thoughtfully.

All six of them arrayed themselves along the beach, squarely between Rhy and Salena, and their clothes. "King Isyn," Rhy said respectfully, trying for an appeal to a reasonable authority who was not one of their diabolical former friends, "would you intervene?"

Isyn cleared his throat, on the receiving end of a significant glare from Gen. "I am new to this group dynamic," he explained diplomatically, "but I have been in similar situations where I can confirm the traditional move upon finding skinny-dipping lovers is to hide their clothes. Or," he added with a helpful smile, "hold that clothing hostage for an agreed-upon ransom."

"I thought we'd become friends," Rhy said to him in disgust.

Isyn grinned, wicked mischief in it that Rhy hadn't seen in the reserved mage before. "Exactly. You'd do it to me."

He wasn't wrong, unfortunately.

"Astar," Salena inserted levelly, "I'm appealing to you as our leader and my future high king."

"Don't you *dare* do the right thing here." Zeph gave Astar a meaningful glare along with the warning.

Astar shrugged. "Zephyr, darling—you say that like you don't know me. I can't possibly behave so callously to a lady. Everyone will turn around to allow Lena to emerge, dry off, and dress."

"And Rhy?" Gen pounced, giving Rhy a saucy glance over the water.

"Rhy is on his own," Astar answered with a flash of a grin. "Is that a fair compromise?"

"Yes," Zeph decided.

"No," Salena said at the same time. "Rhyian is my fiancée now and I'm asserting my rights as he's promised to me. Only *I* see him naked henceforth."

That certainly shut them up.

"Congratulations to you both," Stella said warmly, the first to find a response. "This is very good news indeed."

"Is it?" Astar's dark tone made it sound definitively otherwise, his grin gone. "We all know about Rhy's promises—and how long they don't last."

"I'd take exception to that, if it weren't true," Rhy returned, more lightly than he felt. This, too, seemed to be part of his new path. Keeping his word and holding to vows, those came with all sorts of brutal honesty. "But that *is* in the past," he added firmly. "I've made Salena a number of vows, which I will keep on pain of death. That includes any ceremony or formal pledging of vows she asks for."

His friends exchanged dubious glances, so very doubtful that he regretted the keenness of his night vision. Then Salena squeezed his hand under the water, a gesture of solidarity that meant almost more than any of the promises they'd exchanged.

"Is he telling the truth, Nilly?" Astar asked his twin with a frown of concern. Zeph huffed out a breath, shaking her head at Astar in clear disapproval.

Stella seemed to agree, frowning at her brother. "Ask Lena," she answered.

"Rhyian has changed," Salena said very clearly. "I believe him and I've accepted the vows he's made to me, including a proposal of marriage. That's all any of you need to know."

Gen snorted softly. "But not all we're *going* to know," she muttered under her breath to Zeph, who agreed emphatically, sending them a sunny smile.

Astar held up his hands, both in surrender and to silence them all. "All right, then. This is officially none of our business. Everyone will turn around and allow Rhy and Lena to emerge from the water and dress. *Then* we are going to have a serious talk."

~ 23 ~

ONE DISADVANTAGE—ALL RIGHT, one of the several disadvantages—of being a mossback among shapeshifters was that Lena missed some of the nonverbal exchanges in the moonlit darkness. She'd be severely irritated that her sharp-nosed friends had instantly picked up the smell of sex, except that would be hypocritical as they had indeed used that same information to make Stella spill about her heating affair with Jak early on.

Her female friends had formed a shielding circle around Lena so she could dress discreetly, and had even produced a drying cloth from the supplies they'd brought through the portal. That was kind of them, but Lena still felt encircled by predators, whether the three of them could produce claws and talons at the moment or not. Their sharp minds and even keener curiosity were poised to extract every detail from her. With her body still throbbing from Rhyian's intense lovemaking and the non-physical bits of her still reeling from the rapid changes in their relationship, Lena wasn't quite ready to articulate all that had happened between them. Perhaps she superstitiously didn't want to put it all into words just yet. Also, it had all seemed much more rational when it had been her and Rhyian, alone in all the world. Explaining it to everyone else suddenly seemed far more daunting.

Looking around at their expectant faces, their avid interest apparent in the moonlight even to her non-enhanced vision, she sighed, knowing she couldn't escape. "What goes around, comes around, I suppose," she muttered to herself.

"So very true," Stella agreed brightly, with none of her usual gentle compassion—although she did hand Lena a flask of fresh water, which was most welcome. "I distinctly recall you grilling me on the incident in the carriage with Jak—to my intense discomfort—so I'm not inclined to let you escape these particular claws."

"Remind me," Zeph inquired with mock innocence, "was that the incident when Jak unveiled his impressive cock and jerked off for you?"

"You know it was," Gen said before Stella could reply. "Now shut up so we can hear what happened with Lena and Rhy before Willy makes us all convene to talk about the boring mission."

"The mission is hardly boring when all of our lives and the fate of the world is at stake," Zeph retorted.

"Compared to hearing about how Rhy and Lena reconciled after these bitter seven years it is," Gen insisted.

"Gen has a point," Stella, the blithely uncompassionate traitor noted.

"Accepted." Zeph turned her face toward Lena. "Start talking."

"We're not exactly private," Lena said, stalling.

"As private as we're going to get tonight," Gen replied.

"There's nothing all that much to tell," Lena tried in a last-ditch effort.

The three sent up a unified hoot of patent disbelief, drawing attention from the guys, who were building a campfire. Zeph looked over her shoulder and back. "They're not listening. Jak has broken out the whiskey and they're doing man-boasting."

"I would *love* a whiskey," Lena said, suddenly desperate for a draught.

"That can be your reward for telling us what we want to know," Zeph replied insistently.

"Soonest begun, soonest done," Stella chimed in, using one of Astar's favorite phrases with relentless cheer.

"We should make her describe Rhy's member," Gen suggested.

Fortunately, Stella shook her head emphatically. "No, thank you. He's my cousin."

"Yeah, practically a brother," Zeph agreed with a note of disgust, and Lena felt a little bad that she'd ever assumed Zeph had been one of Rhyian's many lovers.

"Besides," Lena pointed out, "I knew all about Rhyian's body from before. That's not the salient information here."

"Right. The *salient* information is how this happened," Stella said, her eyes reflecting silver moonlight. "I'm with Zeph and Gen: start talking. Tell us everything."

"Don't you know?" Lena shot back. "I thought you saw our future. You could have warned me."

Stella shook her head, no longer teasing. "Things could have gone either way. In fact, the odds were against it. And I could never see what exactly spurred the change that enabled this happy outcome."

Lena only hoped it would be a happy outcome. *The odds were against it.* Chewing her lip, she looked around at her closest friends in all the world. "Have I made a terrible mistake?" she asked plaintively.

"Oh, honey." Gen immediately relented, putting an arm around her, as did Stella and Zeph, all of them gathering close. "Don't say that. I'm sorry we teased you."

"Do you regret it?" Zeph asked without bite.

Did she? "Not yet," Lena ventured, testing the feeling as she said it.

"You feel really happy to me," Stella observed. "Happier than you've felt in a long time. It's natural to be afraid, especially in this instance, to fear losing that again."

"To fear being hurt again," Gen added with feeling.

"But you were dead set against giving Rhy another chance to hurt you," Zeph pointed out. "So something changed that you did."

They all waited, no less expectant than before, just with their curiosity-claws somewhat more sheathed. Lena sighed out a long breath, hoping it wouldn't sound absurd, saying it aloud. "He vowed the equivalent of the *Elskathorrl* to me."

A stunned silence greeted her and she wished again she could see their expressions more clearly.

"The *Elskathorrl*," Zeph repeated, sounding it out. "I know I've heard of that before, but…"

"Of course you have," Gen replied, then released a dreamy sigh. "It's so romantic. Prince Harlan swore it to High Queen

Ursula on the same day he met her. It was love at first sight."

"It was more than that," Stella correctly, almost sternly. "Uncle Harlan was a man of experience and strenuous training. He recognized that Auntie Essla would be a queen he could follow always, regardless of their romantic relationship. He could forswear all others because he knew what he was getting into. Not to introduce further doubt, Lena, but does Rhy even know what the *Elskathorrl* entails? He hasn't completed the *Skablykrr* training."

Somehow Lena hadn't expected sweet, loving, compassionate Nilly to be the voice of dissent. "I'm the one who compared Rhyian's promise to the *Elskathorrl*," she said, rather too tersely. Perhaps defensively? "And I brought up the *Skablykrr*. Rhyian thought he'd come up with making this kind of promise and, like Zeph, only recalled Harlan's vow when I pointed out the similarities."

"He... made it up?" Gen still sounded dreamy. "That is even *more* romantic."

"What, *exactly*, did he say?" Zeph demanded. "Because this does not sound the Rhy we know."

Lena had just known she wasn't ready to talk about this, to expose their tender and fledgling trust to the harsh light of criticism. She felt rather as if her mother were questioning her on the specifics of a hypothesis she hadn't quite worked out all the details for yet. She took a breath. She might not be ready for this thesis-defense, but she would do it. For Rhyian's sake.

"He was trying to figure out what he could do so that I'd trust him again. We were arguing, as always—and let me mention at this juncture that we were both non-corporeal,

Rhyian having appealed to Moranu for assistance in coming to my rescue, and we all know what kind of sacrifice that was for him—and he suddenly decided that he'd promise fidelity to me for the rest of his life, whether I ever took him back or not. And *then*, when I brought up those exact same points, Nilly, that Harlan has done the *Skablykrr* training and Rhyian hasn't, Rhyian actually listened, acknowledged the problem, and vowed that, as soon as our mission is done, he'll do the training—either ask Harlan if he'll teach it or, failing that, Rhyian vowed to go to Dasnaria to learn. Because he's determined to do whatever it takes to be a better person, the kind who doesn't break promises, stated or implied, and I believe him. Maybe it's because I *want* to believe him so badly, but this is a huge step for him and I think it could be the making of him, so I think, if I can forgive and forget and move on—after all, we've all grown up a lot, both on this mission and since we were arguably still kids back then—then all of you can at least give him enough rope to hang himself with. Although I don't think he will. I think he'll surprise everyone. That's what I think," she finished, a bit anticlimactically.

"That was quite a long speech," Zeph observed. "Take a breath."

Stella stroked Lena's cheek, rare skin-to-skin contact from her empath friend, calming and cooling energy in it. "Forgive me for pressing you," Stella murmured. "I wanted to be sure how deep your conviction went, so I could be ready."

To pick up the pieces again, she meant, as Stella had all those years ago. Or… perhaps something more. "I didn't think he could ever say anything to me that would change my mind, but that turned out to be it."

"I *still* say it's terribly romantic," Gen said stubbornly. "Especially knowing that he appealed to Moranu."

"All we knew on our end was that Rhy's spirit left his body," Stella added somberly. "Both of you were dead without my magic keeping you alive. Then, when your *bodies* simply vanished..." She trailed off, her voice choked with tears.

"I'm sorry, Nilly," Lena said, stricken, wishing she could hug her friend without hurting her. She'd been so absorbed in her relationship drama that she hadn't thought about what the others had been through. "Thank you for keeping me alive. I owe you so much."

"Yes, you do." Stella's voice cleared and went silver-sharp, more like her powerful aunts in their warrior and sorceress ways than Lena had ever before witnessed. "You disobeyed a direct order from Astar not to fling your consciousness after the intelligence. You have a great deal of explaining to do."

"Burrrrnnnn," Zeph whispered, and Gen giggled at the irreverence.

"I *am* sorry," Lena said, squirming in her lately realized contrition. It hadn't felt like disobedience at the time. But then, she'd never been any more of a good soldier than Rhyian was.

"Tell it to Astar," Stella advised. Then she unbent, throwing her arms around Lena, embracing her fiercely. "I was so worried," she whispered in Lena's ear. "The things I saw... You played a very dangerous game here and it's not over yet."

Lena tried to hold Stella's delicate body with care, taken aback by the physical affection. "I was just trying to fulfill my part of the mission."

"You didn't care if you lived or died," Stella corrected firmly, pulling back, eyes flashing with more than reflected moonlight. "Which is why I'm grateful Rhyian finally pulled his head out of his ass."

"Nilly!" Lena gasped, adding extra shock for emphasis.

"Oh, what?" Stella demanded irritably. "I can say things like that."

"Jak has been a terrible influence on her," Zeph said mournfully.

"Our sweet, innocent, and loving Nilly," Gen agreed with mock sorrow, "now cursing like a sailor."

"Jak says *much* worse things," Stella confided, a wicked lilt in her voice. "But, in all seriousness, I am very glad Rhy found his way. Auntie Andi hoped something like this would occur to him. It will make all the difference, I think."

Well, that confirmed the something deeper Lena had wondered about.

"Plus, now *everyone* gets to have sex now," Zeph put in cheerfully. "Which means no more moratoriums!"

"Unless we're on a sailboat Jak is captaining," Gen pointed out.

"I am *never* getting on a sailboat with Jak as captain, so long as I live," Stella declared emphatically. "Or he's never getting his impressive cock near me again!"

"Nilly!" Lena, Gen, and Zeph all gasped in unison, before they collapsed into laughter.

~ 24 ~

RHY GLANCED ONCE more at the knot of giggling women surrounding Salena and took a healthy swig of whiskey, now that he'd had enough water to quench his thirst.

He really hoped they weren't badgering Salena too much about her wisdom in giving him a second chance. This new reconciliation between them felt too fragile for intense scrutiny—which was maybe a problem—and he'd have liked to have had at least one full night with her for them to find easiness in each other's company again. So much for that.

"Cheers," Jak said, helpfully topping off Rhy's cup and clinking the flask against it. "You'll survive the information exchange. I did."

Rhy studied him with a sideways look. "No recriminations or cautions?"

"From me?" Jak asked in some surprise, then shook his head. "Lena is a smart lady. Smartest of all of us. If she figures you can be trusted again, I'm not going to question her judgment."

"I'm not sure I agree," Astar put in darkly from the other side of the fire.

Isyn looked around the circle of men. "I'm obviously the

284

new guy here—by a lot—but are you all really in each other's personal business this much?"

Astar flicked him an annoyed look. The usually sunny golden prince was certainly in a mood, which was all Rhy's fault, as usual, no doubt. "I am the future high king of the Thirteen Kingdoms," Astar reminded him, "and leader of this mission. It's up to me to protect my people from ill-advised... liaisons."

"Mmm hmm." Isyn sipped his whiskey, then—astonishingly—winked at Rhy. "I'm counting my blessings that Your Highness wasn't there to interfere with my seducing Gendra then. That was certainly ill-advised, if anything was."

Astar gaped at Isyn. "It's not the same."

"No?" Isyn shrugged. "As I said, I don't have the history here."

"Some of the history," Jak put in helpfully, "is that Willy nobly steps in to protect all the ladies from us, whether they ask for it or not. Stella had to tell him to butt our of our relationship."

Astar opened and closed his mouth, then finally said, "That was different, too."

Isyn raised a brow. "I'm with Jak on this one. Lena has a clear and logical mind. I've only known her a few days and I'm certain of that much. If Rhy has persuaded her he's trustworthy, then that's all I need to know."

Astar grunted, bearish in his unhappiness, and eyed Rhy. "How *did* you convince her?"

"It's private," Rhy answered smoothly. "Between Salena and me. You don't need to know."

"I *do* need to know," Astar insisted. "What if this is another bit of trickery from you?"

Rhy set his teeth, determined not to be annoyed. "I'm done with that."

Jak leaned back on one elbow, twirling a dagger between his fingers, looking interested, while Astar actually sputtered. "Wh—what does that mean?" Astar demanded.

"It means Rhy is engaging in a new enterprise," Zeph answered for Rhy, slithering against Astar's side and giving him a lavish kiss. "I'll tell you about it later, grumpy bear."

"Why can't Rhy tell me himself?" Astar complained, though he sounded considerably less grumpy post-kiss.

"Because Rhyian doesn't report to you on his personal decisions," Salena put in, seating herself close beside Rhy. Gen and Stella also joined them, filling out the circle by sitting beside their chosen mates. Now that they were all together, they began passing around the Winter Isles fish the others had brought and the guys had roasted over the campfire while urgent gossip was exchanged.

Salena took a few bites of the hot fish and sighed in rapture. "I'm so glad you all brought food."

"Even if it is fish," Gen said ruefully.

"Both of you are stalling," Astar pointed out.

Shrugging, Salena gave Astar a bland look. "I already told the girls, so they can fill you boys in on the specifics, if you have to know. As I assume you'd rather not discuss it, Rhyian?" She gazed at him with perfect equanimity, slipping her hand into his, no sign of hesitation or concern. Love for her welled in him—along with absolute trust in her—and he knew he shouldn't have doubted for a moment.

"Yes. Thank you." He kissed her, her lips soft and welcoming.

She smiled briefly and turned back to the others. "I believe we have other, more important things to discuss?"

Astar's expression darkened forbiddingly. "All right, Lena. How about we start with how you disobeyed a direct royal command and went after the intelligence on your own?"

"Nilly already mentioned that and I offer a formal apology," Salena answered with regal calm. "However, Your Highness Crown Prince Astar, I'd like to remind the high throne that Nahanau is an independent ally of the Thirteen Kingdoms. As a member of the royal line of Nahanau, I am not subject to your commands."

Rhy struggled to keep the grin from his face, wanting to cheer for his gorgeous, proud, and courageous mate.

Groaning in frustration, Astar scrubbed a hand over his face. "Lena... We were worried sick about you. About *both* of you," he emphasized, looking to Rhy.

"Which is why I'm apologizing," Lena said. "I regret causing you all anxiety, and that Rhyian risked his own life and sanity to rescue me, but—"

"*I* don't regret it," Rhy told her staunchly. "Smartest decision I ever made," he added with fervor, and she rewarded him with a brilliant smile.

"Arguably a low bar," Zeph put in sweetly, grinning when he scowled at her.

"*But,*" Salena inserted with emphasis, "I calculated the risk—and freely admit there were variables I didn't anticipate—and I believe the benefits will outweigh both in your minds, too. Shall I explain?"

Rhy was happy enough to let Salena recount their adventures, watching the expressions of his friends as they listened. It was good to be here with them, clustered around the campfire on the beach, surf in the background, as they'd done so many times growing up together. Even Isyn, despite his caveats of knowing he was new to their circle, seemed to fit right in, Gen snuggled between his knees and lying back against him, absorbed in the tale.

Jak had put his dagger away, playing with a long lock of Stella's hair as she leaned against him, and Zeph had draped herself over Astar's lap, idly stroking his neck, doing an excellent job of keeping him calm, even through the harrowing parts of the story. And Salena held his hand, doing all her eating and gesturing with the other, as if as unwilling to break contact with him as he felt.

It was good. And it was, possibly, the last time they'd all be together like this. Even if they all survived to return home, they'd be scattering again, each to their own pursuits. Zeph and Astar would be at Castle Ordnung, shouldering their duties and behaving like responsible future rulers. Likewise, Gen and Isyn would return to their palace in the Isles of Remus to take up rule there. Rhy realized he had no idea what Stella and Jak planned to do. Probably go to Annfwn, where Stella would continue her training in sorcery, and maybe to be the next Queen of Annfwn.

For the first time, the thought didn't rankle, didn't cause him to feel bitter. He'd go to Aerron with Salena, as she'd almost certainly want to do. After the *Skablykrr* training, of course, however long that would take. Then they'd see. He hated the prospect of being separated from her, but he'd do what was necessary. All those times he'd worried about being unworthy of her, it had somehow never occurred to him to take steps to *become* worthy. Now that he saw the way, he wouldn't shirk. She would wait for him. Knowing that made all the difference.

As if divining his thoughts, Salena gave him a soft, warm, and intimate smile. She'd finished her tale and answered the inevitable questions. Now everyone was thinking.

"It sounds like," Isyn said into the thoughtful silence, "that you very nearly dismantled the intelligence with your storm magic."

"And, in a desperation move," Gen added, "it somehow portaled your bodies to grab your spirits and land you back here."

"Speaking of which," Salena inserted, "how did you find us?"

They all exchanged speaking looks. "It wasn't easy," Stella answered. "We waited a couple of days, to see if you'd return on your own. Then I set to scrying. But nothing I saw made sense. Like I kept seeing you in Nahanau, Lena, which confused me."

"And which we now understand," Jak said. "It would be nice if your visions came with clarifying instructions, like a legend on a map."

She rolled her eyes at him. "I'll write to the authorities about it. Anyway, we finally took a vote and decided to send

Zeph and Jak through to where my intuition insisted you were and…"

"And here we are," Zeph put in with satisfaction. "I want to be on record that I told you all so."

"Yes, darling, you're always right," Astar said without rancor.

She practically purred.

"Interesting how you put that, Rhy," Jak said thoughtfully, "that it seemed like the intelligence grabbed your bodies to tear your spirits from its metaphysical throat."

"Almost a forced shapeshifting, like the priesthood of Deyrr practiced," Gen added. "Who knew it could do that, though?"

"Maybe even it didn't," Stella answered, then looked around the group gravely. "Just as we are discovering new abilities within ourselves in battling this thing, perhaps it is also growing in power and technique, pressed by circumstance."

"Dad always says shapeshifters push themselves most when under pressure," Zeph commented.

"And Ursula says similar," Astar mused, "that you never truly know the mettle of your warriors until they've faced the enemy, and their own mortality."

Not a good enough reason to use the word 'mortality,' Rhy thought to himself, but kept from saying aloud. "Salena would've destroyed it, if she'd had someone besides me to assist her," he said instead.

Stella fixed her sorcerous gaze on him. "So, you're thinking that if Lena, Isyn, and I all team together to attempt the same thing, we might be successful." Not a question.

He nodded and Isyn looked thoughtful.

"You helped more than you realize," Salena put in, her gaze on him serious, no hint of mischief or flattery. "In your non-corporeal form, you were like a raven, and you gripped with talons stronger than my mental clasp. Without you to help, I couldn't have held on so long."

"So the shapeshifters aren't just surplus support after all," Rhy said to Zeph, who cackled at the reminder of their cranky conversation at the outset of the mission.

"Why would you ever think that?" Astar demanded, clearly offended.

"Never mind, darling." Zeph patted his cheek. "An old joke."

"The other consideration," Salena put in, "is finding a window of opportunity. I had the element of surprise, with Rhyian distracting and annoying the intelligence—"

"At last, the perfect application for Rhy's skills," Gen inserted, an impish gleam in her eyes.

"Ha ha," he replied with a narrowed gaze, promising retribution.

"Which allowed me to discern a vulnerability in the intelligence's manifestation," Salena continued without missing a beat. "However, it will now be on guard against a similar strike, if we can even lure it into communicating with us again."

"We need an ambush," Jak said, brightening at the thought.

"And bait," Zeph replied with a like predatory sparkle in her eyes.

Jak deflated, scowling. "Stella is not going to be bait."

"No one said Nilly is going to be bait," Astar growled.

"Though I *am* the logical choice," Stella replied evenly.

"Not true," Salena countered. "I think *I* am."

~ 25 ~

LENA KEPT PART of her attention on Rhyian, keenly aware—if no one else was—of how fiercely he was controlling himself. Well, Stella probably knew, her penetrating gaze lingering on her cousin, assessing and thoughtful. Even without Stella's empathy, Lena knew Rhyian, and he gazed at her now with quiet fury.

"This began with me," she said, mostly to him, then including the group. "The intelligence was watching me, it said, long before the night of the crystalline moon."

"I dreamed of the tower in the field of lilies long before you began weather-working in Aerron," Stella pointed out calmly. "That means the possibility of that future was alive prior to the intelligence's interest in you."

"And we know the intelligence specifically wanted me dead," Isyn put in. "It said so when we confronted one another in the Winter Isles. It had sent me there to die and was surprised I wasn't. Dead, that is." He stroked a hand down Gen's arm, and she looked up at him with a soft smile. "If not for a miracle and a stubborn orca, I would've been dead before much longer."

"Our three magic-workers appear to be the focus of the

intelligence's attention then," Astar said, releasing a heavy sigh.

"Except," Jak countered, "for the phenomenon we've all noted, where our shapeshifter types have been feeling their animal natures more and acting unusually because of it. Now we have this tale from Rhy and Lena where the intelligence was able to pull their bodies through a portal of some sort. We all saw their bodies disappear before our eyes, and Stella sensed a sort of rift a moment before that happened." Stella, her eyes on Jak, nodded thoughtfully. "I hear you shapeshifters talk," he continued, "how shapeshifting is like pulling a body from a different space, which is also how you manage to store stuff so handily. It occurs to me that some of what the intelligence is doing is like that."

"Interesting," Lena commented. "Rhyian certainly equilibrated to that event faster than I did, and said he thought it could be because it was similar to shapeshifting into a new form, learning to use a different kind of body for the first time."

The shapeshifters all exchanged thoughtful looks. Jak nodded crisply. "As the one person here who is neither a shapeshifter nor a magic worker, I'm going to put out there that the intelligence is focused on all of you, which is probably why Queen Andromeda recommended to Her Majesty that you all be included on this quest."

"She specifically included you, also," Stella pointed out.

Jak grinned at her. "Someone had to sail the boat."

"And save Stella's life," Astar put in, with a grateful nod to Jak.

Jak tipped him a jaunty salute, though his eyes held haunted shadows. "All part of the services we provide the high throne," he answered lightly, a dagger once again spinning through his fingers, his expression taut as if he imagined how he'd like to be using it right that moment. "My point, and I do have one, is that any of us can be bait—except perhaps me, but that frees me to stand guard—but only the magic workers can spring the trap. Thus, they can't also be the bait," Jak concluded.

Rhyian, hand tense in Lena's, added his agreement, and she couldn't help but wonder if the two men weren't just thinking in terms of protecting Stella and herself, rather than for the best outcome of their mission. Stella had been very specific on that point, if on little else, that their success and survival would depend upon keeping their mission goals firmly in mind.

"My father," Gen said slowly, "has always been a proponent of appearing to offer the enemy what they want. Once the enemy swallows the bait; it destroys them from the inside."

"So, we're to be packaged up attractively for the intelligence to seize, and once within, we use our magic in tandem to take it apart," Isyn mused. "It could work."

"We have one part already," Lena said, having been contemplating this piece. "In a way, we *are* inside already. We're in the intelligence's home realm. I think that's part of why I could attack it."

"What's to prevent it from fleeing to the other alter-realms, however?" Astar asked, dipping his chin at Stella. "You said you saw us chasing it from realm to realm."

"In some scenarios, yes." She considered gravely. "I shouldn't say more."

"But you think this could work," Astar persisted.

"I think it's a necessary step," she temporized.

Everyone was silent, thinking that through. "How do we package our magic-workers attractively?" Rhyian asked, doing an admirable job of sounding nonchalant, though his hand gripped hers with almost painful ferocity.

"How about the reverse?" Lena proposed. "We spur it into action by doing what we originally attempted in the Winter Isles: we liberate the alter-realms from its control, one by one, until it's forced to retaliate."

Jak whistled low and long. "I don't like it, but we had this argument once already. I'm game."

Stella met his gaze, then looked to Astar. "Back to the grid alter-realm to try again?"

Astar let out an unhappy sigh. "I suppose so." He pointed at Lena. "On the condition that you, Princess Salena Nakoa KauPo, agree to abide by the parameters we set."

Lena inclined her head graciously. "I've learned my lesson."

"She's learned there's something worth living for, she means," Zeph cackled and Lena sent her a narrow glare. Never mind that it was true.

"When do we go?" Isyn asked, deferring to Astar.

"In the morning," Astar declared. "Everyone is worn out and tonight has given us a great deal to think about." His summer-sky blue eyes lingered on Rhyian a moment, then drifted to Lena. He nodded slightly to her, though she wasn't sure what it indicated. Approval? Resignation? Perhaps the simple respect of one heir-in-waiting to allied thrones as she'd requested. "Do as you like for the rest of the night," he said, abruptly springing to his feet, Zeph squealing in delighted surprise as he lifted her. "I'm tired of thinking, arguing, and giving commands."

"I have the perfect antidote for that," Zeph purred, winding her long arms around Astar's neck.

For once, he didn't blush, simply returned her heated gaze. "I'm counting on it." Carrying her, he strode off down the darkened beach.

"Well, that was abrupt," Gen observed.

Stella shook her head. "Not really. It had been building. This is hard on him, too."

Lena acknowledged the point. "I'm sorry I pulled rank on him."

"Don't be," Stella said with a smile. "We're all in this together, and it will take all of us—and everything we can bring to bear—to end it." Her eyes went to Isyn, who didn't mark her attention, busy whispering something in Gen's ear. Lena noticed, however, and wondered what Isyn had forgotten. Stella caught her looking and gave her a sad, slight smile, along with a headshake of warning. Whatever it was, Isyn had to think of it on his own.

"I'm no fool," Jak declared, uncoiling to his feet with sprightly grace, offering a hand down to Stella, who took it with a smile turned knowingly sensual, "and I intend to spend the night before battle in the tradition of my ancestors."

"In misogynistic dick-swinging and *mjed*-swilling with other men?" Stella inquired sweetly, with wide, innocent eyes.

"I'll teach you to be impudent, wench," he declared with a

piratical swagger, then neatly tossed Stella over his shoulder, affectionately smacking her upraised bottom as she giggled, before he wished them all a *very* pleasant night, complete with eyebrow waggle.

"Am I to carry you off into the darkness also?" Isyn asked Gen.

"You don't have to," she assured him. "Your leg is still weak. Don't stress it unnecessarily."

"Weak?" he echoed in shock. "Now you've done it." He got to his feet, indeed a bit stiffly, but far better than he'd been when Lena had last seen him. They really had put the days of accelerated time and waiting in the Winter Isles to good purpose. As soon as Gen gracefully uncoiled to her feet, Isyn swept her up in his arms. He had to take a moment to stabilize on the shifting sand, but carried Gen off admirably enough. Looking over Isyn's shoulder, Gen winked at Lena. "Enjoy the campfire, you two!"

Rhyian gave Lena a long look, the firelight playing over his carved features, the blue deeply shadowed except where glints of flame danced. His perfect lips tempted her to kiss, to lose herself in him, but something in his somber expression held her off. "What's wrong?" she asked quietly.

He let out a breath and smiled crookedly. "What's right? I feel like I just got you back and now I'm having to face the possibility of losing you forever."

"Us," she answered softly. "*We* are right and we have this moment."

"I just feel like I wasted so much time being an irredeemable asshole," he replied with a grimace.

"Not irredeemable, after all," she pointed out, that love for him filling her more warmly and brightly than ever before. In their youth, that love had been born of innocence and lust, now it felt burnished, deeper, all the richer for the trials they'd suffered. She was rewarded by his slow smile, her love reflected back in his eyes as she seen before, and now had the promise to go with it. "I say we don't waste any more time and follow the example of our friends."

She started to stand, but he held onto her hand, tugging her back down. "They all left," he said, his smile turning sultry. "That's why Gen pointed out they'd left the fire to us."

Hesitating, she still allowed him to pull her closer. "Any of them could return at any time."

He shook his head, sliding his fingers through her hair to drape the long fall of it behind her shoulder before placing a lingering kiss there. "They won't. This is their gift to us, see? They all went far out of earshot, and everyone knows this could be our last night... before everything."

Last night alive, he hadn't said, but they both knew it.

Trailing hot lips down her cheek, he took her earlobe in his teeth, nipping just enough to make her gasp, before laving it with his tongue while the shuddering wave of desire burst into flame through her body. "I want to strip you naked and kiss every bit of you," he whispered darkly.

"No," she said, pulling away.

"Love, I promise I'll be able to hear if anyone comes near," he protested, frowning.

"Not that. I think it's time for a test of your new resolve."

"A test?" he echoed, stricken. "You don't think I can keep

my word to you. I suppose that's fair." He sounded disappointed, however.

"Not that. I trust you, Rhyian." Flicking her gaze up to his,
she saw how that simple declaration came as a relief to him,
and also moved him, far more than telling him she loved him.
Perhaps Rhyian had needed this most of all, for someone to
trust and believe in him.

"And I think you'll enjoy this test," she said, busily undoing
his shirt. "It's *my* turn to torment you," she informed him with
a wicked smile. "You will promise to lie still and let me do
whatever I like to you. I'm going to taste every bit of you until
you are begging me." She pressed a kiss to the hollow at the
base of his throat, sucking lightly, savoring the increased thrum
of his pulse in response, his hands coming up to hold her,
vising as she used her teeth on his collarbones.

"Love," he breathed, "can I just start begging now?"

"You can," she answered archly, "but it won't do you any
good. Promise you'll do as I say until I release you."

"As my lady wishes," he replied. "I vow to do so."

With a purr of satisfied delight, she pushed him to his back
and set to enjoying herself with the delicious feast that was her
Prince of Shadows.

~ 26 ~

R HY WOKE IN the early morning hours, animal instinct humming with the approach of dawn. Soon the sky would begin to grow light, and their friends would return. Salena lay warm and naked in his arms, head pillowed on his chest, her silken hair streaming over him like a blanket in the tropical darkness.

He should awaken her soon, as she wouldn't like being caught unawares like this, and yet he couldn't quite make himself move and break the spell. Instead he lay there on his back, looking at the glittering array of stars arching overhead and savoring Salena's scent wrapped around him like the soft stream of her hair. The moment felt enchanted, suspended in time, and he sent up a fervent prayer of thanks to Moranu for making this second chance possible.

As the stars began to fade, he stroked a hand over the velvet skin of Salena's arm, also draped over his chest with all the possessiveness he could wish for, and nuzzled his lips against her hair. "Salena, love," he murmured, "it's almost dawn."

"I don't care," she murmured sleepily, her crimson nails digging into his flesh lightly, the thigh she'd also draped over him rubbing him enticingly, rousing him further.

He laughed, catching her lips with his, savoring the sleepy languor and sweetness of Salena before she brought all her intellectual claws to bear. She'd devastated him the night before, unraveling all his control and testing the limits of his resolve. But he'd kept his promises, though she'd sorely pressed him, and he felt absurdly proud of himself. And beyond delighted with her.

Sliding a hand down his chest, to his abs, she wrapped clever fingers around his shaft firmly. "Is this for me?" she purred.

"Always and ever," he answered, moving himself through the circle of her grip, "and only for you."

"Then I'd best take care of it, hmm?" She began trailing her mouth down his body, following the path of her hand, but he stopped her. "No?" she asked, looking up at him.

He urged her up to straddle him, brushing her hair back from her face so it tumbled down her back, then filled his hands with her generous breasts. In the crepuscular light she was a glory of shades of gray, a goddess of shifting shadows. "I want to see you and be inside you," he said softly, "if that's all right."

She smiled sensually and leaned into his hands, gasping as he toyed with her sensitive nipples. Rising up to impale herself on him, she sank down and scratched her nails down his chest. "It's more than all right," she replied, and began to ride him.

It was slow and sweet and intensely erotic, her glowing gaze locked to his as they found that rhythm that connected them on levels beyond thought or the physical. With her hair cascading around her lush figure, Salena undulated with him, eyes half-lidded in pleasure, and—after the crescendo caught them both up in a languorous wave—she collapsed over him, breast sealed to his. Their hearts beating as one.

WHILE SALENA BATHED in the sea, Rhy built up the campfire again, more for comfort than anything, in the warming morning. Then, going through the packs that had been piled up nearby, he found makings for tea and began boiling water in their one pot. He also set out the nutritious seaweed biscuits the others had brought from the Isles of Remus. "It's not Nahanaun coffee and the biscuit is no flaky cinnamon pastry," he told Salena, handing her a mug of tea and a biscuit when she returned to the fire, her hair streaming long and dark with water.

With a smile—one he remembered well and hadn't seen in far too long, the smile that meant she was perfectly happy—she gave him a lingering kiss. "Of all the breakfasts we shared, this one is my favorite," she said.

Bemused, he raised a brow. "Why is that?"

"Because it's now," she answered. "Present and future. I'm done with the past."

Taking her hand, hot from holding the tea cup, he kissed it reverently. "You are a miracle, love."

She wrinkled her nose impishly. "Just a minor weather witch who's hoping to pull off the impossible."

The others began arriving soon after that, the various couples emerging from their hideaways, looking rumpled, sleepy, and satisfied—and happy enough for the tea and biscuits. "Bless you, Lena," Gen said, cupping the tea like it was precious nectar.

"Don't thank me," Salena replied, dunking her biscuit in her own tea to soften. "Rhyian did all the prep while I was primping."

"The power of true love," Gen observed, throwing Rhy an astonished look. He chucked a biscuit at her.

"I don't think it can be called primping," Zeph declared, combing out her wildly tangled hair, "under these barbarous circumstances. How I long to be able to shapeshift clean and without these snarls!"

"Welcome to the gritty world of mossbacks," Salena replied, going to Zeph and taking the comb from her. "Here, let me."

Rhy watched Salena fix Zeph's hair, deliberately not eavesdropping on their murmured conversation, affection for the both of them and all his companions filling his heart. He felt lighter, easier in his skin, and it wasn't only being on good terms with Salena again. It was as if something that had been awry for a long time—perhaps for seven years, perhaps even longer—had finally been put into place.

"A moment, Rhy?" Astar asked, his expression grave.

"Of course," Rhy answered, his moment of felicity fading. Ah well. It wouldn't be his life if things were easy. He followed Astar a ways down the beach, until they were out of earshot of the others.

Astar stopped, folded his beefy arms, and gazed out at the sea, looking all stern and noble, the incipient high king. Rhy braced for whatever reprimands or cautions were coming his way, trying not to feel like a little kid being summoned by his father for a lecture. He was a different person now, with new resolve. All he had to do was ground himself in his foundation of making decisions and keeping to them, refusing to break vows, and he'd be able to withstand the censure of the kings in his life.

"Cousin," Astar said, then blew out a breath, unfolded his arms, and faced Rhy. "I want to apologize. That is, I do apologize."

Rhy took a moment to respond, bypassing the sarcastic reply that wanted to leap to his lips, searching for the appropriate words. "Accepted," he said, holding out a hand.

Astar clasped it, frowning in puzzlement. "You didn't let me explain what I'm apologizing for."

Rhy shrugged with one shoulder and grinned. This surprising people with sincerity was fun in its own way, too. "Do I need to know the reason for an apology to accept it? You're a fine and noble man, Willy, with integrity oozing out your pores. If you feel the need to apologize, then you have good reason and I'm fine accepting that at face value."

Astar gave him a long look, releasing his hand. "I want to ask who you are and what you've done with my cousin Rhyian, but that would be unworthy of you and this moment."

"Fair, though," Rhy pointed out, not above being amused, "given my history."

Grimacing, Astar nodded. "Well, Zeph spent considerable

time detailing my failure to give you the benefit of the doubt, not giving you credit for a sincere desire to change. We've all made mistakes and had to learn from them. You're doing exactly what I've asked of you, and—instead of being congratulatory and supportive—I did the opposite."

"Yes, well…" At a loss, beset by an unfamiliar and unsettling emotion, Rhy shrugged again. Then laughed. "I wasn't surprised. You have good reason to doubt whether I'll stick this new resolve."

Astar shook his head. "Big of you to give me the out, but I can admit when I'm wrong." This time he clasped Rhy's shoulder, squeezing. "You're a fine man, too, Rhy. I should remember to tell you that more often."

Unaccountably moved, Rhy returned the gesture, wondering if this unfamiliar emotion was what it was like to receive the approval of someone you admire. If that was so, how would it feel if perhaps his father offered the same? Something deep inside wrenched with agonizing intensity, and Rhy had to catch his breath at the realization of how very badly he wanted that. No sense wishing for the impossible, however.

"You all right?" Astar asked, frowning in concern.

"Yes. More than all right. Thank you, Astar," Rhy said, and pulled his cousin into a hug, both of them pounding each other's backs and choking back emotion.

When they returned to the campfire, Salena gave him a questioning look, smiling in relief when he nodded that all was well. Sitting beside her, he took her hand, and they all looked to Astar.

"As soon as everyone is ready," Astar said solemnly, "we'll

set up for the same trio to go to the grid world. The rest of us will remain here on guard for the intelligence. Once Nilly and Lena liberate that world, we'll know more." He coughed a little, not saying what they all understood—that what they'd know was whether the severed alter-realm would survive the process, and whether anyone in it at the time would be able to escape again.

"I suggest one alteration," Salena said, gripping Rhy's hand but otherwise showing no sign of trepidation. "Zeph doesn't need to go."

Zeph sat up straight in indignation. "I'm going!"

"Lena is right," Stella put in gravely. "We learned last time that we don't need you to guard our backs. No sense risking more people than we need to."

"You needed me to carry Lena's body back through the portal," Zeph shot back and Salena winced.

"I will not be repeating that mistake," Salena replied. "I promise. If this works the way I anticipate, we won't be gone long."

"I'm counting on it," Astar said gravely. "In fact, it would be even better if only one of you went, so we have two magic workers in reserve instead of one."

Stella and Salena exchanged glances, Salena shaking her head to Rhy's relief. He might not be able to withstand imagining her alone in the grid world. "I can't do it without Stella's power."

"And Lena has the technique," Stella said, capping it. "This task requires both of us."

"Is that prophecy?" Jak asked in a grating voice, his turbulent gaze on Stella.

"Confidence," she answered. "We both know how you dislike prophecy."

"I have good reason," he muttered.

"And, when Stella and Lena return, then the Winter Isles?" Isyn asked. "If the alter-realm can survive the severing, I'd like to liberate the folk as quickly as possible, just in case."

In case the intelligence came after them, they all understood.

"If the alter-realms survive the severing," Rhy put in, "and Salena and Nilly are able to portal back, then I'd like to suggest we all stay together from there out. We all go to the Winter Isles, and then on to the next alter-realm, and so forth. No more of this splitting up."

"Seconded," Jak declared, flipping a dagger with blurring speed, a set look on his face.

"It's riskier that way," Astar said doubtfully.

"I disagree," Gen said, a stubborn set to her chin. "We were sent on this mission as a team. All of us, including Isyn, who we were told to find. I think we're supposed to be together to finish it."

Astar glanced at Stella, who had a carefully neutral expression on her face, revealing nothing. "So be it then," he said on a sigh. "Whenever you ladies are ready."

Releasing his hand, Salena stood, brushing the sand off her fighting leathers. "Let's get this over with," she said to Stella who nodded and stood also. She turned to Rhy, who'd gotten to his feet with her. "Rhyian," she said, framing his face in her hands, her lovely eyes full of emotion, "I want you to know that—"

He wrapped his hands around her wrists. "Don't, love," he said stopping her. Then, as she raised her brows, he turned his head to kiss her on one palm, then the other. "Don't make this a goodbye. Go, succeed, and come back. I'll be waiting."

~ 27 ~

L ENA FACED STELLA, their interlaced hands cupping the Star
of Annfwn. Locking her gaze with Stella's solemn gray
one, Lena let her storm magic twine with Stella's, smiling as
Stella widened her eyes. "You're stronger," Stella murmured.
"So much stronger, and brighter."

"You were right," Lena replied quietly. "Of course you
were, but still. I gave my heart what it needs and I feel like the
desert after rain."

"Blooming," Stella said with a blossoming smile. "I'm so
glad."

"It makes a difference, doesn't it, Rhyian and me being
together again? To the success of our mission."

Stella's smile faded into a questioning look. "I hope you
didn't do this for that reason."

"No." Lena suppressed the giddy urge to look at Rhyian,
prowling restlessly in his guard position, sleek and mouth-
wateringly sexual. "I was entirely selfish."

"Good." Stella squeezed their joined hands. "Let's do this."

They opened a portal and stepped into the sterile atmosphere of the grid alter-realm. Funny how something so arcane
as portaling between worlds that shouldn't exist to begin with

had begun to feel practiced. Having promised Jak, Stella and Lena had blades in hand and—back to back—turned in a circle to scan the barren landscape. "Clear," Lena said, and Stella confirmed.

"You know what you'll do?" Stella asked.

"I wouldn't go that far," Lena admitted, "but I have an idea."

"I'm going to hold the portal open for us to go back through fast, if worse comes to worst," Stella said.

"Can you do both things at the same time?"

Stella's eyes increased in brilliance, going to fulminous silver. "I'm well rested," she assured Lena. "You do your part and I'll do mine."

All right then. Lena nodded crisply, willing herself to be equally as confident, her storm magic coalescing and interweaving with Stella and the Star. It took little effort this time to build the cube of their awareness and expand it outward. She felt clear-headed, incisive, and ready to brave the beast. Lena recalled Stella's words about Jak, *he somehow fills and soothes the raw and empty places in me... It's transformative.*

She understood exactly what Stella meant. Having this new trust, this deep understanding and commitment with Rhyian changed everything—mostly her. Courageous and bold, whole and healthy as she hadn't felt in years, Lena reached out her storm sense to the connector leading from the grid world. As swiftly as she'd swipe with a dagger, she severed the connector...

And—after a long, hovering moment—plunged along with the grid alter-realm as it tumbled through space. In her mind,

Stella mentally screamed along with her at the rocketing sense of plummeting descent. Forcing herself to concentrate, she focused on useful communication. *"Where are we going?"* Lena shouted to Stella.

"I don't know, but I can't reach the portal."

They were going to die here then. The prospect filled her with a terrible grief, a devastating sense of loss over the future with Rhyian she'd never have now. Ironic that she'd lose her life just when she'd found a reason to live.

"We will *live,"* Stella said grimly in her mind. *"Jak would never forgive me if I screw this up."* Magic billowed and bloomed, Stella's silver with the Star's topaz gold, forming a net that slowed their headlong flight. It wasn't a descent so much as a trajectory, Lena realized, a hurtling through space and time that was oddly familiar...

In fact, she'd experienced something very similar just recently when she and Rhyian were hurled to rejoin their bodies. *"I think this alter-realm is being drawn to wherever it belongs,"* she told Stella, *"like Rhyian and me, when our spirits and bodies meshed again."*

"Then I'll be ready to help," Stella said, sounding confident again, every bit the powerful sorceress. *"And here it comes. Brace!"*

The impact was staggering. Lena felt herself come begin to come apart, held in place only by Stella's intense magical hold. She may have screamed, her mental voice twining with Stella's. Molecules of physical matter screeched and tore, heated and melded, as the collision continued to reverberate.

Then everything stopped. And Lena was firmly in her

body, though splayed on the glossy, polished obsidian surface of the grid world, her hands still joined with Stella's around the Star. Stella laughed, a grating, grateful sound. "I think we're alive." Her voice sounded tinny and echoing in the thin air.

Lena found herself laughing, too, the jarring of her bruised body painful. "I hurt too much to be dead, that's for sure." Her storm senses stirred, warning of upheaval, which made no sense since the grid-world had no weather to speak of.

"I'll heal you once we get back through the portal," Stella promised.

"Is it still there?" Lena asked, hoping against hope that it would be. If not, at least their lives would be short in this place.

"I think so." Stella groaned. "I'm feeling a bit battered. Give me a moment."

Lena certainly sympathized there. "Try shapeshifting," she suggested. "See if you can do that and heal."

"But we can't in the alter-realms—"

"Ah-ah," Lena interrupted, wagging a finger at Stella. Well, wagging it mostly at the colorless sky and in Stella's general direction. "This may no longer be an alter-realm, if the grid-world piece rejoined its home world. This will be a good test."

"Heh. Excellent point." A black jaguar sat where Stella had been, then shifted to Stella's human form—clean and in fresh fighting leathers, Lena noticed with considerable envy. Oh well, she'd do the same if she could. Stella stretched luxurious-ly. "So much better!" Putting a hand on Lena, Stella healed her minor aches bruises with remarkable speed.

Lena stood up to join Stella, looked around for what could be sending her refreshed storm senses in to high alert—and goggled. "Ah, Nilly…"

"The portal seems to be there." Stella frowned at Lena in confusion. "What's wrong?"

Lena simply pointed and Stella's gaze widened in horror.

They stood together, turning in a circle to take in the cataclysmic sight. All around them, fire raged. Like four distant walls, flames shot high into the sky, incandescent and ranging through the hottest colors. "What do you think that is?" Lena asked, feeling with her weather sense. "It's not atmospheric, although see those waves in the sky? That's a massive storm brewing." Even as she said it, a boom of thunder sounded, rolling from all directions, and lightning forked purple across the previously clear sky.

Stella got that distant expression, looking out and *through* the wall of fire, then refocused her gaze on Lena. "I think it's from the excised piece merging again with where it came from. As if the two parts were forced together with such extremity that the energy released was explosive enough to set the margins on fire."

"That would explain the weather disturbance on a such a huge scale, too. Do we think the fire will eventually burn out?" Lena asked with grave misgivings. Weather tended to rebalance itself over time, but that fire…

Stella shrugged, shaking her head slightly. "Maybe. But at least there's no life in this world, no more so than the grid alter-realm had. It's good to confirm that."

"And that's why this was our practice realm," Lena agreed. "One thing is certain—we can't risk this happening with the Winter Isles."

"No," Stella observed glumly. "We'll need to tell the others and see if anyone has a solution to the problem." She held out her hand with the Star cupped in her palm. "Shall we?"

Grateful that they had the ability to escape, Lena clasped her hand over Stella's. "Yes, let's go home. I mean," she said on a laugh, "back to Not-Nahanau."

Stella smiled sweetly. "Home is where he is. Yes?"

"Yes," Lena agreed fervently, grateful Stella understood. "For me, too."

"If we can't save the Winter Isles, maybe we can portal out all the folk?" Gen suggested.

They were gathered around the now-cold campfire, as it was far too warm for a fire in the midday heat, sitting around it mostly out of habit at that point.

"To where though?" Isyn countered. "As much as the Winter Isles seems like our world, I don't think that landscape—or the folk—belong anywhere in our realm."

"There are parts of the world we don't know about," Gen argued. "Even Dafne admits that."

"If grudgingly," Lena agreed with a fond smile for her mother who hated not knowing *everything*. "However, I think we'd know if a chunk had been carved out of our realm and added to the intelligence's collection. That kind of impact on our world would..." She trailed off, looking to Rhyian in alarm. He hadn't left her side since she and Stella returned. Being held by Rhyian was always nice and they'd both needed the physical contact. It had been several hours for those waiting behind—a much greater time differential than when they'd traveled to the grid-world from the Winter Isles, which was an interesting data point about the intelligence's home alter-realm, though Lena didn't know how to interpret it—and their friends had all been frantic with worry. Jak and Rhyian, in particular, had been almost inarticulate with relief at their reappearance.

By unspoken accord, Stella and Lena had glossed how very near to death they had come, emphasizing only the *very* distant violent results of the remerging.

Now Rhyian was returning her alarmed gaze with grim recognition. "It would be cataclysmic?"

"World destroying," Jak said somberly. "Is that what happens—the intelligence grabs a chunk of the Isles of Remus and the after-effects are what Queen Andromeda saw in her visions?"

"The Isles of Remus are already somewhat loosely connected to our world," Isyn pointed out. "It seems like they'd be easy to pluck, as it were."

"It hasn't happened yet," Astar said, matter of factly.

"So far as we know," Zeph cautioned. "We haven't been back to our world for days and days."

"Less than that probably," Gen reminded her. "A day at most, maybe only hours."

"Still," Zeph continued darkly, "we don't know what the intelligence is doing."

"Licking its wounds in some deep cave," Rhyian said with vicious satisfaction.

"Or preparing to take revenge," Zeph shot back. "What if, by chasing the intelligence and attacking it, we are what causes it to take revenge—or make a preemptive strike—by snatching a piece of Isyn and Gen's kingdom?"

They were all silent a moment, contemplating that. Lena had to admit that Zeph's scenario was plausible. Jak drew a dagger and began spinning it with grim focus.

"This is the difficulty," Stella finally said into the expectant quiet, "with sharing visions of the future. By giving you knowledge, I invite you to act upon it—and through those actions you might create the events I foresee." She rubbed her forehead. "I don't know how Aunt Andi does it, to be honest."

The dagger in Jak's hand vanished and he pulled Stella onto his lap, cupping her head and tucking her face against his chest. "It's not your fault, my star," he said, sweeping the group with a defiant look.

"Of course no one is blaming Nilly," Astar said with implacable certainty, "especially since we're discussing something that *still* hasn't happened." He held up a hand to Zeph and added, "So far as we know."

"Besides," Rhyian put in decisively, "this second-guessing serves no one. If Nilly or my mother see something awful in our futures, of course they're going to attempt to warn us and of course we're going to take action. What, we're going to sit around and hope that by doing nothing we'll escape those consequences?" He snorted in disgust. "You know who doesn't try to affect their own fates? Dead people. Much better for us to take action and see it through. Moranu told me that any decision is better than making no decision at all. There's power and magic in deciding on a course of action."

Lena very nearly laughed as everyone stared at Rhyian with varying expressions of consternation and bemusement.

"Moranu told you that," Isyn said. "Moranu the goddess."

Gen elbowed him. "I told you that Rhy appealed to Moranu for help retrieving Lena and that he belongs to Her service."

"Yes," Isyn replied, rubbing his ribs. "I suppose I didn't quite credit it."

"Any decision is better than none," Jak mused. "I like that. I feel like I should point out at this juncture that we already made these decisions. We planned to reconnect the Winter Isles to their parent world, then chase the intelligence through whichever realm it fled to, severing the alter-realms as we went, until we had the intelligence cornered so we could destroy it."

"And this is where we got stuck," Stella said, turning on Jak's lap to face the rest of them. "We might destroy the Winter Isles in trying to reconnect them." She very deliberately did not look at Isyn. Trying not to influence him. *Hmm.*

"Why did the intelligence want Isyn dead, in particular?" Lena wondered aloud, hoping her question might prompt whatever it was Stella believed he should realize on his own.

Isyn returned her questioning gaze, shrugging. "I have no idea. I'm nothing special."

"That's not true," Gen retorted staunchly, earning a smile from him.

"I *wasn't* anything special, Briar Rose," he corrected, running a hand down her arm. "I wasn't anywhere near as magical as my mother, except that I could see and speak with Falada and—" He sat bolt upright, surprising a sound out of Gen. "Falada. We have to find her."

"We always planned to, Isyn," Astar said in a placating tone. "I think we're all hoping she'll be in one of the alter-realms we visit, but we can't—"

"No, no, no," Isyn interrupted with enthusiasm. "You don't get it. Falada is the key to rejoining the worlds. That's the fae magic of my ancestors of the Isles of Remus! They enable the isles to float between realms without disastrous repercussions. If we find Falada, she will be able to heal the pieces of the alter-realms the intelligence stole and restore them to where they belong."

"*If* we find Falada," Gen echoed. "We don't know where to look. We don't even know where to begin."

Jak had an odd look on his face. "Actually... *I* know where to begin."

~ 28 ~

IT TOOK A long time—longer than Rhy had patience for—to settle on who would portal to the icy seas to find their old sailboat. Jak insisted on going, of course, claiming rights as it was his idea and that he knew better than anyone where he left the boat and, he theorized, Falada.

"After all this time, the sailboat is *not* going to be there," Astar nearly shouted, Rhy wincing at the volume.

"If Willy keeps repeating it loudly enough, do you think the message will eventually penetrate Jak's thick skull?" Rhy asked Salena, rewarded by a soft laugh and head shake.

"I know where I left it," Jak persisted, raising his voice more. "A sailor never forgets where he leaves his ship!"

"Gen knows the place as an orca," Stella said with steady calm, although a hint of feline snarl coiled through the words the longer she spoke, "and she can travel faster in circles to triangulate, while you would freeze in that chilly water. I'm not risking you to hypothermia, *again*, when I can go in a winter-hardy form *and* communicate with Falada."

"Isyn is the best to communicate with Falada," Jak snarled back.

"Isyn is also subject to dying in cold water," Gen put in

with considerable asperity. "Stop being an ass, Jak, and let Nilly and me do this."

Jak glared daggers at her, though fortunately he didn't draw any, then threw up his hands before pointing a finger at Stella. "You have no idea how it kills me to stay behind, *waiting* for *hours*, wondering if I'll ever see you again!"

Oh boy. Rhy put an arm around Jak, tightening his grip and using his superior strength when Jak tried to shrug him off. "Never thought I'd be the voice of reason, bro, but it's time to step away before Nilly is tempted to fry you with another of her fireballs."

Jak cursed and twisted violently, but Rhy held firm, letting Jak see the determination in his gaze. "You'll regret it," Rhy said softly. "We're all up against it here. It's high stakes from now on. Remember what Nilly told us: our success and survival depend on keeping our mission goals firmly in mind. We have to have the balls to do that."

Glaring mutinously, Jak bared his teeth. Then he sagged and shook his head sharply. "At least mine are bigger than yours."

Relieved at Jak's capitulation, Rhy changed his grip to clap Jak on the back. "Good man." Behind Jak, Salena gave Rhy a grateful smile—as did Stella—but only Salena's approval mattered. Tipping the backs of his forefingers against his forehead in the *Elskathorrl* salute, he grinned when Salena rolled her eyes at him, because she also blushed with pleasure. "Come on," he said to Jak and beckoning to Astar. "It's time to initiate Isyn into how we men spend our time while the ladies are out saving the world."

"Excellent idea," Astar declared, drawing his broadsword.

Isyn looked dubiously between Astar and Rhy. "I'm not sure I need to be initiated with bloodshed."

Having finished kissing Stella and determinedly letting her go, Jak swaggered up to them, a blade in each hand and a predatory smile on his face. "Yes, let's test that strength and agility you've been working on, Isyn."

"I want in," Salena said, drawing her own blade, and Rhy frowned at the taunting smile Jak aimed at him. Yeah, turnabout sucked.

"Sure, love," Rhy said easily, before Astar could say anything. "As long as it won't distract you from holding the portal open."

"Oh." Salena's face fell. "You're right. Duty calls."

"I'll spar with you later, one on one," he offered as Salena went to join Stella and Gen in forming the portal, well rewarded by her brightening smile.

"Is that what you kids are calling it?" Zeph drawled, examining her nails.

"Look alive, gimpy," Jak declared and launched himself at Isyn, Astar and Rhy whooping and following after.

"Boys," Zeph said with a shake of her head. She hopped off the rock and followed Salena. "Guess I'll guard against any beasties portaling in."

"Call us if you need us," Astar shouted to her, before ducking a wild swing from Isyn.

IT WAS A decent way to spend the waiting, Rhy had to admit. All four of them lay sprawled on the sand, recovering their breath, when Salena called out, "Incoming!"

With renewed vigor, they all leapt to their feet—Jak offering Isyn a helping hand—and ran to where Salena anchored the portal. "Can you tell if it's friendly?" Rhy asked her, and she shook her head, face a picture of concentration.

They brought weapons to bear, waiting tensely while nothing happened.

"Why is it taking so long?" Jak demanded, pacing restlessly.

"I don't know," Salena gritted out. "Holding the portal open just became much more difficult, as if Nilly let go of her end."

"Isyn," Zeph held out a hand. "Shift me." He obliged and a golden gríobhth stood where she'd been. She prowled to the portal, sniffing at it, tail lashing. Before anyone knew what she intended, she leapt through and disappeared.

"Danu's frozen tits!" Astar roared.

Rhy raised a brow at him. He hadn't known sweet Willy knew such curses. "Zeph knows how to navigate the portals," he said calmly.

Astar fastened an enraged blue glare on Rhy. "You're right—since when are *you* the voice of reason?"

Rhy shrugged, elaborately enough to be irritating and keep Astar's ire focused on him. "If I'm the voice of reason, it speaks to how far gone we are into insanity."

Salena laughed, despite her strained expression. "All right, something definitely coming through. Isyn, I could use your help."

The ivory-haired mage stepped up. Rhy couldn't really see what magic they wrought, but Salena's posture eased. Then her eyes flew open wide. "Bigger! We need it *much* bigger."

"Is that wise—" Astar began, but Rhy dragged him backward out of the way of the scrambling magic workers. He might not be a sorcerer, but he knew how they worked. When his mother used that tone of voice, that meant get out of the way, fast.

Salena staggered, nearly falling as she tried to run backward on the sand and maintain her hold on the portal. Sheathing the Silversteel weapon, Rhy leapt to grab her, wrapping his arms around her and lifting her off her feet to haul her backward, using all his speed and elasticity to do it. "I've got you," he breathed.

"I know. Here she comes."

Rhy felt the magic billow through Salena as the portal strained and expanded—and an enormous white dragon flew out, wings folded, at blistering speed and dripping seawater. What had required Gen to take dragon form? Back-winging for balance, she landed on her hind legs in the shallows, cupping something in her huge taloned hands. With an incoherent shout, Jak raced toward them.

"Oh no," Salena breathed.

Isyn was craning his face in Gen's direction, the portal wavering with his inattention, Salena sagging with exhaustion.

"Focus, Isyn. It's all on you two!" Rhy shouted at him. "Keep steady, love," he murmured to her. "You've got this."

"I hope so," she replied grimly.

Then Zeph, still in gríobhth form, blasted through the portal, a white horse galloping beside her, both of them soaking wet, bleeding all over and showing signs of a pitched fight. Black tentacles shot through the portal after them, flailing and grabbing hold. "Close the portal," Rhy told Salena. "Close it now."

"I'm trying!" she snapped. "The tentacle monster is lodged and holding it open."

It was a bizarre sight, for sure. The tentacle monster hung in the air, half-in and half-out of their reality. It seemed to be gripping the edges of the very large portal with more of its thousands of tentacles, so that the bulging center of it moved back and forth with its movements.

"Just let go then," he suggested, feeling that she was weakening dangerously.

"I can't," she panted. "I don't have Stella's finesse. It's all I can do to hold on and it feels like my mental fingernails are breaking."

"What can we do? I know you can come up with a solution. Think with that big brain."

Zeph whirled in the writhing cocoon of tentacles, slashing with beak and talons, using her tail like a whip, but more tentacles replaced the ones she cut away. Astar was helping her, roaring like his grizzly First Form, his broadsword a blur of motion. The white horse—Falada?—dug her hooves in the sand, losing ground as the tentacles wrapping her dragged her inexorably back through the portal.

"Put me down and help Falada," Salena gritted out. "Isyn and I can make the portal smaller again."

Rhy obeyed immediately. "Steady?"

"Go!"

He lost no time drawing the Silversteel sword and hurling himself at the tentacles dragging at Falada. Zeph could hold her own for a while, anyway. Slicing at the tentacles with methodical speed, Rhy ignored the ones lashing at him and drawing blood. He had to mentally thank Jak for insisting he be prepared to fight without teeth or claws. The wolf raged inside him, though, fierce and howling, and Rhy channeled that ferocity to defend his loved ones, freeing the faery horse from the clinging tentacles. Fortunately, Falada was savvy enough to race away in a burst of speed, escaping the tentacles that shot after her.

With grim determination, he fought his way to the center of the beast, leaving a trail of severed tentacles in his wake. Stella must be severely wounded—not only because Gen had clearly had to carry her back through the portal in dragon form—but because Stella would've blasted this thing with her magic by now. Salena had been walking her way toward Isyn, looking as if she fought against a strong wind. The tentacle monster seemed to be bracing itself now, holding the portal open as Salena and Isyn struggled toward each other, battling for every step, their faces pale with exhaustion.

Behind and around the splayed tentacles, bright green monkey-lizards began pouring through. The agile and voracious creatures immediately launched themselves at

Salena and Isyn.

Throttling back the instinct to run to Salena, Rhy grimly battled his way through the lashing tentacles and assessed the situation, trying to think like his father would. They were losing this battle. With one of their magic workers down and the other two exhausted, they were going to lose people to this fight, especially without a functioning healer. They might have lost Stella already. That Jak hadn't joined the fray was a very bad sign.

Astar still fought on the other side of the torrent of tentacles, but they weren't gaining ground, especially with the monkey-lizards harrying them, as well. They needed that portal closed, which meant pushing the tentacle monster back through.

Or pulling it out.

"Zeph!" he yelled. "Pull!"

She screeched something he didn't understand as he danced and dodged to the portal edges. "Astar! Like this!" He swept his sword along the invisible barrier where tentacles met nothingness, cleaving them away in sweeps. "Bring it through!"

Across the bulging mass of the slimy central body, Astar stared with shock. "Are you mad?"

Rhy laughed, feeling the grin stretch his lips. "Possibly."

~ 29 ~

LENA'S VISION WAS going black around the edges, her magic very nearly expended from the drain of the portal. She barely felt the bites of the monkey-lizards. She couldn't bear to think what might've happened to Stella. When she could spare attention, she looked to make sure Rhyian was still on his feet, spinning in a savage dance, as he fought the onslaught of tentacles. This was the hugest tentacle monster she'd ever seen and it had tendrils woven into her magic via the portal, refusing to let go.

Then Rhyian called to Zeph and Astar, leaping to cut the tentacles from the frame of the portal, Astar following his lead. Zeph stopped trying to escape the tentacles, shrugging into their cloying grasp like a living harness as she spread her wings, dug her feet into the sand, and began to pull.

The tentacle monster resisted, its central body almost bubbling as Lena watched with sick fascination, the thing extruding even more tentacles. Rhyian, Astar, and Zeph were almost swathed to the point of indistinguishability as they no longer attempted to free themselves, instead concentrating on severing the thing's grasp of the portal edges and pulling it through.

"Salena, Isyn!" Rhy called with a muffled shout, "Can you squeeze?"

Squeeze? Oh! Lena applied the last dregs of her magic, flexing it like she would in trying to compress an unruly air current threatening the pattern she'd worked to instill. Across from her, the space between them narrower than before, Isyn gazed back at her with lips compressed in a taut line, his face as white as his hair, eyes blazing green. Their magic interlaced like clasped hands and together they squeezed.

Abruptly, with an obscene squelching plop, the tentacle monster burst all the way through, Lena lurching as the portal—suddenly freed of obstruction—slammed shut. Isyn fell face-first to the ground, vanishing under a pile of monkey-lizards, and Lena barely had the presence of mind to defend herself, slicing with her own daggers at the creatures hanging off of and gnawing on her. Trying to reach Rhyian, she forged her way into the tentacles, their too-familiar sting abrading her skin.

Gah, how she loathed these things—but she loved Rhyian more.

"Rhyian!" she yelled at the writhing mass of tentacles where he'd gone down.

"Gen!" he shouted back, momentarily confusing her. "Get Gen to come fry this fucker already!"

IT HAD BEEN tricky for Gen to fry the tentacles and monkey-lizards with specifically directed dragon fire, with the five of them mixed in, but she'd done it. When the tentacle monster and the monkey-lizards were only gray ash blowing along the sand, Gen shapeshifted back to human form with Isyn's assistance and promptly burst into tears. She'd been trying to use her dragon magic, she babbled, to stabilize Stella.

Without success, as Stella was still unconscious and very near death. Jak sat, holding her in his arms, his expression hard, while Astar sat miserably next to them, head in his hands and bleeding from so many places that he looked coated in blood. Zeph, who'd managed to shift and heal with Isyn's help, looked incongruously clean and lovely as she sat beside Astar, wiping the blood away bit by bit, nodding at Gen's instructions on treatment, her face whiter than usual and lined with strain. Falada stood nearby, dripping from a dip in the sea that she'd told Isyn would do her own wounds the most good. Indeed, though pink smears of blood still marred her otherwise flawless white hide, the lacerations appeared to have already sealed over.

Isyn, like Astar and Lena, was a mess of bleeding wounds, Gen grimly and steadily bandaging each one, even as she offered advice to the others applying makeshift medical attention. Rhyian, who'd also shapeshifted to heal at Lena's urging, was performing the same service for her, cleaning her many lacerations and tying them off with strips of ruined clothing, fastening them tightly to attempt to stop the bleeding. "It's not fair you can't shapeshift back to good condition," he muttered savagely, not for the first time. "You need healing, love."

But they both knew she wouldn't get it, not with Stella out of commission. "We'll have to do it the old-fashioned way," she replied wearily. They were all exhausted from the brief, pitched battle and they hadn't even faced the intelligence yet. It was patently clear that the intelligence had recovered and was once-again targeting them.

"Might as well tell us what happened, Gen," Astar said, sounding as defeated as Lena felt.

At that, Jak seemed to partially emerge from his haunted musings, fastening his sharp gaze on Gen, more guilt than accusation in it. "I should have gone," he said, so quietly it was more to himself. "I knew she wasn't telling everything she'd seen. I felt it in my bones."

"You couldn't have changed anything, Jak," Gen said firmly, though she didn't look at him, or the limp form of Stella in his arms. "We got there fine. The sailboat was battered, but in the same vicinity, though it had dragged its anchor a considerable distance." Gen gave the report like her father would, a crisp and dull military recitation. "Stella shifted to human form and rode on my back to use her sorcery to scan for Falada. As Jak suspected, Falada was still in the area, unable to travel without Stella's sorcery."

"A most distressing development," Falada said in a low, melodious voice, startling everyone but Isyn.

"You can talk," Gen blurted, then halted, flushing with embarrassment.

If a horse could lift a single eyebrow, that would be Falada's expression. "Yes," she replied simply. "So you can you."

"I mean," Gen floundered, "only Stella could seem to hear you when you were..." She trailed off uncertainly.

"Incorporeal," Falada suggested, a hint of amusement in her voice. It was fascinating, truly—her mouth appeared to be fully a horse's, which shouldn't allow for human-sounding speech, and indeed didn't move as a human's would to shape the words. And yet clear speech emerged from it. "Yes, that condition was limiting."

Gen gave Isyn an accusing frown. "When you said you spoke with Falada, I assumed you meant mind-to-mind."

He kissed her forehead. "I apologize. I should have said. It came as a surprise to me, too," he said to the group. "Mother always said Falada could talk, before she... ah..."

"Was violently separated from my body?" Falada suggested in the same tone.

Isyn winced in chagrin. "Yes. I somehow never quite credited it."

"Understandable," Falada replied with gentle affection.

"Continue the report, Gen," Astar directed.

"Right. Ah, upon communicating with the then incorporeal Falada, Stella determined that Falada had been unable to pass through the portal with us, due to said incorporeal status and other arcane considerations I don't understand."

"I don't really understand, either," Falada put in, "but it was most aggravating. I also encountered the same limitation as before—without a person to be anchored to, I couldn't travel away from the area. I very much appreciate the rescue and regret the injuries suffered."

They all looked at Stella then, unconscious, bruised, and

bloodied. As if Stella would simply open her eyes, smile at them in her serene way, and expound on the metaphysical considerations of what made Falada manifest as a ghost horse to begin with.

"At any rate," Gen continued on a heavy sigh, returning her attention to a nasty gash on Isyn's calf that had him wincing as she prodded it, "Stella determined that Falada needed flesh to travel back with us, so she used the Star to do that."

Everyone was quiet a moment. Finally Astar muttered, "I didn't even know she knew how to do that."

"She didn't, I'm sure of it," Jak replied bleakly.

"She said it was similar to Deyrr forcing shapeshifting combined with healing magic, Falada's faery nature, and that the intelligence had given her the idea."

"Being fae changes things," Falada agreed placidly.

Gen shrugged. "My job was to keep Nilly afloat while she worked the magic."

"And?" Jak asked softly, a hint of gathering menace in it.

"Don't use that tone with me, Jakral Konyngrr," Gen snapped. "I did my best, but you try balancing a human and a horse newly made flesh on your back in a stormy sea."

"Oh, Briar Rose," Isyn stopped her hands, folding them in his as Gen burst into sobs, "no one is blaming you." He folded Gen into his arms and leveled an accusing glare on Jak, who raked a hand through his short hair.

"I didn't mean to sound like I blame you, sweet Gen," Jak said, adjusting his hold on Stella and gazing down on her with a dismal expression. "I blame myself. I promised Stella I'd always be with her and I failed her."

"Don't be an idiot mossback," Rhyian drawled, his tone insulting enough that Jak jerked up his head, dark eyes snapping with ire. "You did as Nilly asked you to do. You trusted her to handle the situation, which she did." He put a hand behind Lena's neck, squeezing a little and dropping a kiss to her shoulder. "It hurts us all to stay behind while our friends and lovers go into danger, but the solution isn't to cage them up as if they're fragile and *we* know better."

"Well said," Zeph murmured.

Turning to face Rhyian, Lena gave him a kiss on the lips. "Thank you," she said softly, rewarded by his sweet, slight smile.

"Finish the story, Gen," Astar said wearily.

Gen sniffed and wiped her eyes. "Stella was already weakened from the major magic working and had used even more magic to form the portal. She was about to send Falada through, but—and Jak, you *can* yell at us for this—neither of us thought about potential attack via the portal. As soon as she opened our end, two tentacle monsters came through and attacked."

"Wait, *two?*" Isyn demanded.

Nodding, Gen closed her eyes in remembered helplessness. "There I am, utterly useless in orca form. If I shapeshifted, Nilly and Falada would go into the water, and neither of them could swim well in those forms, not to mention being throttled by the tentacle monsters at the same time. Even if the things drowned, they might have taken them down too. While I was dithering, that's—"

"I doubt you were *dithering*, Gen," Rhyian cut in. "That was an impossible choice."

"Dad can't abide dithering in combat, or otherwise," Gen replied glumly, not at all cheered. "So, I finally shifted into dragon form and tried to catch them, which I did, but those tentacles penetrated even my scales and I couldn't use dragon fire with Falada and Stella all wrapped up, not without help. That's when Zeph came through."

Astar growled low at the reminder. Though Zeph gave him a pointedly questioning look, he said nothing.

"The rest you know," Gen continued after a beat. "Zeph attacked one tentacle monster and got it off Falada."

"Thank you, by the way," Falada put in.

"While I peeled the other off Nilly and managed to toast that one. Lena and Isyn made the portal big enough for me to come through, but the tentacle monster did, too, and..." She shrugged sadly, looking defeated. "Here we are. We've lost the battle and the war."

"Nonsense," Astar bit out, giving Gen a hard look. "You *won* that battle. We're all still here, aren't we?"

"But... Nilly is—" Gen stammered.

"Don't say it," Jak interrupted. "Stella is alive and Astar is right—we survived that battle and we are not giving up now. Stella would say the same."

"You did bring Falada through," Lena pointed out. "That was the objective. We can still move ahead with restoring the alter-realms."

"From what I understand, I should be able to help with that," Falada said, giving Isyn an affectionate look. "I wasn't able to assist with Isyn's rescue, but I can do whatever is needed now."

"Then we take Nilly to the Winter Isles for healing," Astar said.

"Not there," Isyn said decisively, expression pinched. "The folk don't understand human physiology. The palaces at the Isles of Remus would be better. There are resources there."

They were all quiet at that. "That seems like going backwards," Zeph said, putting into words what they all were feeling.

"No," Lena said firmly. "If anything, *we* are going in circles."

Gen threw her an unhappy look. "That does not sound any better."

"Allow me to rephrase," Lena said with a comforting smile. "We're triangulating. We had to travel this path to discover what we now know, including retrieving Falada. Now we take Falada to the Winter Isles."

"And we proceed with the plan," Rhyian added approvingly. "Now that you know how to shut down the alter-realms, and have Falada to assist in safely returning them to their origins, it shouldn't take long."

Lena hoped that would be the case.

"But can you do that without Stella?" Astar asked gravely. He was asking for an assessment from the people he led, she realized, not echoing her own doubts.

Gazing over at Isyn, she found him watching her calmly. He dipped his chin in cool confidence she wished she felt. "We can do it," she said, willing herself to believe it.

"We can do it because we have to," Isyn added, patting Gen in reassurance when she dropped her forehead to his shoulder.

"I can assist there," Falada said, "now that I once again have a physical form."

"All right then," Astar said, getting to his feet, wincing as he did. "A good start would be you three portaling us back to the palace on the Isles of Remus."

~ 30 ~

LENA FOUND IT strange—to say the least—to work with Falada in horse form as the third point of their triangle. Especially since, once she laid hands on Falada's back, she and Isyn balancing the Star there in their symmetrically cupped hands, it was blazingly clear to her magical senses that Falada was anything but a regular horse. Even shapeshifters in horse form didn't feel so magically enormous and scintillatingly powerful, as if the sun had been condensed and stuffed inside a horse hide.

Isyn felt it, too, his brows arcing in surprise. "Why do you keep to this form?" he asked, breathing the question in awe.

"There are reasons," Falada replied, her tone making it clear she declined to explain further. "Don't we have somewhere to be?"

"Right," Isyn muttered and pictured the courtyard where he and Gen had gotten married. They'd all agreed they might as well port directly to that place, as it was little used and familiar to them all.

As soon as the portal was open—Astar, Zeph, and Rhyian in guard positions braced for anything unfriendly to come through—Gen stepped through the portal with a dagger in each hand, making sure all was clear. She reappeared in a moment. "Correct location, nighttime, peaceful," she reported, then went back through. Jak, carrying Stella, followed hard on her heels.

One by one, they all went through, Lena anchoring the portal until only she and Rhyian remained on the beach where their relationship had begun, and then began again. Silversteel sword unsheathed, he raised it to his forehead, saluting her with the enduring promise of the *Elskathorrl*, then extended his free hand to her. Together, they stepped through into the wedding courtyard.

ONCE THEY'D ALL returned to the Isles of Remus, they wasted little time. Astar insisted that everyone who hadn't shapeshifted back to perfect health be seen by a proper healer, to have their injuries checked, disinfected, and bandaged or braced as needed—which included himself. There were no magical healers as they'd had in Erie, nor were any Tala healers living in the Isles, though Gen muttered darkly about changing that as soon as possible. Instead Stella was given into the care of a wizened gentleman who Falada noted had a good bit of faery blood. All Stella needed was to wake up so she could shapeshift to heal herself. Lena tried to tell herself that the "all" wasn't as huge a leap as it seemed.

They also ate a good meal, Isyn rousing the palace to have

one made once Gen reminded him that this was a privilege of being king and they needed to eat before chasing the elusive intelligence. To Lena's surprise, Jak joined them at the table where they were eating in silence, not out of poor spirits—though that was a factor—but with an eye to efficiency.

"Soonest begun, soonest done," Astar had noted before applying himself to his plate.

Jak strode in, filled his plate from the buffet, sat and began eating without a word, bolting his food like the trained soldiers did—without pleasure, fueling the machine they intended to become. They all exchanged glances.

"How is Nilly, Jak?" Astar asked.

Jak glanced up and shook his head, expression set. "She's still out, but Isyn's fae healer seems competent." The tepid word said everything about Stella's chances for recovery.

Beside Lena, Rhyian set a hand on her knee under the table. "I thought you'd want to stay with her," Lena said as gently as she could.

Pinning her with a steely dark glare, Jak chewed and swallowed. "I have a duty to all of you, don't I? To our mission," he added bitterly.

"Under the circumstances," Astar said quietly, "I think you could be excused."

Jak barked out a humorless laugh. "I can't do anything for her. I might as well help kill the thing that did this to her. That would at least serve a useful purpose."

Astar opened his mouth, but Rhyian shook his head minutely. Rising, he went around the table to Jak and put a hand on his shoulder, gripping tighter when Jak tried to shrug him off. "You won't do her any good if you get yourself killed or injured. If you're acting out some self-destructive vengeance, you're helping no one, least of all Stella."

Jak sprang to his feet, evading Rhyian's grip with easy agility. "Don't give me advice!" he spat. "You don't know what—"

"I *do* know," Rhyian interrupted. He shot a finger at Lena. "Salena is the most precious thing in all of creation to me and I'd give my life and more to keep her out of danger, but that's not up to me. Salena needs me alive, not sacrificing myself for her. That's true for Stella, too. When she recovers—"

"*If* she recovers!" Jak shouted.

"Despairing already?" Rhyian sneered. "Are you going to reenact some tragic Dasnarian tale? What happens if Stella wakes up and you've gone and killed your fool self? It makes for a fine ballad but a shitty decision on your part."

Jak's face contorted into a rictus of pain, lips curling into a snarl, and Lena tensed, expecting him to launch himself at Rhyian. From the very relaxed way Rhyian held himself, he was ready for it. Then Jak moved, not in attack, instead embracing Rhyian as a sob escaped him. Rhyian put arms around their friend, steering him away from the table. Zeph and Gen had tears in their eyes just as Lena did, and Astar and Isyn both looked on in pained sympathy as the tough Dasnarian broke down.

BY THE TIME they all gathered in the wedding courtyard, day had dawned and Jak had composed himself. He wasn't his usual cocky self, but he'd lost that glittering self-destructive edge. Lena slid an arm around Rhyian's waist, leaning into him as he put a comforting arm around her in return. "Thank you. You're a good friend to Jak."

Rhyian snorted lightly. "I haven't been in the past, but I'm trying to make up for that. At least I know something about emotional tantrums."

She laughed softly. "Never that."

He turned her in his arms, expression somber as he searched her face with his intensely blue gaze. "I meant what I said," he said in a low, fervent voice. "If I could take your place, I would."

"I know," she replied, sliding her hands over his muscled arms, relishing the feel of him. "I have no death wish, I promise."

"You did before," he said, almost, not quite a question.

"Until you reminded me how much I have to live for," she replied with a smile, rising onto tiptoes to kiss him, which he returned with fevered passion that left her gasping.

"All right, everyone," Astar called. "Let's finish this, once and for all."

Falada had joined them, too, looking sleek and well fed. "I can set the portal destination, but Salena will have to give me the images of the alter-realms."

"Why me?" Lena asked, feeling inadequate all over again. "I'm only a weather magician."

Falada gave a very equine snort. "You harness the power of

the elements and you say *only*. Climb on my back and we'll ride through the worlds, Storm Princess."

Lena took in the tall, unsaddled horse dubiously, then squeaked as Rhyian set his hands on her hips and lifted her aboard with his easy shapeshifter strength. "Go get 'em, love," he said with a lingering caress of her leather-clad thigh. "I'll be here, at your back, always and ever."

She gave him a tremulous smile, then met Isyn's calm green gaze as he approached and took up a position at Falada's head. Behind him, Gen shifted into white saber cat form. They'd debated having her take dragon form, but the saber cat fit through the portals more easily. Isyn could shift her on location, if it became necessary. Zeph was in gríobhth form, tail lashing and curved beak clacking with predatory excitement. Rhyian remained in human form to wield the Silversteel sword and Astar likewise had his broadsword ready. Jak had Stella's Silversteel daggers, a slim and lethal figure in his black fighting leathers.

"To the realm of the lilies and that tower," Astar instructed.

Jak muttered something vicious in Dasnarian under his breath.

Falada *thought* she could ease the remerging of the worlds, as long as Lena guided them and calmed the weather disturbances. Isyn could create the portals out again, but ever-cautious Astar wanted one more test case. The alter-realm where Stella had been trapped in the tower was the other they felt sure had less life to jeopardize, should it all go wrong. It was just as well that Stella didn't have to see the place again.

They wove their magic together, creating the rift in the time and space that the intelligence exploited, and Lena reached for those floating spheres she recalled so well. It didn't require much to find them in that nothing place that had become almost familiar. The sense of the connection with Rhyian went with her, his presence like a vast raven, night-dark wings spread to surround her with love and protection.

Sheltered by him, bolstered by Falada and Isyn, guarded by her steadfast company of friends, Lena searched for and found the lily alter-realm. After that, it was simply a matter of stepping through. Jak went first, having called dibs and looking fierce enough about it that no one, not even Rhyian or Astar, attempted to talk him out of it. Falada stepped through, Lena on her back, and Isyn followed last, holding the portal open.

The place looked oddly peaceful—an endless field of lilies in all colors imaginable stretching in all directions, the air filled with the buzz of bees going from blossom to blossom. Had it been simply a lovely place the intelligence wanted to add to its collection? Lena saw no sign of a tower, but Jak had said that was invisible—and that it had been collapsing when he and Stella made their escape. He was looking at her expectantly. "Get it done, Lena," Jak ground out. "And don't worry if you burn it to the ground. Do it for Stella."

She nodded. So be it. She stretched her mind, taking in the small realm—smaller than either the Winter Isles or the grid world—and encompassing its boundaries. Then, without hesitation, she cut the connection to the intelligence, aware this time of how that energy snapped back, recoiling to its source. Would that alert the intelligence as to their actions? If so, it was too late. In the distance, the vast sense of that entity turned in their direction, a soundless howl echoing in the non-space as it rushed toward them.

The hurtling realm took them with it, but this time they were prepared, with Rhyian's buffering wings and Falada's steady presence in place of Stella's magic net. It worked, and rather than a booming crash and fiery re-entry, the field of lilies settled into place with a sigh. Color rippled over the sky, followed by a great wind as atmospheres recombined. Thunder boomed as the different air masses collided, clouds boiling from nowhere. Lightning forked to the ground, followed by a startling and immediate *crack!*

"This part is up to you," Falada said pointedly.

Oh, right. Lena used her storm senses in a more familiar way, reaching into the atmospheric disturbance, defusing the huge static potential. As she directed the energy of the building storm in various directions—mostly away from each other, for expedience—she sensed the expanse of the world out there. It would be fascinating to explore this place, an entire world of different people, ecologies, and life forms.

"Not today," Falada said, intruding on her thoughts, and proving the fae horse could read them.

No, of course not today, but maybe someday. She opened her eyes to a calming landscape, the field of lilies no longer waving like a storm-tossed sea. This world would have unsettled weather for a while, but it would equilibrate as healthy ecologies left to themselves always would. "We can go back through," she told Astar, then looked behind him for Rhyian. He bowed slightly, smiling in admiration.

"That was almost too easy," Jak complained. "I—"

"You know better," Astar snapped, cutting him off. "Never wish for action."

"I'm not." Jak produced a grin, clearly forced. "I just hoped to have a chance at the intelligence."

"You'll get it," Rhyian predicted darkly.

"Isyn, Lena, Falada," Astar said, taking the lead, "can we portal directly to the Winter Isles now? Unless you need to rest first."

Lena exchanged shrugs with Isyn even as Falada snorted equine disgust at the suggestion. "We're good and we have the Star. We can do that."

"All right," Astar declared. "Look lively. Don't be complacent. Jak—you get to be the scout."

As they'd agreed during planning, Lena pictured the spot on the ice where they'd entered the Winter Isles on their previous visit. There was no need to discuss with the folk this time and frankly Lena preferred not to have them as an audience. The peace of the distant spot on the ice would be ideal for the concentration needed.

But peace wasn't to be had. When Falada carried her through the portal, they emerged into chaos.

~ 31 ~

Rhy watched the flip of Falada's tail vanish into nothingness, then exchanged a nod with Isyn who would naturally be the last through. "See you on the other side."

Isyn smiled. "If nothing else, this is good work we're doing."

Yes, it was. And Rhy found himself somewhat bemused to be that person. A live hero, after all. The moment he stepped through the portal, he skidded on something slick, and a tentacle shot around him, shocking all thoughts from his mind. Animal instinct kicked in, spinning his body into a whirl of Silversteel and dagger, cutting the tentacles away as fast as they hit him, adding to the pile of pieces on the ice.

He searched for any sight of Salena. She was still astride Falada, who fought with impressive ferocity, kicking out with front and back hooves. Salena had a dagger in each hand, slicing at the tentacles that flailed at her—and she was bleeding from new lacerations.

Fighting his way toward her, Rhy tried to size up the situation. There looked to be three tentacle monsters arrayed between Jak and everyone else. They must've come through the portal right after Jak, and he was doing his best from his side, but he was one man and separated from the rest of the group. Zeph and Gen, still in gríobhth and saber cat form, each fought a monster, while Astar was taking on the third. The odds weren't good at all. Moranu, how they could use Stella's help right then.

A surprised shout behind Rhy signaled that Isyn had come through. Rhy risked a glance behind him. "Can we get back through? Or toss these things in?"

Grimly, Isyn shook his head. "Dropped it. Need the girls to open another."

Mentally, Rhy calculated what it would take to get Isyn to the embattled Salena and Falada—and he didn't see it happening. Unless they did something, however, they were going down in this last ignominious ambush.

A whooshing sound echoed through the air, one Rhy knew intimately. It was the cupping and releasing of great wings in the dense, cold air. His own raven's wings made that sound, though nothing on this scale. Jerking his head back, he spotted the bronze form of Kiraka arrowing toward them.

Only, there was no way it was Kiraka, not in this place. It was the intelligence—and here its dragon fire would burn very well. And kill them all.

"Incoming!" Rhy shouted, then spun to Isyn. "Get to Gen, then Astar. Trigger dragon form in both."

"Astar?" Isyn echoed. Rhy realized Isyn might not know Astar had attained dragon form once before. Before he could explain, Isyn shook it away as unnecessary and began running toward Gen, calling her name.

Zeph took to the air with a defiant screech, pumping her

great wings to gain altitude to meet the intelligence head on. The false dragon billowed flame, sending Zeph tumbling back, smoke flowing in trails from her wings. Astar roared, the enraged grizzly's voice echoing across the ice from the man's throat. If he hadn't been in an alter-realm, he'd have shapeshifted already.

Then a white dragon billowed into being, flinging herself into the sky and thrusting herself between the false dragon and Zeph, giving the faltering gríobhth time to recover. Isyn was trying to get to Astar, but the tentacle monster had turned on the ivory-haired mage now that Gen wasn't battling it, while the one Zeph had been attacking was free to advance on Salena and Falada. With a ripping sound, a portal opened above them, raining monkey-lizards, just to make this fight that much more miserable.

Above dragons screamed, flames ripping through the sky in infernal roars. Rhy thought about his father's advice—so often offered to unwilling ears and speaking loudly to him now in this dire predicament. They also had Stella's directive: keep their mission goals firmly in mind. The tentacle monsters, as devastating as they might be, were the sideshow, the distraction. The real battle was against the intelligence. Kill it and the other creatures would lose impetus.

They needed to get Astar in the sky and Salena to use her magic against the false dragon.

He ran for Falada, using his shapeshifter speed and agility to leap into the air over the writhing tentacles to land on Falada's back behind Salena. Both woman and horse whuffed in surprise, but he hung on, wrapping an arm tightly around

Salena's waist. "To Isyn, then to Astar!" he urged Falada, hoping her faery magic would lend her the strength needed to carry both of them and Isyn. The fae horse determinedly forged her way to Isyn, Rhy doing his best to slice away the interfering tentacles.

Salena was breathing hard, leaning back against him, her heart thundering. "Too many," she panted. "I can't—"

"Then don't," he said in her ear, pressing a kiss to her cheek. "Let me handle this, love. You need to get up there."

"Up there?" she echoed, craning her neck back to see the vicious aerial battle being waged above. "But—"

"Magic," he urged. "Use the Star. Attack the intelligence like you did before."

"I'll need your help."

"You have it, love. Always and ever."

RIDING A HORSE bareback through a battle with monsters was not conducive to the meditative trance Lena preferred for maximum magic use. She ached and stung everywhere, the exhaustion from blood loss pulling at her. To think she'd been looking forward to the peace of an empty frozen sea. It had been difficult, during the pitched battle, to fend off the equally will-sapping memories of feeling exactly this way before, riding on Falada's back was far too much like riding Zeph through the sky, her blood and life energy slowly dripping away.

But Rhyian was with her this time, holding her in place as they fought their way toward Isyn. "Use the Star. Focus on the intelligence," he chanted in her ear. "That's your only job, love. Trust us do the rest."

She tried, she really did, pulling her magic around her and holding the Star in her cupped palms, her daggers sheathed. Tentacles lashed at her, but Rhyian fended them off, moving in a blur of speed she hadn't known he possessed. They reached Isyn, Rhyian holding out his sword arm as Falada leapt close. Isyn grabbed Rhyian's forearm, using the leverage to swing on behind. Lena prayed Falada could handle the strain. The fae horse indeed leapt away, clearing the tentacles that dragged at her and galloping in a wide circle to escape them.

"Where's Jak?" Isyn shouted.

"Lost sight of him a while ago," Rhyian answered grimly. Falada completed the circle and closed in on Astar. "You know what to do," he told Isyn as they came in at top speed. Lena didn't hear Isyn's answer, but he leapt off Falada's back, Astar catching him to break his high-speed fall.

Falada and Rhyian fought to clear a space while Isyn's magic burst out in a spray of green. The sudden appearance of Astar in dragon form, as golden as his hair, knocked them aside. Then Astar was in the air, surging up to join the battle.

"Isyn!" Rhyian yelled. "To us!" Once again Isyn leapt onto Falada's back, joining them as the fae horse raced away from the tentacle beasts. "How's it coming, love? We need you."

"Jak," she gasped out.

"You worry about the intelligence," Rhy gritted. "Jak would agree. Keep those mission goals firmly in mind."

He was right, but that didn't help. Still, Lena focused on
the Star, trying to find that bubble of space around the Winter
Isles that would lift her consciousness out of her body and into
that other realm where the intelligence drew its strength.
Falada skidded to a stop well away from the tentacle monsters,
which helped. Isyn's and Falada's magic joined hers, focusing
through the Star, but it wasn't quite enough, not with their
magic already drained. They should've been able to face this
battle with their reserves and health fully restored. And with
Stella helping.

But that wasn't to be. And if she failed now, they would fail
forever. Still, she needed more. "Rhyian, help me." She tucked
the Star inside the hand he had clasped firmly around her
waist.

"I can't—"

"You can." And she reached through the connection between them and pulled him into the Star, which blazed up in
brilliant recognition.

RHY'S MIND LIT up in a blaze, the Star like a sun in his consciousness, Salena the pale, full moon glistening with like
radiance. Others were there in that topaz matrix, too—Astar,
shining with nobility, dark Stella, along with Amelia, their
mother, and Rhy's. Andromeda was like a galaxy in the
distance. And there was the first Salena and his Salena, even

High Queen Ursula, all connected through the Star.

His raven First Form seemed to take new life and flight, lifting Salena up, carrying her into the sky along with the bolstering magics belonging to Isyn and Falada. Incorporeal, burgeoning with magic that seemed be exploding to greater and more intense levels, they arrowed into the intelligence powering the false dragon.

As before when they chased the intelligence through non-space, Lena sank her powerfully disruptive storm magic into the essence of that being, drawing on Isyn's magery, on Falada's fae power, and on the magic flowing through Rhy. Magic that had never been in him before now flowed with all the power of Moranu and the night. Black as deepest shadows, it rolled through and out of him—and into Salena. With perfect trust and the commitment of his vow, he gave her everything of himself.

The intelligence shrieked, echoed by the roaring of dragons in the sky in the outer world. Rhy kept his focus on Salena, giving her his wings and talons. The intelligence shriveled under their combined assault—from within and from without—and the roars dimly reaching his external ears escalated. The intelligence tried to flee, but somehow Salena had it surrounded. The barriers around the Winter Isles alter-realm belonged to her now, and she had the intelligence in a cage it couldn't escape, physically or metaphysically. Trapped in an alter-realm, as Stella had foretold.

Beneath his physical body, Falada staggered at the same moment a booming crash echoed through both realities. The false dragon had crashed into the ice, pursued by the others, and the intelligence abandoned that body, allowing it to dissolve as it attempted to flee.

"Oh no you will not!" Salena's mental shout punctuated the surge of power from her. She drilled the entity with lighting and turbulence, wrenching it apart and scattering it to the winds.

With a last howl, the intelligence dissipated. And was gone, drifting on the winds of non-space like ash from an inferno.

A surge of triumph from Salena, and then she faltered, clutching at him. *"Rhyian..."* Salena fainted, the loss of consciousness breaking their melded magics and flinging him into the harsh physical world, even as Falada collapsed under him.

Rhy managed to leap clear and carry the now unconscious Salena with him. Isyn went down with Falada, but staggered free at the last moment. "Problem," Isyn called to him, pointing with his sword. The three tentacle monsters were heading their way. Wonderful.

"I was hoping the intelligence dying would solve that problem," Rhy snarled, laying Salena on the ice beside Falada. Whipping off his fur-lined cloak, he covered her with it, hoping to keep her warm. She was covered in blood, her skin pale as death where it wasn't spattered in crimson. Rhy scanned for the others, hoping to call in reinforcements. It looked like one dragon had gone through the ice, as it was nowhere in sight, the other lay in a crumpled, smoking heap. Rhy couldn't tell if it was Astar or Gen. The way the massive impact had sent up a cloud of snow and ice, everything was coated in white. No sign of Zeph, nor of Jak.

It was looking more like they'd end up dead heroes after all. Victorious, but dead. Jak would get his epic tragic ballad. And none of them would be around to hear it.

Rhy gauged the rapid approach of the tentacle monsters, burbling toward them like boiling black masses over the ice, monkey-lizards raining through the still-open rift, and exchanged a wry look with Isyn. Two men armed with only slim swords, bloodied and battered—Rhy had no doubt he looked as wretched as Isyn did—facing nearly unbeatable monsters, all their allies dead or incapacitated. As Rhy had long suspected, it wasn't in the least romantic. "I feel like we need some clever and brave last words here," Rhy noted.

"You're the clever one," Isyn replied. "The good news is, no one will ever know what we did or didn't say. Maybe the poets will think up something good."

"A bright spot," Rhy acknowledged.

"I'm just seriously pissed that, after everything, it's come to this." Isyn looked off to the distant settlement. "The folk will die, just not as soon as we will."

"Gobbled up by tentacle monsters," Rhy agreed, then sighed as a new onslaught of monkey-lizards poured through the rift nearby. "Even better. The rifts didn't close with the intelligence's destruction either. Now we can choose the manner of our grisly, meaningless deaths."

"Maybe the folk can eat the monkey-lizards," Isyn suggested.

The dark humor did nothing to defray Rhy's despair at the thought that he'd failed Salena in the end. If he knew she'd live, he could face certain death more easily. But without

Stella, they couldn't—

"Wait," he said, almost more for himself, the inspiration coming in such a rush that he had to slow it down to even begin to understand. "Do you have enough magic left to make a portal?"

Isyn shook his head grimly. "Not a useful one. I could maybe stabilize that existing rift long enough for one person to get through, but I can't set the destination." He gazed off over the ice at the unmoving forms of their crashed companions. "I wouldn't leave Gendra anyway. I'd rather die here with her than live without her."

"Noble and pointless," Rhy retorted, shocking the other man. Rhy pointed his sword at the ivory-haired mage. "I am not reporting those as your last words."

"You mean to escape?" Isyn asked in disbelief. Only someone who hadn't known Rhy for very long would be that surprised by the notion, not that Rhy had any intention of abandoning them all. Then realization dawned on Isyn's face as he watched Rhy go to Salena. "Oh, you mean to put Salena through. Good idea. She might live—though you should go with her."

"Not that either." Rhy touched Salena's cheek. "This better work, love," he told her, then faced Isyn with the Star in his hand. "We'll use this. You stabilize that rift. I'll handle the rest."

"And who will handle yon approaching ravenous monsters?" Isyn asked, but he focused on the rift. "Done. But I don't know where it goes, except to monkey-lizard land."

"Hopefully that won't matter and this won't take that

long." Rhy focused on the Star, the illumination and shadows twined within it, and reached with his mind along the lines of blood, sorting through the people he'd sensed in that matrix earlier.

A bright and familiar mind responded, muzzy with sleep. *Wake up,* he told her, and pushed her to shapeshift. She took over, healing herself as she returned to human form, greeting him with welcome, relief, worry, and lots of questions.

No time. Rhy pulled as hard as he could, using those buffering mental wings…

And Stella, in jaguar form, leapt through the rift.

~ 32 ~

L ENA AWOKE COLD, sticky with old blood, but feeling remarkably well for a dead person. She must be dead, because Stella smiled down at her. "Feeling up to some work? I hit you with a lot of healing power all at once, so you may be disoriented, but we need you."

"How are you here?" Lena asked. "Or am I there?"

"Rhy used the Star to bring me through the rift. Long story," she added when Lena opened her mouth, pulling her to a sitting position. "And no time right now. We have people to save."

Lena looked wildly around, a wave of relief making her sag when she spotted Rhyian, not far away, black hair flying as he whirled through a rain of monkey-lizards, Silversteel sword flashing. He paused momentarily, meeting her gaze, awareness zinging between them. He saluted her with the blade in the *Elskathorrl*, flashing a grin, then turned back to his task.

"Close that rift," Stella instructed her, handing her the Star of Annfwn, then lacing her delicate fingers with Lena's so the Star was cupped between them. "I have blasting to do."

As instructed—no time to be confused—Lena focused on the rift the intelligence had opened, using her magic and the

Star to seal it up again. This had fortunately begun to feel like a habitual task. As she worked, she felt Stella's magic focusing outward, and a tentacle monster went up in a blast of purple smoke. Several smoldering piles closer to them showed these weren't the first she'd blasted.

"Well done," Stella told her as the rifts closed. "Falada, we're ready for you!"

The white fae horse trotted up with Isyn on her back, both were caked with dried blood and other gore, but otherwise looked sprightly. Stella stood, pulling Lena inexorably to her feet. "What are we doing now?" Lena asked as Stella set the Star on Falada's back, Isyn putting his fingers around on his side.

"Returning the Winter Isles to its true home," Stella replied gravely.

"Surely we can do that later," Lena protested. "Jak! We lost sight of him during the fighting. And the others, they—"

"Believe me, I know," Stella cut through, eyes flashing with anger and grief. "But if I stand a chance of healing everyone, I need this to be not an alter-realm. Rhy gave us the order of actions and they make sense. Time is not our friend. Please, Lena…" Stella's eyes filled with tears.

Right. "Let's do this then." Lena worked fast, faster than she ever had before. Their friends and beloveds needed them. Feeling as if she flung a net around the Winter Isles alter-realm, Lena encompassed the entirety of it with a thought. It floated free now, no longer tethered to anything with the intelligence gone. And it *was* truly gone—its absence a vast nothingness Lena found both welcome and oddly poignant. Swiftly, Lena cut away the gossamer threads holding the alter-realm separate, aware of how Falada took it from her, settling the Winter Isles into a world lush and green with summer.

Expecting the atmospheric disturbance this time, Lena disbursed the energy immediately, warming the nearby layers of cold at the boundaries so the contrast would be less harsh. Distant cracks, however, warned of the ice breaking. "We don't have long," Lena warned them.

"Rhy!" Stella called. She stretched and became a horse, Isyn leaping aboard as she galloped across the expanse, Falada leading the way. Rhyian, also now a horse, skidded up to Lena, whinnying, and she climbed aboard.

They raced off over the ice, the distant crackling spurring them on. The folk would have a rapid transition to summer. Feeling Rhyian's horse body surging beneath her reminded her viscerally of those long ago and carefree days when she'd ridden him like this, when their greatest concerns had been beach picnics, when their futures had seemed so far away. She was profoundly grateful that Rhyian had survived that last battle. They were together and always would be.

But the others... If they couldn't save Astar, Zeph, Gen, and Jak, then Lena and Rhyian would become the only happy couple left, Stella and Isyn facing a lifetime of mourning.

They couldn't let it happen.

To her surprise, Stella and Falada veered off toward the dragons, carrying Isyn along, while Rhyian angled toward the piles of tentacles littering the ice. Then she understood. They were looking for Jak, while Stella—selfless till the end—went to heal the ones they knew they could find. Rhyian slid to a hoof-clattering stop, waited for her to dismount, then shifted directly into wolf form. She was briefly disappointed that he hadn't taken human form. She wanted to kiss him, to hold onto him for just a moment, and to ask some of her hundreds of questions, but she understood. His wolf nose would be best for sniffing out Jak.

She helped as best she could with the grisly task, using her daggers to stab and clear away the severed tentacles—which retained some of their sting, even in death—afraid of what she might find beneath. With every glistening piled dislodged, she held her breath, terrified of finding Jak's mangled form beneath.

Another reason for Stella to not be doing this. Rhyian had planned well.

He barked, a whuffing, excited wolfish yip, and Lena raced over to where he pawed at a mound, jaws full of dangling tentacles. Her heart thundered with dread. If Jak was dead, perhaps better to let his body disappear into the thawing sea than to have Stella face what likely had been a truly terrible death. Giving up the daggers, Lena used her hands to claw at the tentacles.

In the distance, a triumphant shout went up. Someone had been saved, but who? Rhyian lifted his muzzle, sniffing the air. "Astar," he said immediately upon shifting back to human form. He joined her in cutting away the tentacles, Rhyian using his greater strength and speed to dislocate their heavy masses, now clearly coiled around a cylindrical shape that had to be Jak.

"Is he...?" Lena couldn't finish.

"I don't know," Rhyian answered. "I could barely sniff him out under all of this. The blood smells fresh, at least."

She couldn't bear this, the hope almost worse than the certain grief. Finally they got him unwound, Jak a slim and bloodied figure, skin ash-gray from blood loss, suffocation, and cold. With shaking fingers, she pressed against his pulse point, her own hands too numb to feel much. She met Rhyian's gaze bleakly.

This was too much like when Jak had nearly frozen before, when they thought they hadn't saved him, when they'd been prepared to burn his body until Stella awoke and—despite their protests and fears that she'd lost her mind—had managed to revive him. Rhyian returned her look, a question in his deep blue eyes. "Which should we do—bring her to him, or take Jak to her?" she asked.

Rhyian didn't ask if Jak was dead. By the somber lines of his face, he knew she thought the worst, but he nodded. "Let's take him to her, love."

Another shout of joy went up from the other group, the sound heartening, but also heart-breaking as Lena cradled Jak's limp form in her arms, draping him over Rhyian's equine back as he knelt low in horse form. They wouldn't know who else had been saved until they got there, and that meant they might have lost two of their number. Was it too much to want them all to make it?

She climbed up behind, scooting close enough to wedge her knees under Jak's boneless body—not corpse—and balanced herself. "Ready," she told Rhyian.

He started up slowly, allowing her time to adjust to keeping both herself and Jak in place, then gradually picked up speed. Lena would've urged Rhyian to go faster, but she knew he wouldn't risk her falling off. She kept her gaze trained on the distant group, though they were too far away for her to see much. Astar had dropped dragon form, his bulk no longer visible. No sign of Gen, unless she'd dropped dragon form also, and Zeph's gríobhth form was relatively small from this distance. Much as Lena longed for another shout of joy, there wasn't one.

Would it be two deaths then? Jak and either Zeph or Gen. She should celebrate that it wasn't more, but she couldn't.

She spotted a bird winging to meet them, the nighthawk transforming into Stella with such speed that she slipped on the ice and nearly fell from the momentum. Her flying black hair settled around her, silver eyes wild with hope and dread as she reached up. "Is he…"

"I don't know," Lena answered, scrambling down and helping Stella slide Jak off Rhyian's back as he obligingly knelt. "He's cold," she offered, hoping that would explain everything, and Stella nodded running her hands over Jak, her expression inscrutable.

Rhyian, back in human form, knelt beside Lena, putting his arm around her and she leaned into the contact, even though she wasn't the one who needed support. Stella gave no hint in word or gesture, setting the Star over Jak's heart, bright light flaring from it. Lena desperately wanted to ask about the others—would Stella have left them if she hadn't determined if the last could be saved or was lost forever? Lena doubted it, and the wait to find out if there was any life left in Jak was excruciating, but she didn't dare interrupt Stella's concentration. Lena took a deep breath, hearing the ragged edge as it shuddered out of her. Rhyian pressed a kiss to her temple, reassuring and bolstering.

She became aware of the sounds of hooves on ice, looking past Stella's bent form to see three horses coming their way. Looking at them head on, she couldn't make out if they had riders. Quickly running the math in her head, she realized the three horses had to include Zeph and Gen, because Isyn and Astar didn't have horse forms. At the same moment she let out a relieved breath, the release like water draining from her body, Rhyian said, very quietly in her ear, "All five are there, love. Astar and Isyn are riding Zeph and Gen, Falada unencumbered."

Squeezing his hand in gratitude for his long sight, she focused her hope on Jak. He didn't look any better. In truth, he looked more like a corpse than ever, his skin blue with chill and skin sunken. At what point should they peel Stella away? She began to regret that she and Rhyian had pulled Jak out from those tentacles. It might've been kinder if Stella had never seen him this way, better if she wasn't draining herself to nothing trying to save him, all for naught.

Lena drew in a breath to say something—she wasn't sure what, but something compassionate, suggesting that it was enough—when Stella spoke. "Don't give up on him yet, Lena." She looked up, eyes fulminous silver. "I need your magic, both of you."

"I wouldn't refuse you or Jak," Rhyian replied, taken aback. "Anything you need, but I don't have magic."

Stella pinned him with a ferocious glare. "This is not the time for your self-delusion, Rhy. You woke me up, pushed me to shapeshift back to health, then used the Star to pull me through the portal. That's magic, dear cousin of mine."

Lena gaped at Rhyian. "Is that what happened?"

He shook his head, then nodded. "I don't know how."

"Magic is intuitive. It finds us when it wants to, rather than the reverse," Stella said more gently. "However, right now, I need your magic, so no doubts allowed." When Lena started to untangle her fingers from Rhyian's, Stella narrowed her gaze. "No, keep your hands together. That bond between you will help."

So, they laid their interlaced fingers over the Star with Stella's. For what felt like an eternity, nothing happened. Then Lena felt Rhyian's magic stir. With a start of amazement, she realized she'd always felt it in him, the coiled darkness, twining in the shadows, seductively attractive. It blended with hers seamlessly, further revealing how she'd always sensed it in him without knowing what it was. Their magic, intertwined as their hands, their love, and their fates, flowed into and through the Star, Stella's rusty black hair lifting in the invisible torrent of magic, topaz gold light reflecting on her face as her eyes shone with silver moonlight. It seemed others were present in that richly magical interface—Queen Andromeda and the first Salena.

Immersed in the triad of their magic, Lena sensed, rather than saw or heard, the others arrive and form a loose, silent circle around them. In their fraught vigil, Lena recognized her own agonizing hope and—as the long minutes drug on—their quiet despair.

And yet, Stella didn't flag, as intent on her goal as ever, as if she could fight death itself to drag Jak back from Glorianna's arms. This time Lena didn't consider trying to coax Stella away. As long as Stella wanted to keep trying, Lena would give over every last bit of the magic she possessed.

The sudden gasp startled her, Jak coughing out a great choking sound, convulsing before falling back in a rictus. "Stay with me," Stella barked out. Though Lena wasn't sure if it was directed at her and Rhyian, or Jak, she firmed her grip on the Star.

Jak flung his head back, the cords of his throat strained as he let out a long scream of agony that brought tears to Lena's eyes. "It's all right. Clearly the bastard is too tough to kill," Rhyian murmured, to her or to Jak, Lena didn't know, but she took comfort in Rhyian's cool steadiness. His sardonic detachment served him well in this scenario.

Then color flooded Jak's complexion and his body gradually relaxed. Opening his eyes, he gazed up at Stella bending over him, wonder in his expression. Still weak, he lifted a hand to her cheek, smiling when she rubbed against his fingers, tears flowing freely. "Fuck me," he breathed. "Cheating death a third time has *got* to be worth an epic ballad."

~ 33 ~

THEY TRAVELED BACK to the Isles of Remus, arriving in the wedding courtyard, the cool misty morning air feeling quite balmy after the frigid temperatures of the Winter Isles. Though at the rate the sea had been thawing there, they'd be far warmer soon. Salena seemed to think the weather would balance out all right and she would know. Rhy trusted her implicitly.

Except when she insisted on repatriating the remaining alter-realms immediately. "Are you out of your mind?" he snarled at her. "You're exhausted. Stella nearly killed herself snatching Jak back from Glorianna's arms and—"

"Glorianna held on like the jealous bitch she is, too," Jak put in wearily, barely able to stay on his feet even with his arms slung around Astar and Isyn. "Good thing Moranu and Danu double-teamed her rose-pink ass," he added, winking at Stella, who only shook her head at him in exasperation. She was purely happy though, as they all were, celebrating the miracle that was all nine of them returning alive, with the intelligence defeated and disaster averted.

"Can't we take a day to be glad we survived, love?" Rhy asked Salena, changing his tone to coaxing. "Rest, eat something, wash the blood off." He added that last because, although Salena had been completely healed, her fighting leathers had been sliced nearly to ribbons, and blood still smeared her face, hands and clothing, except where it had caked on thick enough to be crumbling off in chunks. The sight of it filled his animal self with protective fury, even though his human mind knew the immediate danger was over. Unless Salena pursued this idea. "I know you don't want to face that forest realm again right now," he added.

Salena put a hand on his chest, right over his heart, which wasn't playing fair at all. "Now or tomorrow, it will be just as difficult. I'd rather get this done with. Besides, those alter-realms were free-floating without the intelligence to hold them and give them the magical energy to exist on their own as fragments. If we delay, we could be dooming the creatures in those realms."

Rhy didn't much care if all those creatures spun off into non-space, but Salena did. She would always be the one with the soft heart—and good thing for him that she was, as likely no one else would've given him a second chance. He blew out a breath, then covered her hand with his. "I'm coming with you, to guard your back."

She smiled, radiant with relief and love. "I expect nothing less." Her grin widened, twinkling with mischief. "You can help with the magic, too."

IT TOOK HOURS, but Salena, Isyn, Rhyian, and Falada closed down the various alter-realms one by one, returning them to their origins. It boggled Rhy's mind at how many there were that they'd never visited, and that there were worlds upon worlds out there that had been ripped asunder by the intelligence.

While they worked, the others rested, Stella able to heal Jak further once she recovered some. They learned the rest of the story during short breaks between restoring worlds. Gen had been the dragon to go through the ice, with enough force that she'd been knocked unconscious. Fortunately, she woke sometime afterward, having subconsciously shapeshifted to orca form in the familiar water. Isyn had been able to contact her mind and remind her of her humanity, coaxing her to surface and shapeshift back.

Zeph had been in terrible shape, burnt nearly to a crisp. Isyn had used his magery to force Astar out of his damaged dragon form to human so Stella could heal him. He'd then been able to threaten and cajole Zeph into shapeshifting to heal herself.

"Thus the power of love is what saved all of us," Gen pronounced somberly, giving them stern looks when some of them made scoffing sounds. Even Falada, happily grazing on the lush grass during their rest period, snorted sardonically. "You know I'm right," Gen insisted. "Without the power of true love, each of us would've faced a death—or worse—that we couldn't have come back from."

Rhy didn't mind acknowledging the truth of her words. He nestled Salena closer to his side, beyond grateful to have her there. "You're right, Gen. Without Salena's love, I'd be half-alive at best."

Salena smiled up at him, soft and sweetly sensual, her eyes lambent in the candlelight. They'd spent all day restoring the worlds, and Isyn had summoned servants to bring torches and lanterns to the courtyard so they could finish the job. "One world left," she murmured.

"The intelligence's home alter-realm," Stella replied quietly, pursing her lips. "Will it still look like Nahanau, I wonder?"

"I say no," Salena answered.

"Care to put coin on that?" Jak inquired with lively interest. He dug out a handful of gold coins, tossing them in the air and catching them all neatly again, one-handed.

"How do you even have all of that on you?" Zeph demanded.

"I have my ways," Jak answered, winking at her.

"Jak possesses his own form of sorcery" Astar agreed ruefully. "I, however, will not take that bet."

"Already a wise king," Gen teased.

"Or not," Astar cautioned, glancing at Zeph practically draped over his lap. He threaded his fingers through her shining black hair, combing it away from her forehead, and she smiled with lazy, feline pleasure. "Her Majesty may wish to find another heir."

"As if Auntie Essla could find anyone better suited," Rhy

scoffed. "You're a hero of the realm now. She's not going to cut off your tail."

"We can't be acknowledged as heroes, though," Astar replied. "Remember, our mission was secret. Besides, Rhy, you are also the high queen's nephew, you realize, and have an equal claim to the high throne. Has that never once occurred to you?"

It frankly hadn't. Rhy wasn't even bothered by Salena's giggle at his consternation. He couldn't quite seem to find his footing. "That's absurd," he said faintly. "I'm Tala."

"Why do you think everyone always rode you so hard to measure up, Rhy?" Stella asked with arched brows. "They all knew you were the backup heir, if something happened to Willy."

"What about *you*?" he shot back. "You have the same claim or better. Her Majesty High Queen Nilly—has quite the ring to it."

"No, thank you," she replied swiftly, exchanging a long look with Jak. "Can you imagine a high queen who can't abide court?"

Jak picked up her hand and kissed her fingertips. "It would cut out a lot of the talking and posturing. Maybe you should do it and then I can be the next half-Dasnarian prince consort. Imagine the bribes I could garner selling opportunities for a rare audience with the reclusive high queen. I could be a rich man."

"If I were high queen and you were prince consort, you wouldn't need coin," she retorted on a giggle.

"What's the fun in that, though?" he countered, stealing a

kiss.

"We'll find out when we get back," Salena said in her logical way, "and that won't happen until we deal with this final alter-realm." She pushed to her feet, Rhy uncoiling to assist her. "Who all is coming along?"

THEY ALL DID, even Jak—despite Stella's protests that he was weak still—declaring that he wasn't going to miss out on the end game. When Rhy stepped through the portal at Salena's side, the Silversteel sword at the ready, he gazed about in shock. Gone was false Nahanau. Instead, there seemed to be nothing but a dusty, windswept landscape, broken only by a few stunted, scraggly shapes that might once have been mighty trees. A starry sky arced overhead, though a weak sun also shone, the air nearly too thin to breathe.

"What is this place?" he whispered.

Salena's eyes were grave and full of sorrow. "A dead world," she answered, raising her voice for everyone to hear as Isyn stepped through, the last through the portal. "There is nothing alive anywhere here," she added. "It's as if it was all... stripped away."

"A barren alter-realm," Zeph echoed with a frown.

"A barren world," Salena corrected. "For it is an entire world, not a fragment. One that's died." She sounded sorrowful, grieving for the loss of an ecology as only she could. Rhy set a hand on her lower back, caressing her, and she gave him a grateful smile.

"But this is where the false Nahanau was?" Astar asked, studying the bleak landscape with narrowed eyes.

"Yes," Stella answered. "Lena is right that this is a full world, but the Nahanau landscape was superimposed over it somehow. I can feel the magical echo of it."

"Practice," Salena murmured, and Stella nodded crisply.

"This is where it started, where the intelligence began to build its skills," she said.

"Creating worlds and then stealing pieces of other ones, because it didn't have one of its own," Gen added, sounding sad.

"Tell me you're not feeling sorry for it," Jak said with a snort.

Isyn raised a brow. "It's possible to regret the forces that created a warped mind while still recognizing that it was an enemy."

"So we'll never know more than this?" Rhy asked, giving Isyn a nod for that wisdom. Something to remember.

"We could look in that tower," Stella said, then pointed when they all looked at her in confusion. "Can't you see it?"

"Great," Jak groaned. "*Another* invisible tower. I am not climbing this one."

Stella gave him a kiss. "One was plenty."

He tugged her back for a longer, lingering kiss, then grinned. "I take it back. I'd climb any tower, visible or otherwise for you."

"Hopefully this one has a door and a staircase," Salena said, "because my curiosity is stronger than my invisible-tower climbing skills. Lead the way, Nilly."

Rhy wasn't the only one on guard for danger, despite Salena's assurances that they were alone in this world. Jak held Stella's hand, but his other was occupied with a spinning blade. It felt strange to be walking over the dusty soil, the only sound their footsteps and the ever-present wind, no scents to speak of. And he still didn't see a tower.

Falada trotted forward. "I can dispense with this invisibility spell. It's one I recognize." She snorted, pawed the ground, and abruptly a tower appeared, seemingly formed of the same stone as the ground.

Stella craned her neck, gazing up, then exchanged glances with Jak. "It looks the same."

He lifted a shoulder and let it fall. "If you say so."

"Fortunately, there's a door for Lena," Astar noted with a grin, striding up to it. He studied the smooth surface.

Zeph, joining him, extended a claw from one hand and snicked it into a groove. The door swung outwards. "Whoever these people were," she said, "they had different hands."

Gen peered at the groove. "Or tentacles."

"Oh," Isyn breathed. "Good point."

Inside, a ramp spiraled upward, rather than the expected stairs. "I'll take the lead," Astar declared, drawing his broadsword, "just in case. Rhy—rearguard?"

Rhy nodded, even as Salena rolled her eyes. "There's nothing alive here."

"That doesn't mean there aren't magical traps," Stella pointed out, "which means I should go first."

"Now, wait a moment—" Jak began, but Astar held up a hand to stop him, then extended it to Stella.

"Hand in hand, then, Nilly?"

She beamed at him and took his hand, the Star in her other, shining like a beacon. They climbed the ramp, only Falada staying behind, wryly commenting that she wasn't fond of heights.

"It's creepy," Salena commented, weaving her fingers with Rhy's free hand. "Even the grid world didn't feel this dead."

"How could only one entity have survived when nothing else did?" Rhy wondered.

"I think…" Salena's voice trailed off as she gazed around at the windowless walls. They were nearing the top. "Maybe the intelligence wasn't supposed to be able to survive."

"And this was a prison," Rhy finished for her. "A life sentence."

She nodded. "Exactly."

The tower's single room was round, taking up the entire top of the tower. Books and scrolls of all types ringed the room, along with scrying bowls and other various implements that Rhy recognized as tools of sorcery. A few windows looked out on the empty landscape in all directions.

"This is like the room the intelligence kept me in," Stella told them all in a voice that only slightly wobbled, "minus the sorcerous tools."

"And minus the intelligence," Jak added grimly.

"That's a good thing, right?" Gen asked, drifting around and examining things as they caught her eye.

"It would be nice to have answers," Salena observed, joining her and squinting at a shelf of books, her hands folded behind her back. By mutual accord they weren't touching anything. "Some of these languages are unlike anything I've ever seen."

Isyn peered past her. "Worlds upon worlds."

"And that's only the stuff that's written down," Rhy said, knowing that many traditions were oral, and Salena threw him a thoughtful glance.

"Scrying bowls," Stella noted, "which is likely how it watched us. I can look and see if there are any answers."

"Is it safe?" Astar asked, while Jak darted over to peer at the bowl Stella was examining.

"Should be," Stella answered, magic building with her interest. "Does anyone have water?"

They all exchanged bemused looks. "We didn't think we'd be here long enough to need supplies," Zeph pointed out.

Jak heaved a sigh and took out his flask. "I have whiskey."

"Of course you do," Gen said, rolling her eyes.

"Thank you, my only love," Stella said with a radiant smile.

"Better be worth it," he grumbled, taking a quick swig before pouring the rest into the bowl.

~ 34 ~

LOOKING OVER STELLA'S shoulder as the sorceress invoked the magic of the scrying bowl, Lena watched the story unfold and narrated for the others.

"Once this was a lush, green world, bursting with varied life. A race of sorcerers lived here, each with greater or lesser degrees of magical ability, but everyone possessed magical powers. Over time, they built a civilization that covered this world, so much so that they crowded out all of the natural landscape and the ecology began to collapse. So they created magic vessels that allowed them to leave their world and travel to other ones. Eventually, no one remained on this world, and cataclysmic weather conditions erased all evidence of their once thriving society.

"Then, one day, a ship returned. The people from the ship built this tower from the barren stone, then another ship arrived with a youth. This youth was enormously powerful and they were frightened. So they left it here with no ability to leave. They stranded the young magician here and at first the youth despaired. It starved until its body withered away, but it transferred it consciousness into this tower, taking that as its new body. But though it lived, loneliness eroded its sanity, and desperation pushed it to hone its skills. It could see other worlds and lands in the scrying bowls, so it began to recreate them, but the results were never as it wished."

"That's why no sound or scent in the false-Nahanau," Rhyian said. "It only ever saw images."

"Probably," Lena replied, then continued. "Eventually it discovered how to reach out to those other worlds and take a piece of them. The intelligence couldn't transport itself out of its prison, but it could project its consciousness to the alter-realms it acquired. It observed shapeshifters and played with taking forms in those places. When it encountered creatures of interest, it took those and added them to the various alter-realms in its collection."

"The intelligence could read the future, to some extent," Stella put in. "There's a vision of it seeing our final battle in the Winter Isles, and witnessing its own death."

"Thus its attempts to kill Isyn and sequester Stella," Zeph said thoughtfully.

"And why it watched Salena so carefully," Rhyian put in, giving her an intense look.

"And tried to influence the shapeshifters emotionally," Gen said.

"I think maybe it did want love," Jak said. "They starved this being, first of sustenance, then of the companionship that keeps us sane and whole."

They were all quiet a moment. Finally Astar spoke. "Seems to me like its time to leave this place and go home."

Home.

Lena thought she wasn't the only one who wondered

where that might turn out to be. She caught Rhyian's eye, and he held out a hand to her.

That's right. Home was him.

"I'm ready," she said. For wherever their paths would take them.

~ EPILOGUE I ~

ZEPHYR AND ASTAR

ZEPH EYED THE white towers of Ordnung with an apprehensive gaze. She'd never been all that fond of the edifice, but she'd also never felt like she was walking into the dragon's mouth either. The deadly slow advance of their carriages meant that she had a good long time to contemplate what might happen upon their arrival.

With the exception of Falada, their group had retraced their journey. Falada elected to stay in the Isles of Remus, saying something about looking for people she'd lost. With fair weather and the resources of the throne of the Isles of Remus, the eight of them had sailed to Erie. To everyone's great relief and the health of Jak and Stella's love life, the ship already had a captain. Upon landing, they traveled to Castle Marcellum for Isyn to be reunited with his family. They'd spent some happy days there, including a wedding ball to celebrate Gen and Isyn's marriage.

After that, outfitted with new carriages, they journeyed through the spring landscape, far more enjoyable than their previous winter-blasted trip. Isyn and Gen had elected to travel with the rest of them all the way to Ordnung and then Annfwn, to meet Gen's family, and perhaps to see the

Nahanaun Archipelago. If all went well, Zeph and Astar would remain at Ordnung, so he could pick up his training again. And Zeph would start learning how to be high queen. She scowled at the ruby engagement ring. Unless Ursula tossed them out on their ears. Now that they'd almost arrived, the likelihood of that loomed large.

"Don't worry," Astar whispered in her ear, sliding a long lock of her hair out of the way so he could press a kiss to the spot just under her lobe that always gave her the most delicious shivers. "We're coming home after a long absence, which must be celebrated. Her Majesty won't make a scene immediately. If she wants to replace me as her heir, she'll do it after a suitable lapse of time. And *after* she's lined up a replacement."

"She would be a fool to displace you because of me," Zeph snapped, fretting nevertheless. As Danu's avatar, Ursula was so very like the goddess of clear lines and hard and fast rules that Zeph could see the high queen sending Astar away out of principle. She eyed Rhy and Lena, cozied up together on the opposite seat. Lena was reading to him from some book and Rhy had his eyes closed, listening with a half smile. "Do you really think she might name Rhy as her heir instead?" Zeph whispered, very quietly.

"No," Rhy answered firmly.

Lena stopped reading. "It's a possibility."

He opened one eye, studying her. "Do you want to be high queen?"

"Absolutely not."

"This is Salena's ruby," Zeph pointed out, waggling her

fingers. "If Rhy is high king, then you could have your namesake's jewel." And she and Astar could be free.

Lena gave her a wickedly sweet smile. "Nice try, but no." She took Rhy's hand, gazing into his eyes. "We have plans."

Holding her gaze, Rhy lifted their joined hands and pressed a kiss to the back of hers. "Yes, we do, love," he replied fervently, then raised one winged brow at Zeph. "Look for rescue elsewhere."

"Is that what you want?" Astar asked, frowning in concern. "I don't want to condemn you to a life of misery. You are more important to me than the high throne."

"No, silly bear," she said, melting at his words. "I'm only afraid I'll ruin this for you."

"Not possible." He smiled at her, love lighting his summer-sky blue eyes. "You make everything perfect."

She hoped.

THEY WENT THE final stretch on horseback, riding real horses—eight matched black steeds outfitted in tack with the high queen's stooping hawk emblem—sent to meet them from Ordnung, along with fine clothing for them all to change into. Astar, as heir to the high throne, rode at the lead, with Zeph at his side at his insistence. "Begin as we mean to go on," he'd intoned in a somber voice, breaking into laughter when she launched herself at him.

Isyn and Gen rode behind them, as actual reigning monarchs, followed by Stella and Jak, then Rhy and Lena. Zeph rather suspected Rhy of deliberately hiding at the rear so Ursula's steely gaze wouldn't land on him in speculation.

People lined the road, throwing flowers. They rode through the open gates to Ordnung to the shouts of more people lining the ramparts, along with musical fanfare. High Queen Ursula stood before the great doors at the main entrance, looking stern as a blade, while Prince Harlan at her side grinned at them.

"What do you suppose they told everyone we did?" Zeph asked Astar.

"I suspect that we're being celebrated simply for coming home," he replied, then dismounted, waved off the valet who came to help Zeph, and handed her down himself. "She doesn't bite," he murmured in her ear, brushing it with his lips.

"*I* might," Zeph replied sourly, but dutifully pasted on a bright smile.

Astar led her up the steps with formal manners—something else she supposed she'd have to learn. He bowed deeply as the fanfare and cheering dropped to an expectant hush. Resigning herself to the moment, and knowing her mother would expect it, Zeph dropped into a deep, Dasnarian-style curtsy. As she straightened, Ursula caught her eye, a glint of amusement in her gaze.

"If you did try to bite me, Zephyr," Ursula said with a crook of her narrow lips, "I would bite back. Fair warning." She turned her attention to Astar, and Harlan winked at Zeph's chagrin that she'd been overheard.

After that it was welcomes and speeches, more cheering and embraces. As Astar had intuited, no one mentioned heroics. References were made to diplomacy and touring the kingdoms. The introduction of King Isyn and his new queen, one of their own, elicited much excitement as the semi-mythical Isles of Remus became real. Gen blushed and beamed radiantly, much of her father's side of the family in the audience, locals to the township, shouting her name and waving. None of their parents had traveled to Ordnung. Zeph was vaguely disappointed by that, having looked forward to seeing her folks, but Astar whispered to her that it would've seemed like too much for a simple homecoming. Her parents would come to Ordnung soon and she'd have to be patient until then. There would be a lot of exercising of patience in her future. Unless things went very wrong.

Resigned to the subtleties of court and public displays, she nodded and kept a happy smile fixed in place. It should've been fun, rejoicing in their homecoming, but Zeph couldn't quite let go of the tension. They weren't married yet, so there was still time to set Astar free. She thought she'd settled this in herself, but now the question hammered in her mind. If Ursula disinherited Astar, he might pretend to be fine with it, but Zeph knew him better than she knew herself. It would break something in him to lose what he'd spent his entire life working toward. She couldn't be the cause of that.

More, he would be an excellent high king. Looking around at all the people cheering for Astar, their hope, love, and loyalty shining on their faces as they came up to welcome him home, that was more apparent to her than ever. And Astar handled the press of well-wishers with aplomb, offering each person a special word, knowing every name. Zeph couldn't keep up, their faces soon swimming in her overtaxed brain. Though Astar kept her firmly at his side—and though many offered her congratulations on her engagement—she'd never felt more out of place. Once or twice, she caught herself looking around, hoping to see her father slouched against a pillar, raising his brows in question and tipping his head at the open window in invitation to go fly.

Once they sat down to the feast, Zeph determinedly plowed through the endless glasses of sparkling wine the servants thoughtfully supplied her with, hoping that would blunt the keen edge of despair. They were back to reality and she would have to give him up. Even though leaving Astar would feel like ripping out her own heart, she would do it, for him.

Stella gave her several encouraging smiles, though she was too far down the table for conversation. Just as well, because Zeph was only holding onto her composure with the tips of her claws. Any sympathetic word might push her over the edge into tears. And she needed to be strong enough to do this. Right away. *Soonest begun, soonest done.*

Then Rhy, sliding her a mischievous smile, stood and proposed a toast to Astar and Zeph's engagement, something that had only been mentioned thus far in private conversation, and not once by the high queen. Trust Rhy to force the issue. So, she had to stand with Astar, accepting the congratulations, the excellent wine tasting like dust in her mouth. Ursula, on the other side of Astar from Zeph, gave her a sharp look, that steely gaze making her squirm enough that Zeph began to feel more like prey than predator.

Thus Zeph was totally unsurprised when—as the feast wound down, and Ursula stood to dismiss the company—the high queen then requested a private meeting with Zeph.

"I'll join you," Astar said, rising from his chair.

Ursula leveled him with a stern look. "I said private, Willy, which means only Zeph and myself."

"Begging your pardon, Your Majesty, but anything that concerns Zephyr also involves me. She is my fiancée," he added, facing her in all his noble conviction.

"And I am still high queen," she replied implacably, "which means I expect to be obeyed, particularly in my own castle." She lifted one brow in cool expectation of Astar's capitulation.

"Auntie Essla," Astar said in a lowered voice, "please. I'm begging you."

"Oh for Danu's sake," she bit out in irritation, "I'm not going to eat the girl."

"Not after the three babies she roasted for breakfast," Harlan murmured behind her, grinning when Ursula shot him a steely glare. Zeph really didn't know how he could be so irreverent at a time like this, but she gave him a weak smile.

"Enough stalling," Ursula said crisply, turning her back on both men. "Zeph, with me."

She strode away, her brocaded formal coat flapping around the narrow pants and high boots she wore, a slim blade of a woman. Astar squeezed Zeph's hand and kissed her. "Courage," he whispered. "Remember that I love you and that matters more than any of this."

As she'd feared, she nearly started weeping. She tore herself away so he wouldn't see, muttering that she'd better hurry to catch up. Ursula hadn't gotten that far ahead. The high queen was part Tala and that shapeshifter blood made her an especially fierce and agile warrior, but she still couldn't outpace Zeph. Even in her fancy gown and high heels, Zeph could catch up. The thought gave her a very small measure of satisfaction, in the face of all she wasn't handling well.

They went into a small room Zeph hadn't seen before, darkish with the walls lined with shelves of books, and a massive desk Ursula sat behind, telling Zeph to shut the door. When Zeph turned back, Ursula had steepled her fingers under her sharp chin, studying Zeph with a penetrating gaze. With a start of recognition, Zeph noticed how Ursula's gray eyes were very like her sister Andromeda's, and like Stella's—especially when they looked *through* you in that uncomfortable way. Zeph didn't allow herself to flinch, however. She also remained standing and was relieved when Ursula didn't make her sit.

"This was my father's office," Ursula said, never taking her gaze from Zeph. "It took me years after ascending to the high throne to start using it."

This was not the conversation opener Zeph had expected. "Why not? Your Majesty," she added belatedly.

Ursula smiled thinly. "You can dispense with titles for this conversation, though your etiquette needs work. Much to your mother's chagrin, no doubt."

"She tried," Zeph replied, stung into defending her mother.

"But you're stubborn and more than a little wild." Ursula

sat back in her chair with a sigh. "I am not unfamiliar with the Tala nature, remember. As for why I didn't use this office for so long..." Now she looked around, studying the space. "First because it reminded me of him and I didn't want to be him. Later because I knew I could never be him—and that scared me. Being high queen is not an easy job. It's difficult work, with new challenges arising every day. Sometimes I wish I could simply fly away from all the responsibilities." She raised her brows at Zeph, making it clear her word choice wasn't accidental. Somehow she'd divined that Zeph had wanted to fly away earlier. "So," Ursula continued conversationally, "Astar gave you my mother's ring."

Inadvertently, Zeph held out her hand to gaze on Salena's cabochon ruby, the engagement ring Astar had been directed to give to almost anyone but her. "I know I wasn't on the list of suitable brides," she said, her voice coming out less firm than she'd wanted it.

"No, you weren't," Ursula agreed, "and there was a reason for that."

All right, this wasn't anything Zeph hadn't known when she walked into this trap, and she refused to be ashamed of being herself. Lifting her chin and steeling her spine, she met the high queen's opaque gaze. "I'll give him up. You can have the ring back." Twisting it off her finger, the pain of it agonizing, she laid it on the polished wood. It gleamed there in bloodred splendor, like the heart she'd imagined ripping out of her chest.

Ursula looked from it to Zeph in mild surprise. "Just like that—you won't cause a fuss?"

Zeph shook her head, telling herself she would *not* cry. Ursula might not think much of her, but she had her pride and she would express her grief when she was alone. "I already had decided," she said, her voice only a little wobbly. "I know I'm not an appropriate choice. Astar loves me, but he also is the next high king. He's spent his life admiring you, learning from you, and I can't ask him to give that up for me. I can't ask his people to give him up for me, either. So, yes, I'll go quietly. No fuss."

Ursula considered her gravely. "Do you know why you weren't on that list?"

Oh, please, Zeph thought desperately, *I surrendered already! Don't draw out the torture.* "I have an idea," she made herself answer instead.

"You and Astar are much alike," Ursula said thoughtfully. "Both of you with such a strong sense of integrity and self-sacrifice."

Zeph's mouth fell open a little at the description. "That's Astar, yes, but not me."

"Isn't it? I thought you just now offered to give up the love of your life for the good of the Thirteen Kingdoms." Ursula dipped her chin at the ring on the desk. "You removed that ring like you were tearing out your own heart."

The woman was far too perceptive. "What do you want me to say?" Zeph demanded. "That I'm fine walking away from Astar? Well, I'm *not*." The gríobhth ferocity welled up in her, making her want to lash her tail and snap her beak, but she restrained herself. "I am, however, trying to be a better person. Yes, I love Astar with everything in me, so much that

I'm willing to live in this stone cage and devote myself to helping him do what he yearns to do. That also means, if you're going to disinherit him for wanting to marry me, then I have to walk away. That is the measure of the depth and breadth of my love."

"There's the fight I expected," Ursula observed. "As I was saying, you and Astar share a set of characteristics that lead you to decisions such as the one you're proclaiming. I knew that if I gave Astar a list of acceptable brides, that he might be like his father and regard it as his duty and honor to comply. However, he is also his mother's son, and I know my baby sister well." Ursula's lips twisted in a half smile. "The best way to get Ami to do anything is to tell her she can't."

It took Zeph far too long to catch on. When she did, she whistled low and long. "You wily bitch," she breathed in astonishment, then clapped a hand over her mouth. Her mother would be *apoplectic*.

Ursula, however, laughed, slapping the desk with one hand. "And so we dispense with the last of the formalities." She rose and came around the desk. "Welcome to the family," she said, giving the still stunned Zeph a fierce hug, then holding her by the shoulders. "Now that it's official, I can begin teaching you, as well. We'll start with some of that diplomacy and etiquette," she added with a wink. "It was never my strong suit either. I used my sword and training to work out the stress, just as you'll occasionally want to literally fly. We do what we have to do because the job is important."

"I still don't quite understand," Zeph said faintly.

"You'll learn to make long-range plans, lay out the strategy with an eye to decades hence," Ursula said, leaning against the desk and crossing her heels. "Anyone paying attention could see how much Astar longed for you all those years. I knew when you were ready to fold your wings and find a nest that it would be him you wanted. And you are an excellent choice." She picked up the ring and held it out on her open palm. "My mother—not incidentally a wild and obstinate Tala shapeshifter, herself—would approve of you."

Zeph's eyes once again stung with tears though she didn't fight them this time. Taking the ring back, she slid it onto her finger. Like putting her heart back into her breast. "I'll do my utmost to make her—and you—proud."

Ursula smiled, broad and genuine, then held out a hand to shake Zeph's. "I know you will."

~ EPILOGUE 2 ~

JAKRAL AND STELLA

T HE SIX OF them departed Ordnung in style, Astar and Zeph seeing them off. The girls wept freely and embraced repeatedly, and Jak didn't blame them. It felt wrenching and wrong for the eight of them to part after so long together. Rhy was off in deep conversation with Harlan while Isyn listened to something Ursula was explaining, ticking off points on her fingers.

"You're welcome here anytime," Astar said, giving Jak a clap on the back.

"Remember that sinecure you promised me," Jak replied with a lift of his brows.

"For Stella's husband, it goes without saying," Astar replied soberly. "I would be a fortunate ruler indeed to have you both by my side."

Jak grinned easily, hiding how those words made him squirm. *Stella's husband.* He and Stella hadn't ever discussed marriage. For a long time it hadn't come up, what with fighting for their lives and being so crazy happy just to be together. Stella loved him, Jak had no doubt of that, but marriage might not be in the cards for them. Of course, Astar thought in those terms, having always known he'd have to marry for the high throne, and he and Zeph had been down-right giddy the last few days, now that it turned out Ursula not only approved of the match, but had sneakily engineered it.

In truth, Jak didn't know what Stella thought of the concept of marriage and he'd frankly been too much of a coward to ask. She was a princess, potential heir to the thrones of Avonlidgh and Annfwn, both, not to mention carrying the mark of the Tala that destined her to be Queen Andromeda's heir in sorcery. Still, Stella had a way of bucking convention without really trying. She simply walked her own mysterious and arcane path. He'd vowed to always be by her side, but she'd also dodged any conversations about what their life together would look like, deftly avoiding the subject with dreamy canniness.

It could be he was overthinking, and it wouldn't be the first time.

Still, marriage according to Dasnarian custom was something else entirely, involving draconian contracts and women transferred to their husbands' custody like property. Things were changing in Dasnaria, but not that fast—and Jak felt no desire to honor that part of his heritage, much less subject Stella to it. His own parents had never officially married, partly for that reason and partly because Jepp liked her independence and Kral loved her too much to put rules on her. Jak didn't think he was that extreme, but he also wasn't sure *what* he was. He just wanted to be with Stella and he was worried that might be asking too much.

"Give my regards to my mother and Ash," Astar was saying. "She likely will be unhappy that Zephyr and I will marry next midsummer on the Feast of Danu, here at Ordnung. Just keep telling her that if they don't journey to Ordnung for the Feast of Glorianna this autumn, Zephyr and I will come to Windroven for the Feast of Moranu at midwinter, no matter what."

"A whole year since the crystalline moon," Jak observed. "It feels like it's been twice that already."

"Or more," Astar agreed gravely. "I hope we'll see you there."

"At Castle Windroven?" Jak asked faintly. It hadn't occurred to him to think where they might be at midwinter. That was his mother in him, footloose and never wanting to think past the next gambit.

"Where else would you be?" Astar asked, raising a golden brow. "Annfwn?"

It was a genuine question, Jak realized, not at all rhetorical. "I guess we have to figure that out."

Astar grinned easily. "I guess so. Take care of my sister. I trust no one more."

Jak had to swallow a lump at that. "I'll do my best."

"You're not capable of anything less," Astar agreed.

THEY TRAVELED AT a leisurely pace, enjoying the brilliant weather, stopping a night at Lianore with the gracious Lady Veronica. Then it was on to Castle Windroven, rising dramatically against the sky on the Avonlidgh coast. Built into a mostly defunct volcano, and constructed from rock quarried from that same volcano, Castle Windroven looked like it had grown out of the mountain.

Jak had been there only a few times, and all when he was much younger. This time, as they rode horses up the narrow, tortuously winding road that led to the top, he found a new appreciation for the impregnability of the place and the impossibility of an invader making it to the actual castle alive. "It's amazing Rayfe managed to lay a successful siege to this place," he said to Rhy.

"That's my father," Rhy agreed drolly, "able to achieve the impossible."

"And look good doing it," Lena snickered, unabashed by his repressive glare.

"Arguably he only succeeded because Auntie Andi snuck out to meet him and end the war because she couldn't stand to be the cause of so much death," Stella put in.

"*And* because she was already secretly in love with him," Gen added with a dreamy sigh. "She couldn't withstand the yearnings of her own heart."

"My mother was the one to find the castle blueprints," Lena said in an arch tone. "Without the faithful librarian, Rayfe might be still encamped around this mountain and Andromeda stuck inside."

"I think it's fair to say," Isyn said after a moment, "that our efforts are intertwined in ways we don't always realize at the time. Our fates lead us along paths twistier than this road."

"*Hlyti* guides our steps however it likes," Jak agreed. It

certainly had had its fun with him.

"The Dasnarian concept of fate is an interesting one." Isyn craned his neck back at the castle towering overhead, surf crashing on the nearby cliffs. "Whatever the force that's brought me here, I certainly never expected to see this legendary place. Nor that I'd be traveling to the magical land of Annfwn after."

Rhy snorted. "You'll see how magical it is when they're grilling us for every detail of the trip."

Jak grunted in agreement. They'd all spent several days at Castle Ordnung being relentlessly interrogated about their experiences by Ursula and Harlan. Now they could look forward to the same here. He glanced at Stella and found her watching him solemnly, an inscrutable expression on her face. She'd clearly sensed his recent emotional turmoil, and likely guessed the reason for it, but she hadn't asked and he hadn't offered. They'd taken to dancing carefully around one another. He wasn't at all sure what to make of it. So, he sent her a charming smile, and she nodded.

Though what they'd just agreed to, he didn't know either.

IN A REPEAT of their reception at Ordnung, Queen Amelia and her consort Ash stood at the open gates to Windroven, ready to receive them. Jak had heard the tale many times of how his mother, Jepp, had accompanied Ursula to Windroven, bringing

Queen Amelia's dead first husband's body home. Ami had stood at the gates, defiant, heartbroken, pregnant with Astar and Stella, watching as Ursula's Hawks laid Hugh's body at her feet. The image had always stuck in Jak's head, constructed from his mother's tale, of the incredibly beautiful young queen and how she didn't shed a tear.

Today, Queen Amelia held herself with similar dignity, though the emotion she restrained was clearly eagerness and maternal joy under the thin layer of regal formality. Besides which, the tumult of children bouncing out around the pair of them destroyed any sense of ceremony. Jak had lost track of how many younger siblings Astar and Stella had now, largely because Ash and Ami seemed intent on continually adding to the brood—and hadn't stopped, given Ami's obviously pregnant belly. She certainly was taking her role as avatar of Glorianna-as-mother seriously.

If he was going to be a part of Stella's life from now on, he supposed he'd better start memorizing names and ages.

Before Stella's siblings could swarm her, Jak had hopped off his horse and was at Stella's knee, handing her down. *Begin as you mean to go on*—even if he wasn't sure exactly what that would look like. Stella gave him a sweet smile, no doubt reading his uncertainty. When he made to let go and walk behind her, Stella held on, lacing her fingers with his and bringing him along at her side. Queen Amelia narrowed her eyes at the sight, then focused on her daughter.

"Nilly, darling!" she gushed, exploding out of her regal demeanor and launching herself at Stella, seizing her in such an enthusiastic embrace she tore them apart. Jak considered his options, fairly certain that hadn't been an accident. "Look at you," Ami continued, framing her daughter's face in her hands, then trying to neaten her hair. "You haven't been plucking your widow's peak," she chided. "If anything there's more of it than ever and—"

"I think it's beautiful," Jak said staunchly. Oh, he stayed back in his place, but he wasn't going to abandon Stella entirely. "I hope she never again plucks out a single hair."

Stella threw him a grateful smile, then held out her hand to him. "Mother, Ash, you of course remember Jak, but I'd like to reintroduce you to him as my lover and one true love."

Ami's pretty pink lips dropped into an O of surprise, feigned or real, he couldn't tell, and she looked him up and down as if seeing him for the first time. Those famous twilight-blue eyes held a sparkle of calculation, however, and Jak didn't forget his mother's tales of how Ami used her goddess-given beauty to make people forget what a clever mind she possessed under the veneer of harmless loveliness.

Jak could wish Stella had left out specifying the "lover" part, but his star never did like to lie. He swept Ami a gallant bow, making a leg and holding the pose. "Your Highness Queen Amelia, Consort Ash." He thought about saying something more, but decided anything he might add would sound cheeky. Also, though his fingers twitched, he resisted drawing a dagger to spin.

"Little Jakral Konyngrr," Ami cooed, batting her lashes as he straightened. "I can't recall if you have any sort of title?"

"Ami," Ash said in a warning tone, his fire-scarred voice rough as broken glass.

She flashed him an innocent smile. "You know how forget-ful I am. Didn't Essla make Kral into a general at some point? Though I suppose that's not a title. No land or wealth attached to a military appointment. A pity."

"Mother," Stella said, an exact echo of Ash's tone. Her magic stirred restlessly and Jak squeezed her hand, projecting a sense of wellbeing. Not that Stella would use sorcery on her mother, but in case her empathic senses needed some balancing against whatever her mother was emanating.

Ami's gaze lingered on their joined hands and the way Stella had moved closer. "Lover, you say? I thought you had difficulty with anyone touching you except family." She made it into an accusation, as if Stella had been prevaricating.

"Jak *is* family," Stella said firmly. "He also saved my life, more than once, so take that into your accounting."

"Well, I'm grateful, of course, but you're not some princess trophy who has to be the hero's reward," Ami replied tartly. "You don't have to pay for being rescued by offering up your—"

"Are we to stand on the doorstep all day?" Stella interrupt-ed in a mild tone that didn't fool Jak—nor her mother, by the look of it. Just as well, as Jak's resolve to keep his mouth shut had weakened dangerously at the implication that he'd extorted Stella into a relationship. It came a bit too close to the truth, when he had worked relentlessly to get past her guard to seduce her. "You have other guests," Stella continued, "including the new King and Queen of the Isles of Remus."

"Oh, fine," Ami muttered irritably. "But we're not done here. At least *Gen* married well."

Jak felt Stella's wince and he opened his mouth, but Ash

shook his head minutely. The scarred warrior stood with a straight spine and hands folded behind his back, his apple-green gaze uncanny. He drew Jak to the side with him, giving the others room to approach the queen and be introduced by Stella. "Ami is an emotional woman," Ash confided quietly to Jak, "and she feels slighted that Astar didn't come home to introduce his new fiancée to us before he did with Ursula."

"But you all know Zeph," Jak replied in some surprise. Of course, they knew him nearly as well. Giving into the restless urge, Jak drew a blade and spun it discreetly through his fingers by his side.

Ash shrugged a little. "Even after all these years, Ami's mind and heart remain a mystery to me." Abruptly he grinned, the expression somewhat startling on his scarred visage, lifting only one side of his mouth. "It keeps things interesting. You'll see. Nilly is mercurial in her own way, though she keeps more of it inside. I'm very happy for you, by the way. I think you'll make a splendid husband for her."

Jak coughed, almost bobbling the blade as he never did. *Butterfingers.* "Ah..." He cleared his throat. "We haven't discussed... that."

"I see." Ash looked amused. "I see also that you have the Silversteel daggers I gave Nilly."

"Erm, yes." Why in Danu was he stammering like this? He was more nervous than when his own father was riding him. "Just a loan. Stella still isn't proficient with them, no matter how I've made her learn and practice, so she prefers I hold onto them for her."

"You actually coaxed Nilly into learning to *use* the blades?"

Ash sounded astonished now. "I never could get anywhere with teaching her self-defense. She's always so concerned about hurting anyone."

"Tell me about it," Jak said in heartfelt agreement. "It wasn't easy to get her to do it, but she has the basics now. Enough to keep herself alive long enough for me to get to her. She's actually gotten quite good at using her sorcery as a weapon, too. Her power and accuracy with these fireballs she can call up at a moment's notice is quite impressive."

Ash gazed at him with gratifying respect, then he coughed out a laugh and clapped Jak on the shoulder. "Well, now I know it's true love. Don't be concerned about Ami. She had too many years feeling like someone's trophy, so it's a sore point for her. I'll make her see reason. Perhaps being able to host and plan *your* wedding will take her mind off Astar and Zeph's engagement, and the wedding Ursula will no doubt insist on having at Ordnung."

"Ah, about that..." And Jak was right back into troubled waters. "Like I said, we haven't discussed, um, marriage."

"Ash, darling," Ami called, "we're giving our guests a tour of Windroven."

"I just promised to show Jak the armory," Ash replied. "We'll catch up."

"Oh, I'll go with you," Rhy said, before Lena hauled him back.

"I need you with me," she said to him pointedly.

Rhy looked at her, then back at Jak. For his part, Jak wasn't sure if he wanted rescuing or not. He lifted a shoulder and let it fall. *Hlyti* would have her way with him. Rhy grinned in sympathy, then turned away with the others.

Ash strolled through to an interior courtyard, veering away from the rest of the group, and firmly pointing at some of his many progeny trying to tail them to go with their mother. "Did you know I left Ami once?" he asked conversationally.

"What? No?" Jak answered in considerable surprise.

"Not many people do know the story. It was a long time ago, when Willy and Nilly were little tykes, and horrid little monsters, too." Despite his words, Ash smiled with such fond nostalgia that it softened his harsh features. "I picked a series of fights with Ami, refused to meet her halfway on any number of things, then we had a huge argument which culminated in me agreeing to leave her sight forever."

They walked on a while in silence.

"Aren't you going to ask why?" Ash finally asked, sliding Jak a sharp glance.

"You don't have to talk about it," Jak assured him, though he was wildly curious.

"I brought it up," Ash reminded him mildly. "You see, I was an escaped ex-convict, an outlaw who burned the prisoner's brand from his own face to avoid recapture."

Jak knew that part, and the terrible history behind it. "You being branded a criminal in the first place was a tragic relic of the worst of Uorsin's reign, and Her Majesty gave amnesty immediately upon ascending to the high throne."

"Oh, yes," Ash said in a stern and fervent tone. "She *owed* me that favor."

Ah, Jak hadn't known that part. He filed that tidbit away for future reference.

"She likely would've done it anyway," Ash admitted. "Ursula has been a good monarch, even if we don't always get along. At any rate, what the law says doesn't change what's in our hearts and I was convinced I wasn't good enough for Ami. The most beautiful woman in the Thirteen Kingdoms, the Queen of Avonlidgh, brilliantly alive, passionate, and the most fascinating person I ever met. Who was I, hideously scarred and from the lowest dregs of society, to reach so high? I thought I was doing her a favor by removing myself from her life, and I very nearly succeeded."

"What happened?" Jak didn't need prompting this time. It was all too clear why Ash was telling him this story.

"We got snowed in." Ash huffed out a laugh. "Right here at Windroven, with almost no one on staff because the place had been closed up for months, and Ami... Well, let's say she educated me in the error of my ways. A harsh, but effective lesson in me learning to value myself and what I brought to our relationship."

Jak nodded, spinning his blade thoughtfully. "And you've been happily married ever since."

Ash snorted. "Glorianna, no! Have you met my wife? She's like being married to a gorgeous hurricane. But we've never lacked for passion and I've never once regretted being her husband. Nor of being stepfather to Astar and Stella, along with all the children Ami and I made together. You'll be good for our Nilly. Still, you'll need to get over yourself and propose. She's not the sort to do it for you."

"I don't know if she wants me to," Jak confessed.

"Don't you?" Ash raised a brow. "Then perhaps you don't

know her as well as you think."

"I know Stella better than anyone, even her brother," Jak retorted, stung.

"Then you know," Ash replied simply. "I looked at Nilly today and saw her happier than I've ever seen her in her life, and I was there when she was born. She's made her choice. Don't hold it back from her because you're afraid."

Afraid. Jak nearly scoffed at that, before he caught himself. What *was* he afraid of? This was Stella, the love of his life.

"Ami was testing you, by the way," Ash added in a conspiratorial whisper. "She already had the gossip from Ordnung and knew about your relationship. Remember, this is the woman who defied all expectations and social norms to marry the likes of me. She just wants to be sure you have the spine to stand up to those who will disapprove. And there *will* be plenty of those."

"I don't care about what people say," Jak said with perfect honesty, knowing that Stella wouldn't either.

"Good," Ash said, clapping him on the shoulder. "You'll be doing me a favor by letting Ami absorb herself with planning that wedding. How does the autumn Feast of Glorianna sound?"

"Let me propose first," Jak answered weakly.

"Before dinner." Ash gave him that crooked grin. "No sense delaying any longer. Ask Ami for one of rings she had made from Salena's rubies. Nilly will like that."

Jak groaned. "Is that necessary?"

"It will make Ami happy, which is good for me, and you'll have to brave the tiger that is your new heart-mother sooner or later, which will be good for you. Soonest begun is soonest done," Ash added with a wink, and Jak knew then where Astar got it from.

"JAK, IS SOMETHING wrong?" Stella stepped out onto the parapets, the wind off the sea grabbing her long black hair and making it fly like a pennant, the lowering sun coaxing the red glints out of it, like banked coals flaring to fiery life. "Why are you up here?"

She was dressed for dinner, wearing a slim silver gown he hadn't seen before. "You look beautiful in that," he told her sincerely.

Smoothing her hands over the fine silk that hugged her delicate figure, she wrinkled her nose. "Mother can be a trial, but she does have excellent taste."

"And she loves you."

"Of course she does." Stella sighed, giving him a long look. "You're acting strangely. What did Ash say to you?"

"A bit of stepfatherly advice." Jak took a deep breath. He'd faced and cheated death three times, so this should not be difficult. "How would you feel about staying here at Windroven until autumn?"

She raised her elegant black brows. "I think Mother would love it and I wouldn't mind staying in one place for a few months, especially with the summers here so beautiful. Why, where are you planning to go?" She was keeping her voice steady, but her gray eyes were somber. "I understand that you're probably anxious to get back to your life," she added quickly, twisting her fingers in the fine silk and leaving wrinkles. "Chasing Kooncelund pirates, as I recall."

The woman never forgot a thing. And he was fucking this up. Deciding it could hardly go worse, he went down on one knee and held up the ring Ami had let him select from a jewelry hoard worthy of a dragon—*after* she interrogated him with a thoroughness even Her Majesty couldn't match. The jewel wasn't a large one like Zeph's, but the silver filigree setting and deep bloodred color of the faceted stone seemed to suit both Stella's delicacy and darkly brooding magic.

Stella gazed at the ring in open-mouthed shock. "What is this?" she breathed.

"One of Salena's rubies. Ash said you'd like that." Was he doing this all wrong?

"I do like it, but how did you get it?"

"Your mother gave it to me." He was starting to get exasperated with her obtuseness. "I picked this one out because I thought it suited you, but if you'd rather have something else, we can do that. I'm not entirely without resources. I can buy you any jewel you take a fancy to."

"She gave this ring to you... when? Why?"

"This afternoon," he answered with some impatience, "because I asked her for it so I could propose to you."

"Propose what?" She looked between him and the ring, a line between her brows.

"Marriage, Stella," he ground out. "I'm an open book to

you so don't pretend you didn't see this coming, Lady I Can See the Future."

"I didn't see this," she murmured, "and you've been feeling a lot of things lately, so I haven't been at all sure what was going on in your head. But Jak, you—"

"Oh no you don't," he warned her. "Remember the rule: no 'but Jaks' without whiskey present."

She huffed out a breath. "You don't owe me forever, Jak. We talked about this."

Now he was getting seriously pissed that she was back to this. "Yes, and I told you I go where you go. I'm an excellent bladesman and I'll carve out a place in your life. It doesn't have to be as your husband, however. I didn't think it was the best idea, but Ash talked me into it."

Stella folded arms and raised a brow. "He had to talk you into it? So this isn't *your* idea, but my mother and stepfather interfering in my life as usual."

Jak practically gnashed his teeth. Plus he felt like an idiot, down on one knee. "It *is* my idea. I want this, but only if you do, too."

She tapped an impatient foot. "I'm not convinced. I feel I should point out that thrusting a ring at me doesn't automatically equal a marriage proposal. You're usually smoother than this."

He usually was, it was true. All ability to be charming seemed to have fled, however. "Stella," he bit out, setting his teeth, "I'm down on one knee. Will you marry me or not?"

She sniffed. "See? That wasn't exactly the most romantic phrasing."

Starting to retort, he caught the glint of mischief in her gaze, the very dry sense of humor she'd begun to nurture and share with him. He popped to his feet. Grabbing her hand, he thrust the ring onto her finger. "You will be the death of me. There, you're going to marry me or else."

She surveyed the ring. As he'd imagined, it looked perfect on her. Lifting her fulminous silver gaze to his, she smiled tauntingly. "Or else… what?"

"I'll hold you down and torment you until you agree."

"Not exactly a scary prospect," she noted, then twined her arms around his neck, leaning her shimmeringly lovely body against him. "We don't have to get married," she said, very seriously.

"You're not escaping me that easily," he promised, settling his hands on her slim waist, stroking her subtly flared hips. "I want all the world to know you're mine."

"Isn't enough for me to know it?"

Yes. Yes, it was. And now he finally knew it in his heart, too. "Yes, but your mother wants to plan a wedding, since she's deprived of Astar's."

"Ah, well." Stella rolled her eyes. "As long as it makes my *mother* happy."

"It would make me happy, too," he whispered, kissing her.

"Even though I'll be the death of you?"

"You're also the life of me." He kissed her more deeply. "How many kids do you want?"

She gave a little shudder. "Not as many as my mother has."

He laughed. "Deal."

"After the wedding, maybe we can go sailing on the

Hákyrling with your parents," she said.

That surprised him. "You'd want to do that?"

"I'm sure a sorceress would come in handy chasing pirates," she replied, eyes sparkling with interest. "And I'd like to see more of the world. Or other worlds. I've developed a taste for travel, as long as it doesn't involve fighting for our lives every moment."

"You'll still have to practice your self-defense," he warned her.

She pouted sensually, an expression straight from Ami's playbook. "But I'll have you to protect me."

"Yes, you will, always and forever," he vowed. "If you like sailing, I'll build you a ship of our own."

"I would love that. And Jak?"

"What, my star?"

"I love you."

"I love you, my sun, my moon, and the brightest star in my sky."

She sighed happily. "Much smoother that time."

"Did you say *other* worlds?" he asked, his brain finally clear enough to catch that one.

Tipping her head back, she smiled with serene delight. "Why not? There are so many of them."

Why not indeed.

~ EPILOGUE 3 ~

GENDRA AND ISYN

FLYING IN DRAGON form to Annfwn from Castle Windroven felt a bit over the top, Gen fretted. Was it too much to return home flaunting that she'd finally nailed dragon form? In truth, left to herself, she wouldn't have shown up as a dragon. But Rhy and Lena pronounced themselves done with riding in carriages or on horseback, and Rhy didn't have a winged form big enough to carry Lena, much less the bags of things Isyn and Lena needed. Also, while Isyn wouldn't complain, Gen knew he was getting restless about getting back to the Isles of Remus, to begin the long work of putting his kingdom back together. He still wanted to visit Annfwn, and Nahanau, but he didn't want to waste time unnecessarily.

Gen was definitely looking forward to settling into their life together, but she felt like an imposter every time someone addressed her as queen. Even Ursula had included her in conversations about diplomatic relations between the Thirteen Kingdoms and the Isles, which had only added to her feeling like a fraud. Having Zeph attend those meetings, too, had oddly helped, the two of them occasionally trading wide-eyed glances at their changed circumstances. Who'd have thought when they were little girls fighting all the time, competing relentlessly, playing I Eat You, that someday they'd be seated at the same table with the high queen talking politics?

Well, the others had talked politics; Gen pretty much had kept her mouth shut, despite Isyn's repeated urging for her to speak up. Lena had also assured Gen that she was as intelligent as anyone at those meetings, but knowledge wasn't the same as experience, and she had none of that. It had been a lot easier to be Isyn's wife and set aside thoughts of what being queen would mean when they'd been running around, portaling between worlds, and fighting monsters.

Visiting her father's side of the family on the land outside the Ordnung township had been the best part of the visit. Isyn had fit right in with her family, so unassuming in his ways after long years among the folk, and they soon forgot he was born a prince and had become a king. Her parents were over in Annfwn, so she and Isyn had stayed in the cottage on the lake that Marskal had built for Zynda, adding on over the years. Gen had spent at least half of her childhood in that house, many happy times, and she could have stayed longer.

But the others had been impatient to get on to Windroven, and Isyn was beyond excited to finally see Annfwn. Back in the Winter Isles, holed up in his small, cozy bedchamber, dreaming of showing him Annfwn had been simpler. The reality loomed large and precarious now.

Isyn, perched on her back, stroked the soft scales on her shoulder, as if sensing her nerves. Probably he did—he'd been giving her assessing looks the last several days—but she'd been determinedly cheerful. This was the trip of a lifetime for him, and she would not ruin it.

They crested the final range of mountains, and everyone exclaimed at the vista of the tranquil aquamarine sea along the Annfwn coastline. Coming from this direction, especially on the wing, the contrast between the snowy peaks of the Wild Lands and the tropical loveliness of Annfwn was startling. If Gen had been in human form, she'd have drawn a breath at the vista. Home, at long last.

Rhy pointed out the sights to Isyn, the two of them having become great friends, which came as something of a surprise to Gen. He'd elected to ride with Isyn and Lena to speed up the trip, as his raven form couldn't keep up with her dragon and part of the point of her taking them dragonback was to shorten the trip.

She spiraled over the towering cliff city, taking her time to give Isyn the best view possible. Built into the white cliffs and dripping with flowering vines, tropical blossoms, and laden fruit trees, the city was truly an impressive sight. Staymachs in rainbow colors flew up in greeting, swirling about her and singing songs of welcome. Isyn laughed in pure delight, which made everything worth it right there.

Then a sapphire-blue dragon appeared in the sky, trumpeting in triumph, and brushing wing tips with her. Her mother, Zynda, with Marskal on her back. He saluted Gen, fist over heart in the Hawks' style, and her heart overflowed with the joy of homecoming, nerves entirely forgotten.

By the time she landed on the sparkling white sand of the wide beach, a huge group had assembled, King Rayfe and Queen Andromeda at the forefront. Discharging her passengers, she shifted back to human form in a gown appropriate for greeting royalty, but barefoot—because this was Annfwn, after all. Her parents were quick. Her mom, back in human form also, clad in a simple sheath dress, grabbed her in a fierce embrace.

"I knew you could do it, my brilliant daughter," she whispered in Gen's ear, then cupped Gen's face in her hands, searching with her wild blue gaze. "Was it terrible, what you had to sacrifice?"

Gen nearly said no, but she nodded. "We all had terrible trials, but in the end, the gain was worth it. Mom, Dad, I'd like you to meet my husband, Isyn."

"King of the Isles of Remus," Marskal said, giving the Hawks' salute, then bowing.

"Just your new heart-son," Isyn replied, holding out a hand to shake Marskal's.

Zynda ignored the hand Isyn offered her, hugging him instead and kissing him on both cheeks. Then she took his hands and held them out to either side, studying him. "He's very pretty," she said to Gen. "Excellent choice, if you had to marry a mossback."

"Don't start," Marskal growled, though he had a fond smile on his face, and Zynda grinned cheekily at him.

"I can see where Gendra gets her beauty," Isyn told her. "She is the spitting image of you, heart-mother."

Gen nearly choked at that, fully aware she looked much more like her brown and brown, square-jawed father, but Zynda dimpled in delight. "Charming and discerning, too. I look forward to spending more time with you. But now go greet the royals and get that done with, then you can go play a while." She cupped Gen's cheek, kissing her brow. "You deserve some fun in paradise, my sweet."

Marskal gave her one last hug, murmuring how proud he was of her, then released her to go with Isyn to speak with Rayfe and Andromeda, Rhy and Lena already in apparently intense conversation with them. "I hope Rhy can keep his temper," Gen said quietly to Isyn. "His parents tend to rub him the wrong way."

"Rhy will be fine," Isyn murmured back. "He's a different man now."

WITH THE FORMALITIES over, the beach clearing of people, and Rhy and Lena off with his parents, Gen shapeshifted into a more comfortable, light dress, and offered to give Isyn the tour. She had a special place she wanted to show him. He eyed her, then his heavier, formal garments ruefully. "I envy you being able to change clothes so easily, especially in this heat. I'd love to change into something lighter, but I don't know where our bags went."

She shrugged, feeling the languid, elaborate Tala style return. "Probably spirited off to our rooms, but I think we can do something. Boots off first. No one wears shoes in Annfwn if they don't have to."

Isyn gave her a bemused look, but obligingly toed off his fancy boots. "Now what?"

"Wiggle your toes in the sand," she instructed, keeping a very serious mien. "It's part of the ritual."

"The ritual, huh?" His green eyes sparkled with amusement, his mouth twitching into a smile.

"The ritual to shapeshift you into one of the Tala," she agreed, moving to help him out of the tailored coat he'd already unbuttoned. She tossed it on top of his boots and eyed his shirt. "Yes, let's get rid of this, too." Swiftly undoing the laces, she stripped him out of the shirt and took a moment to run her hands over the smooth, pale skin of his muscular chest. Dusted with ivory hair, the clean lines of him shone clearly, the trail of hair narrowing as it disappeared under the waist of his pants. When she settled her fingers there, he stopped her with his hands on hers. "Briar Rose, do you plan to strip me naked on this beach?" he asked softly, fire warming the cool green of his eyes.

"No one would mind," she answered, trying to keep a straight face and failing as a giggle burst out of her.

"Ah ha, I thought so. Is this a standard Tala trick to play on newcomers, or am I special?"

"You are very special, Isyn," she murmured, twining her arms about his neck and slithering up against him. With his chest bare and only the thin material of her gown between them, her nipples peaked at the contact, sending shivers of delight through her, intensified when he lowered his mouth to hers in a deep, lingering kiss.

"You're the special one," he breathed against her lips. "My miracle. Briar Rose."

She laughed, giddy with the joy of being home and having

her love with her. "I want to show you something."

He caressed the length of her back under the long fall of her hair. "Here, on the beach?" he teased.

"Not that." She swatted him, then took his hand. "This way."

"What about my clothes?" He gestured to the pile on the sand.

"You won't need them, and no one here is going to bother with *things*," she replied loftily.

"I see I have much to learn."

They strolled along the beach, hand in hand, just as Gen had always fantasized she might do some day. Isyn rolled up the cuffs of his pants, wading into the gentle surf with bright-eyed enthusiasm. He drank in everything about Annfwn with sincere wonder, asking questions and treating each discovery with purest joy that was infectious.

Aside from her wedding, it was the best day of her life.

She led him to an outcropping of rocks, high above the sea, where moss formed a thick carpet around a shallow pool. A waterfall poured down in a glassy ribbon, making rainbows in the late afternoon light, trees and vines screening them on three sides, nothing but the glittering sea on the other. "This was my special place," she told Isyn. "I'd come here to practice."

He threaded long fingers through her hair, smiling slightly. "To be alone. To dream, perhaps?"

"That, too," she acknowledged. How well he knew her.

"What did you dream of here, Briar Rose?" He pressed a kiss to her forehead, then to each eyelid as she closed them.

"True love," she admitted on a sigh, then opened her eyes, watching his gorgeous face. "I didn't know to dream of you, though."

"I'd love to paint you here," he murmured, stepping back to arrange the hair around her face, tugging one loose strap from her shoulder and pressing a kiss to the skin he revealed, as he undid the tie. She dropped her head back, releasing a dreamy breath as pleasure shivered through her. "Two paintings," he amended, his artist's fingers nimbly untying the other strap so the shift puddled at her feet, leaving her naked. "One of you as a little girl, dreaming, surrounded by all the forms you learned to take—a hummingbird in the tree, fish in the pond, a white saber cat lounging on the moss."

"And the dragon?" she asked breathily as he took her nipple in his mouth, teasing the sensitive tip with teeth and tongue, making her arch into him in longing.

"That's the second painting," he answered, shucking his pants and easing her onto the moss. Lowering himself beside her, he ran a hand over the curve of breast, waist, and thigh. "You now, all voluptuous woman, naked and alluring, the dragon peering through the vines behind you."

"That one might not be appropriate to hang in the palace," she noted dreamily, nearly purring under his caresses.

"For our bedroom," he replied, trailing lips down her belly, and parting her thighs. "I might also do one of you from this angle." He spread her nether lips and licked her, smiling wickedly at her dual gasp of shock and sensual pleasure. "Naked, pink sex slick with arousal, wearing only your crown."

"Isyn," she groaned, embarrassed and unbearably titillated

by the image he painted, not to mention the erotic havoc his lips, tongue, and teeth worked on her. "I don't have a crown," she said, though that wasn't the point, gripping his ivory hair in her hands and urging him upward.

"You do," he purred, obliging her by sliding up her body, pausing here and there to shower her with more tantalizing kisses and caresses. "Or, rather, you will. I commissioned them before we left. Matching crowns, that I designed myself."

"Ohhh," she breathed, moved and also shivering from his teasing. "I don't know, Isyn."

"*I* know," he answered, pressing into her and filling her gloriously. "You'll be as brilliant a queen as you are at everything, my Briar Rose, my fairy princess, my fearsome dragon."

"I'm happy just to be your wife and your love," she answered, gazing up at him as he moved inside her, rocking her with waves of intimate, shuddering pleasure.

He smiled and kissed her. "Always that, and more."

She wound her legs around his narrow hips, yielding to the delirious joy of being joined to this perfect man. Gazing up at the blue Annfwn sky past his shoulder, she allowed her eyes to drift shut, giving herself over to the ecstasy he brought her. No, she'd never known to dream of this, because this was beyond what that girl she'd been could imagine, and for that she would be forever grateful.

~ EPILOGUE 4 ~
RHYIAN AND SALENA

R HY'S PARENTS MIGHT not be formally posed at the gates of a castle, but King Rayfe and Queen Andromeda looked no less intimidating for all that they stood barefoot on a beach. His father's intent and expectant gaze had fastened on Rhy the moment they came in sight on Gen's back—and hadn't left. Tall, lean, long black hair catching the breeze, Rayfe measured his son and only child with keen insight.

An insight that had always left Rhy coming up wanting in the past. Beside Rayfe, Andromeda was smaller, slighter, and shimmering with magic, her storm-gray eyes looking *through* him and seeing everything. At first, he'd thought that she was Stella and Rhy had to remind himself that they'd left Stella with Jak back at Windroven. He hadn't realized until this moment how much Stella had matured over the course of their journeys, gaining confidence and growing into her power. He supposed he'd changed, too, which was heartening.

"Courage," Salena murmured, taking his hand and interlacing her slender fingers with his. "You've faced worse than your parents."

"Nobody warns you that the toughest beasts are waiting for you when you return home," he replied just as quietly, "ready to lay your guts open with a few well-chosen words."

Salena laughed. "And you're not allowed to kill them."

"I *can* fight back, however," he mused. Since Gen was introducing Isyn to Zynda and Marskal, Rhy went to greet his parents, Salena by his side.

"Mother, Father," he said, bowing formally. "I know you remember Salena, but I'm reintroducing her as my future bride."

Andi's eyes widened, shining with emotion. "Oh, I'm so happy you two finally worked it out. Lena, you've grown into such a lovely young woman. Come here." Andi embraced Salena, then gasped, holding her by the arms. "And your storm magic is truly impressive—both potent and controlled. I see my visions of your future came true." Andi slid her gaze to Rhy, something enigmatic glinting there.

"Thank you," Salena said. "I've learned a great deal on our journeys." She glanced back to Rhy. "We all have."

"We very much look forward to hearing every detail," Rayfe said with keen interest, embracing Salena also.

Rhy snorted to himself. At least this would be almost the last retelling of their experiences. Until they decided to torment their own children with tales of their glorious adventures. Watching Salena exchange quiet words with his father, he caught a sudden vision of Salena's lush body swollen with child, then her teaching several children to body surf, laughing and golden in the sun, and then the both of them telling those children stories by the fire, the young faces rapt with wonder.

"Have you a hug for your mother?" Andi's voice startled

him out of the reverie, her expression wryly amused, her eyes holding wariness and hope. He'd lacked as a son that she even had to ask, and that she so clearly braced for his refusal.

He seized her in a fierce embrace, keenly aware of both her potent magic and slighter frame. That he was taller than his powerful mother continued to come as a surprise. "I love you so much, Mom," he whispered against her hair. "I'm sorry I've been such a bad son."

"Oh, Rhyian," she gasped, her voice breaking with emotion. She pulled back and framed his face in her hands, eyes silver with the tears that flowed down her cheeks. "You have never been a bad son."

"I blamed you," he replied, "for pledging me to Moranu. I was unkind to you."

She gave him a wobbly smile. "You are so much like your father, both of you so determined to forge your own path, to not be controlled by your fate."

"I'm like my mother that way, too," he pointed out, smiling at her consternation. "I seem to recall more than a few stories of you trying to escape the traps laid for you by circumstance."

Swatting at him lightly, she laughed. "I suppose that's true, though at the time everyone thought I was just being difficult."

"I know the feeling," he replied fervently.

"Yes, I suppose you would. I never thought of it that way—you expressed your restlessness and dissatisfaction differently than I did—but we both followed similar paths." She sobered, looking *through* him again with that sorcerous intensity. "I see you found your magic."

He should have realized she'd see it immediately. "Did you always know it was in me?" he demanded.

"Yes." She shrugged. "You and I are much alike that way also. Late bloomers. I didn't know when, or if, yours would awaken, though."

"Why didn't you tell me?"

"Because it was yours to find, Rhyian. I always thought Lena would be part of it, and when you were estranged for so long, I began to wonder. It's good to see it all fall into place for you now."

"It's more like I took the shattered pieces and glued them back together with sheer force of will," he remarked drily.

"Yes, well." She laughed, rolling her eyes. "All I can say is I know the feeling, yes?"

He'd never imagined having this kind of rapport with his mother. Lowering to realize that he'd been the one preventing it all these years. "I called on Moranu."

"Ah." A world of understanding in that one breathed sound. "And how are you?"

"I'm good," he said, realizing it was true. "I spent a lot of years dreading something for no reason, I discovered."

"The goddess is a tricky bitch," Andi confided, "and serving Her is not always easy, but I know you'll find it rewarding."

"You know?" he asked. "Or do you *know*?"

She wagged a finger at him. "Not telling. What was in the vision you saw just now?"

Startled he blinked at her. "That was a real vision?"

"Probably." She shrugged it off cheerfully. "Now you understand how it is." She patted his arm. "You'll get better at discerning the difference with practice."

"Will you teach me?" he asked impulsively, rewarded by her misty smile, and a few more tears.

"I would be delighted, my son," she answered with quiet emotion.

"I have something to show you." He shapeshifted to First Form, then back, with the Star of Annfwn in his palm.

Andi clasped her hands in pure delight. "You've learned to take things and cache them. Well done!"

"Stella, Gen, and Zeph all tutored me on the journey home," he confided. "I've accrued a few more forms, too. I'm working on even more."

"I'm so proud. But why did Stella send the Star with you?"

"She and Jak are getting married, did you know?"

"Not officially, but I'm not surprised."

No, she wouldn't be. "They're spending the summer at Windroven planning the wedding and being Auntie Ami's dress-up dolls to take the heat off Zeph and Astar."

"Ah." Andi sighed. "Martyrs to the cause. Good of them."

"And... Stella thought," he said hesitantly, "not to over-step, but that if you agreed to teach me, I could learn to use the Star, too."

"I'd like that." She blinked back renewed tears.

"I have to go back and forth to Ordnung, though," Rhy added, "and Aerron, too, since—"

"What's this?" Rayfe demanded, striding over, a sharp look on his face. "My son has only just arrived home and you're already talking about going back to Ordnung of all places? Hasn't Her Majesty acquired enough heirs and trainees?"

"Rayfe, my wolf…" Andi began, half in affection and half in warning.

Once upon a time, Rhy would have snarled back, asking his father what he cared whether Rhy stayed or went. Now he saw more behind his father's cool façade. He could see the leader keeping a brave face, the emotion he ruthlessly restrained. Impulsively, he hugged his father, unable to remember the last time he'd done it. After a stunned moment, Rayfe hugged him back, still stiff and hesitant with it. "I love you, too, Dad," Rhy said.

His father softened, then returned the embrace with fervor, clasping a hand to the back of Rhy's head, a gesture of love he called from his boyhood. After another moment, he pulled back. "We plan to stay a few days," Rhy said, "so you can hear the stories, then Gen will fly us over to Nahanau." He held out a hand to Salena, who took it, lush mouth curved in a warm and approving smile. "Isyn wants to see the islands and I have to ask the dragon king for permission to marry his daughter," Rhy added drily. "If I survive that—"

"Really, it's Mom you have to worry about," Salena put in. "She hasn't forgotten the pranks you pulled on her as a naughty schoolboy."

"True," Andi mused. "Dafne will likely expect you to pass an exam."

Rhy sighed, figuring they weren't wrong. "I'll do what I have to." He tipped the backs of his fingers to his forehead in the *Elskathorrl*, smiling at Salena as he did so.

His mother caught her breath. "The *Elskathorrl*… what? How?"

"It's a long story," Rhy explained, "and we will tell you all of it, but the short answer is that Uncle Harlan has agreed to train me in the *Skablykrr*."

Rayfe made a scoffing sound. "Are you Dasnarian now—is this your latest dabbling?"

Rhy reined in the reflexive anger, instead calmly meeting his father's intense blue gaze. "I'm doing what I need to in order to be a better person, to learn to keep my word no matter what, to be decisive." He allowed a sardonic smile to cross his lips. "To be someone you can be proud of, someday."

Rayfe stared a moment, eyes flashing in annoyance, until Andi set a hand on his arm. She gave him a meaningful look. "Rayfe," was all she said.

He glanced at her and softened in a way Rhy rarely saw him do, especially in public. He caught her fingers in his and kissed them. "Right," he muttered, then met Rhy's gaze. "I look forward to seeing what you do with your various efforts then," he said, somewhat stiffly. Then he dashed a hand across his eyes, and Rhy nearly goggled. Surely his father wasn't tearing up? "But, Rhyian, I have always, always been proud of you."

Rhy swallowed hard. He didn't think that had always been the case, but his father's words were sincere in the moment, and he felt the truth of them. "Thank you," he told his father, feeling awkward. "I shall endeavor to earn that pride."

Andi cleared her throat meaningfully, and Rayfe held up a hand, nodding. "I'm sure it will come as no surprise to you that Andromeda has been watching your adventures as much as possible."

"Which doesn't mean we don't want to hear it all from you," Andi inserted hastily.

"True," Rayfe acknowledged. "There are tantalizing holes we are eager to have filled. Still, each evening, your mother has told me what you all did that day, so I have a good idea of how you've conducted yourself, Rhyian."

Rhy winced, Salena squeezing his hand in sympathy. "I know I have a great deal to apologize for—" he began.

"You miss my meaning, Son," Rayfe interrupted. "What I heard, what your mother saw, was the emergence of a real leader." He clasped Rhy's shoulder and squeezed. "No one ever expected you to be perfect; just to learn from your mistakes. And that's what you've done. I'm proud to name you heir to the throne of Annfwn." He smiled at Salena, a warm and charming grin. "Both of you, which should help with the negotiations in Nahanau."

Rhy was still grappling with the astonishing words that made no sense. "Your heirs? But... But the Tala don't have a hereditary succession."

Rayfe grimaced, exchanging a long-suffering look with Andi. "Your esteemed Auntie Essla has been at us to assimilate more of the Thirteen Kingdoms laws."

"In the name of egality across the realms," Andi replied soothingly. "She's not asking for the moon."

"She might as well be," Rayfe grumbled. "But we've had this argument too many times to count. Suffice to say, this particular concession was an easy one, as both your mother and I hoped you'd follow in our footsteps. Though, Lena, you might tell Dafne and Nakoa to watch themselves—with a princess of Nahanau marrying the Prince of Annfwn, that hawk on the high throne might try the same thing with them next."

"Prince of Annfwn," Rhy echoed, still grappling with the sudden shift, amazed at how much it meant to him.

Salena nudged his arm, grinning. "Really a prince!"

"And, eventually, King of Annfwn," Rayfe said, an odd half smile on his face.

"Part of your service to Moranu," Andi said solemnly, "leading Her children."

"But will the Tala fall into line so easily?" Rhy wondered. "This is bucking a long tradition."

"Oh, you'll have to work for it," Rayfe agreed cheerfully. "That's part of why I'm aggravated with you, Rhyian. I want you here so I can guide you, hone those alpha skills."

"Well, he'll be here part time studying sorcery with me," Andi put in placidly, though her eyes danced with mischief at her husband's double-take. "Rhyian's magic came in, just as I knew it would."

Rayfe smiled, the two of them sharing an intimate look. "You did tell me so."

"Didn't you know that already," Salena asked, "if you were watching us?"

Andi rolled her eyes. "Those final days were a serious muddle! You all kept popping in and out of alter-realms, I couldn't make sense of half of it."

"Which is another reason we are eager to hear the whole tale," Rayfe added meaningfully.

"Then let's not keep them standing out here on the beach,"

Andi said crisply. "I'm sure refreshments would be welcome. Let's greet Gen and her new husband, then go relax with some wine. Do you think they'll join us?"

"I think Gen has *other* plans for today," Salena answered with a sly smile. "Maybe this evening."

"Fair enough," Rayfe replied, tugging Andi's long hair, a smoldering look on his face. "I'd feel the same I'm sure."

Rhy cleared his throat. "Will you two stop?"

"Never," they answered as one, then cracked up laughing.

"So," Rayfe asked, beckoning the waiting Gen and Isyn over from their spot down the beach a ways, "dividing your time between Annfwn, Ordnung, and Aerron, I heard you say? Does that mean you'll continue your work Salena?"

"Yes, I feel a few more years of effort will have the rainfall patterns stabilized." She gave Rhy a loving smile. "I appreciate that Rhyian will make the effort to come see me so I can finish that project to my satisfaction."

Rhy lifted their joined hands and kissed her fingers, aware as he did that it was an echo of his father's gesture of affection. "It's not far as the crow flies. Or, as the raven flies, as it were."

She lifted one brow. "As the dragon flies, perhaps?"

"Let's not get ahead of ourselves," he answered wryly. "I've already got years of study ahead of me."

"Some of that study could be practicing opening portals," Salena reminded him. "I know Stella and Isyn want to. Then we could all visit each other more."

"Auntie Essla wants us to keep that secret for the time being." He caught his mother's restrained eyeroll at that.

"I'll handle Essla," Andi said. "And there's time for all of this."

"Yes," Rayfe agreed. "We're not handing over the throne anytime soon."

"We're not decrepit, after all!" Andi added before turning to hug Gen. "You'll be busy."

Salena squeezed his hand and he kissed her lush lips. "Yes," he said, brushing her mouth with his, feeling the curve of her smile. "In the best way possible."

Yes. They had their whole lives ahead of them and all that mattered was that they spend those lives together. The future looked bright, indeed.

TITLES BY JEFFE KENNEDY

FANTASY ROMANCES

BONDS OF MAGIC
Dark Wizard
Bright Familiar
Grey Magic
Familiar Winter Magic (In Fire of the Frost)

HEIRS OF MAGIC
The Long Night of the Crystalline Moon
(also available in *Under a Winter Sky*)
The Golden Gryphon and the Bear Prince
The Sorceress Queen and the Pirate Rogue
The Dragon's Daughter and the Winter Mage
The Storm Princess and the Raven King (May 2022)

THE FORGOTTEN EMPIRES
The Orchid Throne
The Fiery Crown
The Promised Queen

THE TWELVE KINGDOMS
Negotiation
The Mark of the Tala
The Tears of the Rose
The Talon of the Hawk
Heart's Blood
The Crown of the Queen

THE UNCHARTED REALMS
The Pages of the Mind
The Edge of the Blade
The Snows of Windroven
The Shift of the Tide
The Arrows of the Heart
The Dragons of Summer
The Fate of the Tala
The Lost Princess Returns

THE CHRONICLES OF DASNARIA
Prisoner of the Crown
Exile of the Seas
Warrior of the World

SORCEROUS MOONS
Lonen's War
Oria's Gambit
The Tides of Bára
The Forests of Dru
Oria's Enchantment
Lonen's Reign

A COVENANT OF THORNS

Rogue's Pawn

Rogue's Possession

Rogue's Paradise

CONTEMPORARY ROMANCES

Shooting Star

MISSED CONNECTIONS

Last Dance

With a Prince

Since Last Christmas

CONTEMPORARY EROTIC ROMANCES

Exact Warm Unholy

The Devil's Doorbell

FACETS OF PASSION

Sapphire

Platinum

Ruby

Five Golden Rings

FALLING UNDER

Going Under

Under His Touch

Under Contract

EROTIC PARANORMAL

MASTER OF THE OPERA E-SERIAL

Thank you for reading!

ABOUT JEFFE KENNEDY

Jeffe Kennedy is a multi-award-winning and best-selling author of epic fantasy romance. She is the current president of the Science Fiction and Fantasy Writers Association (SFWA) and is a member of Romance Writers of America (RWA), and Novelists, Inc. (NINC). She is best known for her RITA® Award-winning novel, *The Pages of the Mind*, the recent trilogy, *The Forgotten Empires*, and the wildly popular, *Dark Wizard*. Jeffe lives in Santa Fe, New Mexico.

Jeffe can be found online at her website: JeffeKennedy.com, on her podcast First Cup of Coffee, every Sunday at the popular SFF Seven blog, on Facebook, on Goodreads, on BookBub, and pretty much constantly on Twitter @jeffekennedy. She is represented by Sarah Younger of Nancy Yost Literary Agency.

jeffekennedy.com

facebook.com/Author.Jeffe.Kennedy

twitter.com/jeffekennedy

goodreads.com/author/show/1014374.Jeffe_Kennedy

bookbub.com/profile/jeffe-kennedy

Sign up for her newsletter here.

jeffekennedy.com/sign-up-for-my-newsletter